The Best
Short Stories of
O. Henry

歐亨利

短篇小說選

原著雙語彩圖本

歐·亨利（O. Henry）—著　　丁宥榆—譯

U0025417

CONTENTS

1 The Last Leaf

In a little district west of Washington Square the streets have run crazy and broken themselves into small strips called "places." These "places" make strange angles and curves. One Street crosses itself a time or two. An artist once discovered a valuable possibility in this street. Suppose a collector with a bill for paints, paper and canvas should, in traversing this route, suddenly meet himself coming back, without a cent having been paid on account!

So, to quaint old Greenwich Village the art people soon came prowling, hunting for north windows and eighteenth-century gables and Dutch attics and low rents. Then they imported some pewter mugs and a chafing dish or two from Sixth Avenue, and became a "colony."

At the top of a squatty, three-story brick Sue and Johnsy had their studio. "Johnsy" was familiar for Joanna. One was from Maine; the other from California. They had met at the table *d' hôte* of an Eighth Street "Delmonico's," and found their tastes in art, chicory salad and bishop sleeves so congenial that the joint studio resulted.

That was in May. In November a cold, unseen stranger, whom the doctors called Pneumonia, stalked about the colony, touching one here and there with his icy fingers. Over on the east side this ravager strode boldly, smiting his victims by scores, but his feet trod slowly through the maze of the narrow and moss-grown "places."

Mr. Pneumonia was not what you would call a chivalric old gentleman. A mite of a little woman with blood thinned by California zephyrs was hardly fair game for the red-fisted, short-breathed old duffer. But Johnsy he smote; and she lay, scarcely moving, on her painted iron bedstead, looking through the small Dutch window-panes at the blank side of the next brick house.

One morning the busy doctor invited Sue into the hallway with a shaggy, gray eyebrow.

"She has one chance in—let us say, ten," he said, as he shook down the mercury in his clinical thermometer. "And that chance is for her to want to live. This way people have of lining-up on the side of the undertaker makes the entire pharmacopoeia look silly. Your little lady has made up her mind that she's not going to get well. Has she anything on her mind?"

"She—she wanted to paint the Bay of Naples some day." said Sue.

"Paint?—bosh! Has she anything on her mind worth thinking about twice—a man, for instance?"

"A man?" said Sue, with a jew's-harp twang in her voice. "Is a man worth—but, no, doctor; there is nothing of the kind."

"Well, it is the weakness, then," said the doctor. "I will do all that science, so far as it may filter through my efforts, can accomplish. But whenever my patient begins to count the carriages in her funeral procession I subtract 50 per cent from the curative power of medicines. If you will get her to ask one question about the new winter styles in cloak sleeves I will promise you a one-in-five chance for her, instead of one in ten."

After the doctor had gone Sue went into the workroom and cried a Japanese napkin to a pulp. Then she swaggered into Johnsy's room with her drawing board, whistling ragtime.

Johnsy lay, scarcely making a ripple under the bedclothes, with her face toward the window. Sue stopped whistling, thinking she was asleep.

She arranged her board and began a pen-and-ink drawing to illustrate a magazine story. Young artists must pave their way to Art by drawing pictures for magazine stories that young authors write to pave their way to Literature.

As Sue was sketching a pair of elegant horseshow riding trousers and a monocle on the figure of the hero, an Idaho cowboy, she heard a low sound, several times repeated. She went quickly to the bedside.

Johnsy's eyes were open wide. She was looking out the window and counting—counting backward.

"Twelve," she said, and little later "eleven"; and then "ten," and "nine"; and then "eight" and "seven", almost together.

Sue look solicitously out of the window. What was there to count? There was only a bare, dreary yard

to be seen, and the blank side of the brick house twenty feet away. An old, old ivy vine, gnarled and decayed at the roots, climbed half way up the brick wall. The cold breath of autumn had stricken its leaves from the vine until its skeleton branches clung, almost bare, to the crumbling bricks.

"What is it, dear?" asked Sue.

"Six," said Johnsy, in almost a whisper. "They're falling faster now. Three days ago there were almost a hundred. It made my head ache to count them. But now it's easy. There goes another one. There are only five left now."

"Five what, dear? Tell your Sudie."

"Leaves. On the ivy vine. When the last one falls I must go, too. I've known that for three days. Didn't the doctor tell you?"

"Oh, I never heard of such nonsense," complained Sue, with magnificent scorn. "What have old ivy leaves to do with your getting well? And you used to love that vine so, you naughty girl. Don't be a goosey. Why, the doctor told me this morning that your chances for getting well real soon were—let's see exactly what he said—he said the chances were ten to one! Why, that's almost as good a chance as we have in New York when we ride on the street cars or walk past a new building. Try to take some broth now, and let Sudie go back to her drawing, so she can sell the editor man with it, and buy port wine for her sick child, and pork chops for her greedy self."

"You needn't get any more wine," said Johnsy, keeping her eyes fixed out the window. "There goes another. No, I don't want any broth. That leaves just four. I want to see the last one fall before it gets dark. Then I'll go, too."

"Johnsy, dear," said Sue, bending over her, "will you promise me to keep your eyes closed, and not look out the window until I am done working? I must hand those drawings in by tomorrow. I need the light, or I would draw the shade down."

"Couldn't you draw in the other room?" asked Johnsy, coldly.

"I'd rather be here by you," said Sue. "Beside, I don't want you to keep looking at those silly ivy leaves."

"Tell me as soon as you have finished," said Johnsy, closing her eyes, and lying white and still as fallen statue, "because I want to see the last one fall. I'm tired of waiting. I'm tired of thinking. I want to turn loose my hold on everything, and go sailing down, down, just like one of those poor, tired leaves."

"Try to sleep," said Sue. "I must call Behrman up to be my model for the old hermit miner. I'll not be gone a minute. Don't try to move 'til I come back."

Old Behrman was a painter who lived on the ground floor beneath them. He was past sixty and had a Michael Angelo's Moses beard curling down from the head of a satyr along with the body of an imp. Behrman was a failure in art. Forty years he had wielded the brush without getting near enough to touch the hem of his Mistress's robe. He had been always about to paint a masterpiece, but had never yet begun it. For several years he had painted nothing except now and then a daub in the line of commerce or advertising. He earned a little by serving as a model to those young artists in the colony who could not pay the price of a professional. He drank gin to excess, and still talked of his coming masterpiece. For the rest he was a fierce little old man, who scoffed terribly at softness in any one, and who regarded himself as especial mastiff-in-waiting to protect the two young artists in the studio above.

Sue found Behrman smelling strongly of juniper berries in his dimly lighted den below. In one corner was a blank canvas on an easel that had been waiting there for twenty-

five years to receive the first line of the masterpiece. She told him of Johnsy's fancy, and how she feared she would, indeed, light and fragile as a leaf herself, float away, when her slight hold upon the world grew weaker.

Old Behrman, with his red eyes plainly streaming, shouted his contempt and derision for such idiotic imaginings.

"Vass!" he cried. "Is dere people in de world mit der foolishness to die because leafs dey drop off from a confounded vine? I haf not heard of such a thing. No, I will not bose as a model for your fool hermit-dunderhead. Vy do you allow dot silly pusiness to come in der brain of her? Ach, dot poor leetle Miss Yohnsy."

"She is very ill and weak," said Sue, "and the fever has left her mind morbid and full of strange fancies. Very well, Mr. Behrman, if you do not care to pose for me, you needn't. But I think you are a horrid old—old flibbertigibbet."

"You are just like a woman!" yelled Behrman. "Who said I will not bose? Go on. I come mit you. For half an hour I haf peen trying to say dot I am ready to bose. Gott! dis is not any blace in which one so goot as Miss Yohnsy shall lie sick. Some day I vill baint a masterpiece, and ve shall all go away. Gott! yes."

Johnsy was sleeping when they went upstairs. Sue pulled the shade down to the window-sill, and motioned Behrman into the other room. In there they peered out the window fearfully at the ivy vine. Then they looked at each other for a moment without speaking. A persistent, cold rain was falling, mingled with snow. Behrman, in his old blue shirt, took his seat as the hermit miner on an upturned kettle for a rock.

When Sue awoke from an hour's sleep the next morning she found Johnsy with dull, wide-open eyes staring at the drawn green shade.

"Pull it up; I want to see," she ordered, in a whisper.

Wearily Sue obeyed.

But, lo! after the beating rain and fierce gusts of wind that had endured through the livelong night, there yet stood out against the brick wall one ivy leaf. It was the last one on the vine. Still dark green near its stem, but with its serrated edges tinted with the yellow of dissolution and decay, it hung bravely from the branch some twenty feet above the ground.

"It is the last one," said Johnsy. "I thought it would surely fall during the night. I heard the wind. It will fall today, and I shall die at the same time."

"Dear, dear!" said Sue, leaning her worn face down to the pillow, "think of me, if you won't think of yourself. What would I do?"

But Johnsy did not answer. The lonesomest thing in all the world is a soul when it is making ready to go on its mysterious, far journey. The fancy seemed to possess her more strongly as one by one the ties that bound her to friendship and to earth were loosed.

The day wore away, and even through the twilight they could see the lone ivy leaf clinging to its stem against the wall. And then, with the coming of the night the north wind was again loosed, while the rain still beat against the windows and pattered down from the low Dutch eaves.

When it was light enough Johnsy, the merciless, commanded that the shade be raised.

The ivy leaf was still there.

Johnsy lay for a long time looking at it. And then she called to Sue, who was stirring her chicken broth over the gas stove.

"I've been a bad girl, Sudie," said Johnsy. "Something has made that last leaf stay there to show me how wicked I was. It is a sin to want to die. You may bring a me a little

broth now, and some milk with a little port in it, and—no; bring me a hand-mirror first, and then pack some pillows about me, and I will sit up and watch you cook."

An hour later she said:

"Sudie, some day I hope to paint the Bay of Naples."

The doctor came in the afternoon, and Sue had an excuse to go into the hallway as he left.

"Even chances," said the doctor, taking Sue's thin, shaking hand in his. "With good nursing you'll win. And now I must see another case I have downstairs. Behrman, his name is—some kind of an artist, I believe. Pneumonia, too. He is an old, weak man, and the attack is acute. There is no hope for him; but he goes to the hospital today to be made more comfortable."

The next day the doctor said to Sue: "She's out of danger. You've won. Nutrition and care now—that's all."

And that afternoon Sue came to the bed where Johnsy lay, contentedly knitting a very blue and very useless woollen shoulder scarf, and put one arm around her, pillows and all.

"I have something to tell you, white mouse," she said. "Mr. Behrman died of pneumonia today in the hospital. He was ill only two days. The janitor found him the morning of the first day in his room downstairs helpless with pain. His shoes and clothing were wet through and icy cold. They couldn't imagine where he had been on such a dreadful night. And then they found a lantern, still lighted, and a ladder that had been dragged from its place, and some scattered brushes, and a palette with green and yellow colors mixed on it, and—look out the window, dear, at the last ivy leaf on the wall. Didn't you wonder why it never fluttered or moved when

the wind blew? Ah, darling, it's Behrman's masterpiece—he painted it there the night that the last leaf fell."

2 The Gift of the Magi

One dollar and eighty-seven cents. That was all. And sixty cents of it was in pennies. Pennies saved one and two at a time by bulldozing the grocer and the vegetable man and the butcher until one's cheeks burned with the silent imputation of parsimony that such close dealing implied. Three times Della counted it. One dollar and eighty-seven cents. And the next day would be Christmas.

There was clearly nothing to do but flop down on the shabby little couch and howl. So Della did it. Which instigates the moral reflection that life is made up of sobs, sniffles, and smiles, with sniffles predominating.

While the mistress of the home is gradually subsiding from the first stage to the second, take a look at the home. A furnished flat at $8 per week. It did not exactly beggar description, but it certainly had that word on the lookout for the mendicancy squad.

In the vestibule below was a letter-box into which no letter would go, and an electric button from which no mortal finger could coax a ring. Also appertaining thereunto was a card bearing the name "Mr. James Dillingham Young."

The "Dillingham" had been flung to the breeze during a former period of prosperity when its possessor was being paid $30 per week. Now, when the income was shrunk to $20, the letters of "Dillingham" looked blurred, as though they were thinking seriously of contracting to a modest and unassuming D. But whenever Mr. James Dillingham Young came home and reached his flat above he was called "Jim" and greatly hugged by Mrs. James Dillingham Young, already introduced to you as Della. Which is all very good.

Della finished her cry and attended to her cheeks with the powder rag. She stood by the window and looked out dully at a gray cat walking a gray fence in a gray backyard. Tomorrow would be Christmas Day, and she had only $1.87 with which to buy Jim a present. She had been saving every penny she could for months, with this result. Twenty dollars a week doesn't go far. Expenses had been greater than she had calculated. They always are. Only $1.87 to buy a present for Jim. Her Jim. Many a happy hour she had spent planning for something nice for him. Something fine and rare and sterling—something just a little bit near to being worthy of the honor of being owned by Jim.

There was a pier-glass between the windows of the room. Perhaps you have seen a pier-glass in an $8 flat. A very thin and very agile person may, by observing his reflection in a rapid sequence of longitudinal strips, obtain a fairly accurate conception of his looks. Della, being slender, had mastered the art.

Suddenly she whirled from the window and stood before the glass. Her eyes were shining brilliantly, but her face had lost its color within twenty seconds. Rapidly she pulled down her hair and let it fall to its full length.

Now, there were two possessions of the James Dillingham Youngs in which they both took a mighty pride. One was Jim's gold watch that had been his father's and his grandfather's. The other was Della's hair. Had the

Queen of Sheba lived in the flat across the airshaft, Della would have let her hair hang out the window some day to dry just to depreciate Her Majesty's jewels and gifts. Had King Solomon been the janitor, with all his treasures piled up in the basement, Jim would have pulled out his watch every time he passed, just to see him pluck at his beard from envy.

So now Della's beautiful hair fell about her rippling and shining like a cascade of brown waters. It reached below her knee and made itself almost a garment for her. And then she did it up again nervously and quickly. Once she faltered for a minute and stood still while a tear or two splashed on the worn red carpet.

On went her old brown jacket; on went her old brown hat. With a whirl of skirts and with the brilliant sparkle still in her eyes, she fluttered out the door and down the stairs to the street.

Where she stopped the sign read: "Mme. Sofronie. Hair Goods of All Kinds." One flight up Della ran, and collected herself, panting. Madame, large, too white, chilly, hardly looked the "Sofronie."

"Will you buy my hair?" asked Della.

"I buy hair," said Madame. "Take yer hat off and let's have a sight at the looks of it."

Down rippled the brown cascade.

"Twenty dollars," said Madame, lifting the mass with a practiced hand.

"Give it to me quick," said Della.

Oh, and the next two hours tripped by on rosy wings. Forget the hashed metaphor. She was ransacking the stores for Jim's present.

She found it at last. It surely had been made for Jim and no one else. There was no other like it in any of the stores, and she had turned all of them inside out. It was a platinum fob chain simple and chaste in design, properly proclaiming its value by substance alone and not by meretricious ornamentation—as all good things should do. It was even worthy of The Watch. As soon as she saw it she knew that it must be Jim's. It was like him. Quietness and value—the description applied to both. Twenty-one dollars they took from her for it, and she hurried home with the 87 cents. With that chain on his watch Jim might be properly anxious about the time in any company. Grand as the watch was, he sometimes looked at it on the sly on account of the old leather strap that he used in place of a chain.

When Della reached home her intoxication gave way a little to prudence and reason. She got out her curling irons and lighted the gas and went to work repairing the ravages made by generosity added to love. Which is always a tremendous task, dear friends—a mammoth task.

Within forty minutes her head was covered with tiny, close-lying curls that made her look wonderfully like a truant schoolboy. She looked at her reflection in the mirror long, carefully, and critically.

"If Jim doesn't kill me," she said to herself, "before he takes a second look at me, he'll say I look like a Coney

Island chorus girl. But what could I do—oh! what could I do with a dollar and eighty-seven cents?"

At 7 o'clock the coffee was made and the frying-pan was on the back of the stove hot and ready to cook the chops.

Jim was never late. Della doubled the fob chain in her hand and sat on the corner of the table near the door that he always entered. Then she heard his step on the stair away down on the first flight, and she turned white for just a moment. She had a habit for saying little silent prayers about the simplest everyday things, and now she whispered: "Please God, make him think I am still pretty."

The door opened and Jim stepped in and closed it. He looked thin and very serious. Poor fellow, he was only twenty-two—and to be burdened with a family! He needed a new overcoat and he was without gloves.

Jim stopped inside the door, as immovable as a setter at the scent of quail. His eyes were fixed upon Della, and there was an expression in them that she could not read, and it terrified her. It was not anger, nor surprise, nor disapproval, nor horror, nor any of the sentiments that she had been prepared for. He simply stared at her fixedly with that peculiar expression on his face.

Della wriggled off the table and went for him.

"Jim, darling," she cried, "don't look at me that way. I had my hair cut off and sold it because I couldn't have lived through Christmas without giving you a present. It'll grow out again—you won't mind, will you? I just had to do it. My hair grows awfully fast. Say 'Merry Christmas!' Jim, and let's be happy. You don't know what a nice— what a beautiful, nice gift I've got for you."

"You've cut off your hair?" asked Jim, laboriously, as if he had not arrived at that patent fact yet even after the hardest mental labor.

"Cut it off and sold it," said Della. "Don't you like me just as well, anyhow? I'm me without my hair, ain't I?"

Jim looked about the room curiously.

"You say your hair is gone?" he said, with an air almost of idiocy.

"You needn't look for it," said Della. "It's sold, I tell you—sold and gone, too. It's Christmas Eve, boy. Be good to me, for it went for you. Maybe the hairs of my head were numbered," she went on with sudden serious sweetness, "but nobody could ever count my love for you. Shall I put the chops on, Jim?"

Out of his trance Jim seemed quickly to wake. He enfolded his Della. For ten seconds let us regard with discreet scrutiny some inconsequential object in the other direction. Eight dollars a week or a million a year—what is the difference? A mathematician or a wit would give you the wrong answer. The magi brought valuable gifts, but that was not among them. This dark assertion will be illuminated later on.

Jim drew a package from his overcoat pocket and threw it upon the table.

"Don't make any mistake, Dell," he said, "about me. I don't think there's anything in the way of a haircut or a shave or a shampoo that could make me like my girl any less. But if you'll unwrap that package you may see why you had me going a while at first."

White fingers and nimble tore at the string and paper. And then an ecstatic scream of joy; and then, alas! a quick feminine change to hysterical tears and wails, necessitating the immediate employment of all the comforting powers of the lord of the flat.

For there lay The Combs—the set of combs, side and back, that Della had worshipped for long in a Broadway window. Beautiful combs, pure tortoise shell, with jeweled rims—just the shade to wear in the beautiful vanished hair. They were expensive combs, she knew, and her heart had simply craved and yearned over them without the least hope of possession. And now, they were hers, but the tresses that should have adorned the coveted adornments were gone.

But she hugged them to her bosom, and at length she was able to look up with dim eyes and a smile and say: "My hair grows so fast, Jim!"

And then Della leaped up like a little singed cat and cried, "Oh, oh!"

Jim had not yet seen his beautiful present. She held it out to him eagerly upon her open palm. The dull precious metal seemed to flash with a reflection of her bright and ardent spirit.

"Isn't it a dandy, Jim? I hunted all over town to find it. You'll have to look at the time a hundred times a day now. Give me your watch. I want to see how it looks on it."

Instead of obeying, Jim tumbled down on the couch and put his hands under the back of his head and smiled.

"Dell," said he, "let's put our Christmas presents away and keep 'em a while. They're too nice to use just at present. I sold the watch to get the money to buy your combs. And now suppose you put the chops on."

The magi, as you know, were wise men—wonderfully wise men—who brought gifts to the Babe in the manger. They invented the art of giving Christmas presents. Being wise, their gifts were no doubt wise ones, possibly bearing the privilege of exchange in case of duplication. And here I have lamely related to you the uneventful chronicle of two foolish children in a flat who most unwisely sacrificed for each other the greatest treasures of their house. But in a last word to the wise of these days let it be said that of all who give gifts these two were the wisest. Of all who give and receive gifts, such as they are wisest. Everywhere they are wisest. They are the magi.

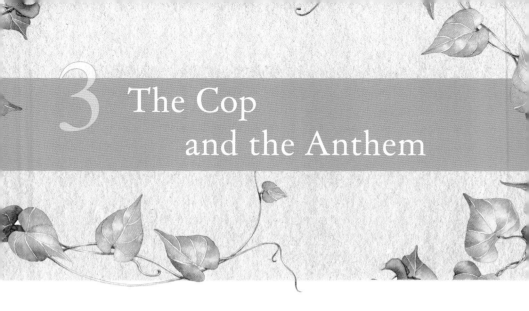

3 The Cop and the Anthem

On his bench in Madison Square Soapy moved uneasily. When wild geese honk high of nights, and when women without sealskin coats grow kind to their husbands, and when Soapy moves uneasily on his bench in the park, you may know that winter is near at hand.

A dead leaf fell in Soapy's lap. That was Jack Frost's card. Jack is kind to the regular denizens of Madison Square, and gives fair warning of his annual call. At the corners of four streets he hands his pasteboard to the North Wind, footman of the mansion of All Outdoors, so that the inhabitants thereof may make ready.

Soapy's mind became cognizant of the fact that the time had come for him to resolve himself into a singular Committee of Ways and Means to provide against the coming rigor. And therefore he moved uneasily on his bench.

The hibernatorial ambitions of Soapy were not of the highest. In them there were no considerations of Mediterranean cruises, of soporific Southern skies or drifting in the Vesuvian Bay. Three months on the Island was what his soul craved. Three months of assured board and bed and congenial company, safe from Boreas and bluecoats, seemed to Soapy the essence of things desirable.

For years the hospitable Blackwell's had been his winter quarters. Just as his more fortunate fellow New Yorkers had bought their tickets to Palm Beach and the Riviera each winter, so Soapy had made his humble arrangements for his annual hegira to the Island. And now the time was come. On the previous night three Sabbath newspapers, distributed beneath his coat, about his ankles and over his lap, had failed to repulse the cold as he slept on his bench near the spurting fountain in the ancient square. So the Island loomed big and timely in Soapy's mind. He scorned the provisions made in the name of charity for the city's dependents. In Soapy's opinion the Law was more benign than Philanthropy. There was an endless round of institutions, municipal and eleemosynary, on which he might set out and receive lodging and food accordant with the simple life. But to one of Soapy's proud spirit the gifts of charity are encumbered. If not in coin you must pay in humiliation of spirit for every benefit received at the hands of philanthropy. As Caesar had his Brutus, every bed of charity must have its toll of a bath, every loaf of bread its compensation of a private and personal inquisition. Wherefore it is better to be a guest of the law, which, though conducted by rules, does not meddle unduly with a gentleman's private affairs.

Soapy, having decided to go to the Island, at once set about accomplishing his desire. There were many easy ways of doing this. The pleasantest was to dine luxuriously at some expensive restaurant; and then, after declaring insolvency, be handed over quietly and without uproar to a policeman. An accommodating magistrate would do the rest.

Soapy left his bench and strolled out of the square and across the level sea of asphalt, where Broadway and Fifth Avenue flow together. Up Broadway he turned, and halted at a glittering café, where are gathered together nightly the choicest products of the grape, the silkworm and the protoplasm.

Soapy had confidence in himself from the lowest button of his vest upward. He was shaven, and his coat was decent and his neat black, ready-tied four-in-hand had been presented to him by a lady missionary on Thanksgiving Day. If he could reach a table in the restaurant unsuspected success would be his. The portion of him that would show above the table would raise no doubt in the waiter's mind. A roasted mallard duck, thought Soapy, would be about the thing—with a bottle of Chablis, and then Camembert, a demi-tasse and a cigar. One dollar for the cigar would be enough. The total would not be so high as to call forth any supreme manifestation of revenge from the café management; and yet the meat would leave him filled and happy for the journey to his winter refuge.

But as Soapy set foot inside the restaurant door the head waiter's eye fell upon his frayed trousers and decadent shoes. Strong and ready hands turned him about and conveyed him in silence and haste to the sidewalk and averted the ignoble fate of the menaced mallard.

Soapy turned off Broadway. It seemed that his route to the coveted Island was not to be an epicurean one. Some other way of entering limbo must be thought of.

At a corner of Sixth Avenue electric lights and cunningly displayed wares behind plate-glass made a shop window conspicuous. Soapy took a cobblestone and dashed it through the glass. People came running around the corner, a policeman in the lead. Soapy stood still, with his hands in his pockets, and smiled at the sight of brass buttons.

"Where's the man that done that?" inquired the officer, excitedly.

"Don't you figure out that I might have had something to do with it?" said Soapy, not without sarcasm, but friendly, as one greets good fortune.

The policeman's mind refused to accept Soapy even as a clue. Men who smash windows do not remain to parley with the law's minions. They take to their heels. The policeman saw a man halfway down the block running to catch a car. With drawn club he joined in the pursuit. Soapy, with disgust in his heart, loafed along, twice unsuccessful.

On the opposite side of the street was a restaurant of no great pretensions. It catered to large appetites and modest purses. Its crockery and atmosphere were thick; its soup and napery thin. Into this place Soapy took his accusive shoes and telltale trousers without challenge. At a table he sat and consumed beefsteak, flapjacks, doughnuts and pie. And then to the waiter be betrayed the fact that the minutest coin and himself were strangers.

"Now, get busy and call a cop," said Soapy. "And don't keep a gentleman waiting."

"No cop for youse," said the waiter, with a voice like butter cakes and an eye like the cherry in a Manhattan cocktail. "Hey, Con!"

Neatly upon his left ear on the callous pavement two waiters pitched Soapy. He arose joint by joint, as a carpenter's rule opens, and beat the dust from his clothes. Arrest seemed but a rosy dream. The Island seemed very far away. A policeman who stood before a drug store two doors away laughed and walked down the street.

Five blocks Soapy traveled before his courage permitted him to woo capture again. This time the opportunity presented what he fatuously termed to himself a "cinch." A young woman of a modest and pleasing guise was standing before a show window gazing with sprightly interest at its display of shaving mugs and inkstands, and two yards from the window a large policeman of severe demeanour leaned against a water plug.

It was Soapy's design to assume the role of the despicable and execrated "masher." The refined and elegant appearance of his victim and the contiguity of the conscientious cop encouraged him to believe that he would soon feel the pleasant official clutch upon his arm that would insure his winter quarters on the right little, tight little isle.

Soapy straightened the lady missionary's ready-made tie, dragged his shrinking cuffs into the open, set his hat at a killing cant and sidled toward the young woman. He made eyes at her, was taken with sudden coughs and "hems," smiled, smirked and went brazenly through the impudent and contemptible litany of the "masher." With half an eye Soapy saw that the policeman was watching him fixedly. The young woman moved away a few steps, and again bestowed her absorbed attention upon the shaving mugs. Soapy followed, boldly stepping to her side, raised his hat and said:

"Ah there, Bedelia! Don't you want to come and play in my yard?"

The policeman was still looking. The persecuted young woman had but to beckon a finger and Soapy would be practically en route for his insular haven. Already he imagined he could feel the cozy warmth of the station-house. The young woman faced him and, stretching out a hand, caught Soapy's coat sleeve.

"Sure, Mike," she said joyfully, "if you'll blow me to a pail of suds. I'd have spoke to you sooner, but the cop was watching."

With the young woman playing the clinging ivy to his oak Soapy walked past the policeman overcome with gloom. He seemed doomed to liberty.

At the next corner he shook off his companion and ran. He halted in the district where by night are found the lightest streets, hearts, vows and librettos. Women in furs and men in greatcoats moved gaily in the wintry air. A sudden fear seized Soapy that some dreadful enchantment had rendered him immune to arrest. The thought brought a little of panic upon it, and when he came upon another policeman lounging grandly in front of a transplendent theater he caught at the immediate straw of "disorderly conduct."

On the sidewalk Soapy began to yell drunken gibberish at the top of his harsh voice. He danced, howled, raved and otherwise disturbed the welkin.

The policeman twirled his club, turned his back to Soapy and remarked to a citizen.

"'Tis one of them Yale lads celebratin' the goose egg they give to the Hartford College. Noisy; but no harm. We've instructions to lave them be."

Disconsolate, Soapy ceased his unavailing racket. Would never a policeman lay hands on him? In his fancy the Island seemed an unattainable Arcadia. He buttoned his thin coat against the chilling wind.

In a cigar store he saw a well-dressed man lighting a cigar at a swinging light. His silk umbrella he had set by the door on entering. Soapy stepped inside, secured the umbrella and sauntered off with it slowly. The man at the cigar light followed hastily.

"My umbrella," he said, sternly.

"Oh, is it?" sneered Soapy, adding insult to petit larceny. "Well, why don't you call a policeman? I took it. Your umbrella! Why don't you call a cop? There stands one on the corner."

The umbrella owner slowed his steps. Soapy did likewise, with a presentiment that luck would again run against him. The policeman looked at the two curiously.

"Of course," said the umbrella man—"that is—well, you know how these mistakes occur—I—f it's your umbrella I hope you'll excuse me—I picked it up this morning in a restaurant—If you recognize it as yours, why—I hope you'll—"

"Of course it's mine," said Soapy, viciously.

The ex-umbrella man retreated. The policeman hurried to assist a tall blonde in an opera cloak across the street in front of a street car that was approaching two blocks away.

Soapy walked eastward through a street damaged by improvements. He hurled the umbrella wrathfully into an excavation. He muttered against the men who wear helmets and carry clubs. Because he wanted to fall into their clutches, they seemed to regard him as a king who could do no wrong.

At length Soapy reached one of the avenues to the east where the glitter and turmoil was but faint. He set his face down this toward Madison Square, for the homing instinct survives even when the home is a park bench.

But on an unusually quiet corner Soapy came to a standstill. Here was an old church, quaint and rambling and gabled. Through one violet-stained window a soft light glowed, where, no doubt, the organist loitered over the keys, making sure of his mastery of the coming Sabbath anthem. For there drifted out to Soapy's ears sweet music that caught and held him transfixed against the convolutions of the iron fence.

The moon was above, lustrous and serene; vehicles and pedestrians were few; sparrows twittered sleepily in the eaves—for a little while the scene might have been a country churchyard. And the anthem that the organist played cemented Soapy to the iron fence, for he had known it well in the days when his life contained such things as mothers and roses and ambitions and friends and immaculate thoughts and collars.

The conjunction of Soapy's receptive state of mind and the influences about the old church wrought a sudden and wonderful change in his soul. He viewed with swift horror the pit into which he had tumbled, the degraded days, unworthy desires, dead hopes, wrecked faculties and base motives that made up his existence.

And also in a moment his heart responded thrillingly to this novel mood. An instantaneous and strong impulse moved him to battle with his desperate fate. He would pull himself out of the mire; he would make a man of himself again; he would conquer the evil that had taken possession of him. There was time; he was comparatively young yet; he would resurrect his old eager ambitions and pursue them without faltering. Those solemn but sweet organ notes had set up a revolution in him. Tomorrow he would go into the roaring downtown district and find work. A fur importer had once offered him a place as driver. He would find him tomorrow and ask for the position. He would be somebody in the world. He would—

Soapy felt a hand laid on his arm. He looked quickly around into the broad face of a policeman.

"What are you doin' here?" asked the officer.

"Nothin'," said Soapy.

"Then come along," said the policeman.

"Three months on the Island," said the Magistrate in the Police Court the next morning.

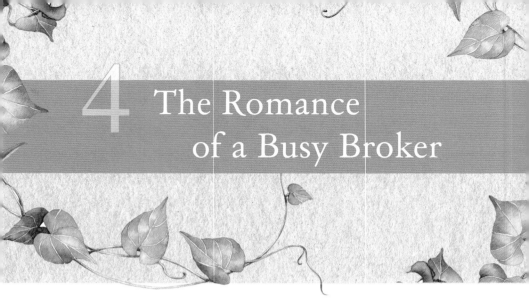

4 The Romance of a Busy Broker

Pitcher, confidential clerk in the office of Harvey Maxwell, broker, allowed a look of mild interest and surprise to visit his usually expressionless countenance when his employer briskly entered at half-past nine in company with his young lady stenographer. With a snappy "Good-morning, Pitcher," Maxwell dashed at his desk as though he were intending to leap over it, and then plunged into the great heap of letters and telegrams waiting there for him.

The young lady had been Maxwell's stenographer for a year. She was beautiful in a way that was decidedly unstenographic. She forewent the pomp of the alluring pompadour. She wore no chains, bracelets or lockets. She had not the air of being about to accept an invitation to luncheon. Her dress was grey and plain, but it fitted her figure with fidelity and discretion. In her neat black turban hat was the gold-green wing of a macaw. On this morning she was softly and shyly radiant. Her eyes were dreamily bright, her cheeks genuine peach-blow, her expression a happy one, tinged with reminiscence.

Pitcher, still mildly curious, noticed a difference in her ways this morning. Instead of going straight into the adjoining room, where her desk was, she lingered, slightly irresolute, in the outer office. Once she moved over by Maxwell's desk, near enough for him to be aware of her presence.

The machine sitting at that desk was no longer a man; it was a busy New York broker, moved by buzzing wheels and uncoiling springs.

"Well—what is it? Anything?" asked Maxwell sharply. His opened mail lay like a bank of stage snow on his crowded desk. His keen gray eye, impersonal and brusque, flashed upon her half impatiently.

"Nothing," answered the stenographer, moving away with a little smile.

"Mr. Pitcher," she said to the confidential clerk, "did Mr. Maxwell say anything yesterday about engaging another stenographer?"

"He did," answered Pitcher. "He told me to get another one. I notified the agency yesterday afternoon to send over a few samples this morning. It's 9.45 o'clock, and not a single picture hat or piece of pineapple chewing gum has showed up yet."

"I will do the work as usual, then," said the young lady, "until some one comes to fill the place." And she went to her desk at once and hung the black turban hat with the gold-green macaw wing in its accustomed place.

He who has been denied the spectacle of a busy Manhattan broker during a rush of business is handicapped for the profession of anthropology. The poet sings of the "crowded hour of glorious life." The broker's hour is not only crowded, but the minutes and seconds are hanging to all the straps and packing both front and rear platforms.

And this day was Harvey Maxwell's busy day. The ticker began to reel out jerkily its fitful coils of tape, the desk telephone had a chronic attack of buzzing. Men began to throng into the office and call at him over the railing, jovially, sharply, viciously, excitedly. Messenger boys ran in and out with messages and telegrams. The clerks in the office jumped about like sailors during a storm. Even Pitcher's face relaxed into something resembling animation.

On the Exchange there were hurricanes and landslides and snowstorms and glaciers and volcanoes, and those elemental disturbances were reproduced in miniature in the broker's offices. Maxwell shoved his chair against the wall and transacted business after the manner of a toe dancer. He jumped from ticker to 'phone, from desk to door with the trained agility of a harlequin.

In the midst of this growing and important stress the broker became suddenly aware of a high-rolled fringe of golden hair under a nodding canopy of velvet and ostrich tips, an imitation sealskin sacque and a string of beads as large as hickory nuts, ending near the floor with a silver heart. There was a self-possessed young lady connected with these accessories; and Pitcher was there to construe her.

"Lady from the Stenographer's Agency to see about the position," said Pitcher.

Maxwell turned half around, with his hands full of papers and ticker tape.

"What position?" he asked, with a frown.

"Position of stenographer," said Pitcher. "You told me yesterday to call them up and have one sent over this morning."

"You are losing your mind, Pitcher," said Maxwell. "Why should I have given you any such instructions? Miss Leslie has given perfect satisfaction during the year she has been here. The place is hers as long as she chooses to retain it. There's no place open here, madam. Countermand that order with the agency, Pitcher, and don't bring any more of 'em here."

The silver heart left the office, swinging and banging itself independently against the office furniture as it indignantly departed. Pitcher seized a moment to remark to the bookkeeper that the "old man" seemed to get more absent-minded and forgetful every day of the world.

The rush and pace of business grew fiercer and faster. On the floor they were pounding half a dozen stocks in which Maxwell's customers were heavy investors. Orders to buy and sell were coming and going as swift as the flight of swallows. Some of his own holdings were imperilled, and the man was working like some high-geared, delicate, strong machine—strung to full tension, going at full speed, accurate, never hesitating, with the proper word and decision and act ready and prompt as clockwork. Stocks and bonds, loans and mortgages, margins and securities—here was a world of finance, and there was no room in it for the human world or the world of nature.

When the luncheon hour drew near there came a slight lull in the uproar.

Maxwell stood by his desk with his hands full of telegrams and memoranda, with a fountain pen over his right ear and his hair hanging in disorderly strings over his forehead. His window was open, for the beloved janitress, Spring had turned on a little warmth through the waking registers of the earth.

And through the window came a wandering—perhaps a lost—odor—a delicate, sweet odor of lilac that fixed the broker for a moment immovable. For this odor belonged to Miss Leslie; it was her own, and hers only.

The odor brought her vividly, almost tangibly before him. The world of finance dwindled suddenly to a speck. And she was in the next room— twenty steps away.

"By George, I'll do it now," said Maxwell, half aloud. "I'll ask her now. I wonder I didn't do it long ago."

He dashed into the inner office with the haste of a short trying to cover. He charged upon the desk of the stenographer.

She looked up at him with a smile. A soft pink crept over her cheek, and her eyes were kind and frank. Maxwell leaned one elbow on her desk. He still clutched fluttering papers with both hands and the pen was above his ear.

"Miss Leslie," he began hurriedly, "I have but a moment to spare. I want to say something in that moment. Will you be my wife? I haven't had time to make love to you in the ordinary way, but I really do love you. Talk quick, please—those fellows are clubbing the stuffing out of Union Pacific."

"Oh, what are you talking about?" exclaimed the young lady. She rose to her feet and gazed upon him, round-eyed.

"Don't you understand?" said Maxwell, restively. "I want you to marry me. I love you, Miss Leslie. I wanted to tell you, and I snatched a minute when things had slackened up a bit. They're calling me for the 'phone now. Tell 'em to wait a minute, Pitcher. Won't you, Miss Leslie?"

The stenographer acted very queerly. At first she seemed overcome with amazement; then tears flowed from her wondering eyes; and then she smiled sunnily through them, and one of her arms slid tenderly about the broker's neck.

"I know now," she said, softly. "It's this old business that has driven everything else out of your head for the time. I was frightened at first. Don't you remember, Harvey? We were married last evening at 8 o'clock in the Little Church Around the Corner."

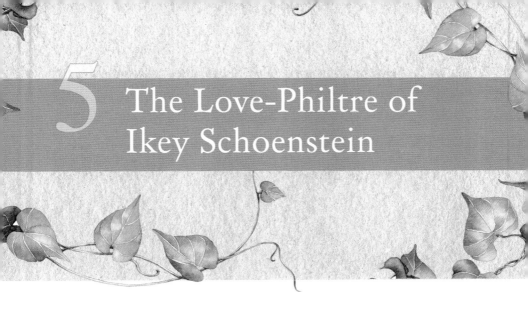

5 The Love-Philtre of Ikey Schoenstein

The Blue Light Drug Store is downtown, between the Bowery and First Avenue, where the distance between the two streets is the shortest. The Blue Light does not consider that pharmacy is a thing of bric-à-brac, scent and ice-cream soda. If you ask it for pain-killer it will not give you a bonbon.

The Blue Light scorns the labor-saving arts of modern pharmacy. It macerates its opium and percolates its own laudanum and paregoric. To this day pills are made behind its tall prescription desk—pills rolled out on its own pill-tile, divided with a spatula, rolled with the finger and thumb, dusted with calcined magnesia and delivered in little round pasteboard pill-boxes. The store is on a corner about which coveys of ragged-plumed, hilarious children play and become candidates for the cough drops and soothing syrups that wait for them inside.

Ikey Schoenstein was the night clerk of the Blue Light and the friend of his customers. Thus it is on the East Side, where the heart of pharmacy is not glacé. There, as it should be, the druggist is a counsellor, a confessor, an adviser, an able and willing missionary and mentor whose learning is respected, whose occult wisdom is venerated and whose medicine is often poured, untasted, into the gutter. Therefore Ikey's corniform, bespectacled nose and narrow, knowledge-bowed figure was well known in the vicinity of the Blue Light, and his advice and notice were much desired.

Ikey roomed and breakfasted at Mrs. Riddle's two squares away. Mrs. Riddle had a daughter named Rosy. The circumlocution has been in vain—you must have guessed it—Ikey adored Rosy. She tinctured all his thoughts; she was the compound extract of all that was chemically pure and official—the dispensatory contained nothing equal to her. But Ikey was timid, and his hopes remained insoluble in the menstruum of his backwardness and fears. Behind his counter he was a superior being, calmly conscious of special knowledge and worth; outside he was a weak-kneed, purblind, motorman-cursed rambler, with ill-fitting clothes stained with chemicals and smelling of socotrine aloes and valerianate of ammonia.

The fly in Ikey's ointment (thrice welcome, pat trope!) was Chunk McGowan.

Mr. McGowan was also striving to catch the bright smiles tossed about by Rosy. But he was no out-fielder as Ikey was; he picked them off the bat. At the same time he was Ikey's friend and customer, and often dropped in at the Blue Light Drug Store to have a bruise painted with iodine or get a cut rubber-plastered after a pleasant evening spent along the Bowery.

One afternoon McGowan drifted in in his silent, easy way, and sat, comely, smooth-faced, hard, indomitable, good-natured, upon a stool.

"Ikey," said he, when his friend had fetched his mortar and sat opposite, grinding gum benzoin to a powder, "get busy with your ear. It's drugs for me if you've got the line I need."

Ikey scanned the countenance of Mr. McGowan for the usual evidences of conflict, but found none.

"Take your coat off," he ordered. "I guess already that you have been stuck in the ribs with a knife. I have many times told you those Dagoes would do you up."

Mr. McGowan smiled. "Not them," he said. "Not any Dagoes. But you've located the diagnosis all right enough—it's under my coat, near the ribs. Say! Ikey—Rosy and me are goin' to run away and get married tonight."

Ikey's left forefinger was doubled over the edge of the mortar, holding it steady. He gave it a wild rap with the pestle, but felt it not. Meanwhile Mr. McGowan's smile faded to a look of perplexed gloom.

"That is," he continued, "if she keeps in the notion until the time comes. We've been layin' pipes for the getaway for two weeks. One day she says she will; the same evenin' she says nixy. We've agreed on tonight, and Rosy's stuck to the affirmative this time for two whole days. But it's five hours yet till the time, and I'm afraid she'll stand me up when it comes to the scratch."

"You said you wanted drugs," remarked Ikey.

Mr. McGowan looked ill at ease and harassed—a condition opposed to his usual line of demeanour. He made a patent-medicine almanac into a roll and fitted it with unprofitable carefulness about his finger.

"I wouldn't have this double handicap make a false start tonight for a million," he said. "I've got a little flat up in Harlem all ready, with chrysanthemums on the table and a kettle ready to boil. And I've engaged a pulpit pounder to be ready at his house for us at 9.30. It's got to come off. And if Rosy don't change her mind again!"—Mr. McGowan ceased, a prey to his doubts.

"I don't see then yet," said Ikey, shortly, "what makes it that you talk of drugs, or what I can be doing about it."

"Old man Riddle don't like me a little bit," went on the uneasy suitor, bent upon marshalling his arguments. "For a week he hasn't let Rosy step outside the door with me. If it wasn't for losin' a boarder they'd have bounced me long ago. I'm makin' $20 a week and she'll never regret flyin' the coop with Chunk McGowan."

"You will excuse me, Chunk," said Ikey. "I must make a prescription that is to be called for soon."

"Say," said McGowan, looking up suddenly, "say, Ikey, ain't there a drug of some kind—some kind of powders that'll make a girl like you better if you give 'em to her?"

Ikey's lip beneath his nose curled with the scorn of superior enlightenment; but before he could answer, McGowan continued:

"Tim Lacy told me he got some once from a croaker uptown and fed 'em to his girl in soda water. From the very first dose he was ace-high and everybody else looked like thirty cents to her. They was married in less than two weeks."

Strong and simple was Chunk McGowan. A better reader of men than Ikey was could have seen that his tough frame was strung upon fine wires. Like a good general who was about to invade the enemy's territory he was seeking to guard every point against possible failure.

"I thought," went on Chunk hopefully, "that if I had one of them powders to give Rosy when I see her at supper tonight it might brace her up and keep her from reneging on the proposition to skip. I guess she don't need a mule team to drag her away, but women are better at coaching than they are at running bases. If the stuff'll work just for a couple of hours it'll do the trick."

"When is this foolishness of running away to be happening?" asked Ikey.

"Nine o'clock," said Mr. McGowan. "Supper's at seven. At eight Rosy goes to bed with a headache. At nine old Parvenzano lets me through to his backyard, where there's a board off Riddle's fence, next door. I go under her window and help her down the fire-escape. We've got to make it early on the preacher's account. It's all dead easy if Rosy don't balk when the flag drops. Can you fix me one of them powders, Ikey?"

Ikey Schoenstein rubbed his nose slowly.

"Chunk," said he, "it is of drugs of that nature that pharmaceutists must have much carefulness. To you alone of my acquaintance would I intrust a powder like that. But for you I shall make it, and you shall see how it makes Rosy to think of you."

Ikey went behind the prescription desk. There he crushed to a powder two soluble tablets, each containing a quarter of a grain of morphia. To them he added a little sugar of milk to increase the bulk, and folded the mixture neatly in a white paper. Taken by an adult this powder would insure several hours of heavy slumber without danger to the sleeper. This he handed to Chunk McGowan, telling him to administer it in a liquid if possible, and received the hearty thanks of the backyard Lochinvar.

The subtlety of Ikey's action becomes apparent upon recital of his subsequent move. He sent a messenger for Mr. Riddle and disclosed the plans of Mr. McGowan for eloping with Rosy. Mr. Riddle was a stout man, brick-dusty of complexion and sudden in action.

"Much obliged," he said, briefly, to Ikey. "The lazy Irish loafer! My own room's just above Rosy's. I'll just go up there myself after supper and load the shot-gun and wait. If he comes in my backyard he'll go away in a ambulance instead of a bridal chaise."

With Rosy held in the clutches of Morpheus for a many-hours deep slumber, and the blood-thirsty parent waiting, armed and forewarned, Ikey felt that his rival was close, indeed, upon discomfiture.

All night in the Blue Light Drug Store he waited at his duties for chance news of the tragedy, but none came.

At eight o'clock in the morning the day clerk arrived and Ikey started hurriedly for Mrs. Riddle's to learn the outcome. And, lo! as he stepped out of the store who but Chunk McGowan sprang from a passing street car and grasped his hand—Chunk McGowan with a victor's smile and flushed with joy.

"Pulled it off," said Chunk with Elysium in his grin. "Rosy hit the fire-escape on time to a second, and we was under the wire at the Reverend's at 9.30 1/4. She's up at the flat—she cooked eggs this mornin' in a blue kimono—Lord! how lucky I am! You must pace up some day, Ikey, and feed with us. I've got a job down near the bridge, and that's where I'm heading for now."

"The—the—powder?" stammered Ikey.

"Oh, that stuff you gave me!" said Chunk, broadening his grin; "well, it was this way. I sat down at the supper table last night at Riddle's, and I looked at Rosy, and I says to myself, 'Chunk, if you get the girl get her on the square—don't try any hocus-pocus with a thoroughbred like her.' And I keeps the paper you give me in my pocket. And then my lamps fall on another party present, who, I says to myself, is failin' in a proper affection toward his comin' son-in-law, so I watches my chance and dumps that powder in old man Riddle's coffee—see?"

6 Springtime à la Carte

It was a day in March.

Never, never begin a story this way when you write one. No opening could possibly be worse. It is unimaginative, flat, dry, and likely to consist of mere wind. But in this instance it is allowable. For the following paragraph, which should have inaugurated the narrative, is too wildly extravagant and preposterous to be flaunted in the face of the reader without preparation.

Sarah was crying over her bill of fare.

Think of a New York girl shedding tears on the menu card!

To account for this you will be allowed to guess that the lobsters were all out, or that she had sworn ice-cream off during Lent, or that she had ordered onions, or that she had just come from a Hackett matinée. And then, all these theories being wrong, you will please let the story proceed.

The gentleman who announced that the world was an oyster which he with his sword would open made a larger hit than he deserved. It is not difficult to open an oyster with a sword. But did you ever notice any one try to open the terrestrial bivalve with a typewriter? Like to wait for a dozen raw opened that way?

Sarah had managed to pry apart the shells with her unhandy weapon far enough to nibble a wee bit at the cold and clammy world within. She knew no more shorthand than if she had been a graduate in stenography just let slip upon the world by a business college. So, not being able to stenog, she could not enter that bright galaxy of office talent. She was a free-lance typewriter and canvassed for odd jobs of copying.

The most brilliant and crowning feat of Sarah's battle with the world was the deal she made with Schulenberg's Home Restaurant. The restaurant was next door to the old red brick in which she hall-roomed. One evening after dining at Schulenberg's 40-cent, five-course *table d'hôte* (served as fast as you throw the five baseballs at the colored gentleman's head) Sarah took away with her the bill of fare. It was written in an almost unreadable script neither English nor German, and so arranged that if you were not careful you began with a toothpick and rice pudding and ended with soup and the day of the week.

The next day Sarah showed Schulenberg a neat card on which the menu was beautifully typewritten with the viands temptingly marshalled under their right and

proper heads from "hors d'oeuvre" to "not responsible for overcoats and umbrellas."

Schulenberg became a naturalized citizen on the spot. Before Sarah left him she had him willingly committed to an agreement. She was to furnish typewritten bills of fare for the twenty-one tables in the restaurant—a new bill for each day's dinner, and new ones for breakfast and lunch as often as changes occurred in the food or as neatness required.

In return for this Schulenberg was to send three meals per diem to Sarah's hall room by a waiter—an obsequious one if possible—and furnish her each afternoon with a pencil draft of what Fate had in store for Schulenberg's customers on the morrow.

Mutual satisfaction resulted from the agreement. Schulenberg's patrons now knew what the food they ate was called even if its nature sometimes puzzled them. And Sarah had food during a cold, dull winter, which was the main thing with her.

And then the almanac lied, and said that spring had come. Spring comes when it comes. The frozen snows of January still lay like adamant in the cross-town streets. The hand-organs still played "In the Good Old Summertime," with their December vivacity and expression. Men began to make thirty-day notes to buy Easter dresses. Janitors shut off steam. And when these things happen one may know that the city is still in the clutches of winter.

One afternoon Sarah shivered in her elegant hall bedroom; "house heated; scrupulously clean; conveniences; seen to be appreciated." She had no work to do except Schulenberg's menu cards. Sarah sat in her squeaky willow rocker, and looked out the window. The calendar on the wall kept crying to her: "Springtime is here, Sarah—springtime is here, I tell you. Look at me, Sarah, my figures show it. You've got a neat figure yourself, Sarah—a—nice springtime figure—why do you look out the window so sadly?"

Sarah's room was at the back of the house. Looking out the window she could see the windowless rear brick wall of the box factory on the next street. But the wall was clearest crystal; and Sarah was looking down a grassy lane shaded with cherry trees and elms and bordered with raspberry bushes and Cherokee roses.

Spring's real harbingers are too subtle for the eye and ear. Some must have the flowering crocus, the wood-starring dogwood, the voice of bluebird—even so gross a reminder as the farewell handshake of the retiring buckwheat and oyster before they can welcome the Lady in Green to their dull bosoms. But to old earth's choicest kin there come straight, sweet messages from his newest bride, telling them they shall be no stepchildren unless they choose to be.

On the previous summer Sarah had gone into the country and loved a farmer. (In writing your story never hark back thus. It is bad art, and cripples interest. Let it march, march.)

Sarah stayed two weeks at Sunnybrook Farm. There she learned to love old Farmer Franklin's son Walter. Farmers have been loved and wedded and turned out to grass in less time. But young Walter Franklin was a modern agriculturist. He had a telephone in his cow house, and he could figure up exactly what effect next year's Canada wheat crop would have on potatoes planted in the dark of the moon.

It was in this shaded and raspberried lane that Walter had wooed and won her. And together they had sat and woven a crown of dandelions for her hair. He had immoderately praised the effect of the yellow blossoms against her brown tresses; and she had left the chaplet there, and walked back to the house swinging her straw sailor in her hands.

They were to marry in the spring—at the very first signs of spring, Walter said. And Sarah came back to the city to pound her typewriter.

A knock at the door dispelled Sarah's visions of that happy day. A waiter had brought the rough pencil draft of the Home Restaurant's next day fare in old Schulenberg's angular hand.

Sarah sat down to her typewriter and slipped a card between the rollers. She was a nimble worker. Generally in an hour and a half the twenty-one menu cards were written and ready.

Today there were more changes on the bill of fare than usual. The soups were lighter; pork was eliminated from the entrées, figuring only with Russian turnips among the roasts. The gracious spirit of spring pervaded the entire menu. Lamb, that lately capered on the greening hillsides, was becoming exploited with the sauce that commemorated its gambols. The song of the oyster, though not silenced, was *diminuendo con amore.* The frying-pan seemed to be held, inactive, behind the beneficent bars of the broiler. The pie list swelled; the richer puddings had vanished; the sausage, with his drapery wrapped about him, barely lingered in a pleasant thanatopsis with the buckwheats and the sweet but doomed maple.

Sarah's fingers danced like midgets above a summer stream. Down through the courses she worked, giving each item its position according to its length with an accurate eye. Just above the desserts came the list of vegetables. Carrots and peas, asparagus on toast, the perennial tomatoes and corn and succotash, lima beans, cabbage—and then—

Sarah was crying over her bill of fare. Tears from the depths of some divine despair rose in her heart and gathered to her eyes. Down went her head on the little typewriter stand; and the keyboard rattled a dry accompaniment to her moist sobs.

For she had received no letter from Walter in two weeks, and the next item on the bill of fare was dandelions—dandelions with some kind of egg—but bother the egg!—dandelions, with whose golden blooms Walter had crowned her his queen of love and future bride—dandelions, the harbingers of spring, her sorrow's crown of sorrow—reminder of her happiest days.

Madam, I dare you to smile until you suffer this test: Let the Marechal Niel roses that Percy brought you on the night you gave him your heart be served as a salad with French dressing before your eyes at a Schulenberg *table d'hôte*. Had Juliet so seen her love tokens dishonored the sooner would she have sought the lethean herbs of the good apothecary.

But what a witch is Spring! Into the great cold city of stone and iron a message had to be sent. There was none to convey it but the little hardy courier of the fields with his rough green coat and modest air. He is a true soldier of fortune, this *dent-de-lion*—this lion's tooth, as the French chefs call him. Flowered, he will assist at love-making, wreathed in my lady's nut-brown hair; young and callow and unblossomed, he goes into the boiling pot and delivers the word of his sovereign mistress.

By and by Sarah forced back her tears. The cards must be written. But, still in a faint, golden glow from her dandelionan dream, she fingered the typewriter keys absently for a little while, with her mind and heart in the meadow lane with her young farmer. But soon she came swiftly back to the rock-bound lanes of Manhattan, and the typewriter began to rattle and jump like a strike-breaker's motor car.

At 6 o'clock the waiter brought her dinner and carried away the typewritten bill of fare. When Sarah ate she set aside, with a sigh, the dish of dandelions with its crowning ovarious accompaniment. As this dark mass had been transformed from a bright and love-indorsed flower to be an ignominious vegetable, so had her summer hopes wilted and perished. Love may, as Shakespeare said, feed on itself: but Sarah could not bring herself to eat the dandelions that had graced, as ornaments, the first spiritual banquet of her heart's true affection.

At 7.30 the couple in the next room began to quarrel: the man in the room above sought for A on his flute; the gas went a little lower; three coal wagons started to unload—the only sound of which the phonograph is jealous; cats on the back fences slowly retreated toward Mukden. By these signs Sarah knew that it was time for her to read. She got out "The Cloister and the Hearth," the best non-selling book of the month, settled her feet on her trunk, and began to wander with Gerard.

The front door bell rang. The landlady answered it. Sarah left Gerard and Denys treed by a bear and listened. Oh, yes; you would, just as she did!

And then a strong voice was heard in the hall below, and Sarah jumped for her door, leaving the book on the floor and the first round easily the bear's.

You have guessed it. She reached the top of the stairs just as her farmer came up, three at a jump, and reaped and garnered her, with nothing left for the gleaners.

"Why haven't you written—oh, why?" cried Sarah.

"New York is a pretty large town," said Walter Franklin. "I came in a week ago to your old address. I found that you went away on a Thursday. That consoled some; it eliminated the possible Friday bad luck. But it didn't prevent my hunting for you with police and otherwise ever since!"

"I wrote!" said Sarah, vehemently.

"Never got it!"

"Then how did you find me?"

The young farmer smiled a springtime smile.

"I dropped into that Home Restaurant next door this evening," said he. "I don't care who knows it; I like a dish of some kind of greens at this time of the year. I ran my eye down that nice typewritten bill of fare looking for something in that line. When I got below cabbage I turned my chair over and hollered for the proprietor. He told me where you lived."

"I remember," sighed Sarah, happily. "That was dandelions below cabbage."

"I'd know that cranky capital W 'way above the line that your typewriter makes anywhere in the world," said Franklin.

"Why, there's no W in dandelions," said Sarah in surprise.

The young man drew the bill of fare from his pocket, and pointed to a line.

Sarah recognized the first card she had typewritten that afternoon. There was still the rayed splotch in the upper right-hand corner where a tear had fallen. But over the spot where one should have read the name of the meadow plant, the clinging memory of their golden blossoms had allowed her fingers to strike strange keys.

Between the red cabbage and the stuffed green peppers was the item:

"DEAREST WALTER, WITH HARD-BOILED EGG."

7 The Ransom of Red Chief

It looked like a good thing: but wait till I tell you. We were down South, in Alabama—Bill Driscoll and myself—when this kidnapping idea struck us. It was, as Bill afterward expressed it, "during a moment of temporary mental apparition"; but we didn't find that out till later.

There was a town down there, as flat as a flannel-cake, and called Summit, of course. It contained inhabitants of as undeleterious and self-satisfied a class of peasantry as ever clustered around a Maypole.

Bill and me had a joint capital of about six hundred dollars, and we needed just two thousand dollars more to pull off a fraudulent town-lot scheme in Western Illinois with. We talked it over on the front steps of the hotel. Philoprogenitiveness, says we, is strong in semi-rural communities; therefore, and for other reasons, a kidnapping project ought to do better there than in the radius of newspapers that send reporters out in plain clothes to stir up talk about such things. We knew that Summit couldn't get after us with anything stronger than constables and, maybe, some lackadaisical bloodhounds and a diatribe or two in the *Weekly Farmers' Budget*. So, it looked good.

We selected for our victim the only child of a prominent citizen named Ebenezer Dorset. The father was respectable and tight, a mortgage fancier and a stern, upright collection-plate passer and forecloser. The kid was a boy of ten, with bas-relief freckles, and hair the color of the cover of the magazine you buy at the news-stand when you want to catch a train. Bill and me figured that Ebenezer would melt down for a ransom of two thousand dollars to a cent. But wait till I tell you.

About two miles from Summit was a little mountain, covered with a dense cedar brake. On the rear elevation of this mountain was a cave. There we stored provisions.

One evening after sundown, we drove in a buggy past old Dorset's house. The kid was in the street, throwing rocks at a kitten on the opposite fence.

"Hey, little boy!" says Bill, "would you like to have a bag of candy and a nice ride?"

The boy catches Bill neatly in the eye with a piece of brick.

"That will cost the old man an extra five hundred dollars," says Bill, climbing over the wheel.

That boy put up a fight like a welter-weight cinnamon bear; but, at last, we got him down in the bottom of the buggy and drove away. We took him up to the cave, and I hitched the horse in the cedar brake. After dark I drove the buggy to the little village, three miles away, where we had hired it, and walked back to the mountain.

Bill was pasting court-plaster over the scratches and bruises on his features. There was a fire burning behind the big rock at the entrance of the cave, and the boy was watching a pot of boiling coffee, with two buzzard tailfeathers stuck in his red hair. He points a stick at me when I come up, and says:

"Ha! cursed paleface, do you dare to enter the camp of Red Chief, the terror of the plains?"

"He's all right now," says Bill, rolling up his trousers and examining some bruises on his shins. "We're playing Indian. We're making Buffalo Bill's show look like magic-lantern views of Palestine in the town hall. I'm Old Hank, the Trapper, Red Chief's captive, and I'm to be scalped at daybreak. By Geronimo! that kid can kick hard."

Yes, sir, that boy seemed to be having the time of his life. The fun of camping out in a cave had made him forget that he was a captive himself. He immediately christened me Snake-eye, the Spy, and announced that, when his braves returned from the warpath, I was to be broiled at the stake at the rising of the sun.

Then we had supper; and he filled his mouth full of bacon and bread and gravy, and began to talk. He made a during-dinner speech something like this:

"I like this fine. I never camped out before; but I had a pet 'possum once, and I was nine last birthday. I hate to go to school. Rats ate up sixteen of Jimmy Talbot's aunt's speckled hen's eggs. Are there any real Indians in these woods? I want some more gravy. Does the trees moving make the wind blow? We had five puppies. What makes your nose so red, Hank? My father has lots of money. Are the stars hot? I whipped Ed Walker twice, Saturday. I don't like girls. You dassent catch toads unless with a string. Do oxen make any noise? Why are oranges round? Have you got beds to sleep on in this cave? Amos Murray has got six toes. A parrot can talk, but a monkey or a fish can't. How many does it take to make twelve?"

Every few minutes he would remember that he was a pesky redskin, and pick up his stick rifle and tiptoe to the mouth of the cave to rubber for the scouts of the hated paleface. Now and then he would let out a war-whoop that made Old Hank the Trapper shiver. That boy had Bill terrorized from the start.

"Red Chief," says I to the kid, "would you like to go home?"

"Aw, what for?" says he. "I don't have any fun at home. I hate to go to school. I like to camp out. You won't take me back home again, Snake-eye, will you?"

"Not right away," says I. "We'll stay here in the cave awhile."

"All right!" says he. "That'll be fine. I never had such fun in all my life."

We went to bed about eleven o'clock. We spread down some wide blankets and quilts and put Red Chief between us. We weren't afraid he'd run away. He kept us awake for three hours, jumping up and reaching for his rifle and screeching: "Hist! pard," in mine and Bill's ears, as the fancied crackle of a twig or the rustle of a leaf revealed to his young imagination the stealthy approach of the outlaw band. At last, I fell into a troubled sleep, and dreamed that I had been kidnapped and chained to a tree by a ferocious pirate with red hair.

Just at daybreak, I was awakened by a series of awful screams from Bill. They weren't yells, or howls, or shouts, or whoops, or yawps, such as you'd expect from a manly set of vocal organs—they were simply indecent, terrifying, humiliating screams, such as women emit when they see ghosts or caterpillars. It's an awful thing to hear a strong, desperate, fat man scream incontinently in a cave at daybreak.

I jumped up to see what the matter was. Red Chief was sitting on Bill's chest, with one hand twined in Bill's hair. In the other he had the sharp case-knife we used for slicing bacon; and he was industriously and realistically trying to take Bill's scalp, according to the sentence that had been pronounced upon him the evening before.

I got the knife away from the kid and made him lie down again. But, from that moment, Bill's spirit was broken. He laid down on his side of the bed, but he never closed an eye again in sleep as long as that boy was with us. I dozed off for a while, but along toward sun-up I remembered that Red Chief had said I was to be burned at the stake at the rising of the sun. I wasn't nervous or afraid; but I sat up and lit my pipe and leaned against a rock.

"What you getting up so soon for, Sam?" asked Bill.

"Me?" says I. "Oh, I got a kind of a pain in my shoulder. I thought sitting up would rest it."

"You're a liar!" says Bill. "You're afraid. You was to be burned at sunrise, and you was afraid he'd do it. And he would, too, if he could find a match. Ain't it awful, Sam? Do you think anybody will pay out money to get a little imp like that back home?"

"Sure," said I. "A rowdy kid like that is just the kind that parents dote on. Now, you and the Chief get up and cook breakfast, while I go up on the top of this mountain and reconnoiter."

I went up on the peak of the little mountain and ran my eye over the contiguous vicinity. Over toward Summit I expected to see the sturdy yeomanry of the village armed with scythes and pitchforks beating the countryside for the dastardly kidnappers. But what I saw was a peaceful landscape dotted with one man ploughing with a dun mule. Nobody was dragging the creek; no couriers dashed hither and yon, bringing tidings of no news to the distracted parents. There was a sylvan attitude of somnolent sleepiness pervading that section of the external outward surface of Alabama that lay exposed to my view. "Perhaps," says I to myself, "it has not yet been discovered that the wolves have borne away the tender lambkin from the fold. Heaven help the wolves!" says I, and I went down the mountain to breakfast.

When I got to the cave I found Bill backed up against the side of it, breathing hard, and the boy threatening to smash him with a rock half as big as a cocoanut.

"He put a red-hot boiled potato down my back," explained Bill, "and then mashed it with his foot; and I boxed his ears. Have you got a gun about you, Sam?"

I took the rock away from the boy and kind of patched up the argument. "I'll fix you," says the kid to Bill. "No man ever yet struck the Red Chief but what he got paid for it. You better beware!"

After breakfast the kid takes a piece of leather with strings wrapped around it out of his pocket and goes outside the cave unwinding it.

"What's he up to now?" says Bill, anxiously. "You don't think he'll run away, do you, Sam?"

"No fear of it," says I. "He don't seem to be much of a home body. But we've got to fix up some plan about the ransom. There don't seem to be much excitement around Summit on account of his disappearance; but maybe they haven't realized yet that he's gone. His folks may think he's spending the night with Aunt Jane or one of the neighbors. Anyhow, he'll be missed today. Tonight we must get a message to his father demanding the two thousand dollars for his return."

Just then we heard a kind of war-whoop, such as David might have emitted when he knocked out the champion Goliath. It was a sling that Red Chief had pulled out of his pocket, and he was whirling it around his head.

I dodged, and heard a heavy thud and a kind of a sigh from Bill, like a horse gives out when you take his saddle off. A niggerhead rock the size of an egg had caught Bill just behind his left ear. He loosened himself all over and fell in the fire across the frying pan of hot water for washing the dishes. I dragged him out and poured cold water on his head for half an hour.

By and by, Bill sits up and feels behind his ear and says: "Sam, do you know who my favorite Biblical character is?"

"Take it easy," says I. "You'll come to your senses presently."

"King Herod," says he. "You won't go away and leave me here alone, will you, Sam?"

I went out and caught that boy and shook him until his freckles rattled.

"If you don't behave," says I, "I'll take you straight home. Now, are you going to be good, or not?"

"I was only funning," says he sullenly. "I didn't mean to hurt Old Hank. But what did he hit me for? I'll behave, Snake-eye, if you won't send me home, and if you'll let me play the Black Scout today."

"I don't know the game," says I. "That's for you and Mr. Bill to decide. He's your playmate for the day. I'm going away for a while, on business. Now, you come in and make friends with him and say you are sorry for hurting him, or home you go, at once."

I made him and Bill shake hands, and then I took Bill aside and told him I was going to Poplar Grove, a little village three miles from the cave, and find out what I could about how the kidnapping had been regarded in Summit. Also, I thought it best to send a peremptory letter to old man Dorset that day, demanding the ransom and dictating how it should be paid.

"You know, Sam," says Bill, "I've stood by you without batting an eye in earthquakes, fire and flood—in poker games, dynamite outrages, police raids, train robberies, and cyclones. I never lost my nerve yet till we kidnapped that two-legged skyrocket of a kid. He's got me going. You won't leave me long with him, will you, Sam?"

"I'll be back some time this afternoon," says I. "You must keep the boy amused and quiet till I return. And now we'll write the letter to old Dorset."

Bill and I got paper and pencil and worked on the letter while Red Chief, with a blanket wrapped around him, strutted up and down, guarding the mouth of the cave. Bill begged me tearfully to make the ransom fifteen hundred dollars instead of two thousand. "I ain't attempting," says he, "to decry the celebrated moral aspect of parental affection, but we're dealing with humans, and it ain't human for anybody to give up two thousand dollars for that forty-pound chunk of freckled wildcat. I'm willing to take a chance at fifteen hundred dollars. You can charge the difference up to me."

So, to relieve Bill, I acceded, and we collaborated a letter that ran this way:

Ebenezer Dorset, Esq.:

We have your boy concealed in a place far from Summit. It is useless for you or the most skilful detectives to attempt to find him. Absolutely, the only terms on which you can have him restored to you are these: We demand fifteen hundred dollars in large bills for his return; the money to be left at midnight tonight at the same spot and in the same box as your reply--as hereinafter described. If you agree to these terms, send your answer in writing by a solitary messenger tonight at half-past eight o'clock. After crossing Owl Creek, on the road to Poplar Grove, there are three large trees about a hundred yards apart, close to the fence of the wheat field on the right-hand side. At the bottom of the fence-post, opposite the third tree, will be found a small pasteboard box.

The messenger will place the answer in this box and return immediately to Summit.

If you attempt any treachery or fail to comply with our demand as stated, you will never see your boy again.

If you pay the money as demanded, he will be returned to you safe and well within three hours. These terms are final, and if you do not accede to them no further communication will be attempted.

TWO DESPERATE MEN.

I addressed this letter to Dorset, and put it in my pocket. As I was about to start, the kid comes up to me and says:

"Aw, Snake-eye, you said I could play the Black Scout while you was gone."

"Play it, of course," says I. "Mr. Bill will play with you. What kind of a game is it?"

"I'm the Black Scout," says Red Chief, "and I have to ride to the stockade to warn the settlers that the Indians are coming. I'm tired of playing Indian myself. I want to be the Black Scout."

"All right," says I. "It sounds harmless to me. I guess Mr. Bill will help you foil the pesky savages."

"What am I to do?" asks Bill, looking at the kid suspiciously.

"You are the hoss," says Black Scout. "Get down on your hands and knees. How can I ride to the stockade without a hoss?"

"You'd better keep him interested," said I, "till we get the scheme going. Loosen up."

Bill gets down on his all fours, and a look comes in his eye like a rabbit's when you catch it in a trap.

"How far is it to the stockade, kid?" he asks, in a husky manner of voice.

"Ninety miles," says the Black Scout. "And you have to hump yourself to get there on time. Whoa, now!"

The Black Scout jumps on Bill's back and digs his heels in his side.

"For Heaven's sake," says Bill, "hurry back, Sam, as soon as you can. I wish we hadn't made the ransom more than a thousand. Say, you quit kicking me or I'll get up and warm you good."

I walked over to Poplar Grove and sat around the post-office and store, talking with the chawbacons that came in to trade. One whiskerand says that he hears Summit is all upset on account of Elder Ebenezer Dorset's boy having been lost or stolen. That was all I wanted to know. I bought some smoking tobacco, referred casually to the price of black-eyed peas, posted my letter surreptitiously, and came away. The postmaster said the mail-carrier would come by in an hour to take the mail on to Summit.

When I got back to the cave Bill and the boy were not to be found. I explored the vicinity of the cave, and risked a yodel or two, but there was no response.

So I lighted my pipe and sat down on a mossy bank to await developments.

In about half an hour I heard the bushes rustle, and Bill wabbled out into the little glade in front of the cave. Behind him was the kid, stepping softly like a scout, with a broad grin on his face. Bill stopped, took off his hat, and wiped his face with a red handkerchief. The kid stopped about eight feet behind him.

"Sam," says Bill, "I suppose you'll think I'm a renegade, but I couldn't help it. I'm a grown person with masculine proclivities and habits of self-defence, but there is a time when all systems of egotism and predominance fail. The boy is gone. I sent him home. All is off. There was martyrs in old times," goes on Bill, "that suffered death rather than give up the particular graft they enjoyed. None of 'em ever was subjugated to such supernatural tortures as I have been. I tried to be faithful to our articles of depredation; but there came a limit."

"What's the trouble, Bill?" I asks him.

"I was rode," says Bill, "the ninety miles to the stockade, not barring an inch. Then, when the settlers was rescued, I was given oats. Sand ain't a palatable substitute. And then, for an hour I had to try to explain to him why there was nothin' in holes, how a road can run both ways, and what makes the grass green. I tell you, Sam, a human can only stand so much. I takes him by the neck of his clothes and drags him down the mountain. On the way he kicks my legs black-and-blue from the knees down; and I've got two or three bites on my thumb and hand cauterized.

"But he's gone"—continues Bill—"gone home. I showed him the road to Summit and kicked him about eight feet nearer there at one kick. I'm sorry we lose the ransom; but it was either that or Bill Driscoll to the madhouse."

Bill is puffing and blowing, but there is a look of ineffable peace and growing content on his rose-pink features.

"Bill," says I, "there isn't any heart disease in your family, is there?"

"No," says Bill, "nothing chronic except malaria and accidents. Why?"

"Then you might turn around," says I, "and have a look behind you."

Bill turns and sees the boy, and loses his complexion and sits down plump on the ground and begins to pluck aimlessly at grass and little sticks. For an hour I was afraid of his mind. And then I told him that my scheme was to put the whole job through immediately and that we would get the ransom and be off with it by midnight if old Dorset fell in with our proposition. So Bill braced up enough to give the kid a weak sort of a smile and a promise to play the Russian in a Japanese war with him as soon as he felt a little better.

I had a scheme for collecting that ransom without danger of being caught by counterplots that ought to commend itself to professional kidnappers. The tree under which the answer was to be left—and the money later on—was close to the road fence with big, bare fields on all sides. If a gang of constables should be watching for any one to come for the note, they could see him a long way off crossing the fields or in the road. But no, sirree! At half-past eight I was up in that tree as well hidden as a tree toad, waiting for the messenger to arrive.

Exactly on time, a half-grown boy rides up the road on a bicycle, locates the pasteboard box at the foot of the fence-post, slips a folded piece of paper into it, and pedals away again back toward Summit.

I waited an hour and then concluded the thing was square. I slid down the tree, got the note, slipped along the fence till I struck the woods, and was back at the cave in another half an hour. I opened the note, got near the lantern, and read it to Bill. It was written with a pen in a crabbed hand, and the sum and substance of it was this:

Two Desperate Men.

Gentlemen: I received your letter today by post, in regard to the ransom you ask for the return of my son. I think you are a little high in your demands, and I hereby make you a counter-proposition, which I am inclined to believe you will accept. You bring Johnny home and pay me two hundred and fifty dollars in cash, and I agree to take him off your hands. You had better come at night, for the neighbors believe he is lost, and I couldn't be responsible for what they would do to anybody they saw bringing him back.

Very respectfully,

EBENEZER DORSET.

"Great pirates of Penzance!" says I; "of all the impudent—"

But I glanced at Bill, and hesitated. He had the most appealing look in his eyes I ever saw on the face of a dumb or a talking brute.

"Sam," says he, "what's two hundred and fifty dollars, after all? We've got the money. One more night of this kid will send me to a bed in Bedlam. Besides being a thorough gentleman, I think Mr. Dorset is a spendthrift for making us such a liberal offer. You ain't going to let the chance go, are you?"

"Tell you the truth, Bill," says I, "this little he ewe lamb has somewhat got on my nerves too. We'll take him home, pay the ransom, and make our getaway."

We took him home that night. We got him to go by telling him that his father had bought a silver-mounted rifle and a pair of moccasins for him, and we were going to hunt bears the next day.

It was just twelve o'clock when we knocked at Ebenezer's front door. Just at the moment when I should have been abstracting the fifteen hundred dollars from the box under the tree, according to the original proposition, Bill was counting out two hundred and fifty dollars into Dorset's hand.

When the kid found out we were going to leave him at home he started up a howl like a calliope and fastened himself as tight as a leech to Bill's leg. His father peeled him away gradually, like a porous plaster.

"How long can you hold him?" asks Bill.

"I'm not as strong as I used to be," says old Dorset, "but I think I can promise you ten minutes."

"Enough," says Bill. "In ten minutes I shall cross the Central, Southern and Middle Western States, and be legging it trippingly for the Canadian border."

And, as dark as it was, and as fat as Bill was, and as good a runner as I am, he was a good mile and a half out of Summit before I could catch up with him.

8 The Pendulum

"Eighty-first Street—let 'em out, please," yelled the shepherd in blue.

A flock of citizen sheep scrambled out and another flock scrambled aboard. Ding-ding! The cattle cars of the Manhattan Elevated rattled away, and John Perkins drifted down the stairway of the station with the released flock.

John walked slowly toward his flat. Slowly, because in the lexicon of his daily life there was no such word as "perhaps." There are no surprises awaiting a man who has been married two years and lives in a flat. As he walked John Perkins prophesied to himself with gloomy and downtrodden cynicism the foregone conclusions of the monotonous day.

Katy would meet him at the door with a kiss flavored with cold cream and butter-scotch. He would remove his coat, sit upon a macadamized lounge and read, in the evening paper, of Russians and Japs slaughtered by the deadly linotype. For dinner there would be pot roast, a salad flavored with a dressing warranted not to crack or injure the leather, stewed rhubarb and the bottle of strawberry marmalade blushing at the certificate of chemical purity on its label. After dinner Katy would show him the new patch in her crazy quilt that the iceman had cut for her off the end of his four-in-hand. At half-past seven they would spread newspapers over the furniture to catch the pieces of plastering that fell when the fat man in the flat overhead began to take his physical culture exercises. Exactly at eight Hickey & Mooney, of the vaudeville team (unbooked) in the flat across the hall, would yield to the gentle influence of delirium tremens and begin to overturn chairs under the delusion that Hammerstein was pursuing them with a five-hundred-dollar-a-week contract. Then the gent at the window across the air-shaft would get out his flute; the nightly gas leak would steal forth to frolic in the highways; the dumbwaiter would slip off its trolley; the janitor would drive Mrs. Zanowitski's five children once more across the Yalu, the lady with the champagne shoes and the Skye terrier would trip downstairs and paste her Thursday name over her bell and letter-box—and the evening routine of the Frogmore flats would be under way.

John Perkins knew these things would happen. And he knew that at a quarter past eight he would summon his nerve and reach for his hat, and that his wife would deliver this speech in a querulous tone:

"Now, where are you going, I'd like to know, John Perkins?"

"Thought I'd drop up to McCloskey's," he would answer, "and play a game or two of pool with the fellows."

Of late such had been John Perkins's habit. At ten or eleven he would return. Sometimes Katy would be asleep; sometimes waiting up, ready to melt in the crucible of her ire a little more gold plating from the wrought steel chains of matrimony. For these things Cupid will have to answer when he stands at the bar of justice with his victims from the Frogmore flats.

Tonight John Perkins encountered a tremendous upheaval of the commonplace when he reached his door. No Katy was there with her affectionate, confectionate kiss. The three rooms seemed in portentous disorder. All about lay her things in confusion. Shoes in the middle of the floor, curling tongs, hair bows, kimonos, powder box, jumbled together on dresser and chairs—this was not Katy's way. With a sinking heart John saw the comb with a curling cloud of her brown hair among its teeth. Some unusual hurry and perturbation must have possessed her, for she always carefully placed these combings in the little blue vase on the mantel to be some day formed into the coveted feminine "rat."

Hanging conspicuously to the gas jet by a string was a folded paper. John seized it. It was a note from his wife running thus:

Dear John,

I just had a telegram saying mother is very sick. I am going to take the 4.30 train. Brother Sam is going to meet me at the depot there. There is cold mutton in the icebox. I hope it isn't her quinsy again. Pay the milkman 50 cents. She had it bad last spring. Don't forget to write to the company about the gas meter, and your good socks are in the top drawer. I will write tomorrow.

Hastily,

KATY.

Never during their two years of matrimony had he and Katy been separated for a night. John read the note over and over in a dumbfounded way. Here was a break in a routine that had never varied, and it left him dazed.

There on the back of a chair hung, pathetically empty and formless, the red wrapper with black dots that she always wore while getting the meals. Her week-day clothes had been tossed here and there in her haste. A little paper bag of her favorite butter-scotch lay with its string yet unwound. A daily paper sprawled on the floor, gaping rectangularly where a railroad time-table had been clipped from it. Everything in the room spoke of a loss, of an essence gone, of its soul and life departed. John Perkins stood among the dead remains with a queer feeling of desolation in his heart.

He began to set the rooms tidy as well as he could. When he touched her clothes a thrill of something like terror went through him. He had never thought what existence would be without Katy. She had become so thoroughly annealed into his life that she was like the air he breathed—necessary but scarcely noticed. Now, without warning, she was gone, vanished, as completely absent as if she had never existed. Of course it would be only for a few days, or at most a week or two, but it seemed to him as if the very hand of death had pointed a finger at his secure and uneventful home.

John dragged the cold mutton from the ice-box, made coffee and sat down to a lonely meal face to face with the strawberry marmalade's shameless certificate of purity. Bright among withdrawn blessings now appeared to him the ghosts of pot roasts and the salad with tan polish dressing. His home was dismantled. A quinsied mother-in-law had knocked his lares and penates sky-high. After his solitary meal John sat at a front window.

He did not care to smoke. Outside the city roared to him to come join in its dance of folly and pleasure. The night was his. He might go forth unquestioned and thrum the strings of jollity as free as any gay bachelor there. He might carouse and wander and have his fling until dawn if he liked; and there would be no wrathful Katy waiting for him, bearing the chalice that held the dregs of his joy. He might play pool at McCloskey's with his roistering friends until Aurora dimmed the electric bulbs if he chose. The hymeneal strings that had curbed him always when the Frogmore flats had palled upon him were loosened. Katy was gone.

John Perkins was not accustomed to analyzing his emotions. But as he sat in his Katy-bereft 10x12 parlor he hit unerringly upon the keynote of his discomfort. He knew now that Katy was necessary to his happiness. His feeling for her, lulled into unconsciousness by the dull round of domesticity, had been sharply stirred by the loss of her presence. Has it not been dinned into us by proverb and sermon and fable that we never prize the music till the sweet-voiced bird has flown—or in other no less florid and true utterances?

"I'm a double-dyed dub," mused John Perkins, "the way I've been treating Katy. Off every night playing pool and bumming with the boys instead of staying home with her. The poor girl here all alone with nothing to amuse her, and me acting that way! John Perkins, you're the worst kind of a shine. I'm going to make it up for the little girl. I'll take her out and let her see some amusement. And I'll cut out the McCloskey gang right from this minute."

Yes, there was the city roaring outside for John Perkins to come dance in the train of Momus. And at McCloskey's the boys were knocking the balls idly into the pockets against the hour for the nightly game. But no primrose way nor clicking cue could woo the remorseful soul of Perkins the bereft. The thing that was his, lightly held and half scorned, had been taken away from him, and he wanted it. Backward to a certain man named Adam, whom the cherubim bounced from the orchard, could Perkins, the remorseful, trace his descent.

Near the right hand of John Perkins stood a chair. On the back of it stood Katy's blue shirtwaist. It still retained something of her contour. Midway of the sleeves were fine, individual wrinkles made by the movements of her arms in working for his comfort and pleasure. A delicate but impelling odor of bluebells came from it. John took it and looked long and soberly at the unresponsive grenadine. Katy had never been unresponsive. Tears:—

yes, tears— came into John Perkins's eyes. When she came back things would be different. He would make up for all his neglect. What was life without her?

The door opened. Katy walked in carrying a little hand satchel. John stared at her stupidly.

"My! I'm glad to get back," said Katy. "Ma wasn't sick to amount to anything. Sam was at the depot, and said she just had a little spell, and got all right soon after they telegraphed. So I took the next train back. I'm just dying for a cup of coffee."

Nobody heard the click and rattle of the cog-wheels as the third-floor front of the Frogmore flats buzzed its machinery back into the Order of Things. A band slipped, a spring was touched, the gear was adjusted and the wheels revolve in their old orbit.

John Perkins looked at the clock. It was 8.15. He reached for his hat and walked to the door.

"Now, where are you going, I'd like to know, John Perkins?" asked Katy, in a querulous tone.

"Thought I'd drop up to McCloskey's," said John, "and play a game or two of pool with the fellows."

9 The Green Door

Suppose you should be walking down Broadway after dinner, with ten minutes allotted to the consummation of your cigar while you are choosing between a diverting tragedy and something serious in the way of vaudeville. Suddenly a hand is laid upon your arm. You turn to look into the thrilling eyes of a beautiful woman, wonderful in diamonds and Russian sables. She thrusts hurriedly into your hand an extremely hot buttered roll, flashes out a tiny pair of scissors, snips off the second button of your overcoat, meaningly ejaculates the one word, "parallelogram!" and swiftly flies down a cross street, looking back fearfully over her shoulder.

That would be pure adventure. Would you accept it? Not you. You would flush with embarrassment; you would sheepishly drop the roll and continue down Broadway,

fumbling feebly for the missing button. This you would do unless you are one of the blessed few in whom the pure spirit of adventure is not dead.

True adventurers have never been plentiful. They who are set down in print as such have been mostly business men with newly invented methods. They have been out after the things they wanted—golden fleeces, holy grails, lady loves, treasure, crowns and fame. The true adventurer goes forth aimless and uncalculating to meet and greet unknown fate. A fine example was the Prodigal Son—when he started back home.

Half-adventurers—brave and splendid figures—have been numerous. From the Crusades to the Palisades they have enriched the arts of history and fiction and the trade of historical fiction. But each of them had a prize to win, a goal to kick, an axe to grind, a race to run, a new thrust in tierce to deliver, a name to carve, a crow to pick—so they were not followers of true adventure.

In the big city the twin spirits Romance and Adventure are always abroad seeking worthy wooers. As we roam the streets they slyly peep at us and challenge us in twenty different guises. Without knowing why, we look up suddenly to see in a window a face that seems to belong to our gallery of intimate portraits; in a sleeping thoroughfare we hear a cry of agony and fear coming from an empty and shuttered house; instead of at our familiar curb, a cab-driver deposits us before a strange door, which one, with a smile, opens for us and bids us enter; a slip of paper, written upon, flutters down to our feet from the high lattices of Chance; we exchange glances of instantaneous hate, affection and fear with hurrying strangers in the passing crowds; a sudden douse of rain— and our umbrella may be sheltering the daughter of the Full Moon and first cousin of the Sidereal System; at every corner handkerchiefs drop, fingers beckon, eyes besiege, and the lost, the lonely, the rapturous, the mysterious, the perilous, changing clues of adventure are slipped into our fingers. But few of us are willing to hold and follow them. We are grown stiff with the ramrod of convention down our backs. We pass on; and some day we come, at the end of a very dull life, to reflect that our romance has been a pallid thing of a marriage or two, a satin rosette kept in a safe-deposit drawer, and a lifelong feud with a steam radiator.

Rudolf Steiner was a true adventurer. Few were the evenings on which he did not go forth from his hall bedchamber in search of the unexpected and the egregious. The most interesting thing in life seemed to him to be what might lie just around the next corner. Sometimes his willingness to tempt fate led him into strange paths. Twice he had spent the night in a station-house; again and again he had found himself the dupe of ingenious and mercenary tricksters; his watch and money had been the price of one flattering allurement. But with undiminished ardor he picked up every glove cast before him into the merry lists of adventure.

One evening Rudolf was strolling along a cross-town street in the older central part of the city. Two streams of people filled the sidewalks—the home-hurrying, and that restless contingent that abandons home for the specious welcome of the thousand-candle-power *table d'hôte*.

The young adventurer was of pleasing presence, and moved serenely and watchfully. By daylight he was a salesman in a piano store. He wore his tie drawn through a topaz ring instead of fastened with a stick pin; and once he had written to the editor of a magazine that "Junie's Love Test" by Miss Libbey, had been the book that had most influenced his life.

During his walk a violent chattering of teeth in a glass case on the sidewalk seemed at first to draw his attention (with a qualm) to a restaurant before which it was set; but a second glance revealed the electric letters of a dentist's sign high above the next door. A giant negro, fantastically dressed in a red embroidered coat, yellow trousers and a military cap, discreetly distributed cards to those of the passing crowd who consented to take them.

This mode of dentistic advertising was a common sight to Rudolf. Usually he passed the dispenser of the dentist's cards without reducing his store; but tonight the African slipped one into his hand so deftly that he retained it there smiling a little at the successful feat.

When he had traveled a few yards further he glanced at the card indifferently. Surprised, he turned it over and looked again with interest. One side of the card was blank; on the other was written in ink three words, "The Green Door." And then Rudolf saw, three steps in front of him, a man throw down the card the negro had given him as he passed. Rudolf picked it up. It was printed with the dentist's name and address and the usual schedule of "plate work" and "bridge work" and "crowns," and specious promises of "painless" operations.

The adventurous piano salesman halted at the corner and considered. Then he crossed the street, walked down a block, recrossed and joined the upward current of people again. Without seeming to notice the negro as he passed the second time, he carelessly took the

card that was handed him. Ten steps away he inspected it. In the same handwriting that appeared on the first card "The Green Door" was inscribed upon it. Three or four cards were tossed to the pavement by pedestrians both following and leading him. These fell blank side up. Rudolf turned them over. Every one bore the printed legend of the dental "parlors."

Rarely did the arch sprite Adventure need to beckon twice to Rudolf Steiner, his true follower. But twice it had been done, and the quest was on.

Rudolf walked slowly back to where the giant negro stood by the case of rattling teeth. This time as he passed he received no card. In spite of his gaudy and ridiculous garb, the Ethiopian displayed a natural barbaric dignity as he stood, offering the cards suavely to some, allowing others to pass unmolested. Every half minute he chanted a harsh, unintelligible phrase akin to the jabber of car conductors and grand opera. And not only did he withhold a card this time, but it seemed to Rudolf that he received from the shining and massive black countenance a look of cold, almost contemptuous disdain.

The look stung the adventurer. He read in it a silent accusation that he had been found wanting. Whatever the mysterious written words on the cards might mean, the black had selected him twice from the throng for their recipient; and now seemed to have condemned him as deficient in the wit and spirit to engage the enigma.

Standing aside from the rush, the young man made a

rapid estimate of the building in which he conceived that his adventure must lie. Five stories high it rose. A small restaurant occupied the basement.

The first floor, now closed, seemed to house millinery or furs. The second floor, by the winking electric letters, was the dentist's. Above this a polyglot babel of signs struggled to indicate the abodes of palmists, dressmakers, musicians, and doctors. Still higher up draped curtains and milk bottles white on the window sills proclaimed the regions of domesticity.

After concluding his survey Rudolf walked briskly up the high flight of stone steps into the house. Up two flights of the carpeted stairway he continued; and at its top paused. The hallway there was dimly lighted by two pale jets of gas—one far to his right, the other nearer, to his left. He looked toward the nearer light and saw, within its wan halo, a green door. For one moment he hesitated; then he seemed to see the contumelious sneer of the African juggler of cards; and then he walked straight to the green door and knocked against it.

Moments like those that passed before his knock was answered measure the quick breath of true adventure. What might not be behind those green panels! Gamesters at play; cunning rogues baiting their traps with subtle skill; beauty in love with courage, and thus planning to be sought by it; danger, death, love, disappointment, ridicule—any of these might respond to that temerarious rap.

A faint rustle was heard inside, and the door slowly opened. A girl not yet twenty stood there, white-faced and tottering. She loosed the knob and swayed weakly, groping with one hand. Rudolf caught her and laid her on a faded couch that stood against the wall. He closed the door and took a swift glance around the room by the light of a flickering gas jet. Neat, but extreme poverty was the story that he read.

The girl lay still, as if in a faint. Rudolf looked around the room excitedly for a barrel. People must be rolled upon a barrel who—no, no; that was for drowned persons. He began to fan her with his hat. That was successful, for he struck her nose with the brim of his derby and she opened her eyes. And then the young man saw that hers, indeed, was the one missing face from his heart's gallery of intimate portraits. The frank, grey eyes, the little nose, turning pertly outward; the chestnut hair, curling like the tendrils of a pea vine, seemed the right end and reward of all his wonderful adventures. But the face was wofully thin and pale.

The girl looked at him calmly, and then smiled.

"Fainted, didn't I?" she asked, weakly. "Well, who wouldn't? You try going without anything to eat for three days and see!"

"Himmel!" exclaimed Rudolf, jumping up. "Wait till I come back."

He dashed out the green door and down the stairs. In twenty minutes he was back again, kicking at the door with his toe for her to open it. With both arms he hugged an array of wares from the grocery and the restaurant. On the table he laid them—bread and butter, cold meats, cakes, pies, pickles, oysters, a roasted chicken, a bottle of milk and one of redhot tea.

"This is ridiculous," said Rudolf, blusteringly, "to go without eating. You must quit making election bets of this kind. Supper is ready." He helped her to a chair at the table and asked: "Is there a cup for the tea?" "On the shelf by the window," she answered. When he turned again with the cup he saw

her, with eyes shining rapturously, beginning upon a huge dill pickle that she had rooted out from the paper bags with a woman's unerring instinct. He took it from her, laughingly, and poured the cup full of milk. "Drink that first" he ordered, "and then you shall have some tea, and then a chicken wing. If you are very good you shall have a pickle tomorrow. And now, if you'll allow me to be your guest we'll have supper."

He drew up the other chair. The tea brightened the girl's eyes and brought back some of her color. She began to eat with a sort of dainty ferocity like some starved wild animal. She seemed to regard the young man's presence and the aid he had rendered her as a natural thing—not as though she undervalued the conventions; but as one whose great stress gave her the right to put aside the artificial for the human. But gradually, with the return of strength and comfort, came also a sense of the little conventions that belong; and she began to tell him her little story. It was one of a thousand such as the city yawns at every day—the shop girl's story of insufficient wages, further reduced by "fines" that go to swell the store's profits; of time lost through illness; and then of lost positions, lost hope, and—the knock of the adventurer upon the green door.

But to Rudolf the history sounded as big as the Iliad or the crisis in "Junie's Love Test."

"To think of you going through all that," he exclaimed.

"It was something fierce," said the girl, solemnly.

"And you have no relatives or friends in the city?"

"None whatever."

"I am all alone in the world, too," said Rudolf, after a pause.

"I am glad of that," said the girl, promptly; and somehow it pleased the young man to hear that she approved of his bereft condition.

Very suddenly her eyelids dropped and she sighed deeply.

"I'm awfully sleepy," she said, "and I feel so good."

Rudolf rose and took his hat.

"Then I'll say good-night. A long night's sleep will be fine for you."

He held out his hand, and she took it and said "good-night." But her eyes asked a question so eloquently, so frankly and pathetically that he answered it with words.

"Oh, I'm coming back tomorrow to see how you are getting along. You can't get rid of me so easily."

Then, at the door, as though the way of his coming had been so much less important than the fact that he had come, she asked: "How did you come to knock at my door?"

He looked at her for a moment, remembering the cards, and felt a sudden jealous pain. What if they had fallen into other hands as adventurous as his? Quickly he decided that she must never know the truth. He would never let her know that he was aware of the strange expedient to which she had been driven by her great distress.

"One of our piano tuners lives in this house," he said. "I knocked at your door by mistake."

The last thing he saw in the room before the green door closed was her smile.

At the head of the stairway he paused and looked curiously about him. And then he went along the hallway to its other end; and, coming back, ascended to the floor above and continued his puzzled explorations. Every door that he found in the house was painted green.

Wondering, he descended to the sidewalk. The fantastic African was still there. Rudolf confronted him with his two cards in his hand.

"Will you tell me why you gave me these cards and what they mean?" he asked.

In a broad, good-natured grin the negro exhibited a splendid advertisement of his master's profession.

"Dar it is, boss," he said, pointing down the street. "But I 'spect you is a little late for de fust act."

Looking the way he pointed Rudolf saw above the entrance to a theater the blazing electric sign of its new play, "The Green Door."

"I'm informed dat it's a fust-rate show, sah," said the negro. "De agent what represents it pussented me

with a dollar, sah, to distribute a few of his cards along with de doctah's. May I offer you one of de doctah's cards, suh?"

At the corner of the block in which he lived Rudolf stopped for a glass of beer and a cigar. When he had come out with his lighted weed he buttoned his coat, pushed back his hat and said, stoutly, to the lamp post on the corner:

"All the same, I believe it was the hand of Fate that doped out the way for me to find her."

Which conclusion, under the circumstances, certainly admits Rudolf Steiner to the ranks of the true followers of Romance and Adventure.

10 The Furnished Room

Restless, shifting, fugacious as time itself is a certain vast bulk of the population of the red brick district of the lower West Side. Homeless, they have a hundred homes. They flit from furnished room to furnished room, transients forever—transients in abode, transients in heart and mind. They sing "Home, Sweet Home" in ragtime; they carry their Poplar Grove in a bandbox; their vine is entwined about a picture hat; a rubber plant is their fig tree.

Hence the houses of this district, having had a thousand dwellers, should have a thousand tales to tell, mostly dull ones, no doubt; but it would be strange if there could not be found a ghost or two in the wake of all these vagrant guests.

One evening after dark a young man prowled among these crumbling red mansions, ringing their bells. At the twelfth he rested his lean hand-baggage upon the step and wiped the dust from his hatband and forehead. The bell sounded faint and far away in some remote, hollow depths.

To the door of this, the twelfth house whose bell he had rung, came a housekeeper who made him think of an unwholesome, surfeited worm that had eaten its nut to a hollow shell and now sought to fill the vacancy with edible lodgers.

He asked if there was a room to let.

"Come in," said the housekeeper. Her voice came from her throat; her throat seemed lined with fur. "I have the third-floor back, vacant since a week back. Should you wish to look at it?"

The young man followed her up the stairs. A faint light from no particular source mitigated the shadows of the halls. They trod noiselessly upon a stair carpet that its own loom would have forsworn. It seemed to have become vegetable; to have degenerated in that rank, sunless air to lush lichen or spreading moss that grew in patches to the stair-case and was viscid under the foot like organic matter. At each turn of the stairs were vacant niches in the wall. Perhaps plants had once been set within them. If so they had died in that foul and tainted air. It may be that statues of the saints had stood there, but it was not difficult to conceive that imps and devils had dragged them forth in the darkness and down to the unholy depths of some furnished pit below.

"This is the room," said the housekeeper, from her furry throat. "It's a nice room. It ain't often vacant. I had some most elegant people in it last summer—no trouble at all, and paid in advance to the minute. The water's at the end of the hall. Sprowls and Mooney kept it three months. They done a vaudeville sketch. Miss B'retta Sprowls—you may have heard of her—Oh, that was just the stage names—right there over the dresser is where the marriage certificate hung, framed. The gas is here, and you see there is plenty of closet room. It's a room everybody likes. It never stays idle long."

"Do you have many theatrical people rooming here?" asked the young man.

"They comes and goes. A good proportion of my lodgers is connected with the theaters. Yes, sir, this is the theatrical district. Actor people never stays long anywhere. I get my share. Yes, they comes and they goes."

He engaged the room, paying for a week in advance. He was tired, he said, and would take possession at once. He counted out the money. The room had been made ready, she said, even to towels and water. As the housekeeper moved away he put, for the thousandth time, the question that he carried at the end of his tongue.

"A young girl—Miss Vashner—Miss Eloise Vashner—do you remember such a one among your lodgers? She would be singing on the stage, most likely. A fair girl, of medium height and slender, with reddish, gold hair and a dark mole near her left eyebrow."

"No, I don't remember the name. Them stage people has names they change as often as their rooms. They comes and they goes. No, I don't call that one to mind."

No. Always no. Five months of ceaseless interrogation and the inevitable negative. So much time spent by day in questioning managers, agents, schools and choruses; by night among the audiences of theaters from all-star casts down to music halls so low that he dreaded to find what he most hoped for. He who had loved her best had tried to find her. He was sure that since her disappearance from home this great, water-girt city held her somewhere, but it was like a monstrous quicksand, shifting its particles constantly, with no foundation, its upper granules of today buried tomorrow in ooze and slime.

The furnished room received its latest guest with a first glow of pseudo-hospitality, a hectic, haggard, perfunctory welcome like the specious smile of a demirep. The sophistical comfort came in reflected gleams from the decayed furniture, the ragged brocade upholstery of a couch and two chairs, a foot-wide cheap pier-glass between the two windows, from one or two gilt picture frames and a brass bedstead in a corner.

The guest reclined, inert, upon a chair, while the room, confused in speech as though it were an apartment in Babel, tried to discourse to him of its divers tenantry.

A polychromatic rug like some brilliant-flowered, rectangular, tropical islet lay surrounded by a billowy sea of soiled matting. Upon the gay-papered wall were those pictures that pursue the homeless one from house to house—The Huguenot Lovers, The First Quarrel, The Wedding Breakfast, Psyche at the Fountain. The mantel's chastely severe outline was ingloriously veiled behind some pert drapery drawn rakishly askew like the sashes of the Amazonian ballet. Upon it was some desolate flotsam cast aside by the room's marooned when a lucky sail had borne them to a fresh port—a trifling vase or two, pictures of actresses, a medicine bottle, some stray cards out of a deck.

One by one, as the characters of a cryptograph became explicit, the little signs left by the furnished rooms' procession of guests developed a significance. The threadbare space in the rug in front of the dresser told that lovely woman had marched in the throng. The tiny fingerprints on the wall spoke of little prisoners trying to feel their way to sun and air. A splattered stain, raying like the shadow of a bursting bomb, witnessed where a hurled glass or bottle had splintered with its contents against the wall. Across the pier-glass had been scrawled with a diamond in staggering letters the name "Marie." It seemed that the succession of dwellers in the furnished room had turned in fury—perhaps tempted beyond forbearance by its garish coldness—and wreaked upon it their passions. The furniture was chipped and bruised; the couch, distorted by bursting springs, seemed a horrible monster that had been slain during the stress of some grotesque convulsion. Some more potent upheaval had cloven a great slice from the marble mantel. Each plank in the floor owned its particular cant and shriek as from a separate and individual agony. It seemed incredible that all this malice and injury had been wrought upon the room by those who had called it for a time their home; and yet it may have been the cheated home instinct surviving blindly, the resentful rage at false household gods that had kindled their wrath. A hut that is our own we can sweep and adorn and cherish.

The young tenant in the chair allowed these thoughts to file, soft-shod, through his mind, while there drifted into the room furnished sounds and furnished scents. He heard in one room a tittering and incontinent, slack laughter; in others the monologue of a scold, the rattling of dice, a lullaby, and one crying dully; above him a banjo tinkled with spirit. Doors banged somewhere; the elevated

trains roared intermittently;
a cat yowled miserably
upon a back fence. And
he breathed the breath of
the house—a dank savor
rather than a smell—a cold,
musty effluvium as from
underground vaults mingled
with the reeking exhalations
of linoleum and mildewed
and rotten woodwork.

Then suddenly, as he
rested there, the room was
filled with the strong, sweet odor of mignonette. It came
as upon a single buffet of wind with such sureness and
fragrance and emphasis that it almost seemed a living
visitant. And the man cried aloud: "What, dear?" as if he
had been called, and sprang up and faced about. The rich
odor clung to him and wrapped him around. He reached
out his arms for it, all his senses for the time confused
and commingled. How could one be peremptorily called
by an odor? Surely it must have been a sound. But, was it
not the sound that had touched, that had caressed him?

"She has been in this room," he cried, and he sprang to
wrest from it a token, for he knew he would recognize the
smallest thing that had belonged to her or that she had
touched. This enveloping scent of mignonette, the odor
that she had loved and made her own—whence came it?

The room had been but carelessly set in order. Scattered upon the flimsy dresser scarf were half a dozen hairpins— those discreet, indistinguishable friends of womankind, feminine of gender, infinite mood and uncommunicative of tense. These he ignored,  conscious of their triumphant lack of identity. Ransacking the drawers of the dresser he came upon a discarded, tiny, ragged handkerchief. He pressed it to his face. It was racy and insolent with heliotrope; he hurled it to the floor. In another drawer he found odd buttons, a theater program, a pawnbroker's card, two lost marshmallows, a book on the divination of dreams. In the last was a woman's black satin hair bow, which halted him, poised between ice and fire. But the black satin hair bow also is femininity's demure, impersonal common ornament and tells no tales.

And then he traversed the room like a hound on the scent, skimming the walls, considering the corners of the bulging matting on his hands and knees, rummaging mantel and tables, the curtains and hangings, the drunken cabinet in the corner, for a visible sign, unable to perceive that she was there beside, around, against, within, above him, clinging to him, wooing him, calling him so poignantly through the finer senses that even his grosser ones became cognizant of the call. Once again he answered loudly: "Yes, dear!" and turned, wild-eyed, to gaze on vacancy, for he could not yet discern form and color and love and outstretched arms in the odor of mignonette. Oh, God! whence that odor, and since when have odors had a voice to call? Thus he groped.

He burrowed in crevices and corners, and found corks and cigarettes. These he passed in passive contempt. But once he found in a fold of the matting a half-smoked cigar, and this he ground beneath his heel with a green and trenchant oath. He sifted the room from end to end. He found dreary and ignoble small records of many a peripatetic tenant; but of her whom he sought, and who may have lodged there, and whose spirit seemed to hover there, he found no trace.

And then he thought of the housekeeper.

He ran from the haunted room downstairs and to a door that showed a crack of light. She came out to his knock. He smothered his excitement as best he could.

"Will you tell me, madam," he besought her, "who occupied the room I have before I came?"

"Yes, sir. I can tell you again. 'Twas Sprowls and Mooney, as I said. Miss B'retta Sprowls it was in the theaters, but Missis Mooney she was. My house is well known for respectability. The marriage certificate hung, framed, on a nail over—"

"What kind of a lady was Miss Sprowls—in looks, I mean?"

"Why, black-haired, sir, short, and stout, with a comical face. They left a week ago Tuesday."

"And before they occupied it?"

"Why, there was a single gentleman connected with the draying business. He left owing me a week. Before him was Missis Crowder and her two children, that stayed four months; and back of them was old Mr. Doyle, whose sons paid for him. He kept the room six months. That goes back a year, sir, and further I do not remember."

He thanked her and crept back to his room. The room was dead. The essence that had vivified it was gone. The perfume of mignonette had departed. In its place was the old, stale odor of mouldy house furniture, of atmosphere in storage.

The ebbing of his hope drained his faith. He sat staring at the yellow, singing gaslight. Soon he walked to the bed and began to tear the sheets into strips. With the blade of his knife he drove them tightly into every crevice around windows and door. When all was snug and taut he turned out the light, turned the gas full on again and laid himself gratefully upon the bed.

     *   *   *   *   *   *   *

It was Mrs. McCool's night to go with the can for beer. So she fetched it and sat with Mrs. Purdy in one of those subterranean retreats where housekeepers foregather and the worm dieth seldom.

"I rented out my third-floor-back, this evening," said Mrs. Purdy, across a fine circle of foam. "A young man took it. He went up to bed two hours ago."

"Now, did ye, Mrs. Purdy, ma'am?" said Mrs. McCool, with intense admiration. "You do be a wonder for rentin' rooms of that kind. And did ye tell him, then?" she concluded in a husky whisper laden with mystery.

"Rooms," said Mrs. Purdy, in her furriest tones, "are furnished for to rent. I did not tell him, Mrs. McCool."

"'Tis right ye are, ma'am; 'tis by renting rooms we kape alive. Ye have the rale sense for business, ma'am. There be many people will rayjict the rentin' of a room if they be tould a suicide has been after dyin' in the bed of it."

"As you say, we has our living to be making," remarked Mrs. Purdy.

"Yis, ma'am; 'tis true. 'Tis just one wake ago this day I helped ye lay out the third-floor-back. A pretty slip of a colleen she was to be killin' herself wid the gas—a swate little face she had, Mrs. Purdy, ma'am."

"She'd a-been called handsome, as you say," said Mrs. Purdy, assenting but critical, "but for that mole she had a-growin' by her left eyebrow. Do fill up your glass again, Mrs. McCool."

11 The Count and the Wedding Guest

One evening when Andy Donovan went to dinner at his Second Avenue boarding-house, Mrs. Scott introduced him to a new boarder, a young lady, Miss Conway. Miss Conway was small and unobtrusive. She wore a plain, snuffy-brown dress, and bestowed her interest, which seemed languid, upon her plate. She lifted her diffident eyelids and shot one perspicuous, judicial glance at Mr. Donovan, politely murmured his name, and returned to her mutton. Mr. Donovan bowed with the grace and beaming smile that were rapidly winning for him social, business and political advancement, and erased the snuffy-brown one from the tablets of his consideration.

Two weeks later Andy was sitting on the front steps enjoying his cigar. There was a soft rustle behind and above him and Andy turned his head—and had his head turned.

Just coming out the door was Miss Conway. She wore a night-black dress of *crêpe de—crêpe de*—oh, this thin black goods. Her hat was black, and from it drooped and fluttered an ebon veil, filmy as a spider's web. She stood on the top step and drew on black silk gloves. Not a speck of white or a spot of color about her dress anywhere. Her rich golden hair was drawn, with scarcely a ripple, into a shining, smooth knot low on her neck. Her face was plain rather than pretty, but it was now illuminated and made almost beautiful by her large gray eyes that gazed above the houses across the street into the sky with an expression of the most appealing sadness and melancholy.

Gather the idea, girls—all black, you know, with the preference for *crêpe de*—oh, *crêpe de Chine*—that's it. All black, and that sad, faraway look, and the hair shining under the black veil (you have to be a blonde, of course), and try to look as if, although your young life had been blighted just as it was about to give a hop-skip-and-a-jump over the threshold of life, a walk in the park might do you good, and be sure to happen out the door at the right moment, and—oh, it'll fetch 'em every time. But it's fierce, now, how cynical I am, ain't it?—to talk about mourning costumes this way.

Mr. Donovan suddenly reinscribed Miss Conway upon the tablets of his consideration. He threw away the remaining inch-and-a-quarter of his cigar, that would have been good for eight minutes yet, and quickly shifted his center of gravity to his low-cut patent leathers.

"It's a fine, clear evening, Miss Conway," he said; and if the Weather Bureau could have heard the confident emphasis of his tones it would have hoisted the square white signal, and nailed it to the mast.

"To them that has the heart to enjoy it, it is, Mr. Donovan," said Miss Conway, with a sigh.

Mr. Donovan, in his heart, cursed fair weather. Heartless weather! It should hail and blow and snow to be consonant with the mood of Miss Conway.

"I hope none of your relatives—I hope you haven't sustained a loss?" ventured Mr. Donovan.

"Death has claimed," said Miss Conway, hesitating—"not a relative, but one who—but I will not intrude my grief upon you, Mr. Donovan."

"Intrude?" protested Mr. Donovan. "Why, say, Miss Conway, I'd be delighted, that is, I'd be sorry—I mean I'm sure nobody could sympathize with you truer than I would."

Miss Conway smiled a little smile. And oh, it was sadder than her expression in repose.

"'Laugh, and the world laughs with you; weep, and they give you the laugh,'" she quoted. "I have learned that, Mr. Donovan. I have no friends or acquaintances in this city. But you have been kind to me. I appreciate it highly."

He had passed her the pepper twice at the table.

"It's tough to be alone in New York—that's a cinch," said Mr. Donovan. "But, say—whenever this little old town does loosen up and get friendly it goes the limit. Say you took a little stroll in the park, Miss Conway—don't you think it might chase away some of your mullygrubs? And if you'd allow me—"

"Thanks, Mr. Donovan. I'd be pleased to accept of your escort if you think the company of one whose heart is filled with gloom could be anyways agreeable to you."

Through the open gates of the iron-railed, old, downtown park, where the elect once took the air, they strolled, and found a quiet bench.

There is this difference between the grief of youth and that of old age; youth's burden is lightened by as much of it as another shares; old age may give and give, but the sorrow remains the same.

"He was my fiancé," confided Miss Conway, at the end of an hour. "We were going to be married next spring. I don't want you to think that I am stringing you, Mr. Donovan, but he was a real Count. He had an estate and a castle in Italy. Count Fernando Mazzini was his name. I never saw the beat of him for elegance. Papa objected, of course, and once we eloped, but Papa overtook us, and took us back. I thought sure papa and Fernando would fight a duel. Papa has a livery business—in P'kipsee, you know."

"Finally, Papa came 'round, all right, and said we might be married next spring. Fernando showed him proofs of his title and wealth, and then went over to Italy to get the castle fixed up for us. Papa's very proud and, when Fernando wanted to give me several thousand dollars for my trousseau he called him down something awful. He wouldn't even let me take a ring or any presents from him. And when Fernando sailed I came to the city and got a position as cashier in a candy store."

"Three days ago I got a letter from Italy, forwarded from P'kipsee, saying that Fernando had been killed in a gondola accident."

"That is why I am in mourning. My heart, Mr. Donovan, will remain forever in his grave. I guess I am poor company, Mr. Donovan, but I cannot take any interest in no one. I should not care to keep you from gayety and your friends who can smile and entertain you. Perhaps you would prefer to walk back to the house?"

Now, girls, if you want to observe a young man hustle out after a pick and shovel, just tell him that your heart is in some other fellow's grave. Young men are grave-robbers by nature. Ask any widow. Something must be done to restore that missing organ to weeping angels in crêpe de Chine. Dead men certainly get the worst of it from all sides.

"I'm awfully sorry," said Mr. Donovan, gently. "No, we won't walk back to the house just yet. And don't say you haven't no friends in this city, Miss Conway. I'm awful sorry, and I want you to believe I'm your friend, and that

I'm awful sorry."

"I've got his picture here in my locket," said Miss Conway, after wiping her eyes with her handkerchief. "I never showed it to anybody; but I will to you, Mr. Donovan, because I believe you to be a true friend."

Mr. Donovan gazed long and with much interest at the photograph in the locket that Miss Conway opened for him. The face of Count Mazzini was one to command interest. It was a smooth, intelligent, bright, almost a handsome face—the face of a strong, cheerful man who might well be a leader among his fellows.

"I have a larger one, framed, in my room," said Miss Conway. "When we return I will show you that. They are all I have to remind me of Fernando. But he ever will be present in my heart, that's a sure thing."

A subtle task confronted Mr. Donovan—that of supplanting the unfortunate Count in the heart of Miss Conway. This his admiration for her determined him to do. But the magnitude of the undertaking did not seem to weigh upon his spirits. The sympathetic but cheerful friend was the role he essayed; and he played it so successfully that the next half-hour found them conversing pensively across two plates of ice-cream, though yet there was no diminution of the sadness in Miss Conway's large gray eyes.

Before they parted in the hall that evening she ran upstairs and brought down the framed photograph wrapped lovingly in a white silk scarf. Mr. Donovan surveyed it with inscrutable eyes.

"He gave me this the night he left for Italy," said Miss Conway. "I had the one for the locket made from this."

"A fine-looking man," said Mr. Donovan, heartily. "How would it suit you, Miss Conway, to give me the pleasure of your company to Coney next Sunday afternoon?"

A month later they announced their engagement to Mrs. Scott and the other boarders. Miss Conway continued to wear black.

A week after the announcement the two sat on the same bench in the downtown park, while the fluttering leaves of the trees made a dim kinetoscopic picture of them in the moonlight. But Donovan had worn a look of abstracted gloom all day. He was so silent tonight that love's lips could not keep back any longer the questions that love's heart propounded.

"What's the matter, Andy, you are so solemn and grouchy tonight?"

"Nothing, Maggie."

"I know better. Can't I tell? You never acted this way before. What is it?"

"It's nothing much, Maggie."

"Yes it is; and I want to know. I'll bet it's some other girl you are thinking about. All right. Why don't you go get her if you want her? Take your arm away, if you please."

"I'll tell you then," said Andy, wisely, "but I guess you won't understand it exactly. You've heard of Mike Sullivan, haven't you? 'Big Mike' Sullivan, everybody calls him."

"No, I haven't," said Maggie. "And I don't want to, if he makes you act like this. Who is he?"

"He's the biggest man in New York," said Andy, almost reverently. "He can about do anything he wants to with Tammany or any other old thing in the political line. He's a mile high and as broad as East River. You say anything against Big Mike, and you'll have a million men on your collarbone in about two seconds. Why, he made a visit over to the old country awhile back, and the kings took to their holes like rabbits."

"Well, Big Mike's a friend of mine. I ain't more than deuce-high in the district as far as influence goes, but Mike's as good a friend to a little man, or a poor man as he is to a big one. I met him today on the Bowery, and what do you think he does? Comes up and shakes hands. 'Andy,' says he, 'I've been keeping cases on you. You've

been putting in some good licks over on your side of the street, and I'm proud of you. What'll you take to drink?" He takes a cigar and I take a highball. I told him I was going to get married in two weeks. 'Andy,' says he, 'send me an invitation, so I'll keep in mind of it, and I'll come to the wedding.' That's what Big Mike says to me; and he always does what he says.

"You don't understand it, Maggie, but I'd have one of my hands cut off to have Big Mike Sullivan at our wedding. It would be the proudest day of my life. When he goes to a man's wedding, there's a guy being married that's made for life. Now, that's why I'm maybe looking sore tonight."

"Why don't you invite him, then, if he's so much to the mustard?" said Maggie, lightly.

"There's a reason why I can't," said Andy, sadly. "There's a reason why he mustn't be there. Don't ask me what it is, for I can't tell you."

"Oh, I don't care," said Maggie. "It's something about politics, of course. But it's no reason why you can't smile at me."

"Maggie," said Andy, presently, "do you think as much of me as you did of your—as you did of the Count Mazzini?"

He waited a long time, but Maggie did not reply. And then, suddenly she leaned against his shoulder and began to cry—to cry and shake with sobs, holding his arm tightly, and wetting the *crêpe de Chine* with tears.

"There, there, there!" soothed Andy, putting aside his own trouble. "And what is it, now?"

"Andy," sobbed Maggie. "I've lied to you, and you'll never marry me, or love me any more. But I feel that I've got to tell. Andy, there never was so much as the little finger of a count. I never had a beau in my life. But all the other girls had; and they talked about 'em; and that seemed to make the fellows like 'em more. And, Andy, I look swell in black—you know I do. So I went out to a photograph store and bought that picture, and had a little one made for my locket, and made up all that story about the Count and about his being killed, so I could wear black. And nobody can love a liar, and you'll shake me, Andy, and I'll die for shame. Oh, there never was anybody I liked but you—and that's all."

But instead of being pushed away, she found Andy's arm folding her closer. She looked up and saw his face cleared and smiling.

"Could you—could you forgive me, Andy?"

"Sure," said Andy. "It's all right about that. Back to the cemetery for the Count. You've straightened everything out, Maggie. I was in hopes you would before the wedding-day. Bully girl!"

"Andy," said Maggie, with a somewhat shy smile, after she had been thoroughly assured of forgiveness, "did you believe all that story about the Count?"

"Well, not to any large extent," said Andy, reaching for his cigar case, "because it's Big Mike Sullivan's picture you've got in that locket of yours."

12 One Thousand Dollars

"One thousand dollars," repeated Lawyer Tolman, solemnly and severely, "and here is the money."

Young Gillian gave a decidedly amused laugh as he fingered the thin package of new fifty-dollar notes.

"It's such a confoundedly awkward amount," he explained, genially, to the lawyer. "If it had been ten thousand a fellow might wind up with a lot of fireworks and do himself credit. Even fifty dollars would have been less trouble."

"You heard the reading of your uncle's will," continued Lawyer Tolman, professionally dry in his tones. "I do not know if you paid much attention to its details. I must remind you of one. You are required to render to us an account of the manner of expenditure of this $1,000 as soon as you have disposed of it. The will stipulates that. I trust that you will so far comply with the late Mr. Gillian's wishes."

"You may depend upon it," said the young man politely, "in spite of the extra expense it will entail. I may have to engage a secretary. I was never good at accounts."

Gillian went to his club. There he hunted out one whom he called Old Bryson.

Old Bryson was calm and forty and sequestered. He was in a corner reading a book, and when he saw Gillian approaching he sighed, laid down his book and took off his glasses.

"Old Bryson, wake up," said Gillian. "I've a funny story to tell you."

"I wish you would tell it to someone in the billiard room," said Old Bryson. "You know how I hate your stories."

"This is a better one than usual," said Gillian, rolling a cigarette; "and I'm glad to tell it to you. It's too sad and funny to go with the rattling of billiard bars. I've just come from my late uncle's firm of legal corsairs. He leaves me an even thousand dollars. Now, what can a man possibly do with a thousand dollars?"

"I thought," said Old Bryson, showing as much interest as a bee shows in a vinegar cruet, "that the late Septimus Gillian was worth something like half a million."

"He was," assented Gillian, joyously, "and that's where the joke comes in. He's left his whole cargo of doubloons to a microbe. That is, part of it goes to the man who invents a new bacillus and the rest to establish a hospital for doing away with it again. There are one or two trifling bequests on the side. The butler and the housekeeper get

a seal ring and $10 each. His nephew gets $1,000."

"You've always had plenty of money to spend," observed Old Bryson.

"Tons," said Gillian. "Uncle was the fairy god-mother as far as an allowance was concerned."

"Any other heirs?" asked Old Bryson.

"None." Gillian frowned at his cigarette and kicked the upholstered leather of a divan uneasily. "There is a Miss Hayden, a ward of my uncle, who lived in his house. She's a quiet thing—musical—the daughter of somebody who was unlucky enough to be his friend. I forgot to say that she was in on the seal ring and $10 joke, too. I wish I had been. Then I could have had two bottles of brut, tipped the waiter with the ring, and had the whole business off my hands. Don't be superior and insulting, Old Bryson—tell me what a fellow can do with a thousand dollars."

Old Bryson rubbed his glasses and smiled. And when Old Bryson smiled, Gillian knew that be intended to be more offensive than ever.

"A thousand dollars," he said, "means much or little. One man may buy a happy home with it and laugh at Rockefeller. Another could send his wife South with it and save her life. A thousand dollars would buy pure milk for one hundred babies during June, July, and August and save fifty of their lives. You could count upon a half hour's diversion with it at faro in one of the fortified art galleries. It would furnish an education to an ambitious boy. I am told that a genuine Corot was secured for that amount in an auction room yesterday. You could move to a New Hampshire town and live respectably two years on it. You could rent Madison Square Garden for one evening with it, and lecture your audience, if you should have one, on the precariousness of the profession of heir presumptive."

"People might like you, Old Bryson," said Gillian, always unruffled, "if you wouldn't moralize. I asked you to tell me what I could do with a thousand dollars."

"You?" said Bryson, with a gentle laugh. "Why, Bobby Gillian, there's only one logical thing you could do. You can go buy Miss Lotta Lauriere a diamond pendant with the money, and then take yourself off to Idaho and inflict your presence upon a ranch. I advise a sheep ranch, as I have a particular dislike for sheep."

"Thanks," said Gillian, rising, "I thought I could depend upon you, Old Bryson. You hit on the very scheme. I wanted to chuck the money in a lump, for I've got to turn in an account for it, and I hate itemizing."

Gillian phoned for a cab and said to the driver: "The stage entrance of the Columbine Theater."

Miss Lotta Lauriere was assisting nature with a powder puff, almost ready for her call at a crowded matinée, when her dresser mentioned the name of Mr. Gillian.

"Let it in," said Miss Lauriere. "Now, what is it, Bobby? I'm going on in two minutes."

"Rabbit-foot your right ear a little," suggested Gillian, critically. "That's better. It won't take two minutes for me. What do you say to a little thing in the pendant line? I can stand three ciphers with a figure one in front of 'em."

"Oh, just as you say," caroled Miss Lauriere. "My right glove, Adams. Say, Bobby, did you see that necklace Della Stacey had on the other night? Twenty-two hundred dollars it cost at Tiffany's. But, of course—pull my sash a little to the left, Adams."

"Miss Lauriere for the opening chorus!" cried the call boy without.

Gillian strolled out to where his cab was waiting.

"What would you do with a thousand dollars if you had it?" be asked the driver.

"Open a s'loon," said the cabby promptly and huskily. "I know a place I could take money in with both hands. It's a four-story brick on a corner. I've got it figured out. Second story— Chinks and chop suey; third floor—manicures and foreign missions; fourth floor—poolroom. If you was thinking of putting up the cap—"

"Oh, no," said Gillian, I merely asked from curiosity. I take you by the hour. Drive 'til I tell you to stop."

Eight blocks down Broadway Gillian poked up the trap with his cane and got out. A blind man sat upon a stool on the sidewalk selling pencils. Gillian went out and stood before him.

"Excuse me," he said, "but would you mind telling me what you would do if you had a thousand dollars?"

"You got out of that cab that just drove up, didn't you?" asked the blind man.

"I did," said Gillian.

"I guess you are all right," said the pencil dealer, "to ride in a cab by daylight. Take a look at that, if you like."

He drew a small book from his coat pocket and held it out. Gillian opened it and saw that it was a bank deposit book. It showed a balance of $1,785 to the blind man's credit.

Gillian returned the book and got into the cab.

"I forgot something," he said. "You may drive to the law offices of Tolman & Sharp, at—Broadway."

Lawyer Tolman looked at him hostilely and inquiringly through his gold-rimmed glasses.

"I beg your pardon," said Gillian, cheerfully, "but may I ask you a question? It is not an impertinent one, I hope. Was Miss Hayden left anything by my uncle's will besides the ring and the $10?"

"Nothing," said Mr. Tolman.

"I thank you very much, sir," said Gillian, and out he went to his cab. He gave the driver the address of his late uncle's home.

Miss Hayden was writing letters in the library. She was small and slender and clothed in black. But you would have noticed her eyes. Gillian drifted in with his air of regarding the world as inconsequent.

"I've just come from old Tolman's," he explained. "They've been going over the papers down there. They found a"—Gillian searched his memory for a legal term—"they found an amendment or a postscript or something to the will. It seemed that the old boy loosened up a little on second thoughts and willed you a thousand dollars. I was driving up this way and Tolman asked me to bring you the money. Here it is. You'd better count it to see if it's right."

Gillian laid the money beside her hand on the desk.

Miss Hayden turned white. "Oh!" she said, and again "Oh !"

Gillian half turned and looked out the window.

"I suppose, of course," he said, in a low voice, that you know I love you."

"I am sorry," said Miss Hayden, taking up her money.

"There is no use?" asked Gillian, almost light-heartedly.

"I am sorry," she said again.

"May I write a note?" asked Gillian, with a smile. He seated himself at the big library table. She supplied him with paper and pen, and then went back to her secrétaire.

Gillian made out his account of his expenditure of the thousand dollars in these words:

Paid by the black sheep, Robert Gillian, $1,000 on account of the eternal happiness, owed by Heaven to the best and dearest woman on earth.

Gillian slipped his writing into an envelope, bowed and went his way.

His cab stopped again at the offices of Tolman & Sharp.

"I have expended the thousand dollars," he said cheerily, to Tolman of the gold glasses, "and I have come to render account of it, as I agreed. There is quite a feeling of summer in the air—do you not think so, Mr. Tolman?" He tossed a white envelope on the lawyer's table. "You will find there a memorandum, sir, of the modus operandi of the vanishing of the dollars."

Without touching the envelope, Mr. Tolman went to a door and called his partner, Sharp. Together they explored the caverns of an immense safe. Forth they dragged as trophy of their search a big envelope sealed with wax. This they forcibly invaded, and wagged their venerable heads together over its contents. Then Tolman became spokesman.

"Mr. Gillian," he said, formally, "there was a codicil to your uncle's will. It was intrusted to us privately, with instructions that it be not opened until you had furnished us with a full account of your handling of the $1,000 bequest in the will. As you have fulfilled the conditions, my partner and I have read the codicil. I do not wish to encumber your understanding with its legal phraseology, but I will acquaint you with the spirit of its contents.

"In the event that your disposition of the $1,000 demonstrates that you possess any of the qualifications that deserve reward, much benefit will accrue to you. Mr. Sharp and I are named as the judges, and I assure you that we will do our duty strictly according to justice— with liberality. We are not at all unfavorably disposed toward you, Mr. Gillian. But let us return to the letter of the codicil. If your disposal of the money in question has been prudent, wise, or unselflish, it is in our power to hand you over bonds to the value of $50,000, which have been placed in our hands for that purpose. But if—as our client, the late Mr. Gillian, explicitly provides—you have used this money as you have used money in the past— I quote the late Mr. Gillian—in reprehensible dissipation among disreputable associates—the $50,000 is to be paid to Miriam Hayden, ward of the late Mr. Gillian, without delay. Now, Mr. Gillian, Mr. Sharp and I will examine your account in regard to the $1,000. You submit it in writing, I believe. I hope you will repose confidence in our decision."

Mr. Tolman reached for the envelope. Gillian was a little the quicker in taking it up. He tore the account and its cover leisurely into strips and dropped them into his pocket.

"It's all right," he said, smilingly. "There isn't a bit of need to bother you with this. I don't suppose you'd understand these itemized bets, anyway. I lost the thousand dollars on the races. Good-day to you, gentlemen."

Tolman & Sharp shook their heads mournfully at each other when Gillian left, for they heard him whistling gayly in the hallway as he waited for the elevator.

13 The Duplicity of Hargraves

When Major Pendleton Talbot, of Mobile, sir, and his daughter, Miss Lydia Talbot, came to Washington to reside, they selected for a boarding place a house that stood fifty yards back from one of the quietest avenues. It was an old-fashioned brick building, with a portico upheld by tall white pillars. The yard was shaded by stately locusts and elms, and a catalpa tree in season rained its pink and white blossoms upon the grass. Rows of high box bushes lined the fence and walks. It was the Southern style and aspect of the place that pleased the eyes of the Talbots.

In this pleasant, private boarding house they engaged rooms, including a study for Major Talbot, who was adding the finishing chapters to his book, "Anecdotes and Reminiscences of the Alabama Army, Bench, and Bar."

Major Talbot was of the old, old South. The present day had little interest or excellence in his eyes. His mind lived in that period before the Civil War, when the Talbots owned thousands of acres of fine cotton land and the slaves to till them; when the family mansion was the scene of princely hospitality, and drew its guests from the aristocracy of the South. Out of that period he had brought all its old pride and scruples of honor, an antiquated and punctilious politeness, and (you would think) its wardrobe.

Such clothes were surely never made within fifty years. The major was tall, but whenever he made that wonderful, archaic genuflexion he called a bow, the corners of his frock coat swept the floor. That garment was a surprise even to Washington, which has long ago ceased to shy at the frocks and broad-brimmed hats of Southern congressmen. One of the boarders christened it a "Father Hubbard," and it certainly was high in the waist and full in the skirt.

But the major, with all his queer clothes, his immense area of plaited, ravelling shirt bosom, and the little black string tie with the bow always slipping on one side, both was smiled at and liked in Mrs. Vardeman's select boarding house. Some of the young department clerks would often "string him," as they called it, getting him started upon the subject dearest to him—the traditions and history of his beloved Southland.

During his talks he would quote freely from the "Anecdotes and Reminiscences." But they were very careful not to let him see their designs, for in spite of his sixty-eight years, he could make the boldest of them uncomfortable under the steady regard of his piercing gray eyes.

Miss Lydia was a plump, little old maid of thirty-five, with smoothly drawn, tightly twisted hair that made her look still older. Old fashioned, too, she was; but ante-bellum glory did not radiate from her as it did from the major. She possessed a thrifty common sense; and it was she who handled the finances of the family, and met all comers when there were bills to pay. The major regarded board bills and wash bills as contemptible nuisances. They kept coming in so persistently and so often. Why, the major wanted to know, could they not be filed and paid in a lump sum at some convenient period—say when the "Anecdotes and Reminiscences" had been published and paid for? Miss Lydia would calmly go on with her sewing and say, "We'll pay as we go as long as the money lasts, and then perhaps they'll have to lump it."

Most of Mrs. Vardeman's boarders were away during the day, being nearly all department clerks and business men; but there was one of them who was about the house a great deal from morning to night. This was a young man named Henry Hopkins Hargraves—every one in the house addressed him by his full name—who was engaged at one of the popular vaudeville theaters. Vaudeville has risen to such a respectable plane in the last few years, and Mr. Hargraves was such a modest and well-mannered person, that Mrs. Vardeman could find no objection to enrolling him upon her list of boarders.

At the theater Hargraves was known as an all-round dialect comedian, having a large repertoire of German, Irish, Swede, and black-face specialties. But Mr. Hargraves was ambitious, and often spoke of his great desire to succeed in legitimate comedy.

This young man appeared to conceive a strong fancy for Major Talbot. Whenever that gentleman would begin his Southern reminiscences, or repeat some of the liveliest of the anecdotes, Hargraves could always be found, the most attentive among his listeners.

For a time the major showed an inclination to discourage the advances of the "play actor," as he privately termed him; but soon the young man's agreeable manner and indubitable appreciation of the old gentleman's stories completely won him over.

It was not long before the two were like old chums. The major set apart each afternoon to read to him the manuscript of his book. During the anecdotes Hargraves never failed to laugh at exactly the right point. The major was moved to declare to Miss Lydia one day that young Hargraves possessed remarkable perception and a gratifying respect for the old regime. And when it came to talking of those old days—if Major Talbot liked to talk, Mr. Hargraves was entranced to listen.

Like almost all old people who talk of the past, the major loved to linger over details. In describing the splendid, almost royal, days of the old planters, he would hesitate until he had recalled the name of the Negro who held his horse, or the exact date of certain minor happenings, or the number of bales of cotton raised in such a year; but Hargraves never grew impatient or lost interest. On the contrary, he would advance questions on a variety of subjects connected with the life of that time, and he never failed to extract ready replies.

The fox hunts, the 'possum suppers, the hoe downs and jubilees in the Negro quarters, the banquets in the plantation-house hall, when invitations went for fifty miles around; the occasional feuds with the neighboring gentry; the major's duel with Rathbone Culbertson about Kitty Chalmers, who afterward married a Thwaite of South Carolina; and private yacht races for fabulous sums on Mobile Bay; the quaint beliefs, improvident habits, and loyal virtues of the old slaves—all these were subjects that held both the major and Hargraves absorbed for hours at a time.

Sometimes, at night, when the young man would be coming upstairs to his room after his turn at the theater was over, the major would appear at the door of his study and beckon archly to him. Going in, Hargraves would find a little table set with a decanter, sugar bowl, fruit, and a big bunch of fresh green mint.

"It occurred to me," the major would begin—he was always ceremonious—"that perhaps you might have found your duties at the—at your place of occupation—sufficiently arduous to enable you, Mr. Hargraves, to appreciate what the poet might well have had in his mind when he wrote, 'tired Nature's sweet restorer,'—one of our Southern juleps."

It was a fascination to Hargraves to watch him make it. He took rank among artists when he began, and he never varied the process. With what delicacy he bruised the mint; with what exquisite nicety he estimated the ingredients; with what solicitous care he capped the compound with the scarlet fruit glowing against the dark green fringe! And then the hospitality and grace with which he offered it, after the selected oat straws had been plunged into its tinkling depths!

After about four months in Washington, Miss Lydia discovered one morning that they were almost without money. The "Anecdotes and Reminiscences" was completed, but publishers had not jumped at the collected gems of Alabama sense and wit. The rental of a small house which they still owned in Mobile was two months in arrears. Their board money for the month would be due in three days. Miss Lydia called her father to a consultation.

"No money?" said he with a surprised look. "It is quite annoying to be called on so frequently for these petty sums. Really, I—"

The major searched his pockets. He found only a two-dollar bill, which he returned to his vest pocket.

"I must attend to this at once, Lydia," he said. "Kindly get me my umbrella and I will go down town immediately. The congressman from our district, General Fulghum, assured me some days ago that he would use his influence to get my book published at an early date. I will go to his hotel at once and see what arrangement has been made."

With a sad little smile Miss Lydia watched him button his "Father Hubbard" and depart, pausing at the door, as he always did, to bow profoundly.

That evening, at dark, he returned. It seemed that Congressman Fulghum had seen the publisher who had the major's manuscript for reading. That person had said that if the anecdotes, etc., were carefully pruned down about one half, in order to eliminate the sectional and class prejudice with which the book was dyed from end to end, he might consider its publication.

The major was in a white heat of anger, but regained his equanimity, according to his code of manners, as soon as he was in Miss Lydia's presence.

"We must have money," said Miss Lydia, with a little wrinkle above her nose. "Give me the two dollars, and I will telegraph to Uncle Ralph for some tonight."

The major drew a small envelope from his upper vest pocket and tossed it on the table.

"Perhaps it was injudicious," he said mildly, "but the sum was so merely nominal that I bought tickets to the theater tonight. It's a new war drama, Lydia. I thought you would be pleased to witness its first production in Washington. I am told that the South has very fair treatment in the play. I confess I should like to see the performance myself."

Miss Lydia threw up her hands in silent despair.

Still, as the tickets were bought, they might as well be used. So that evening, as they sat in the theater listening to the lively overture, even Miss Lydia was minded to relegate their troubles, for the hour, to second place. The major, in spotless linen, with his extraordinary coat showing only where it was closely buttoned, and his white hair smoothly roached, looked really fine and distinguished. The curtain went up on the first act of "A Magnolia Flower," revealing a typical Southern plantation scene. Major Talbot betrayed some interest.

"Oh, see!" exclaimed Miss Lydia, nudging his arm, and pointing to her program.

The major put on his glasses and read the line in the cast of characters that her finger indicated.

COL. WEBSTER CALHOUN

. . . . . . H. Hopkins Hargraves.

"It's our Mr. Hargraves," said Miss Lydia. "It must be his first appearance in what he calls 'the legitimate.' I'm so glad for him."

Not until the second act did Col. Webster Calhoun appear upon the stage. When he made his entry Major Talbot gave an audible sniff, glared at him, and seemed to freeze solid. Miss Lydia uttered a little, ambiguous squeak and crumpled her program in her hand. For Colonel Calhoun was made up as nearly resembling Major Talbot as one pea does another. The long, thin, white hair, curly at the ends, the aristocratic beak of a nose, the crumpled, wide, ravelling shirt front, the string tie, with the bow nearly under one ear, were almost exactly duplicated. And then, to clinch the imitation, he wore the twin to the major's supposed to be unparalleled coat. High-collared, baggy, empire-waisted, ample-skirted, hanging a foot lower in front than behind, the garment could have been designed from no other pattern. From then on, the major and Miss Lydia sat bewitched, and saw the counterfeit presentment of a haughty Talbot "dragged," as the major afterward expressed it, "through the slanderous mire of a corrupt stage."

Mr. Hargraves had used his opportunities well. He had caught the major's little idiosyncrasies of speech, accent, and intonation and his pompous courtliness to perfection—exaggerating all to the purposes of the stage. When he performed that marvelous bow that the major fondly imagined to be the pink of all salutations, the audience sent forth a sudden round of hearty applause.

Miss Lydia sat immovable, not daring to glance toward her father. Sometimes her hand next to him would be laid against her cheek, as if to conceal the smile which, in spite of her disapproval, she could not entirely suppress.

The culmination of Hargraves's audacious imitation took place in the third act. The scene is where Colonel Calhoun entertains a few of the neighboring planters in his "den."

Standing at a table in the center of the stage, with his friends grouped about him, he delivers that inimitable, rambling, character monologue so famous in "A Magnolia Flower," at the same time that he deftly makes juleps for the party.

Major Talbot, sitting quietly, but white with indignation, heard his best stories retold, his pet theories and hobbies advanced and expanded, and the dream of the "Anecdotes and Reminiscences" served, exaggerated and garbled. His favorite narrative—that of his duel with Rathbone Culbertson—was not omitted, and it was delivered with more fire, egotism, and gusto than the major himself put into it.

The monologue concluded with a quaint, delicious, witty little lecture on the art of concocting a julep, illustrated by the act. Here Major Talbot's delicate but showy science was reproduced to a hair's breadth— from his dainty handling of the fragrant weed—"the one-thousandth part of a grain too much pressure, gentlemen, and you extract the bitterness, instead of the aroma, of this heaven-bestowed plant"—to his solicitous selection of the oaten straws.

At the close of the scene the audience raised a tumultuous roar of appreciation. The portrayal of the type was so exact, so sure and thorough, that the leading characters in the play were forgotten. After repeated calls, Hargraves came before the curtain and bowed, his rather boyish face bright and flushed with the knowledge of success.

At last Miss Lydia turned and looked at the major. His thin nostrils were working like the gills of a fish. He laid both shaking hands upon the arms of his chair to rise.

"We will go, Lydia," he said chokingly. "This is an abominable—desecration."

Before he could rise, she pulled him back into his seat. "We will stay it out," she declared. "Do you want to advertise the copy by exhibiting the original coat?" So they remained to the end.

Hargraves's success must have kept him up late that night, for neither at the breakfast nor at the dinner table did he appear.

About three in the afternoon he tapped at the door of Major Talbot's study. The major opened it, and Hargraves walked in with his hands full of the morning papers— too full of his triumph to notice anything unusual in the major's demeanour.

"I put it all over 'em last night, major," he began exultantly. "I had my inning, and, I think, scored. Here's what *the Post* says:

His conception and portrayal of the old-time Southern colonel, with his absurd grandiloquence, his eccentric garb, his quaint idioms and phrases, his moth-eaten pride of family, and his really kind heart, fastidious sense of honor, and lovable simplicity, is the best delineation of a character role on the boards today. The coat worn by Colonel Calhoun is itself nothing less than an evolution of genius. Mr. Hargraves has captured his public.

"How does that sound, major, for a first nighter?"

"I had the honor"—the major's voice sounded ominously frigid—"of witnessing your very remarkable performance, sir, last night."

Hargraves looked disconcerted.

"You were there? I didn't know you ever—I didn't know you cared for the theater. Oh, I say, Major Talbot," he exclaimed frankly, "don't you be offended. I admit I did get a lot of pointers from you that helped me out wonderfully in the part. But it's a type, you know—not individual. The way the audience caught on shows that. Half the patrons of that theater are Southerners. They recognized it."

"Mr. Hargraves," said the major, who had remained standing, "you have put upon me an unpardonable insult. You have burlesqued my person, grossly betrayed my confidence, and misused my hospitality. If I thought you possessed the faintest conception of what is the sign manual of a gentleman, or what is due one, I would call you out, sir, old as I am. I will ask you to leave the room, sir."

The actor appeared to be slightly bewildered, and seemed hardly to take in the full meaning of the old gentleman's words.

"I am truly sorry you took offence," he said regretfully. "Up here we don't look at things just as you people do. I know men who would buy out half the house to have their personality put on the stage so the public would recognize it."

"They are not from Alabama, sir," said the major haughtily.

"Perhaps not. I have a pretty good memory, major; let me quote a few lines from your book. In response to a toast at a banquet given in Milledgeville, I believe—you uttered, and intend to have printed these words:

> The Northern man is utterly without sentiment or warmth except in so far as the feelings may be turned to his own commercial profit. He will suffer without resentment any imputation cast upon the honor of himself or his loved ones

that does not bear with it the consequence of pecuniary loss. In his charity, he gives with a liberal hand; but it must be heralded with the trumpet and chronicled in brass.

"Do you think that picture is fairer than the one you saw of Colonel Calhoun last night?"

"The description," said the major frowning, "is—not without grounds. Some exag—latitude must be allowed in public speaking."

"And in public acting," replied Hargraves.

"That is not the point," persisted the major, unrelenting. "It was a personal caricature. I positively decline to overlook it, sir."

"Major Talbot," said Hargraves, with a winning smile, "I wish you would understand me. I want you to know that I never dreamed of insulting you. In my profession, all life belongs to me. I take what I want, and what I can, and return it over the footlights. Now, if you will, let's let it go at that. I came in to see you about something else. We've been pretty good friends for some months, and I'm going to take the risk of offending you again. I know you are hard up for money—never mind how I found out; a boarding house is no place to keep such matters secret—and I want you to let me help you out of the pinch. I've been there often enough myself. I've been getting a fair salary all the season, and I've saved some money. You're welcome to a couple hundred—or even more—until you get—"

"Stop!" commanded the major, with his arm outstretched. "It seems that my book didn't lie, after all. You think your money salve will heal all the hurts of honor. Under no circumstances would I accept a loan from a casual acquaintance; and as to you, sir, I would starve before I would consider your insulting offer of a financial adjustment of the circumstances we have discussed. I beg to repeat my request relative to your quitting the apartment."

Hargraves took his departure without another word. He also left the house the same day, moving, as Mrs. Vardeman explained at the supper table, nearer the vicinity of the down-town theater, where "A Magnolia Flower" was booked for a week's run.

Critical was the situation with Major Talbot and Miss Lydia. There was no one in Washington to whom the major's scruples allowed him to apply for a loan. Miss Lydia wrote a letter to Uncle Ralph, but it was doubtful whether that relative's constricted affairs would permit him to furnish help. The major was forced to make an apologetic address to Mrs. Vardeman regarding the delayed payment for board, referring to "delinquent rentals" and "delayed remittances" in a rather confused strain.

Deliverance came from an entirely unexpected source.

Late one afternoon the door maid came up and announced an old colored man who wanted to see Major Talbot. The major asked that he be sent up to his study.

Soon an old darkey appeared in the doorway, with his hat in hand, bowing, and scraping with one clumsy foot. He was quite decently dressed in a baggy suit of black. His big, coarse shoes shone with a metallic luster suggestive of stove polish. His bushy wool was gray—almost white. After middle life, it is difficult to estimate the age of a Negro. This one might have seen as many years as had Major Talbot.

"I be bound you don't know me, Mars' Pendleton," were his first words.

The major rose and came forward at the old, familiar style of address. It was one of the old plantation darkeys without a doubt; but they had been widely scattered, and he could not recall the voice or face.

"I don't believe I do," he said kindly—"unless you will assist my memory."

"Don't you 'member Cindy's Mose, Mars' Pendleton, what 'migrated 'mediately after de war?"

"Wait a moment," said the major, rubbing his forehead with the tips of his fingers. He loved to recall everything connected with those beloved days. "Cindy's Mose," he reflected. "You worked among the horses—breaking the colts. Yes, I remember now. After the surrender, you took the name of—don't prompt me—Mitchell, and went to the West—to Nebraska."

"Yassir, yassir,"—the old man's face stretched with a delighted grin—"dat's him, dat's it. Newbraska. Dat's me—Mose Mitchell. Old Uncle Mose Mitchell, dey calls me now. Old mars', your pa, gimme a pah of dem mule colts when I lef' fur to staht me goin' with. You 'member dem colts, Mars' Pendleton?"

"I don't seem to recall the colts," said the major. "You know I was married the first year of the war and living at the old Follinsbee place. But sit down, sit down, Uncle Mose. I'm glad to see you. I hope you have prospered."

Uncle Mose took a chair and laid his hat carefully on the floor beside it.

"Yassir; of late I done mouty famous. When I first got to Newbraska, dey folks come all roun' me to see dem mule colts. Dey ain't see no mules like dem in Newbraska. I sold dem mules for three hundred dollars. Yassir—three hundred.

"Den I open a blacksmith shop, suh, and made some money and bought some lan'. Me and my old 'oman done raised up seb'm chillun, and all doin' well 'cept two of 'em what died. Fo' year ago a railroad come along and staht a town slam ag'inst my lan', and, suh, Mars' Pendleton, Uncle Mose am worth leb'm thousand dollars in money, property, and lan'."

"I'm glad to hear it," said the major heartily. "Glad to hear it."

"And dat little baby of yo'n, Mars' Pendleton—one what you name Miss Lyddy—I be bound dat little tad done growed up tell nobody wouldn't know her."

The major stepped to the door and called: "Lydia, dear, will you come?"

Miss Lydia, looking quite grown up and a little worried, came in from her room.

"Dar, now! What'd I tell you? I knowed dat baby done be plum growed up. You don't 'member Uncle Mose, child?"

"This is Aunt Cindy's Mose, Lydia," explained the major. "He left Sunnymead for the West when you were two years old."

"Well," said Miss Lydia, "I can hardly be expected to remember you, Uncle Mose, at that age. And, as you say, 'I'm 'plum growed up,' and was a blessed long time ago. But I'm glad to see you, even if I can't remember you."

And she was. And so was the major. Something alive and tangible had come to link them with the happy past. The three sat and talked over the olden times, the major and Uncle Mose, correcting or prompting each other as they reviewed the plantation scenes and days.

The major inquired what the old man was doing so far from his home.

"Uncle Mose am a delicate," he explained, "to de grand Baptis' convention in dis city. I never preached none, but bein' a residin' elder in de church, and able fur to pay my own expenses, dey sent me along."

"And how did you know we were in Washington?" inquired Miss Lydia.

"Dey's a cullud man works in de hotel whar I stops, what comes from Mobile. He told me he seen Mars' Pendleton comin' outen dish here house one mawnin'.

"What I come fur," continued Uncle Mose, reaching into his pocket—"besides de sight of home folks—was to pay Mars' Pendleton what I owes him."

"Owe me?" said the major, in surprise.

"Yassir—three hundred dollars." He handed the major a roll of bills. "When I lef' old mars' says: 'Take dem mule colts, Mose, and, if it be so you gits able, pay fur 'em.' Yas sir—dem was his words. De war had done lef' old mars' po' hisself. Old mars' bein' 'long ago dead, de debt descends to Mars' Pendleton. Three hundred dollars. Uncle Mose is plenty able to pay now. When dat railroad buy my lan' I laid off to pay fur dem mules. Count de money, Mars' Pendleton. Dat's what I sold dem mules fur. Yassir."

Tears were in Major Talbot's eyes. He took Uncle Mose's hand and laid his other upon his shoulder.

"Dear, faithful old servitor," he said in an unsteady voice, "I don't mind saying to you that 'Mars' Pendleton' spent his last dollar in the world a week ago. We will accept this money, Uncle Mose, since, in a way, it is a sort of payment, as well as a token of the loyalty and devotion of the old regime. Lydia, my dear, take the money. You are better fitted than I to manage its expenditure."

"Take it, honey," said Uncle Mose. "Hit belongs to you. Hit's Talbot money."

After Uncle Mose had gone, Miss Lydia had a good cry—for joy; and the major turned his face to a corner, and smoked his clay pipe volcanically.

The succeeding days saw the Talbots restored to peace and ease. Miss Lydia's face lost its worried look. The major appeared in a new frock coat, in which he looked like a wax figure personifying the memory of his golden age. Another publisher who read the manuscript of the "Anecdotes and Reminiscences" thought that, with a little retouching and toning down of the high lights, he could make a really bright and salable volume of it. Altogether, the situation was comfortable, and not without the touch of hope that is often sweeter than arrived blessings.

One day, about a week after their piece of good luck, a maid brought a letter for Miss Lydia to her room. The postmark showed that it was from New York. Not knowing any one there, Miss Lydia, in a mild flutter of wonder, sat down by her table and opened the letter with her scissors. This was what she read:

Dear Miss Talbot:

I thought you might be glad to learn of my good fortune. I have received and accepted an offer of two hundred dollars per week by a New York stock company to play Colonel Calhoun in "A Magnolia Flower."

There is something else I wanted you to know. I guess you'd better not tell Major Talbot. I was anxious to make him some amends for the great help he was to me in studying the part, and for the bad humor he was in *about it. He refused to let me, so I did it anyhow. I could easily spare the three hundred.*

Sincerely yours,

H. Hopkins Hargraves
P.S. How did I play Uncle Mose?

Major Talbot, passing through the hall, saw Miss Lydia's door open and stopped.

"Any mail for us this morning, Lydia dear?" he asked.

Miss Lydia slid the letter beneath a fold of her dress.

"The Mobile Chronicle came," she said promptly. "It's on the table in your study."

A guard came to the prison shoe-shop, where Jimmy Valentine was assiduously stitching uppers, and escorted him to the front office. There the warden handed Jimmy his pardon, which had been signed that morning by the governor. Jimmy took it in a tired kind of way. He had served nearly ten months of a four year sentence. He had expected to stay only about three months, at the longest. When a man with as many friends on the outside as Jimmy Valentine had is received in the "stir" it is hardly worth while to cut his hair.

"Now, Valentine," said the warden, "you'll go out in the morning. Brace up, and make a man of yourself. You're not a bad fellow at heart. Stop cracking safes, and live straight."

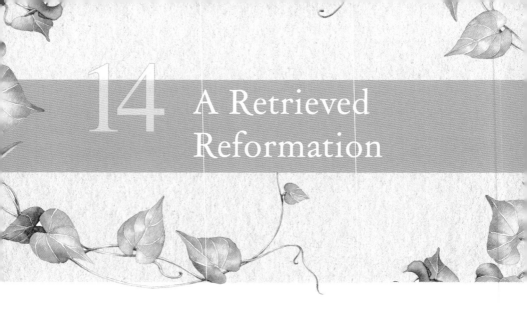

14 A Retrieved Reformation

"Me?" said Jimmy, in surprise. "Why, I never cracked a safe in my life."

"Oh, no," laughed the warden. "Of course not. Let's see, now. How was it you happened to get sent up on that Springfield job? Was it because you wouldn't prove an alibi for fear of compromising somebody in extremely high-toned society? Or was it simply a case of a mean old jury that had it in for you? It's always one or the other with you innocent victims."

"Me?" said Jimmy, still blankly virtuous. "Why, warden, I never was in Springfield in my life!"

"Take him back, Cronin!" smiled the warden, "and fix him up with outgoing clothes. Unlock him at seven in the morning, and let him come to the bull-pen. Better think over my advice, Valentine."

At a quarter past seven on the next morning Jimmy stood in the warden's outer office. He had on a suit of the villainously fitting, ready-made clothes and a pair of the stiff, squeaky shoes that the state furnishes to its discharged compulsory guests.

The clerk handed him a railroad ticket and the five-dollar bill with which the law expected him to rehabilitate himself into good citizenship and prosperity. The warden gave him a cigar, and shook hands. Valentine, 9762, was chronicled on the books, "Pardoned by Governor," and Mr. James Valentine walked out into the sunshine.

Disregarding the song of the birds, the waving green trees, and the smell of the flowers, Jimmy headed straight for a restaurant. There he tasted the first sweet joys of liberty in the shape of a broiled chicken and a bottle of white wine—followed by a cigar a grade better than the one the warden had given him. From there he proceeded leisurely to the depot. He tossed a quarter into the hat of a blind man sitting by the door, and boarded his train. Three hours set him down in a little town near the state line. He went to the café of one Mike Dolan and shook hands with Mike, who was alone behind the bar.

"Sorry we couldn't make it sooner, Jimmy, me boy," said Mike. "But we had that protest from Springfield to buck against, and the governor nearly balked. Feeling all right?"

"Fine," said Jimmy. "Got my key?"

He got his key and went upstairs, unlocking the door

of a room at the rear. Everything was just as he had left it. There on the floor was still Ben Price's collar-button that had been torn from that eminent detective's shirt-band when they had overpowered Jimmy to arrest him.

Pulling out from the wall a folding-bed, Jimmy slid back a panel in the wall and dragged out a dust-covered suitcase. He opened this and gazed fondly at the finest set of burglar's tools in the East. It was a complete set, made of specially tempered steel, the latest designs in drills, punches, braces and bits, jimmies, clamps, and augers, with two or three novelties, invented by Jimmy himself, in which he took pride. Over nine hundred dollars they had cost him to have made at—, a place where they make such things for the profession.

In half an hour Jimmy went downstairs and through the café. He was now dressed in tasteful and well-fitting clothes, and carried his dusted and cleaned suitcase in his hand.

"Got anything on?" asked Mike Dolan, genially.

"Me?" said Jimmy, in a puzzled tone. "I don't understand. I'm representing the New York Amalgamated

Short Snap Biscuit Cracker and Frazzled Wheat Company."

This statement delighted Mike to such an extent that Jimmy had to take a seltzer-and-milk on the spot. He never touched "hard" drinks.

A week after the release of Valentine, 9762, there was a neat job of safe-burglary done in Richmond, Indiana, with no clue to the author. A scant eight hundred dollars was all that was secured. Two weeks after that a patented, improved, burglar-proof safe in Logansport was opened like a cheese to the tune of fifteen hundred dollars, currency; securities and silver untouched. That began to interest the rogue-catchers. Then an old-fashioned bank-safe in Jefferson City became active and threw out of its crater an eruption of bank-notes amounting to five thousand dollars. The losses were now high enough to bring the matter up into Ben Price's class of work. By comparing notes, a remarkable similarity in the methods of the burglaries was noticed. Ben Price investigated the scenes of the robberies, and was heard to remark:

"That's Dandy Jim Valentine's autograph. He's resumed business. Look at that combination knob—jerked out as easy as pulling up a radish in wet weather. He's got the only clamps that can do it. And look how clean those tumblers were punched out! Jimmy never has to drill but one hole. Yes, I guess I want Mr. Valentine. He'll do his bit next time without any short-time or clemency foolishness."

Ben Price knew Jimmy's habits. He had learned them while working up the Springfield case. Long jumps, quick get-aways, no confederates, and a taste for good society—these ways had helped Mr. Valentine to become noted as a successful dodger of retribution. It was given out that Ben Price had taken up the trail of the elusive cracksman, and other people with burglar-proof safes felt more at ease.

One afternoon Jimmy Valentine and his suitcase climbed out of the mail-hack in Elmore, a little town five miles off the railroad down in the black-jack country of Arkansas. Jimmy, looking like an athletic young senior just home from college, went down the board sidewalk toward the hotel.

A young lady crossed the street, passed him at the corner and entered a door over which was the sign "The Elmore Bank." Jimmy Valentine looked into her eyes, forgot what he was, and became another man. She lowered her eyes and colored slightly. Young men of Jimmy's style and looks were scarce in Elmore.

Jimmy collared a boy that was loafing on the steps of the bank as if he were one of the stockholders, and began to ask him questions about the town, feeding him dimes at intervals. By and by the young lady came out, looking royally unconscious of the young man with the suitcase, and went her way.

"Isn't that young lady Miss Polly Simpson?" asked Jimmy, with specious guile.

"Naw," said the boy. "She's Annabel Adams. Her pa owns this bank. What'd you come to Elmore for? Is that a gold watch-chain? I'm going to get a bulldog. Got any more dimes?"

Jimmy went to the Planters' Hotel, registered as Ralph D. Spencer, and engaged a room. He leaned on the desk and declared his platform to the clerk. He said he had come to Elmore to look for a location to go into business. How was the shoe business, now, in the town? He had thought of the shoe business. Was there an opening?

The clerk was impressed by the clothes and manner of Jimmy. He, himself, was something of a pattern of fashion to the thinly gilded youth of Elmore, but he now perceived his shortcomings. While trying to figure out Jimmy's manner of tying his four-in-hand he cordially gave information.

Yes, there ought to be a good opening in the shoe line. There wasn't an exclusive shoe-store in the place. The dry-goods and general stores handled them. Business in all lines was fairly good. Hoped Mr. Spencer would decide to locate in Elmore. He would find it a pleasant town to live in, and the people very sociable.

Mr. Spencer thought he would stop over in the town a few days and look over the situation. No, the clerk needn't call the boy. He would carry up his suitcase, himself; it was rather heavy.

Mr. Ralph Spencer, the phoenix that arose from Jimmy Valentine's ashes—ashes left by the flame of a sudden and alterative attack of love—remained in Elmore, and prospered. He opened a shoe-store and secured a good run of trade.

Socially he was also a success, and made many friends. And he accomplished the wish of his heart. He met Miss Annabel Adams, and became more and more captivated by her charms.

At the end of a year the situation of Mr. Ralph Spencer was this: he had won the respect of the community, his shoe-store was flourishing, and he and Annabel were engaged to be married in two weeks. Mr. Adams, the typical, plodding, country banker, approved of Spencer. Annabel's pride in him almost equaled her affection. He was as much at home in the family of Mr. Adams and that of Annabel's married sister as if he were already a member.

One day Jimmy sat down in his room and wrote this letter, which he mailed to the safe address of one of his old friends in St. Louis:

Dear Old Pal:

I want you to be at Sullivan's place, in Little Rock, next Wednesday night at nine o'clock. I want you to wind up some little matters for me. And, also, I want to make you a present of my kit of tools. I know you'll be glad to get them— you couldn't duplicate the lot for a thousand dollars. Say, Billy, I've quit the old business— a year ago. I've got a nice store. I'm making an honest living, and I'm going to marry the finest girl on earth two weeks from now. It's the only life, Billy—the straight one. I wouldn't touch a dollar of another man's money now for a million. After I get married I'm going to sell out and go West, where there won't be so much danger of having old scores brought up against me. I tell you, Billy, she's an angel. She believes in me; and I wouldn't do another crooked thing for the whole world. Be sure to be at Sully's, for I must see you. I'll bring along the tools with me.

                              Your old friend,

                              Jimmy.

On the Monday night after Jimmy wrote this letter, Ben Price jogged unobtrusively into Elmore in a livery buggy. He lounged about town in his quiet way until he found out what he wanted to know. From the drug-store across the street from Spencer's shoe-store he got a good look at Ralph D. Spencer.

"Going to marry the banker's daughter are you, Jimmy?" said Ben to himself, softly. "Well, I don't know!"

The next morning Jimmy took breakfast at the Adamses. He was going to Little Rock that day to order his wedding-suit and buy something nice for Annabel. That would be the first time he had left town since he came to Elmore. It had been more than a year now since those last professional "jobs," and he thought he could safely venture out.

After breakfast quite a family party went downtown together—Mr. Adams, Annabel, Jimmy, and Annabel's married sister with her two little girls, aged five and nine. They came by the hotel where Jimmy still boarded, and he ran up to his room and brought along his suitcase. Then they went on to the bank. There stood Jimmy's horse and buggy and Dolph Gibson, who was going to drive him over to the railroad station.

All went inside the high, carved oak railings into the banking-room—Jimmy included, for Mr. Adams's future son-in-law was welcome anywhere. The clerks were pleased to be greeted by the good-looking, agreeable

young man who was going to marry Miss Annabel. Jimmy set his suitcase down. Annabel, whose heart was bubbling with happiness and lively youth, put on Jimmy's hat and picked up the suitcase. "Wouldn't I make a nice drummer?" said Annabel. "My! Ralph, how heavy it is? Feels like it was full of gold bricks."

"Lot of nickel-plated shoe-horns in there," said Jimmy, coolly, "that I'm going to return. Thought I'd save express charges by taking them up. I'm getting awfully economical."

The Elmore Bank had just put in a new safe and vault. Mr. Adams was very proud of it, and insisted on an inspection by every one. The vault was a small one, but it had a new patented door. It fastened with three solid steel bolts thrown simultaneously with a single handle, and had a time-lock. Mr. Adams beamingly explained its workings to Mr. Spencer, who showed a courteous but not too intelligent interest. The two children, May and Agatha, were delighted by the shining metal and funny clock and knobs.

While they were thus engaged Ben Price sauntered in and leaned on his elbow, looking casually inside between the railings. He told the teller that he didn't want anything; he was just waiting for a man he knew.

Suddenly there was a scream or two from the women, and a commotion. Unperceived by the elders, May, the nine-year-old girl, in a spirit of play, had shut Agatha in the vault. She had then shot the bolts and turned the knob of the combination as she had seen Mr. Adams do.

The old banker sprang to the handle and tugged at it for a moment. "The door can't be opened," he groaned. "The clock hasn't been wound nor the combination set."

Agatha's mother screamed again, hysterically.

"Hush!" said Mr. Adams, raising his trembling hand. "All be quite for a moment. Agatha!" he called as loudly as he could: "Listen to me." During the following silence they could just hear the faint sound of the child wildly shrieking in the dark vault in a panic of terror.

"My precious darling!" wailed the mother. "She will die of fright! Open the door! Oh, break it open! Can't you men do something?"

"There isn't a man nearer than Little Rock who can open that door," said Mr. Adams, in a shaky voice. "My God! Spencer, what shall we do? That child—she can't stand it long in there. There isn't enough air, and, besides, she'll go into convulsions from fright."

Agatha's mother, frantic now, beat the door of the vault with her hands. Somebody wildly suggested dynamite. Annabel turned to Jimmy, her large eyes full of anguish, but not yet despairing. To a woman nothing seems quite impossible to the powers of the man she worships.

"Can't you do something, Ralph—*try*, won't you?"

He looked at her with a queer, soft smile on his lips and in his keen eyes.

"Annabel," he said, "give me that rose you are wearing, will you?"

Hardly believing that she heard him aright, she unpinned the bud from the bosom of her dress, and placed it in his hand. Jimmy stuffed it into his vest-pocket, threw off his coat and pulled up his shirt-sleeves. With that act Ralph D. Spencer passed away and Jimmy Valentine took his place.

"Get away from the door, all of you," he commanded, shortly.

He set his suitcase on the table, and opened it out flat. From that time on he seemed to be unconscious of the presence of any one else. He laid out the shining, queer implements swiftly and orderly, whistling softly to himself as he always did when at work. In a deep silence and immovable, the others watched him as if under a spell.

In a minute Jimmy's pet drill was biting smoothly into the steel door. In ten minutes—breaking his own burglarious record—he threw back the bolts and opened the door.

Agatha, almost collapsed, but safe, was gathered into her mother's arms.

Jimmy Valentine put on his coat, and walked outside the railings towards the front door. As he went he thought he heard a far-away voice that he once knew call "Ralph!" But he never hesitated.

At the door a big man stood somewhat in his way.

"Hello, Ben!" said Jimmy, still with his strange smile. "Got around at last, have you? Well, let's go. I don't know that it makes much difference, now."

And then Ben Price acted rather strangely.

"Guess you're mistaken, Mr. Spencer," he said. "Don't believe I recognize you. Your buggy's waiting for you, ain't it?"

And Ben Price turned and strolled down the street.

15 Roads of Destiny

I go to seek on many roads
What is to be.
True heart and strong, with love to light—
Will they not bear me in the fight
To order, shun or wield or mould
My Destiny?

Unpublished poems of David Mignot.

The song was over. The words were David's; the air,
one of the countryside. The company about the inn table
applauded heartily, for the young poet paid for the wine.
Only the notary, M. Papineau, shook his head a little at the
lines, for he was a man of books, and he had not drunk
with the rest.

David went out into the village street, where the night air drove the wine vapor from his head. And then he remembered that he and Yvonne had quarreled that day, and that he had resolved to leave his home that night to seek fame and honor in the great world outside.

"When my poems are on every man's tongue," he told himself, in a fine exhilaration, "she will, perhaps, think of the hard words she spoke this day."

Except the roysterers in the tavern, the village folk were abed. David crept softly into his room in the shed of his father's cottage and made a bundle of his small store of clothing. With this upon a staff, he set his face outward upon the road that ran from Vernoy.

He passed his father's herd of sheep huddled in their nightly pen—the sheep he herded daily, leaving them to scatter while he wrote verses on scraps of paper. He saw a light yet shining in Yvonne's window, and a weakness shook his purpose of a sudden. Perhaps that light meant that she rued, sleepless, her anger, and that morning might—But, no! His decision was made. Vernoy was no place for him. Not one soul there could share his thoughts. Out along that road lay his fate and his future.

Three leagues across the dim, moonlit champaign ran the road, straight as a plowman's furrow. It was believed in the village that the road ran to Paris, at least; and this name the poet whispered often to himself as he walked. Never so far from Vernoy had David traveled before.

THE LEFT BRANCH

Three leagues, then, the road ran, and turned into a puzzle. It joined with another and a larger road at right angles. David stood, uncertain, for a while, and then took the road to the left.

Upon this more important highway were, imprinted in the dust, wheel tracks left by the recent passage of some vehicle. Some half an hour later these traces were verified by the sight of a ponderous carriage mired in a little brook at the bottom of a steep hill. The driver and postilions were shouting and tugging at the horses' bridles. On the road at one side stood a huge, black-clothed man and a slender lady wrapped in a long, light cloak.

David saw the lack of skill in the efforts of the servants. He quietly assumed control of the work. He directed the outriders to cease their clamor at the horses and to exercise their strength upon the wheels. The driver alone urged the animals with his familiar voice; David himself heaved a powerful shoulder at the rear of the carriage, and with one harmonious tug the great vehicle rolled up on solid ground. The outriders climbed to their places.

David stood for a moment upon one foot. The huge gentleman waved a hand. "You will enter the carriage," he said, in a voice large, like himself, but smoothed by art and habit. Obedience belonged in the path of such a voice. Brief as was the young poet's hesitation, it was cut shorter still by a renewal of the command. David's foot went to the step. In the darkness he perceived dimly the form of the lady upon the rear seat. He was about to seat himself opposite, when the voice again swayed him to its will. "You will sit at the lady's side."

The gentleman swung his great weight to the forward seat. The carriage proceeded up the hill. The lady was shrunk, silent, into her corner. David could not estimate whether she was old or young, but a delicate, mild perfume from her clothes stirred his poet's fancy to the belief that there was loveliness beneath the mystery. Here was an adventure such as he had often imagined. But as yet he held no key to it, for no word was spoken while he sat with his impenetrable companions.

In an hour's time David perceived through the window that the vehicle traversed the street of some town. Then it stopped in front of a closed and darkened house, and a postilion alighted to hammer impatiently upon the door. A latticed window above flew wide and a night-capped head popped out.

"Who are ye that disturb honest folk at this time of night? My house is closed. 'Tis too late for profitable travelers to be abroad. Cease knocking at my door, and be off."

"Open!" spluttered the postilion, loudly; "open for Monseigneur, the Marquis de Beaupertuys."

"Ah!" cried the voice above. "Ten thousand pardons, my lord. I did not know—the hour is so late—at once shall the door be opened, and the house placed at my lord's disposal."

Inside was heard the clink of chain and bar, and the door was flung open. Shivering with chill and apprehension, the landlord of the Silver Flagon stood, half clad, candle in hand, upon the threshold.

David followed the marquis out of the carriage. "Assist the lady," he was ordered. The poet obeyed. He felt her small hand tremble as he guided her descent. "Into the house," was the next command.

The room was the long dining-hall of the tavern. A great oak table ran down its length. The huge gentleman seated himself in a chair at the nearer end. The lady sank into another against the wall, with an air of great weariness. David stood, considering how best he might now take his leave and continue upon his way.

"My lord," said the landlord, bowing to the floor, "h-had I ex-expected this honor, entertainment would have been ready. T-t-there is wine and cold fowl and m-m-maybe—"

"Candles," said the marquis, spreading the fingers of one plump white hand in a gesture he had.

"Y-yes, my lord." He fetched half a dozen candles, lighted them, and set them upon the table.

"If monsieur would, perhaps, deign to taste a certain Burgundy—there is a cask—"

"Candles," said the monsieur, spreading his fingers.

"Assuredly—quickly—I fly, my lord."

A dozen more lighted candles shone in the hall. The great bulk of the marquis overflowed his chair. He was dressed in fine black from head to foot save for the snowy ruffles at his wrist and throat. Even the hilt and scabbard of his sword were black. His expression was one of sneering pride. The ends of his upturned moustache reached nearly to his mocking eyes.

The lady sat motionless, and now David perceived

that she was young, and possessed a pathetic and appealing beauty. He was startled from the contemplation of her forlorn loveliness by the booming voice of the marquis.

"What is your name and pursuit?"

"David Mignot. I am a poet."

The moustache of the marquis curled nearer to his eyes.

"How do you live?"

"I am also a shepherd; I guarded my father's flock," David answered, with his head high, but a flush upon his cheek.

"Then listen, master shepherd and poet, to the fortune you have blundered upon tonight. This lady is my niece, Mademoiselle Lucie de Varennes. She is of noble descent and is possessed of ten thousand francs a year in her own right. As to her charms, you have but to observe for yourself. If the inventory pleases your shepherd's heart, she becomes your wife at a word. Do not interrupt me. Tonight I conveyed her to the château of the Comte de Villemaur, to whom her hand had been promised. Guests were present; the priest was waiting; her marriage to one eligible in rank and fortune was ready to be accomplished. At the altar this demoiselle, so meek and dutiful, turned upon me like a leopardess, charged me with cruelty and crimes, and broke, before the gaping priest, the troth I had plighted for her. I swore there and then, by ten thousand devils, that she should marry the first man we met after leaving the château, be he prince, charcoal burner, or thief. You, shepherd, are the first. Mademoiselle must be wed this night. If not you, then another. You have ten minutes in which to make your decision. Do not vex me with words or questions. Ten minutes, shepherd; and they are speeding."

The marquis drummed loudly with his white fingers upon the table. He sank into a veiled attitude of waiting. It was as if some great house had shut its doors and windows against approach. David would have spoken, but the huge man's bearing stopped his tongue. Instead, he stood by the lady's chair and bowed.

"Mademoiselle," he said, and he marveled to find his words flowing easily before so much elegance and beauty. "You have heard me say I was a shepherd. I have also had the fancy, at times, that I am a poet. If it be the test of a poet to adore and cherish the beautiful, that fancy is now strengthened. Can I serve you in any way, mademoiselle?"

The young woman looked up at him with eyes dry and mournful. His frank, glowing face, made serious by the gravity of the adventure, his strong, straight figure and the liquid sympathy in his blue eyes, perhaps, also, her imminent need of long-denied help and kindness, thawed her to sudden tears.

"Monsieur,' she said, in low tones, "you look to be true and kind. He is my uncle, the brother of my father, and my only relative. He loved my mother, and he hates me because I am like her. He has made my life one long terror. I am afraid of his very looks, and never before dared to disobey him. But tonight he would have married me to a man three times my age. You will forgive me for bringing this vexation upon you, monsieur. You will, of course, decline this mad act he tries to force upon you. But let me thank you for your generous words, at least. I have had none spoken to me in so long."

There was now something more than generosity in the poet's eyes. Poet he must have been, for Yvonne was forgotten; this fine, new loveliness held him with its freshness and grace. The subtle perfume from her filled him with strange emotions. His tender look fell warmly upon her. She leaned to it thirstily.

"Ten minutes," said David, "is given me in which to do what I would devote years to achieve. I will not say I pity you, mademoiselle; it would not be true—I love you. I cannot ask love from you yet, but let me rescue you from this cruel man, and, in time, love may come. I think I have a future, I will not always be a shepherd. For the present I will cherish you with all my heart and make your life less sad. Will you trust your fate to me, mademoiselle?"

"Ah, you would sacrifice yourself from pity!"

"From love. The time is almost up, mademoiselle."

"You will regret it, and despise me."

"I will live only to make you happy, and myself worthy of you!"

Her fine small hand crept into his from beneath her cloak.

"I will trust you," she breathed, "with my life. And—and love—may not be so far off as you think. Tell him. Once away from the power of his eyes I may forget."

David went and stood before the marquis. The black figure stirred, and the mocking eyes glanced at the great hall clock.

"Two minutes to spare. A shepherd requires eight minutes to decide whether he will accept a bride of beauty and income! Speak up, shepherd, do you consent to become mademoiselle's husband?"

"Mademoiselle," said David, standing proudly, "has done me the honor to yield to my request that she become my wife."

"Well said!" said the marquis. "You have yet the making of a courtier in you, master shepherd. Mademoiselle could have drawn a worse prize, after all. And now to be done with the affair as quick as the Church and the devil will allow!"

He struck the table soundly with his sword hilt. The landlord came, knee-shaking, bringing more candles in the hope of anticipating the great lord's whims. "Fetch a priest," said the marquis, "a priest; do you understand? In ten minutes have a priest here, or—"

The landlord dropped his candles and flew.

The priest came, heavy-eyed and muffled. He made David Mignot and Lucie de Varennes man and wife, pocketed a gold piece that the marquis tossed him, and shuffled out again into the night.

"Wine," ordered the marquis, spreading his ominous fingers at the host.

"Fill glasses," he said, when it was brought. He stood up at the head of the table in the candlelight, a black mountain of venom and conceit, with something like the memory of an old love turned to poison in his eye, as it fell upon his niece.

"Monsieur Mignot," he said, raising his wine-glass, "drink after I say this to you: You have taken to be your wife one who will make your life a foul and wretched thing. The blood in her is an inheritance running black lies and red ruin. She will bring you shame and anxiety. The devil that descended to her is there in her eyes and skin and mouth that stoop even to beguile a peasant. There is your promise, monsieur poet, for a happy life. Drink your wine. At last, mademoiselle, I am rid of you."

The marquis drank. A little grievous cry, as if from a sudden wound, came from the girl's lips. David, with his glass in his hand, stepped forward three paces and faced the marquis. There was little of a shepherd in his bearing.

"Just now," he said calmly, "you did me the honor to call me 'monsieur.' May I hope, therefore, that my marriage to mademoiselle has placed me somewhat nearer to you in—let us say, reflected rank—has given me the right to stand more as an equal to monseigneur in a certain little piece of business I have in my mind?"

"You may hope, shepherd," sneered the marquis.

"Then," said David, dashing his glass of wine into the contemptuous eyes that mocked him, "perhaps you will condescend to fight me."

The fury of the great lord outbroke in one sudden curse like a blast from a horn. He tore his sword from its black sheath; he called to the hovering landlord: "A sword there, for this lout!" He turned to the lady, with a laugh that chilled her heart, and said: "You put much labor upon me, madame. It seems I must find you a husband and make you a widow in the same night."

"I know not sword-play," said David. He flushed to make the confession before his lady.

"I know not sword-play," mimicked the marquis. "Shall we fight like peasants with oaken cudgels? Hola! Francois, my pistols!"

A postilion brought two shining great pistols ornamented with carven silver from the carriage holsters. The marquis tossed one upon the table near David's hand. "To the other end of the table," he cried; "even a shepherd may pull a trigger. Few of them attain the honor to die by the weapon of a De Beaupertuys."

The shepherd and the marquis faced each other from the ends of the long table. The landlord, in an ague of terror, clutched the air and stammered: "M-M-Monseigneur, for the love of Christ! not in my house!—do not spill blood—it will ruin my custom—" The look of the marquis, threatening him, paralyzed his tongue.

"Coward," cried the lord of Beaupertuys, "cease chattering your teeth long enough to give the word for us, if you can."

Mine host's knees smote the floor. He was without a vocabulary. Even sounds were beyond him. Still, by gestures he seemed to beseech peace in the name of his house and custom.

"I will give the word," said the lady, in a clear voice. She went up to David and kissed him sweetly. Her eyes were sparkling bright, and color had come to her cheek. She stood against the wall and the two men leveled their pistols for her count.

"*Un—deux—trois!*"

The two reports came so nearly together that the candles flickered but once. The marquis stood, smiling, the fingers of his left hand resting, outspread, upon the end of the table. David remained erect, and turned his head very slowly, searching for his wife with his eyes. Then, as a garment falls from where it is hung, he sank, crumpled, upon the floor.

With a little cry of terror and despair, the widowed maid ran and stooped above him. She found his wound, and then looked up with her old look of pale melancholy. "Through his heart," she whispered. "Oh, his heart!"

"Come," boomed the great voice of the marquis, "out with you to the carriage Daybreak shall not find you on my hands. Wed you shall be again, and to a living husband, this night. The next we come upon, my lady, highwayman or peasant. If the road yields no other, than the churl that opens my gates. Out with you to the carriages."

The marquis, implacable and huge, the lady wrapped again in the mystery of her cloak, the postilion bearing the weapons—all moved out to the waiting carriage. The sound of its ponderous wheels rolling away echoed through the slumbering village. In the hall of the Silver Flagon the distracted landlord wrung his hands above the slain poet's body, while the flames of the four and twenty candles danced and flickered on the table.

THE RIGHT BRANCH

Three leagues, then, the road ran, and turned into a puzzle. It joined with another and a larger road at right angles. David stood, uncertain, for a while, and then took the road to the right.

Whither it led he knew not, but he was resolved to leave Vernoy far behind that night. He traveled a league and then passed a large château which showed testimony of recent entertainment. Lights shone from every window; from the great stone gateway ran a tracery of wheel tracks drawn in the dust by the vehicles of the guests.

Three leagues farther and David was weary. He rested and slept for a while on a bed of pine boughs at the roadside. Then up and on again along the unknown way.

Thus for five days he traveled the great road, sleeping upon Nature's balsamic beds or in peasants' ricks, eating of their black, hospitable bread, drinking from streams or the willing cup of the goat-herd.

At length he crossed a great bridge and set his foot within the smiling city that has crushed or crowned more poets than all the rest of the world. His breath came quickly as Paris sang to him in a little undertone her vital chant of greeting—the hum of voice and foot and wheel.

High up under the eaves of an old house in the Rue Conti, David paid for lodging, and set himself, in a wooden chair, to his poems. The street, once sheltering citizens of import and consequence, was now given over to those who ever follow in the wake of decline.

The houses Were tall and still possessed of a ruined dignity, but many of them were empty save for dust and the spider. By night there was the clash of steel and the cries of brawlers straying restlessly from inn to inn. Where once gentility abode was now but a rancid and rude incontinence. But here David found housing commensurate to his scant purse. Daylight and candlelight found him at pen and paper.

One afternoon he was returning from a foraging trip to the lower world, with bread and curds and a bottle of thin wine. Halfway up his dark stairway he met—or rather came upon, for she rested on the stair—a young woman of a beauty that should balk even the justice of a poet's imagination. A loose, dark cloak, flung open, showed a rich gown beneath. Her eyes changed swiftly with every little shade of thought. Within one moment they would be round and artless like a child's, and long and cozening like a gypsy's. One hand raised her gown, undraping a little shoe, high-heeled, with its ribbons dangling, untied. So heavenly she was, so unfitted to stoop, so qualified to charm and command! Perhaps she had seen David coming, and had waited for his help there.

Ah, would monsieur pardon that she occupied the stairway, but the shoe!—the naughty shoe! Alas! It would not remain tied. Ah! if monsieur would be so gracious!

The poet's fingers trembled as he tied the contrary ribbons. Then he would have fled from the danger of her presence, but the eyes grew long and cozening, like a gypsy's, and held him. He leaned against the balustrade, clutching his bottle of sour wine.

"You have been so good," she said, smiling. "Does monsieur, perhaps, live in the house?"

"Yes, madame. I-I think so, madame."

"Perhaps in the third story, then?"

"No, madame; higher up."

The lady fluttered her fingers with the least possible gesture of impatience.

"Pardon. Certainly I am not discreet in asking. Monsieur will forgive me? It is surely not becoming that I should inquire where he lodges:'

"Madame, do not say so. I live in the—"

"No, no, no; do not tell me. Now I see that I erred. But I cannot lose the interest I feel in this house and all that is in it. Once it was my home. Often I come here but to dream of those happy days again. Will you let that be my excuse?"

"Let me tell you, then, for you need no excuse," stammered the poet. "I live in the top floor—the small room where the stairs turn."

"In the front room?" asked the lady, turning her head sidewise.

"The rear, madame."

The lady sighed, as if with relief.

"I will detain you no longer, then, monsieur," she said, employing the round and artless eye. "Take good care of my house. Alas! only the memories of it are mine now. Adieu, and accept my thanks for your courtesy."

She was gone, leaving but a smile and a trace of sweet perfume. David climbed the stairs as one in slumber. But he awoke from it, and the smile and the perfume lingered with him and never afterward did either seem quite to leave him. This lady of whom he knew nothing drove him to lyrics of eyes, chansons of swiftly conceived love, odes to curling hair, and sonnets to slippers on slender feet.

Poet he must have been, for Yvonne was forgotten; this fine, new loveliness held him with its freshness and grace. The subtle perfume about her filled him with strange emotions.

On a certain night three persons were gathered about a table in a room on the third floor of the same house. Three chairs and the table and a lighted candle upon it was all the furniture. One of the persons was a huge man, dressed in black. His expression was one of sneering pride. The ends of his upturned moustache reached nearly to his mocking eyes. Another was a lady, young and beautiful, with eyes that could be round and artless, like a child's, or long and cozening, like a gypsy's, but were now keen and ambitious, like any other conspirator's. The third was a man of action, a combatant, a bold and impatient executive, breathing fire and steel. He was addressed by the others as Captain Desrolles.

This man struck the table with his fist, and said, with controlled violence:

"Tonight. Tonight as he goes to midnight mass. I am tired of the plotting that gets nowhere. I am sick of signals and ciphers and secret meetings and such *baragouin*. Let us be honest traitors. If France is to be rid of him, let us kill in the open, and not hunt with snares and traps. Tonight, I say. I back my words. My hand will do the deed. Tonight, as he goes to mass."

The lady turned upon him a cordial look. Woman, however wedded to plots, must ever thus bow to rash courage. The big man stroked his upturned moustache.

"Dear captain," he said, in a great voice, softened by habit, "this time I agree with you. Nothing is to be gained by waiting. Enough of the palace guards belong to us to make the endeavor a safe one."

"Tonight," repeated Captain Desrolles, again strikng the table. "You have heard me, marquis; my hand will do the deed."

"But now," said the huge man, softly, "comes a question. Word must be sent to our partisans in the palace, and a signal agreed upon. Our staunchest men must accompany the royal carriage. At this hour what messenger can penetrate so far as the south doorway? Ribout is stationed there; once a message is placed in his hands, all will go well."

"I will send the message," said the lady.

"You, countess?" said the marquis, raising his eyebrows. "Your devotion is great, we know, but—"

"Listen!" exclaimed the lady, rising and resting her hands upon the table; "in a garret of this house lives a youth from the provinces as guileless and tender as the lambs he tended there. I have met him twice or thrice upon the stairs. I questioned him, fearing that he might dwell too near the room in which we are accustomed to meet. He is mine, if I will. He writes poems in his garret, and I think he dreams of me. He will do what I say. He shall take the message to the palace."

The marquis rose from his chair and bowed. "You did not permit me to finish my sentence, countess," he said. "I would have said: 'Your devotion is great, but your wit and charm are infinitely greater.'"

While the conspirators were thus engaged, David was polishing some lines addressed to his *amorette d'escalier.*

He heard a timorous knock at his door, and opened it, with a great throb, to behold her there, panting as one in straits, with eyes wide open and artless, like a child's.

"Monsieur," she breathed, "I come to you in distress. I believe you to be good and true, and I know of no other help. How I flew through the streets among the swaggering men! Monsieur, my mother is dying. My uncle is a captain of guards in the palace of the king. Some one must fly to bring him. May I hope—"

"Mademoiselle," interrupted David, his eyes shining with the desire to do her service, "your hopes shall be my wings. Tell me how I may reach him."

The lady thrust a sealed paper into his hand.

"Go to the south gate—the south gate, mind—and say to the guards there, 'The falcon has left his nest.' They will pass you, and you will go to the south entrance to the palace. Repeat the words, and give this letter to the man who will reply 'Let him strike when he will.' This is the password, monsieur, entrusted to me by my uncle, for now when the country is disturbed and men plot against the king's life, no one without it can gain entrance to the palace grounds after nightfall. If you will, monsieur, take him this letter so that my mother may see him before she closes her eyes."

"Give it me," said David, eagerly. "But shall I let you return home through the streets alone so late? I—"

"No, no—fly. Each moment is like a precious jewel. Some time," said the lady, with eyes long and cozening, like a gypsy's, "I will try to thank you for your goodness."

The poet thrust the letter into his breast, and bounded down the stairway. The lady, when he was gone, returned to the room below.

The eloquent eyebrows of the marquis interrogated her.

"He is gone," she said, "as fleet and stupid as one of his own sheep, to deliver it."

The table shook again from the batter of Captain Desrolles's fist.

"Sacred name!" he cried; "I have left my pistols behind! I can trust no others."

"Take this,"said the marquis, drawing from beneath his cloak a shining, great weapon, ornamented with carven silver. "There are none truer. But guard it closely, for it bears my arms and crest, and already I am suspected. Me, I must put many leagues between myself and Paris this night. Tomorrow must find me in my château. After you, dear countess."

The marquis puffed out the candle. The lady, well cloaked, and the two gentlemen softly descended the stairway and flowed into the crowd that roamed along the narrow pavements of the Rue Conti.

David sped. At the south gate of the king's residence a halberd was laid to his breast, but he turned its point with the words: "The falcon has left his nest."

"Pass, brother," said the guard, "and go quickly."

On the south steps of the palace they moved to seize him, but again the mot de passe charmed the watchers. One among them stepped forward and began: "Let him strike—" But a flurry among the guards told of a surprise.

A man of keen look and soldierly stride suddenly pressed through them and seized the letter which David held in his hand. "Come with me,' he said, and led him inside the great hall. Then he tore open the letter and read it. He beckoned to a man uniformed as an officer of musketeers, who was passing. "Captain Tetreau, you will have the guards at the south entrance and the south gate arrested and confined. Place men known to be loyal in their places." To David he said: "Come with me."

He conducted him through a corridor and an anteroom into a spacious chamber, where a melancholy man, somberly dressed, sat brooding in a great leather-covered chair. To that man he said:

"Sire, I have told you that the palace is as full of traitors and spies as a sewer is of rats. You have thought, sire, that it was my fancy. This man penetrated to your very door by their connivance. He bore a letter which I have intercepted. I have brought him here that your majesty may no longer think my zeal excessive."

"I will question him," said the king, stirring in his chair. He looked at David with heavy eyes dulled by an opaque film. The poet bent his knee.

"From where do you come?'" asked the king.

"From the village of Vernoy, in the province of Eure-et-Loir, sire."

"What do you follow in Paris?"

"I—I would be a poet, sire."

"What did you in Vemoy?"

"I minded my father's flock of sheep."

The king stirred again, and the film lifted from his eyes.

"Ah! in the fields?"

"Yes, sire."

"You lived in the fields; you went out in the cool of the morning and lay among the hedges in the grass. The flock distributed itself upon the hillside; you drank of the living stream; you ate your sweet brown bread in the shade; and you listened, doubtless, to blackbirds piping in the grove. Is not that so, shepherd?"

"It is, sire," answered David, with a sigh; "and to the bees at the flowers, and, maybe, to the grape gatherers singing on the hill."

"Yes, yes," said the king, impatiently; "maybe to them; but surely to the blackbirds. They whistled often, in the grove, did they not?"

"Nowhere, sire, so sweetly as in Eure-et-Loir. I have endeavored to express their song in some verses that I have written."

"Can you repeat those verses?" asked the king, eagerly. "A long time ago I listened to the blackbirds. It would be something better than a kingdom if one could rightly construe their song. And at night you drove the sheep to the fold and then sat, in peace and tranquillity, to your pleasant bread. Can you repeat those verses, shepherd?"

"They run this way, sire," said David, with respectful ardor:

Lazy shepherd, see your lambkins
Skip, ecstatic, on the mead;
See the firs dance in the breezes,
Hear Pan blowing at his reed.

"Hear us calling from the tree-tops,
See us swoop upon your flock;
Yield us wool to make our nests warm
In the branches of the—

"If it please your majesty," interrupted a harsh voice, "I will ask a question or two of this rhymester. There is little time to spare. I crave pardon, sire, if my anxiety for your safety offends."

"The loyalty," said the king, "of the Duke d'Aumale is too well proven to give offense." He sank into his chair, and the film came again over his eyes.

"First," said the duke, "I will read you the letter he brought:

"Tonight is the anniversary of the dauphin's death. If he goes, as is his custom, to midnight mass to pray for the soul of his son, the falcon will strike, at the corner of the Rue Esplanade. If this be his intention, set a red light in the upper room at the southwest corner of the palace, that the falcon may take heed."

"Peasant," said the duke, sternly, "you have heard these words. Who gave you this message to bring?"

"My lord duke," said David, sincerely, "I will tell you. A lady gave it me. She said her mother was ill, and that this writing would fetch her uncle to her bedside. I do not know the meaning of the letter, but I will swear that she is beautiful and good."

"Describe the woman," commanded the duke, "and how you came to be her dupe."

"Describe her!" said David with a tender smile. "You would command words to perform miracles. Well, she is made of sunshine and deep shade. She is slender, like the alders, and moves with their grace. Her eyes change while you gaze into them; now round, and then half shut as the sun peeps between two clouds. When she comes, heaven is all about her; when she leaves, there is chaos and a scent of hawthorn blossoms. She came to me in the Rue Conti, number twenty-nine."

"It is the house," said the duke, turning to the king, "that we have been watching. Thanks to the poet's tongue, we have a picture of the infamous Countess Quebedaux."

"Sire and my lord duke," said David, earnestly, "I hope my poor words have done no injustice. I have looked into that lady's eyes. I will stake my life that she is an angel, letter or no letter."

The duke looked at him steadily. "I will put you to the proof," he said, slowly. "Dressed as the king, you shall, yourself, attend mass in his carriage at midnight. Do you accept the test?"

David smiled. "I have looked into her eyes," he said. "I had my proof there. Take yours how you will."

Half an hour before twelve the Duke d'Aumale, with his own hands, set a red lamp in a southwest window of the palace. At ten minutes to the hour, David, leaning on his arm, dressed as the king, from top to toe, with his head bowed in his cloak, walked slowly from the royal apartments to the waiting carriage. The duke assisted him inside and closed the door. The carriage whirled away along its route to the cathedral.

On the *qui vive* in a house at the corner of the Rue Esplanade was Captain Tetreau with twenty men, ready to pounce upon the conspirators when they should appear.

But it seemed that, for some reason, the plotters had slightly altered their plans. When the royal carriage had reached the Rue Christopher, one square nearer than the Rue Esplanade, forth from it burst Captain Desrolles, with his band of would-be regicides, and assailed the equipage. The guards upon the carriage, though surprised at the premature attack, descended and fought valiantly. The noise of conflict attracted the force of Captain Tetreau, and they came pelting down the street to the rescue. But, in the meantime, the desperate Desrolles had torn open the door of the king's carriage, thrust his weapon against the body of the dark figure inside, and fired.

Now, with loyal reinforcements at hand, the street rang with cries and the rasp of steel, but the frightened horses had dashed away. Upon the cushions lay the dead body of the poor mock king and poet, slain by a ball from the pistol of Monseigneur, the Marquis de Beaupertuys.

THE MAIN ROAD

Three leagues, then, the road ran, and turned into
a puzzle. It joined with another and a larger road
at right angles. David stood, uncertain, for a while,
and then sat himself to rest upon its side.

Whither those roads led he knew not. Either way there seemed to lie a great world full of chance and peril. And then, sitting there, his eye fell upon a bright star, one that he and Yvonne had named for theirs. That set him thinking of Yvonne, and he wondered if he had not been too hasty. Why should he leave her and his home because a few hot words had come between them? Was love so brittle a thing that jealousy, the very proof of it, could break it? Mornings always brought a cure for the little heartaches of evening. There was yet time for him to return home without any one in the sweetly sleeping village of Vernoy being the wiser. His heart was Yvonne's; there where he had lived always he could write his poems and find his happiness.

David rose, and shook off his unrest and the wild mood that had tempted him. He set his face steadfastly back along the road he had come. By the time he had re-traveled the road to Vernoy, his desire to rove was gone. He passed the sheepfold, and the sheep scurried, with a drumming flutter, at his late footsteps, warming his heart by the homely sound. He crept without noise into his little room and lay there, thankful that his feet had escaped the distress of new roads that night.

How well he knew woman's heart! The next evening Yvonne was at the well in the road where the young congregated in order that the *curé* might have business. The corner of her eye was engaged in a search for David, albeit her set mouth seemed unrelenting. He saw the look; braved the mouth, drew from it a recantation and, later, a kiss as they walked homeward together.

Three months afterward they were married. David's father was shrewd and prosperous. He gave them a wedding that was heard of three leagues away. Both the young people were favorites in the village. There was a procession in the streets, a dance on the green; they had the marionettes and a tumbler out from Dreux to delight the guests.

Then a year, and David's father died. The sheep and the cottage descended to him. He already had the seemliest wife in the village. Yvonnes milk pails and her brass kettles were bright—ouf! they blinded you in the sun when you passed that way. But you must keep your eyes upon her yard, for her flower beds were so neat and gay they restored to you your sight. And you might hear her sing, aye, as far as the double chestnut tree above Père Gruneau's blacksmith forge.

But a day came when David drew out paper from a long-shut drawer, and began to bite the end of a pencil. Spring had come again and touched his heart. Poet he must have been, for now Yvonne was well-nigh forgotten. This fine new loveliness of earth held him with its witchery and grace. The perfume from her woods and meadows stirred him strangely. Daily had he gone forth with his flock, and brought it safe at night. But now he stretched himself under the hedge and pieced words together on his bits of paper. The sheep strayed, and the wolves, perceiving that difficult poems make easy mutton, ventured from the woods and stole his lambs.

David's stock of poems grew larger and his flock smaller. Yvonne's nose and temper waxed sharp and her talk blunt. Her pans and kettles grew dull, but her eyes had caught their flash. She pointed out to the poet that his neglect was reducing the flock and bringing woe upon the household. David hired a boy to guard the sheep, locked himself in the little room in the top of the cottage, and wrote more poems. The boy, being a poet by nature, but not furnished with an outlet in the way of writing, spent his time in slumber. The wolves lost no time in discovering that poetry and sleep are practically the same; so the flock steadily grew smaller. Yvonne's ill temper increased at an equal rate. Sometimes she would stand in the yard and rail at David through his high window. Then you could hear her as far as the double chestnut tree above Père Gruneau's blacksmith forge.

M. Papineau, the kind, wise, meddling old notary, saw this, as he saw everything at which his nose pointed. He went to David, fortified himself with a great pinch of snuff, and said:

"Friend Mignot, I affixed the seal upon the marriage certificate of your father. It would distress me to be obliged to attest a paper signifying the bankruptcy of his son. But that is what you are coming to. I speak as an old friend. Now, listen to what I have to say. You have your heart set, I perceive, upon poetry. At Dreux, I have a friend, one Monsieur Bril—Georges Bril. He lives in a little cleared space in a houseful of books. He is a learned man; he visits Paris each year, he himself has written books. He will tell you when the catacombs were made, how they found out the names of the stars, and why the plover has a long bill. The meaning and the form of poetry is to him as intelligent as the baa of a sheep is to you. I will give you a letter to him; and you shall take him your poems and let him read them. Then you will know if you shall write more, or give your attention to your wife and business."

"Write the letter," said David. "I am sorry you did not speak of this sooner."

At sunrise the next morning he was on the road to Dreux with the precious roll of poems under his arm. At noon he wiped the dust from his feet at the door of Monsieur Bril. That learned man broke the seal of M. Papineau's letter, and sucked up its contents through his gleaming spectacles as the sun draws water. He took David inside to his study and sat him down upon a little island beat upon by a sea of books.

Monsieur Bril had a conscience. He flinched not even at a mass of manuscript the thickness of a finger length and rolled to an incorrigible curve. He broke the back of the roll against his knee and began to read. He slighted nothing; he bored into the lump as a worm into a nut, seeking for a kernel.

Meanwhile, David sat, marooned, trembling in the spray of so much literature. It roared in his ears. He held no chart or compass for voyaging in that sea. Half the world, he thought, must be writing books.

Monsieur Bril bored to the last page of the poems. Then he took off his spectacles and wiped them with his handkerchief.

"My old friend, Papineau, is well?" he asked.

"In the best of health," said David.

"How many sheep have you, Monsieur Mignot?"

"Three hundred and nine, when I counted them yesterday. The flock has had ill fortune. To that number it has decreased from eight hundred and fifty."

"You have a wife and a home, and lived in comfort. The sheep brought you plenty. You went into the fields with them and lived in the keen air and ate the sweet bread of contentment. You had but to be vigilant and recline there upon nature's breast, listening to the whistle of the blackbirds in the grove. Am I right thus far?"

"It was so," said David.

"I have read all your verses," continued Monsieur Bril, his eyes wandering about his sea of books as if he conned the horizon for a sale. "Look yonder, through that window, Monsieur Mignot; tell me what you see in that tree."

"I see a crow," said David, looking.

"There is a bird," said Monsieur Bril, "that shall assist me where I am disposed to shirk a duty. You know that bird, Monsieur Mignot; he is the philosopher of the air. He is happy through submission to his lot. None so merry or full-crawed as he with his whimsical eye and rollicking step. The fields yield him what he desires. He never grieves that his plumage is not gay, like the oriole's. And you have heard, Monsieur Mignot, the notes that nature has given him? Is the nightingale any happier, do you think?'

David rose to his feet. The crow cawed harshly from his tree.

"I thank you, Monsieur Bril," he said, slowly. "There was not, then, one nightingale note among all those croaks?"

"I could not have missed it." said Monsieur Bril. with a

sigh. "I read every word. Live your poetry, man; do not try to write it any more."

"I thank you," said David, again. "And now I will be going back to my sheep."

"If you would dine with me,' said the man of books, "and overlook the smart of it, I will give you reasons at length!'

"No," said the poet, "I must be back in the fields cawing at my sheep."

Back along the road to Vernoy he trudged with his poems under his arm. When he reached his village he turned into the shop of one Zeigler, a Jew out of Armenia, who sold anything that a came to his hand.

"Friend," said David, "wolves from the forest harass my sheep on the hills. I must purchase firearms to protect them. What have you?"

"A bad day, this, for me, friend Mignot," said Zeigler, spreading his hands, "for I perceive that I must sell you a weapon that will not fetch a tenth of its value. Only last week I bought from a peddler a wagon full of goods that he procured at a sale by a *commissionaire* of the crown. The sale was of the château and belongings of a great lord—I know not his title—who has been banished for conspiracy against the king. There are some choice firearms in the lot. This pistol—oh, a weapon fit for a prince!—it shall be only forty francs to you, friend Mignot—if I lost ten by the sale. But perhaps an arquebus—"

"This will do," said David, throwing the money on the counter. "Is it charged?"

"I will charge it," said Zeigler. "And, for ten francs more, add a store of powder and ball."

David laid his pistol under his coat and walked to his cottage. Yvonne was not there. Of late she had taken to gadding much among the neighbors. But a fire was glowing in the kitchen stove. David opened the door of it and thrust his poems in upon the coals. As they blazed up they made a singing, harsh sound in the flue.

"The song of the crow!" said the poet.

He went up to his attic room and closed the door. So quiet was the village that a score of people heard the roar of the great pistol. They flocked thither, and up the stairs where the smoke, issuing, drew their notice.

The men laid the body of the poet upon his bed, awkwardly arranging it to conceal the torn plumage of the poor black crow. The women chattered in a luxury of zealous pity. Some of them ran to tell Yvonne.

M. Papineau, whose nose had brought him there among the first, picked up the weapon and ran his eye over its silver mountings with a mingled air of connoisseurship and grief.

"The arms," he explained, aside, to the curé' "and crest of Monseigneur, the Marquis de Beaupertuys."

Part 2

歐亨利短篇小說選

1 最後一片藤葉

華盛頓廣場的西邊有個小區域，那裡的街道錯綜複雜，叉成一條條叫做「小巷子」的羊腸小徑，這些「小巷子」彎曲的角度很奇怪，一條街自己就會交叉個一兩次。有一次，有位畫家就發現這種街道有一個好處。假如收帳員來這裡收顏料、畫紙和畫布的款，他會先繞個幾圈，結果卻繞回到原地，一毛錢都還沒收到！

所以呢，沒多久時間，這個古色古香的格林威治村就聚集了一堆搞藝術的人。他們尋找荷蘭式的閣樓，窗戶要開向北方，要有三角牆，租金還要便宜。他們從第六街買來白鑞製的杯子和一兩個保溫鍋，這裡儼然形成了一個畫家的「殖民地」。

蘇和蕎西把工作室設在一棟三層樓的矮磚房頂樓。蕎西是蕎安娜的簡稱，她們一個來自緬因州，一個來自加州，是在

第八街的「戴爾摩尼卡」餐廳裡認識的。她們發現彼此志趣相投，都熱愛藝術、苦苣沙拉和斗蓬袖，於是便合組了這間畫室。

那已經是五月的事了。到了十一月時，被醫生稱為「肺炎」的這位隱形而冷面的不速之客，肆虐這個殖民地，用他冰冷的手四處撫過，毫無忌憚地席捲整個東區，受害者不計其數。然而，他通過這些又亂又窄、滿是青苔的「小巷子」時，步伐卻慢了下來。

這位肺炎先生稱不上什麼具有俠義精神的老紳士，一個被加州西風吹得面無血色的瘦弱女子，根本不是這位紅拳頭、呼吸急促的老傢伙的對手。蕎西逃不過他的魔掌，她一動也不動地躺在一張上了漆的鐵床架上，透過小小的荷式窗戶，看著隔壁磚房上那面空蕩蕩的牆。

一日早晨，那位忙碌的醫生挑了挑他花白的濃密眉毛，把蘇叫到走廊上。

　　「她只有一成的機會了。」醫生一邊甩著溫度計的水銀，一邊說：「這一成的機會，只有靠她的意志力了。像她這樣的人，已經在排隊等著料理後事了，這整本藥典看起來毫無用武之地。妳的朋友已經放棄生存的意志了。她有沒有什麼放不下的事？」

　　「她——她希望有朝一日能畫一幅那不勒斯港。」蘇說。

　　「畫畫？——真是的！她腦子裡有沒有一些值得想的事情，譬如想個男人之類的？」

　　「男人？男人哪有什麼——沒有，醫生，沒有什麼男人可想的。」蘇帶著單簧口琴似的鼻音說道。

　　「那這就麻煩了。」醫生說：「我還是會盡我的所能，用各種方法來醫治她。不過病人一旦開始計算自己的送葬行列需要幾輛馬車時，藥效就要打對折了。要是你能讓她至少對冬季新款的披風袖子產生點興趣，願意開口問幾個問題，我保證她治癒的機率就不只一成，而是有五成了。」

　　醫生離開後，蘇躲進工作室，哭得整條張日式手帕都濕成了一團。之後，她打起精神，帶著畫板走進蕎西的房間，一邊吹著爵士曲調的口哨。

　　蕎西靜靜地躺在床上，面向窗戶，棉被沒什麼皺褶。蘇以為她睡著了，便不再吹口哨。

　　蘇把畫板架好，開始為一本雜誌裡的故事畫鋼筆插畫。年輕的畫家都要從繪製雜誌插畫做起，為自己鋪設通往藝術的大道，替雜誌寫文章也是一些年輕作家進入文學殿堂的必經之路。

當蘇正在為一位愛達荷州牛仔畫一件參加馬展穿的華麗馬褲和單片眼鏡時，她聽到了陣反覆的低吟聲，便快步走到床邊。

喬西睜圓了眼睛，望著窗外數數——倒數著。

「十二。」喬西數著，停頓一會兒後接著數道「十一」，然後「十」、「九」，而「八」和「七」幾乎是同時數出來。

蘇急忙往窗外看，那裡有什麼好數的？窗外除了一座冷冷清清的庭院，和二十英尺外那棟磚房的空牆之外，什麼也沒有。有一株老常春藤攀了半面的磚牆，腐壞的根部長滿了癬。冰涼的秋風打落片片藤葉，莖幹光禿禿，緊攀著殘垣。

「親愛的，你在數什麼？」蘇問。

「六。」喬西用微弱的聲音說道：「現在越掉越快了，三天前大概還有一百片，數得我頭都痛了，現在數就不用那麼費勁了。又掉一片了，現在只剩五片了。」

「五片什麼，親愛的？告訴你的蘇兒吧。」

「葉子，常春藤上的葉子。等到最後一片藤葉落下，我也要離開了。這我三天前就知道了，難道醫生沒告訴你嗎？」

「噯，不要胡說了。」蘇一副不以為然的樣子，抱怨著：「那些老藤葉和你能不能康復有什麼關係？你這個淘氣的姑娘，以前好愛那些藤蔓的。你就別說傻話了，你知道嗎，今天早上醫生才告訴我，你復原的機率是——我想想他是怎麼說的——他說機率有九成呢！這就好像我們在紐約街頭搭車或走路

時，隨處走都會路過新蓋的大樓一樣呢。喝點湯吧，好讓蘇兒繼續畫畫，把畫賣給編輯先生，然後買葡萄酒給她那生病的小孩喝，再買豬排給自己吃。」

「不用再買酒了。」蕎西說著，眼睛仍盯著窗外：「又掉一片了，不，我不想喝湯，只剩四片葉子了。我想在天黑前看著最後一片藤葉落下，然後我也要走了。」

「蕎西，親愛的，」蘇彎下身對她說：「答應我，把眼睛閉上，別往窗外看了，等我畫完好嗎？我明天要把這些畫交出去，要不是需要光線，我就要把窗簾拉下來了。」

「你就不能去別的房間畫嗎？」蕎西冷冷地問。

「我還是在這裡陪你比較好，」蘇說：「況且，我不希望你一直看著那些討厭的常春藤葉。」

「等你畫好就叫我。」蕎西說著，慢慢闔上眼睛地躺下。她看起來毫無血色，就像一尊倒下的雕像。「我想看著最後一片藤葉落下，但是我等得好累了，我不想再想了，我什麼都不想要了，我只想像那些凋零的葉子一樣，就這樣飄啊，飄啊的。」

「妳睡一會兒吧。」蘇說：「我得叫包曼上來當我的模特兒，才畫得出隱居的老礦工。我出去一下，你躺著別動，等我回來。」

老包曼住在一樓，也是一位畫家。他已經過了耳順之年，留著米開朗基羅的摩西雕像的那種鬍子，鬍子像是從半人半獸的森林之神頭部，往魔鬼的身軀蓋下來。包曼在藝術領域裡並不成功，他揮灑筆墨四十年，還構不著藝術女神的衣角。他老是說他要開始畫他那幅曠世名作了，但就沒見過他真的開始動筆。數年來，他除了偶爾替商家或廣告塗塗鴉之外，什麼作品也沒有。他在這一區給請不起專業人士的年輕畫家當模特兒，賺一點外快。他毫不節制地喝著他的杜松子酒，滿口漫談他即將問世的曠世名作。此外，他也是個好鬥的小老頭，最瞧不起軟弱的性格。他把自己看成是站哨的獒犬，要保護樓上工作室的那兩位小姑娘。

蘇在樓下昏暗的房間裡找到了渾身酒味的包曼。房間一角的畫架上是一塊空白的油畫布，在那裡等待了二十五年，等著曠世名畫的第一筆。蘇把蕎西所想的告訴包曼，說蕎西已經生命垂危了，再這樣虛弱下去，她怕蕎西真的會像葉子一樣飄落飛走。

老包曼紅色的雙眼泛著淚光，不屑地駁斥這種愚笨的想法。

「啥！」他大吼道：「這世界上會有人笨到因為鬼常春藤的葉子掉下來，就不想活了嗎？真是聽都沒聽過！免了，我才不幫你當什麼笨隱士。你怎麼會讓她的腦袋瓜裡裝進這種愚蠢的想法呢？噯唷，可憐的蕎西小姐唷。」

「她病得很重，身子很虛弱。」蘇說：「發燒把她的腦子燒壞了，老是想些有的沒的。好吧，包曼先生，要是你不想當我的模特兒，我也不勉強，你講話這麼毒，真是個可惡的糟老頭。」

「你這個臭婆娘！」包曼大吼大叫：「誰說我不願意當模特兒了？走就走啊，我跟你去。我一直說我要當模特兒的啊，都說了半個小時了。搞什麼！蕎西小姐這麼好的人，怎麼會在這種鬼地方養病。等哪一天我畫出曠世巨作了，我們就統統搬走。去！就這麼說了。」

他們上樓的時候，蕎西正在睡覺，蘇把窗簾往下拉到窗台，示意包曼到另一個房間去。他們在另一個房間裡，害怕地窺探窗外的常春藤，又互相對看了一會兒，不發一語。一陣冷雨夾雜著雪花綿綿不絕地落下，身著藍色舊襯衫的包曼把水壺翻過來當成岩石，坐在上面扮起隱居的老礦工來了。

那晚蘇只睡了一個小時，第二天早上醒來時，她發現蕎西雙眼瞪得大大的，呆滯地看著拉下的綠色窗簾。

「把窗簾拉起來，我想看。」她用微弱的聲音發出命令。

蘇無奈地照做。

但是你看！經過一整夜的狂風暴雨，竟然還有一片藤葉在磚牆上屹立不搖，那是最後一片藤葉。它的莖部還是深綠色的，鋸齒狀的葉緣因枯萎而泛黃，但這片葉子依舊勇敢地抓緊枝幹，懸在離地二十英尺處。

　　「那是最後一片藤葉。」蕎西說：「我以為經過這一夜，它一定被吹落了，我有聽到風的聲音。那就是今天了，我也將隨它而逝。」

　　「親愛的，親愛的！」蘇將她憔悴的臉龐靠向枕頭，說道：「你就算不為自己著想，也該為我著想啊。我該怎麼辦？」

　　但是蕎西並沒有回應，世上最孤單的，莫過於一個即將踏上神秘而漫長旅程的靈魂了。當她與朋友和世界聯繫的繩索逐一鬆脫之時，她的心靈也被這種幻想抓得更緊。

　　白晝逐漸消逝，透過黃昏的微光，他們還看得見那片孤單的藤葉，緊緊依附著牆上的莖幹。隨著夜幕低垂，北風又開始吹拂，雨水依舊打在窗上，淅瀝嘩啦地從低矮的荷式屋簷上滴落。

　　當天色稍亮，冷酷無情的蕎西又再度要求將窗簾拉起。

　　那片藤葉還在。

　　蕎西躺了好久，一直盯著那片藤葉，然後把正在瓦斯爐前攪拌雞湯的蘇叫了過來。

　　「我好壞，蘇兒。」蕎西說：「一定有什麼力量讓那片藤葉遲遲不落，好讓我明白自己是多麼地懦弱，我不該一心想死的。你幫我倒點湯吧，還要一些加了葡萄酒的牛奶，還要

——不，先給我一面小鏡子，在我身邊堆一些枕頭，我要坐起來看你做飯。」

過了一個小時，喬西開口道：「蘇兒，我希望有一天能畫一幅那不勒斯港。」

醫生下午來了一趟，要離開時，蘇便順勢跟到走廊上。

「機會一半一半吧，照顧得宜的話，你還是會成功的。現在我得去看樓下的另一個病人，包曼，這個名字——聽起來很像畫家。他也得了肺炎，這麼虛弱的老頭，發作得很快，應該是沒望了，不過今天送他去住院，至少能舒服一點。」醫生握著蘇那消瘦、顫抖的手說。

第二天，醫生告訴蘇：「她已經脫離險境了，你成功了。現在只要補充營養，好好照顧就行了。」

那天下午，喬西心滿意足地織著一條不甚實用的湛藍色羊毛披肩，蘇來到她的床邊，把喬西和連同枕被一手抱住。

「告訴你一件事，白老鼠，」她說：「包曼先生今天在醫院因肺炎去世了，他才發病兩天，發病當天的早上，工友在樓下房裡發現他痛苦又無助，衣服和鞋子都濕透了，冷冰冰的。他們想不透那種風雨交加的晚上，他還會上哪兒去。後來他們發現了一盞提燈，還亮著，還有一把被移動過的梯子，和散落一地的畫筆、混著黃綠顏料的調色盤——你看窗外呀，親愛的，你看牆上那最後一片藤葉，你不覺得奇怪嗎？風一直吹，它卻從未被吹動。噢，親愛的，那就是包曼的曠世巨作啊——那是他在最後一片藤葉掉落的那一晚，畫上去的啊。」

2 聖誕禮物

一塊又八角七分錢，就這麼多了，其中六角還是一分一分的銅板，這可是一次一分兩分地跟雜貨店、菜販、肉販老闆軟硬兼施、討價還價來的，這麼個斤斤計較法，弄得自己都為自己的小氣感到羞赧了。黛拉數了三次，一塊又八角七分，明天就是聖誕節了。

黛拉此時唯一能做的，就是在破爛的小沙發上大哭一場。她哭著，心中的感慨油然而生。生命，就是這樣由哭哭啼啼、抽抽噎噎、嬉嬉笑笑所交織而成的，尤其抽抽噎噎的時候是最多的了。

趁著這位家庭主婦心情逐漸平復之際，我們來看看這個家吧。一週租金八塊錢的公寓，附家具，這種田地不難形容，足可以說是乞戶了。

樓下的門廊上有信箱和電鈴，但無人會來信，也無人會按電鈴。門廊上還掛有門牌，上面寫著「詹姆斯·迪林翰·楊公館」。

「迪林翰」幾個字已經字跡模糊，當年屋主正旺時，每週可賺進三十塊，但現在縮水為二十塊了。他們正慎重考慮要把這幾個字改採成縮寫「D.」，比較不招搖。然而，儘管如此，每當詹姆斯·迪林翰·楊先生回到家，一進到屋裡，就聽到剛剛介紹過的黛拉·楊太太嘴裡喚著「吉姆」，還給他一個熱情的擁抱時，一切就又變得不缺了。

黛拉擦乾眼淚，用粉撲在臉頰上補過粉，站在窗口，無精打采地望著一隻灰貓，灰貓正走在灰濛濛院子裡的灰色圍籬上。明天就是聖誕節了，她竟然只有一塊又八角七分的錢能給吉姆買禮物。她東摳西摳地存了好幾個月，竟才存了這麼一點錢。一週二十塊錢的生活費，很吃緊，生活總是捉襟見肘，左支右絀。只有一塊又八角七分錢能給吉姆買禮物，這可是她的吉姆呀。她花了好多時間滿心歡喜地計畫幫吉姆買件好東西，東西一定要精緻、要稀有、要珍貴——至少也要有點配得上吉姆才行。

房間的兩扇窗戶之間有一面鏡子，你大概在一間八塊租金的公寓裡看過這種鏡子。夠瘦又夠輕巧的人，可以在這種狹長的鏡子裡左出右進，瞄到自己的樣子，正確無誤地看到自己的長相。像黛拉這麼苗條的人，就辦得到。

黛拉突然從窗邊跑到鏡子前面，她兩眼炯炯有神，但不一會兒，又黯淡下來。她很快地撥撥頭髮，把頭髮放下來。

這對夫婦有兩樣東西最讓他們自豪，一個是吉姆三代代傳的金錶，另一個就是黛拉的頭髮。天井對面公寓住的如果是席巴女王，黛拉總有一天會將她的秀髮垂在窗外風乾，讓女王陛下的奇珍異寶黯然失色；又如果羅門王守在堆滿寶藏的地下室門前，吉姆路過時會亮出他的金錶，好讓所羅門王嫉妒得直扯鬍子。

此時，黛拉的秀髮如棕色涓瀑傾瀉而下，如波如浪，閃閃發亮。頭髮長及膝蓋，宛若長袍。她神情緊張地又連忙盤起頭髮，躊躇了好一會兒。她直楞楞地站著，眼淚一面撲簌簌地掉了下來，滴在破舊的紅地毯上。

她穿上陳舊的褐色外套，戴上陳舊的褐色帽子，眼裡泛著淚光，轉身裙擺一搖，便焦急地出門，下樓到街上去了。

黛拉停在一個招牌前面，牌子上寫著：「索芙蘿妮夫人——專營各式美髮用品」。她一個箭步直奔上樓，氣喘吁吁。她看到眼前這位夫人身材高大、膚色白晳、冷冷酷酷的，和「索芙蘿妮」這個名字一點也不搭。

「你們買頭髮嗎？」黛拉問。

「買。」夫人說：「把帽子脫掉，讓我看看。」

她的一片棕色瀑布傾瀉而下，波光蕩漾。

「二十塊。」夫人熟練地捧著黛拉的頭髮說。

「快付給我吧。」黛拉說。

喔，接下來的兩個小時猶如添了瑰麗的翅膀，輕快地飛過。別管這個胡謅的比喻了，此時，黛拉正地毯式地搜索各家商店，幫吉姆物色禮物。

找遍了大街小巷，她終於找到一件獨家專賣而且完全為吉姆量身訂做的禮物。這是一條簡單大方的白金錶鍊，光是鍊子本身就可見其價值，不需要靠一些小裝飾來錦上添花——好東西就是這樣。黛拉一看到它，就知道它非吉姆莫屬了。這條錶鍊足以與金錶匹配，而且很有吉姆的味道，沈靜又有氣質。黛拉花了二十一塊錢買下這條錶鍊後，便連忙趕回家，身上只剩八角七分。吉姆的手錶再怎麼氣派，畢竟配的是舊皮帶，他有時看時間都只敢偷瞄一眼而已，如今有了這條錶鍊，吉姆在朋友面前就可以大大方方地看時間了。

黛拉回到家，按住興奮之情，稍微冷靜了下來。她拿出燙頭髮的鐵鉗子，點燃煤氣，開始修補愛情加慷慨所造成的大災難，這一向是個大工程，親愛的朋友——大工程啊。

不到四十分鐘，她的頭皮就貼滿了細密的鬈髮，活像個逃學的小學童。她小心仔細地對著鏡子照來照去，嘴裡自言自語著：

「吉姆看到了，要是沒有氣瘋，他一定會說我像康尼島合唱團裡的小女生。可是我也沒輒啊——我只有一塊八角七分錢，能怎麼辦呢？」

七時許，咖啡已經煮好，火爐後方的油鍋也夠熱，可以準備煎肉排了。

吉姆一向準時回家的。黛拉將錶鍊對折握在手心，然後坐在門邊的桌角，吉姆都是從這扇門進來的。當她聽到樓下樓梯傳來吉姆的腳步聲，她臉色白了一下。黛拉習慣為最平凡的生活瑣事默禱，現在亦是如此：「上帝啊，請讓他覺得我還是很美啊。」

吉姆打開門，走進屋內，把門關上。他身材消瘦，一臉嚴肅，這個可憐的人兒，才二十二歲就要養家活口！他需要一件新大衣，也缺少一雙手套。

吉姆一踏進家門，就像獵犬聞到鵪鶉的氣味似地，他定睛睛地看著黛拉，黛拉看不出那是什麼神情，讓她感到害怕。吉姆的神情，說不上是生氣，也不是驚訝、不喜歡或恐懼，就只是一種奇怪的表情，完全不在她的預期之內。

黛拉從桌椅中間擠出來，走到他面前，哭道：

「親愛的吉姆，你不要那樣看我嘛，我把頭髮剪了，賣了，過聖誕節怎麼能不送你禮物呢？頭髮會再長回來的——你不會生氣吧？我只能賣頭髮啊，不過我頭髮長得很快的，跟我說

『聖誕快樂！』吧，吉姆，我們要快快樂樂的呀，你不知道我給你買了一個多棒的禮物呢。」

「你把頭髮剪了？」吉姆吃力地問道，事實已經擺在眼前，他好像還百思不得其解。

「剪掉了，賣掉了。」黛拉說：「不管怎麼說，你還是一樣愛我吧？就算剪了頭髮，我還是原來的我啊，對不對？」

吉姆好奇地朝著房間東張西望。

「你說你把頭髮剪掉了？」他愚蠢地又問了一次。

「不用找了，已經賣掉了，我跟你說——賣掉了，沒有了。今天是聖誕夜，來嘛，對我好一點，這頭髮可是為你而剪的。」她溫柔而正經地繼續說道：「或許我的頭髮數得出有幾根，但是我對你的愛是無法計量的。吉姆，我要去煎肉排囉？」

吉姆這才恍然大悟，緊緊地將他的黛拉抱個滿懷。現在我們就花個十秒鐘，換個角度仔細想想一些無關緊要的事吧。一週八塊錢和一年一百萬的收入，究竟有什麼差別？數學家或智者都無法給出答案，東方三賢帶來了珍貴的禮物，但禮物中也找不到這個問題的答案。這樣說或許有點模糊，且待稍後分曉。

吉姆從大衣口袋裡掏出一包東西，扔在桌上。

「別誤會，黛拉，剪頭髮也好，修頭髮或洗頭髮也好，都不會減少我對你的愛。你打開這包東西，就知道我剛才為什麼會楞住了。」他說。

黛拉用白晰靈巧的手指解開繩子，拆開包裝紙，她先是欣喜若狂地尖叫，然後又歇斯底里地大哭了起來。噯呀！女人就是女人，看來那一家之主非得使出渾身解數，好好安撫她一番才行。

　　桌上擺著一組全套的髮梳，有分側面用的和後面用的，這就是黛拉在百老匯櫥窗前夢寐以求的那一套髮梳。它們絕美無比，純玳瑁質地，邊緣還鑲了珠寶，色澤和已逝的秀髮很能搭配。她知道這套髮梳十分昂貴，她想都不敢想，然而，現在卻美夢成真了！只不過，要配戴這些飾品的秀髮已不復見。

　　黛拉還是將髮梳摟在胸前，然後抬起淚眼朦朧的雙眸，微笑著說：「我的頭髮長得很快的，吉姆！」然後又像隻被燙到的小貓一樣，一邊跳著，一邊喊道：「哇！喔！」

　　吉姆還沒看到自己的漂亮禮物，黛拉興奮地打開手心，將禮物遞給吉姆。這種不具光澤的金屬似乎也感染了黛拉的開朗與熱情，閃耀出光芒。

　　「是不是很棒啊，吉姆？我找遍大街小巷才找到的呢，你現在一天看一百次時間都沒問題了，快把手錶給我，我看看配不配。」

　　吉姆沒有什麼動靜，只是跌坐在沙發上，雙手放在腦後，一味地笑。

　　「黛兒，我們先把這些聖誕禮物收好吧，這些東西太寶貴，不適合現在用。我把手錶賣了，好為你買髮梳。現在去煎肉排吧。」他說。

諸君應該知道，東方三賢都是智者——聰明絕頂的智者——他們為誕生於馬槽的聖嬰獻上禮物，此舉被視為聖誕禮物的濫觴。他們是聰明人，送的禮自然也很聰明，就算禮物重複了，也有更換的權利。在這裡，我已經簡單地為您講述了一段平淡無奇的故事，一段關於住在公寓的兩個傻孩子的故事，他們不夠明智，為彼此犧牲了家裡最珍貴的寶物。不過，時下的聰明人啊，容我奉上最後一句話，其實像他們這樣，才是最聰明的送禮人，也是最聰明的收禮人啊，不管到哪裡，他們的智慧都無與倫比，他們就是賢人。

3 警察與讚美詩

　　索比在麥迪遜廣場的長椅上動來動去，渾身不自在。你只要聽到野雁在夜空中引吭高歌，看到沒有皮草的妻子開始向丈夫示好，或是發現索比坐在公園椅子上坐立難安，那你就可以知道冬天的腳步近了。

　　一片枯葉落在索比的膝蓋上，這是嚴冬捎來的卡片。嚴冬對麥迪遜廣場的居民還算仁慈，它在每年造訪之前，總不忘先提醒一下。它會在十字路口遞名片給「戶外大廈」的管理員「北風」，好讓住戶有個心理準備。

　　索比意識到該是下定決心成立他個人的「抗寒籌備委員會」的時候了，所以他才會這麼坐立不安。

　　不過索比抗寒的決心還不算誇張，他還沒考慮去地中海巡航，也沒考慮去催人欲眠的南方，更沒想過到去漂浮在維蘇威海灣的海上。他一心只想去「島」上待個三個月，那裡不

愁吃、不愁穿，有人作伴，又能
遠離北風和警察的騷擾，這就教
他心滿意足了。

　　多年以來，好客的布萊克威爾
監獄一直是他冬天時的避風港。每
年的這個時候，運氣好一點的紐約
同胞會到棕櫚灘或里維拉去避寒，索
比也不落人後，只不過他的方式比較
卑微一點，他每年都逃到「島」上過
冬，現在也差不多是時候了。昨天夜
裡，索比睡在老廣場噴泉旁的椅子上，
大衣裡塞了一堆報紙，腳踝和膝蓋的地方
也蓋了幾張。他一共用掉了三份安息日報，
但還是凍得半死，致使他腦海裡隱約又浮現去「島」上避
寒的念頭。公立機構或慈善機構多不勝數，他大可找一間投
靠，過著衣食無缺的單純生活，不過對於自尊心像索比這麼
強的人來說，那種地方是教人難以領受的。他認為「法律」
比「慈善」慈悲多了，因為獲得別人行善、免費施捨的東
西，要付出「屈辱」的代價。那就好像凱撒對待布魯特斯一
樣，想要睡一張以慈善為名的床，就得先被押去沐浴一番，
想塞一條麵包，也得被盤問私人問題，毫無隱私權可言。也
因此，他寧願乖乖地去法律那兒作客吧，雖然繁文縟節一大
堆，至少不會過度侵犯個人隱私。

　　索比下定決心後，便馬上付諸行動。去「島」上有很多簡

單的方法，而最輕鬆愉快的方法，就是找一家高級餐廳吃霸王餐，這麼一來，也不需和警察叫囂，就可以安安靜靜地被移送法辦。接下來的事，熱心的法官自然會搞定一切。

索比起身走出廣場，穿過百老匯街和第五大道交會的平坦柏油路，轉進百老匯，停在一間燈火輝煌的咖啡店前。這一帶每晚都會供應上等的葡萄、絲綢和原生質產品。

索比對於自己從最底下一顆鈕釦到上半身的背心都信心滿滿，他刮過鬍子，大衣也還算體面，脖子上還打了一個整齊的黑色領結，這領結是一位女傳教士在一個感恩節時送給他的。他只要能順利地進入餐廳找到位子坐下，就大功告成了，因為他坐在座位上時的上半身還不至於引人側目。他心想，他要點一隻烤鴨，配上一瓶夏布利酒，再來些卡門貝乳酪、一小杯濃縮黑咖啡和一支雪茄。一塊錢的雪茄應該就夠了，這樣總價不會貴到讓咖啡店經理採取什麼報復性的可怕手段，而且這麼一來，食物的份量也夠他填飽肚子，能讓他滿足地上路了。

然而，索比才剛踏進餐廳大門，領班就注意到他穿著一條破褲和一雙爛鞋，二話不說，便用強壯而敏捷的手架著他轉身，一聲不響地把他丟到人行道上，那隻備受威脅的烤鴨這才躲掉了被白吃的命運。

索比離開百老匯，看來通往「夢中島」的路還真不好走，得想想別的辦法才行。

第六大道街角有一家商店，厚玻璃內展示著各種精品，在路燈的照射下，十分引人注目。索比拾起一塊小石子砸向玻

璃，民眾聞聲紛紛聚集了過來，走在前頭的正是一位警察。索比雙手插著口袋佇在原地，他一看到警察，就笑了出來。

「是誰幹的？」警察激動地問道。

「你難道不認為是我幹的嗎？」索比雖語帶譏諷，卻一臉友善，一副好運當頭的樣子。

但警察卻毫不認為索比有任何嫌疑，如果他是砸破窗子的人，早拔腿就跑了，哪會笨到留在現場和執法人員周旋。這時，半條街外剛好有一個人在追趕一輛車，警察見狀，立刻拔出警棍追了上去。索比只好繼續閒晃，他兩次都失利，心裡嘔得很。

對街有一家不起眼的餐廳，供應大眾化的飲食和清湯，桌上鋪著薄薄的桌巾，擺了粗重的餐具，價位一般，氣氛很凝重。索比穿著剛才攪局壞事的鞋子和褲子，不費吹灰之力就進到餐廳裡。他找了張桌子坐下，吃了牛排、煎餅、甜甜圈和餡餅，然後跟服務生坦承自己身無分文。

「別閒著，快叫警察，別讓一位紳士久等了。」索比說。

「這種事用不著報警，嘿，來人啊！」服務生用奶油蛋糕般的聲音說道，眼神像是曼哈頓雞尾酒裡的櫻桃。

兩名服務生把索比摔在冰冷無情的人行道上，摔得他左耳都貼在地上了。就像木匠在打開折尺那樣，他的身體一節一節地爬起來，然後撣了撣身上的灰塵。要被捕簡直難如登天，「島」彷彿遠在天邊。過兩家店面的藥局前面，有位警察見狀笑了笑，隨後離開。

索比走了五條街，發現一個他自認為易如反掌的大好機會，於是又起了膽子想被捕。在一面展示櫥窗前，站著一位端莊、討人喜歡的女孩，她正興致盎然地看著窗內的刮鬍杯和墨水瓶架，而在兩碼之外，有位高大、一臉正經的警察正靠在消防栓上。

索比鎖定了這位優雅美麗的受害者，打算施展「搭訕良家婦女」的卑劣伎倆，況且這位警察看起來一副盡忠職守的樣子，他相信自己很快就能怡然自得地被捕，這麼一來，他肯定能在小監獄裡過冬了。

索比整頓了一下女傳教士送的領結，拉出縮進去的袖口，把帽子斜戴，側身走向年輕女子。他「嗯哼」地咳了幾聲，拋個媚眼，擠出不自然的笑容，準備展開這次厚顏無恥的「搭訕」行動。索比瞄到警察仍緊盯著他看，而年輕女子的視線沒離開過櫥窗裡的刮鬍杯，她移動了幾步，索比隨之移動，然後大膽地走到她身邊，脫帽說道：

「嗨，貝德莉雅，要不要來我院子裡玩玩啊？」

警察一直在注意他們，被騷擾的小姐只消對警察一招手，索比就得逞了。索比已經開始想像派出所的溫暖和舒適了。年輕女子看著索比，突然伸手抓住他的外套衣袖。

「好啊，麥克，如果你請我喝一桶啤酒，我就去啊。要不是那個警察在盯著我看，我早就跟你說話了。」她愉快地說道。

年輕女子緊緊搭著他，兩人從警察面前走過，索比很沮喪，好像注定想脫去自由身都不可得一樣。

才走了一個路口，索比便甩開女子跑掉，一直跑到街燈通明的地方。這一區盡是羅曼史、誓約和歌劇，身著大衣、皮草的男男女女，在冰冷的空氣中，愉快地走著。索比突然一陣冷顫，他感到有一股恐怖的魔力在從中作梗，讓他連想被補都求之無門。他一時慌張了起來，看到一位警察在美輪美奐的戲院前閒晃，當下就決定來個「妨害治安的舉動」。

索比開始在人行道上裝酒瘋。他聲音刺耳刺刺，胡言亂語，一下跳舞，一下大哭，語無倫次地嚷嚷著，在夜空下大吵大鬧的。

警察轉身背過索比，揮著警棍向民眾喊道：「這個耶魯的小伙子啊，正在慶祝他賞給了哈特福特大學一個大鴨蛋，雖然很吵，但不礙事的，我們上面有交代，准他們這樣鬧。」

　　索比悲傷地停止了這場鬧劇，沒有一位警察願意逮捕他嗎？他夢寐以求的「島」彷彿是個到不了的世外桃源。他扣上薄外套的鈕釦，好擋住凜冽的寒風。

　　索比看見一間雪茄店裡有位衣著筆挺的男士，正就著搖晃的火光點雪茄。男子在進雪茄店之前，把銀色雨傘擱在了門口處。索比走進店門，用身體遮掩住雨傘，然後裝作若無其事地拿著傘緩步離開，點雪茄的男子立刻追了出來。

　　「那是我的雨傘！」他厲聲地說道。

　　「哦，是嗎？」索比冷笑著，用一副不屑這種偷雞摸狗的語氣說道：「那你怎麼不叫警察？我拿走囉，你的雨傘啊！怎麼不叫警察？那邊路口就有一個！」

　　男子慢下腳步，索比也慢下腳步，他有種不祥的預感，這次也不會成功的。警察好奇地看著這兩個人。

「當然，那是……這人免難都會犯錯嘛……我……如果那是你的雨傘，請原諒我……我是今天早上在一間餐廳裡拿的……如果傘是你的，那麼……希望你……」傘主說。

「當然是我的。」索比惡狠狠地說。

前傘主走開後，警察快步地前去協助對街一位身穿歌劇斗蓬的高挑金髮美女過街，兩條街外有一輛電車就要駛過來了。

索比往東走，經過一條因施工弄得坑坑疤疤的街道，氣得把雨傘扔進地上的洞裡。他數落著那些頭戴鋼盔、身配警棍的警察，他想被逮捕，那些警察卻把他當成皇帝一樣，做什麼事都沒有罪。

最後，索比來到東邊的一條街，那裡燈火黯淡，較為寧靜。他望著街底的麥迪遜廣場，發現自己竟下意識地走回來了，即使他的家只是一張公園長椅，回家的本能還是發揮了作用。

索比行經一個路口時，發現那裡靜得出奇，令他不禁駐足。那裡矗立著一棟造型奇特混雜、有著三角牆的老教堂。他靠著迂迴的鐵欄杆，在紫色玻璃窗外往內瞧，教堂內燈光柔和，有位風琴手正在彈著琴鍵，為即將演出的安息日讚美詩勤加練習。悠揚的樂聲，讓索比聽得出神。

夜空裡，月光皎潔而靜謐，路上人車寂寥，屋簷下的麻雀睏倦地吱喳了幾聲——乍看之下，猶如鄉間墓園。風琴手彈奏的讚美詩，撥動了索比的心弦，勾起了他的回憶，讓他想起他的生命中也曾經擁有過母愛、玫瑰、志向、朋友、純真的思想和潔白的衣領。

索比是個善感的人，加上老教堂的這般感化，他的靈魂剎時受到了昇華。他回顧自己所墜入的深淵，心頭一陣顫抖，他的生命，竟是由這些糜爛的生活、一文不值的渴望、墮落的身心和生物的本能動機所組成。

一時之間，這種新生的感覺，令他振奮，一股強烈的衝動湧上心頭，他決定與坎坷的命運對抗。他要將自己拉出泥沼，重新做人，他要征服佔據身心的惡魔。他還年輕，還有時間，他要重拾往日的雄心，勇往直前追尋自己的理想。這段莊嚴悠揚的琴聲為他帶來重生，明天，他就要到喧囂的城鎮找工作，一位毛草進口商曾經有意願雇用他當司機，他明天就要去找這位進口商應徵工作，他要闖出一番名堂，他要——

索比感到有隻手抓著他的手臂，回頭一看，竟是一名警察的寬大臉龐。

「你在這裡做什麼？」警察問。

「沒什麼。」索比說。

「那就跟我走。」警察說。

「『島』上關三個月。」次日早晨，法庭上的法官如是宣判。

4 忙碌證券商的愛情故事

　　皮契是證券經紀人哈維‧麥斯威爾的機要秘書,他平常臉上沒什麼表情,不過,今天早上九點半,看著老闆和年輕女速記員行色匆匆走進辦公室時,他倒是露出了驚奇的神色。麥斯威爾沒好氣地說了聲「早,皮契」,便以一副幾乎要跳過去的態勢,直往辦公桌衝去,埋進滿桌待辦的信件和電報裡。

　　這位年輕女子做麥斯威爾的速記員已經一年了。她很美,美得無法用速記的方式來形容。她不梳華麗誘人的高捲髮,也不配戴項鍊、手鐲或墜子;她完全不做社交式的打扮,只穿素雅的灰色洋裝,這剛好符合她盡責、謹慎的形象;在她整齊的黑色無邊帽上,插有一支黃綠色的金剛鸚鵡毛。今天早上,她看起來臉色紅潤、容光煥發,散發著優雅含蓄的氣質。她的雙眼朦朧而明亮,一臉愉悅的神情,還帶著幾分在回味什麼似地況味。

皮契心裡還在好奇時，又注意到她今天早上的舉止有點異常，她沒有直接進到自己位於隔壁的辦公室，反而在外面的辦公大廳徘徊，有所躊躇的樣子，還一度磨蹭到麥斯威爾的桌邊，好讓他注意到她的存在。

桌前這位紐約證券商已經忙到不能用「人」來形容了，而是像一台由唧唧運轉的輪子和拉開的彈簧所驅動的機器。

拆封的信件在他桌上高高堆起，一看還以為是舞台布景用的雪堆。他用銳利的灰色眼珠，冷淡又不客氣地看著女速記員，不耐煩地尖聲問道：「有事嗎？」

「沒事。」速記員一邊回答，一邊微笑著走開。

「皮契先生，麥斯威爾先生昨天有沒有提到要再請一位速記員？」她對機要秘書說。

「有啊，他交代我再找一個，我昨天下午已經通知職業介紹所找一些合適的人選過來了。現在都九點四十五分了，還沒見到半個戴寬邊帽或嚼鳳梨口香糖的人影。」皮契回答。

「那我就照常工作好了，等有人來接手再說吧。」這位年輕女子說著，便立刻回到座位上，把插著黃綠色金剛鸚鵡毛的帽子掛在平常擺放的地方。

誰想要精通人類學，就得先見識過曼哈頓的證券商在商務繁忙之際的忙碌光景。詩人歌詠著「璀璨人生的擁擠時刻」，此時眼前這位證券商的時刻豈止擁擠，簡直是像車廂吊環或是擠得水洩不通的前後月台，半分半秒都不得閒。

今天正是麥斯威爾大忙的日子。股票行情收報機的帶子吐吐停停的，桌上的電話響個沒完沒了。人群開始湧入交易大廳，隔著柵欄對他大吼大叫，喜怒哀樂，神情各異。信差帶

著信件和電報進進出出，辦事員忙得東奔西走，和遇到暴風雨的水手沒兩樣，連皮契的神情都顯得帶勁。

整個交易所彷彿颶風來襲，又似山崩爆發，暴風雪過境，一下子更是冰川火山交替，這些自然現象的縮影在這裡隨處可見。麥斯威爾把椅子推到牆邊，他像是踮著腳尖跳著舞一般，一下從股票行情收報機跳到電話旁，一下又從桌子跳到門邊，身手之伶俐，可不輸訓練有素的小丑。

即便事務愈見繁忙，壓力倍增，麥斯威爾還是瞄到一片梳得高捲的金色瀏海，髮上的帽子插了鴕鳥毛，綴著搖曳的絲絨，再往下看是仿製的海豹皮衣，搭著一串胡桃大小的珠鍊，幾乎垂到地上，尾端還掛了一顆銀色的心形綴飾。一位神情自若的年輕女性，打扮著這一身行頭，皮契正要為她引薦。

「這位小姐是速記員介紹所介紹來應徵職務的。」皮契說。

麥斯威爾滿手文件和股票行情報表，他略轉過身，皺著眉頭問：「什麼職位來著？」

「速記員啊，你昨天交代我跟他們聯絡，請他們今早介紹人過來的。」皮契說道。

「皮契，你腦袋瓜壞掉了！我怎麼會這麼說呢？萊絲麗小姐這一年來不是做得好好的嗎？除非她不想幹了，否則我不會換人的。小姐，我們這裡不缺人。皮契，跟介紹所取消這個申請，別再介紹人來了。」麥斯威爾說。

戴銀色的心形綴飾的女子氣沖沖地走出辦公室，她搖搖擺擺，一路上弄得辦公室的設備砰砰作響。皮契逮到機會就跟記帳員說，麥斯威爾那老傢伙越來越心不在焉了，忘東忘西的。

　　業務越來越繁忙，他們在交易所裡埋頭處理六張股票，那可都是大客戶的股票。買賣股票的交易聲，迅如燕飛，此起彼落。麥斯威爾自己所持的一些股票告急中，他像一部精密強大的機器，悉力運作中；他就像個鐘錶一樣，上緊發條，全速運轉，下手又快又準，毫不遲疑，決策正確。這是一個金融世界，放眼只見股票、債券、貸款、抵押、定金與證券，人情和自然在這裡毫無容身之地。

　　時近午餐時刻，交易所的喧囂才稍平靜下來。

　　麥斯威爾站在辦公桌旁，他滿手電報和紙條，右耳夾著鋼筆，前額蓋著凌亂的髮絲。他的窗戶敞開著，這是大地的通風口，親愛的春神業已開始送暖。

　　此時窗外撲來一陣芳香，也許那是不經意飄來的吧。這股清新、甜美的百合花香，是萊絲麗身上獨有的芬芳，讓麥斯威爾聞得如癡如醉。

　　香氣繚繞成萊絲麗的身影，栩栩如生得幾乎觸摸得到。金融的世界剎時縮成一個小點，而萊絲麗就在二十步之遙的隔壁辦公室而已。

　　「天啊，就是現在，我馬上去問她，真不知道我怎麼會拖到現在。」麥斯威爾提高音調說。

他以游擊手般的速度，直奔內部的辦公室，衝向速記員的桌子。

萊絲麗面帶笑容地抬頭看他，眼神既溫柔又真誠，雙頰還泛著一抹紅暈。麥斯威爾用一隻手肘撐著桌子，兩手依舊滿是雜亂飛舞的文件，耳上還夾著筆。

「萊絲麗小姐，我只有一點時間，我想利用這個空檔跟你說幾句話。你願意做我的妻子嗎？我沒有時間像一般人一樣對你示愛，但我是真心愛你。快回答我吧——那些人還在搶購大西洋聯盟的股票呢。」他急忙開口道。

「啊，你在說什麼啊？」萊絲麗驚呼道，她站起身，兩眼瞪得圓圓地。

「你難道不明白嗎？」麥斯威爾不肯罷休地說道：「我要你嫁給我啊，我愛你啊，萊絲麗小姐，我一直想告訴你，好不容易逮到業務稍歇的時候了。他們又在叫我接電話了，叫他們等等啊，皮契。你願意嫁給我嗎，萊絲麗小姐？」

這位速記員的反應很古怪，她先是目瞪口呆，接著一臉疑惑，然後不住地掉下眼淚，最後又在淚光中露出笑靨。她用一隻手臂輕柔地環住證券商的脖子，輕聲細語地說：

「現在我明白了，是這門生意讓你患了失憶症，我剛才還嚇了一跳呢。你不記得了嗎，哈維？我們昨晚八點已經在『街角小教堂』完成終身大事啦。」

5 愛情迷幻藥

　　藍光藥局位於商業區的包爾瑞街與第一街之間，這裡是兩條街距離最近的地方。藍光藥局可不會把賣藥當成是在賣什麼小飾品、香水或冰淇淋汽水之類的，你要買止痛藥，他們就不會拿夾心軟糖來權充。

　　現代藥房為了節省勞力所採用的配藥法，藍光藥局可是嗤之以鼻的。在藍光藥局裡，一定要將鴉片泡軟了，才過濾其中的鴉片酊和鎮痛成分。一直到現在，他們的藥丸都還是在高高的處方桌後面配製的。他們將藥丸撒在製藥板上，用刮勺分好份量，再用手指和掌心搓揉，撒上燒成粉末的氧化鎂，最後裝進圓圓的小紙盒裡。藍光藥局開在路口，這裡有許多衣衫襤褸的小孩子嬉嬉鬧鬧的，他們遲早得向藥局報到，買點止咳喉糖和舒緩糖漿。

　　伊基・史恩斯坦是藍光藥局的晚班店員，也是顧客們的好朋友。這家藥局開在東區，這一帶的人很看重配藥這門學問，他們視藥師為顧問、接受告解的神父或是指導老師。伊基既是一位能幹又熱心的傳教士，也是顧客的良師益友，他的學問受到尊敬，深不可測的智慧為人所景仰。他開的藥，管它味道如何，病人一股腦兒就往肚裡吞。因此，伊基那長得像羊角、戴著眼鏡的鼻樑，還有瘦弱、被知識壓得駝背的身子，在藍光這一帶可是赫赫有名的，人們總是爭相向他請益。

伊基住在兩條街外的雷道夫人家，也在她家用早餐。雷道夫人有個女兒，名叫蘿西。用不著我說，你想必也猜到了——伊基暗戀著蘿西，滿腦子想的都是她。她是高純度的藥用複合精華，藥學書裡最上等的處方都無法與她相比。不過伊基很沒膽，他的性格畏縮怕事，只敢想不敢做。他在櫃臺後面或許很嗆，看起來沈著而專業，但一離開櫃臺，他就變得唯唯諾諾又遲鈍，連走在路上都會挨司機的罵。他的衣服既不合身，又被化學藥劑弄得髒兮兮的，渾身都是索哥德拉蘆薈和氨水裡戊酸鹽的臭味。

伊基唯一的肉中刺（這種形容貼切他的行業），就是強克‧麥可高文。

麥可高文先生也在追求蘿西，不過他不像伊基只敢站得遠遠的，他可是主動地贏得了蘿西的青睞。麥可高文是伊基的朋友兼顧客，他傍晚常在包爾瑞街上散步，並且順道光顧藍光藥局，替淤青處擦些碘酒或包紮傷口。

有一天下午，麥可高文又一聲不響、從從容容地進到藥局，找了一張凳子坐下。他的面貌俊秀，鬍子刮得乾乾淨淨，為人正經，很好強，但也很敦厚。

「伊基，聽好了，如果你有這些配方的藥，就幫我配藥吧。」他說道。此時伊基正坐在對面，拿著藥缽將膠狀的安息香磨成粉末。

伊基對著他上下端詳，尋找打鬥的痕跡，不過沒發現什麼異狀。

「把外套脫掉吧，我就猜到你的肋骨被捅了一刀，我告訴你多少次了，那些外國佬一定會修理你的。」伊基命令道。

「不是那些外國佬，和他們無關。不過你差不多猜對位置了──是在外套裡靠近肋骨的地方沒錯。嘿！伊基，蘿西和我決定今晚私奔，完成終身大事哩。」麥可高文微笑道。

伊基的左手食指緊扣住藥缽邊緣，穩穩扶住。他用杵子重重地敲向藥缽，卻沒打著，弄得麥可高文也收起笑容，一臉茫然不知所措。

「我是說，如果她別再三心兩意的話。我們這兩個星期一直在計畫私奔的事，有一天我們都說好了，不料才到傍晚她就變卦。這次蘿西已經同意今晚行動，這個念頭也維持兩天了，不過距離行動的時間還有五個小時，我真怕她又臨陣脫逃。」麥可高文繼續說道。

「你說你要抓藥。」伊基說。

麥可高文看起來侷促不安、滿面愁容，和他以往的行徑很不一樣。他把一本專利藥物年鑑捲成筒狀，小心地把它套進手指上玩弄著。

「私奔這件事很不順利，我不能讓它今晚再有所閃失。

我已經在哈林區買了一間小公寓，桌上都擺了菊花，還準備了一個燒水用的水壺。我約了一位牧師晚上九點半在他家碰面，這次非成功不可，只要蘿西別再改變心意啦！」麥可高文講完又面露愁容。

「我還是不明白，你為什麼會提到配藥的事，我又能幫上什麼忙？」伊基不耐煩地說。

「雷道那老傢伙看我不怎麼順眼。」這位忐忑不安的求婚者決定一吐苦水，繼續說道：「他整整一個星期都不讓蘿西跟我出去，要不是擔心失去一個房客，他們早就把我攆出去了。我週薪二十塊美金耶，蘿西跟著強克·麥可高文，還怕沒有好日子過嗎？」

「失陪一下，強克。我得先配個藥，等會兒有人要來拿。」伊基說。

「喂，伊基，有沒有一種藥——藥粉之類的，能讓一個女人吃了之後更愛你的？」麥可高文突然抬頭說。

伊基輕蔑地揪起嘴唇，發現原來他想幹這種勾當。他還來不及回答，麥可高文又繼續說：「提姆·雷西跟我說，有一次他在非商業區跟一個愛碎嘴的江湖術士買了這種藥，摻在汽水裡給他的女友喝。沒多久，他的地位馬上三級跳，別人在她眼裡變得一文不值。他們不到兩個星期就結婚了耶。」

強克·麥可高文就是這樣四肢發達、頭腦簡單，任何一個比伊基聰明的讀者都看得出他想確保萬無一失，就像一位善戰的將軍一樣，攻城時懂在可能的逃逸路線上先設好兵防。

麥可高文滿懷希望地繼續說：「我想，今晚和蘿西共進晚餐的時候，要是給她吃下這種藥，或許可以堅定她私奔的決心，不會再變卦。應該用不著帶騾子拖著她走吧，不過也很難說，女人啊，說是一回事，做又是一回事。這玩意兒的藥效只要能持續個幾個小時，我的詭計就成功了。」

「你們打算什麼時候私奔？」伊基問。

「九點。」麥可高文說：「我們七點吃晚餐，蘿西八點就會假裝頭痛上床睡覺。隔壁的老帕文札諾答應讓我在九點的時候穿越他家，從那邊進到雷道家的後院，那裡的圍籬掉了一塊木板。然後我再從蘿西的窗戶鑽進去，扶著她從逃生梯爬下來。我已經約了牧師了，一定要早點到。只要蘿西別臨陣退縮，事情就好辦了。伊基，你能幫我配這種藥粉嗎？」

伊基・史恩斯坦緩緩地揉了揉鼻子說：「強克，任何一位藥師對這種藥都必須格外小心。在我的朋友裡，我只賣這種藥給你。我就幫你這個忙，你看看蘿西會有什麼反應。」

伊基走到處方桌後方，把兩片各含十六點二毫克嗎啡的可溶性藥片搗成粉末，再加一點乳糖增加份量，然後仔細地用白紙包好。成人吃了這種藥會沈睡好幾個小時，不過對健康沒什麼大礙。他把藥包遞給麥可高文，吩咐他摻在飲料裡來用，效果比較好，然後接受了這位大情聖的道謝。

伊基接下來的行為，讓人看穿了他的心機。他派人送了口信給雷道先生，揭發麥可高文將挾蘿西私奔的陰謀。雷道先生個子不高，但身材很壯，臉色黝黑而紅潤，動作敏捷。

「感激不盡。」雷道他簡單地向伊基道謝，說道：「這個好吃懶做的愛爾蘭佬！我的房間就在蘿西樓上，等晚餐過後，我就帶著獵槍親自上去等著，要是他敢踏進我家後院，包準他禮車搭不成，反教救護車給抬走。」

蘿西像被睡神召喚了去，沈睡了好幾個小時。知情的雷道先生早就全副武裝地等在那裡，準備大開殺戒。伊基心想，他的情敵必敗無疑了。

伊基整晚在藍光藥局值班的時候，都密切地期待悲劇發生的消息，不過什麼也沒聽到。

早上八點，早班店員一抵達，伊基便一溜煙地直奔雷道家，探個究竟。結果他才剛踏出店門，麥可高文便從一輛駛過的街車中跳了下來，朝他迎面走來，抓住他的手——臉上還露出勝利者的微笑，樂得滿臉通紅。

「成功了！蘿西幾乎準時抵達逃生梯，我們九點三十十五秒趕到牧師家。她現在在公寓裡，今早穿著日式和服煮雞蛋呢。哇！我真是太幸福了！伊基，你哪天一定要來吃個便飯。我在橋邊找到工作了，現在正要去上班。」麥可高文幸福地笑道。

「那個……那個……藥粉？」伊基結結巴巴地問。

「喔，那玩意兒啊！」麥可高文笑得更開心了：「是這樣的，昨晚我坐在雷道家的餐桌前，看著蘿西，然後我對自己說：『強克啊，你要是愛這個女人，就不該對她耍花樣啊，怎麼能對這樣的良家婦女下藥呢？』於是我便把你給我的藥包收在口袋裡。後來我靈機一動，看上在場的另一位當事人，這個人對他的準女婿不懷好意，所以我就趁機把藥粉倒進雷道那老頭兒的咖啡裡了！這樣你瞭解了吧？」

6 春日菜單

這是一個三月天。

說故事的時候，千萬，千萬別用這種開場白，沒有比這更糟的開場方式了，既沒創意又枯燥無味，讀起來正經八百，簡直跟廢話沒兩樣。不過對這篇故事來說，這種開場白還算過得去，因為接下來的故事開頭，其誇張、荒誕的程度，若不先做點準備，怎麼好在讀者面前炫耀呢？

莎拉正看著菜單哭泣。

試想一個紐約女子看著菜單掉眼淚的畫面！

怎麼說呢？你可以猜想龍蝦賣完了，或者她正在齋戒，不能吃冰淇淋；也或者她剛點了洋蔥，或剛看完一齣哈克特的戲碼。不過，這些揣測都不對，請容故事繼續發展下去吧。

有位紳士曾宣稱，世界就像一個牡蠣，用寶劍即可撬開。用劍撬開牡蠣，根本是牛刀小試，不過你看過有人用打字機來撬開陸生貝殼嗎？想見識一打生貝殼被如此撬開的樣子嗎？

莎拉就有此能耐。她用這種彆扭的武器把貝殼撬開，撬的深度剛好夠咬到裡面冰冷、濕黏的小肉塊。她的速記知識並不強，差不多是商學院畢業生的速記程度而已，因此她無法成為一位出色的辦公人員，只能擔任非約聘的自由打字員，招攬零星的打字工作。

在莎拉為了討生活而與世界的大戰中，最英勇的一次事蹟，便是舒倫伯格餐廳之役。這家餐廳位於莎拉所居住的老紅磚屋隔壁。有天晚上，莎拉在舒倫伯格餐廳吃完一頓四十分錢、五道菜的套餐之後（上菜之快，差不多和連丟五顆棒球在小色人頭上的時間一樣），她順手把菜單帶了出來。菜單上面的字跡模糊不清，其文字既不是英文，也不是德文，而且編排的方式很容易讓人點錯順序，一不小心就會從牙籤和布丁開始上菜，最後才看到湯和當天星期幾。

第二天，莎拉交給舒倫柏格一張整潔的卡片，是用打字機打成的精緻菜單，每樣食物都整整齊齊地排列在適當的標題下面，從「開胃菜」開始，看起來就很美味可口，最後則以「概不負責外套及雨傘之保管」作結。

舒倫柏格當場就被她說服了，兩人在莎拉離開之前達成愉快的協定，莎拉答應幫他餐廳裡的二十一張桌子各打一份菜單，每晚更換新的菜色，而早餐和午餐的餐點內容有所更動時，或是菜單破損了，也會適時更新。

　舒倫柏格這邊則必須負責供應莎拉每日三餐，由一位服務生送到她的住處，如果能派嘴巴甜一點的服務生，是最好不過了。此外，每天下午並送來翌日菜單的手稿。

　協議的結果令雙方都滿意。現在舒倫柏格的老主顧終於知道他們吃的東西叫什麼名稱了，雖然有時食物內容還是令人摸不著頭腦。而莎拉在陰冷的冬天裡能得以溫飽，也便心滿意足了。

　年曆報春沒報準，唯有等到春天的氣息出現，春天才算來了。市區街道上的正月冰雪，還像冰磚一樣；手風琴仍用臘月的活力和聲調，演奏著〈夏日情懷〉的曲調；男人開始計畫採購三十天後的復活節新衣，管理員也還關著蒸汽機，這般景象顯示了冬天的腳步尚未離去。

一日午後，莎拉在那精緻的宿舍裡渾身發抖，當初這個房間的廣告還打著「附暖氣，保證清潔，設備齊全，歡迎蒞臨參觀」的標語呢。除了為舒倫柏格餐廳打菜單之外，她便無所事事了。她坐在一張嘎吱作響的藤椅上，凝望著窗外。牆上的月曆不斷地對她呼喊：「春天來啦，莎拉，我說春天來啦。看我就知道了，莎拉，我身上有數字為證啊。你的體態也勻襯起來啦，莎拉，這分明就是春天的體態嘛，何必如此鬱鬱寡歡，直看著窗外呢？」

　　莎拉的房間位於房子後方，從窗外可以看到對街製盒工廠的後牆，這面牆是用最澄澈的錶面玻璃做的，上面沒有窗戶。莎拉看著樓下長滿草的小徑，小徑上櫻桃樹與榆樹成蔭，兩旁還種了木莓和切洛基玫瑰。

　　春天的預兆細微得難以察覺，非得等到番紅花盛開，山茱萸成林，藍色知更鳥報佳音，甚至要等到蕎麥和牡蠣向人們握手道別，退出舞台後，人們才願意敞開胸懷，迎接綠衫春神的到來。不過春神這位古老大地的新娘，仍對他的子民發出直接而甜蜜的訊息，說她將不會冷落他們，除非他們不愛春天的氣息。

　　去年夏天，莎拉愛上了一位鄉下農夫。（寫故事時，千萬別這樣倒述，這種敘事法極不可取，相當掃興，應該讓故事一路發展下去才是。）

　　莎拉在桑尼布魯克農場待了兩個星期，在那裡與老農夫富蘭克林之子華特相戀。一般農夫的生活，多半是盡快完成戀愛和結婚，然後回到牧場工作。不過年輕的華特‧富蘭克林是個現代的農業家，他不但在乳牛棚裡裝電話，還能精確地計算來年加拿大的小麥收成量，會對月黑之夜種植的馬鈴薯產生什麼樣的影響。

華特就是在這條滿是木莓的林蔭小徑中贏得莎拉的芳心的。他們依偎而坐，一起用蒲公英編織莎拉的花冠，華特更不忘極力恭維黃花與她棕色的髮絲是多麼地相得益彰。後來莎拉回家時，並未將花冠帶走，只是手裡一邊搖著草帽，逕自走回家。

他們打算春天結婚，華特說春天一到就立刻結婚，於是莎拉先回到城裡，繼續幹她的活兒。

此時傳來一陣敲門聲，敲醒了沈浸在甜蜜回憶中的莎拉。服務生送來餐廳次日菜單的草稿，上面是老舒倫柏格消瘦的筆跡。

莎拉坐在打字機前，替打字機捲上一張紙卡，以靈巧的手法，不消一個半小時，就把二十一張菜單打好了。

今天菜單的調整比往常多，湯變得較為清淡，主菜刪除了豬肉，烤肉中也只加俄國蕪菁，整個菜單充滿了春天的風味。牠們為小羔羊淋上醬汁，慶祝小羊開始在日漸蒼鬱的山坡上跳躍。牡蠣的歌聲雖然尚未停歇，但已轉稀。油鍋被擱著不用，改以烤肉架取而代之。餡餅的種類增加了，甜膩的布丁消失了。裹著外衣的香腸，夥同蕎麥以及氣味香甜卻氣數已盡的楓葉，一同苟延殘喘著，愉悅地沈浸在死亡的冥想中。

　　莎拉的手指如夏日溪流上跳躍的矮人，她盯著草稿，目測菜名的長度，一道一道地打在正確的位置上，甜點前面要打上蔬菜。胡蘿蔔炒青豆、蘆筍土司、多年生番茄加豆子煮玉米、青豆、甘藍菜，以及……

　　莎拉看著菜單，不禁哭了。淚水自她內心深處泉湧而出，她心中一股絕望。她把頭靠在小小的打字台上，弄得鍵盤喀喀地乾響，正好為她的啜泣聲伴奏。

　　兩個星期以來，她都沒收到華特的隻字片語，菜單上的下一道菜，竟然是蒲公英——蒲公英炒蛋之類的——真討厭的炒蛋！華特曾用金色的蒲公英花，向他的愛人和未來的新娘許下承諾。蒲公英這春天的使者，再度勾起她對往日的美好回憶，令讓她愁上更加愁。

　　女士啊，要是親身經歷過這種折磨，諒你也笑不出來了：想像波西在你倆定情之夜送妳的黃玫瑰，被淋上法式沙拉醬，成為眼前舒倫柏格套餐裡的一道沙拉，你還笑得出來嗎？倘若茱麗葉發現她的愛情信物被如此這般地糟蹋，她一定會找個好藥師配一瓶忘情水啊。

　　春天這位女巫果非等閒之輩！即便在天寒地凍的石頭城裡，她一定也派人捎了春天的訊息。原來蒲公英就是春神的信差，這位來自田野的小壯丁，穿著一身粗糙的綠衣，不疾不徐地進城。蒲公英是不折不扣的命運鬥士，連法國大廚都管他叫「獅牙」呢。當它成熟開了花，就化身花環，在男女歡愛之際助興，妝點女孩的棕色髮絲；若是稚嫩尚未開花的，就這麼走進油鍋報春聲。

不久後，莎拉強忍住淚水，繼續完成菜單。她心不在焉地敲著鍵盤，仍然沈浸在那既朦朧又璀璨的蒲公英之夢裡，想著與愛人徜徉在草原小徑上的點點滴滴。沒一會兒，她又回過神來，回到曼哈頓的石子路上，打字機又像破壞罷工的汽車一般，喀吋喀吋地跳動著。

六時許，服務生送來晚餐，並拿走她打好的菜單。莎拉用餐時，嘆了一口氣，把那盤蒲公英炒蛋推到一邊。一朵許過愛情誓約的鮮花，如今成了一團卑微的黑色蔬菜，她的夏日之夢也同樣地枯萎凋零了。莎士比亞曾說，「愛情，以愛情自身為『食』」，但是莎拉無論如何也嚥不下這道菜，這是曾經為她的真情增添無限光彩的蒲公英啊。

七點半，隔壁房的夫妻開始爭執；樓上男子尋找著長笛上的A音調；煤氣稍稍減弱了；三輛運煤馬車開始卸貨——這是唯一令留聲機嫉妒的聲音；後院圍籬上的貓慢慢地撤退到瀋陽。看到這些景象，莎拉知道該是看書的時候了，她拿出本月最滯銷的書籍《修道院與壁爐》，挪一挪腳的姿勢，開始漫遊傑瑞德的世界。

門鈴響起，房東太太前去開門。莎拉丟下被熊逼到樹上的傑瑞德和丹尼斯，聆聽發生了什麼事。喔，沒錯，你也會和她有相同的反應！

樓下大廳傳來一陣粗獷的聲音，莎拉把書往地上一拋，便往門邊衝去。熊輕鬆地贏得第一回合，想必你也猜到是怎麼回事了。她才剛奔到樓梯口，她的農夫已經三步併作一步地跳上樓來，緊緊地一把摟住她，不留一絲給其他拾穗者。

「為什麼連一封信也沒有，為什麼？」莎拉哭喊著。

「紐約實在太大了，我一個星期前到你以前住的地方找你，才知道你在某個星期四就搬走了。這樣也好，可以避開黑色的星期五。接著，我一路問警察，用盡各種辦法，尋找你的行蹤。」

「我有寫信給你耶！」莎拉激動地說。

「我沒收到啊！」

「那你是怎麼找到我的？」

年輕的農夫微笑中帶著春意，說：「我晚上不經意地走進隔壁的餐廳，並不曉得誰會知情。我看著打得整整齊齊的菜單，想找一道當季的綠色蔬菜來吃，一看到甘藍菜的下一行，便馬上回過身把老闆叫了過來，是他給我你的地址的。」

「我記得，甘藍菜下面是蒲公英。」莎拉幸福地嘆了口氣。

「不管走到哪裡，我都認得出你那台問題打字機打出來的大寫字母『W』。」富蘭克林說。

「怎麼會呢？蒲公英這個字裡並沒有『W』啊？」莎拉訝異地說。

年輕農夫從口袋裡拿出菜單，指著其中一行。

莎拉認得這張菜單，這是她當天下午所打的第一張菜單，右上角還有一塊被淚水暈開的污點。那裡本來應該寫著蒲公英的字樣，可是她當時沈溺在金色花卉的回憶中，竟打出一些奇怪的字母。

　　在紅色甘藍和夾餡青椒的中間，赫然出現一道菜：

　　「摯愛華特配水煮蛋。」

7 紅酋長的贖金

看起來應該行得通，不過諸君且聽我娓娓道來，才知分曉啊。比爾・德瑞斯科和我，在南方的阿拉巴馬州時，興起了綁票這個念頭。後來比爾形容這是「一時財迷心竅」，只是我們當時並不自覺。

那裡有個像煎餅一樣平坦的小鎮，叫做「頂峰鎮」，鎮上的居民就像五朔節時繞著花柱的農人一樣，性格純樸，生活自給自足。

比爾和我已經湊了六百元，還缺兩千元，才能完成這項西伊利諾州的詐騙計畫。我們在飯店的台階上討論這件事，我們認為這種半農業的社區比較有多子多孫的觀念，在這裡執行綁票計畫應該是挺適合的。當然，還有別的原因啦，在這裡，至少沒有便衣報社記者出沒，不會鬧得風風雨雨。頂峰鎮頂多會派幾名警察和懶洋洋的獵犬出來，或者在《農家週報》上罵個幾句。所以呢，看來應該行得通。

　　我們鎖定下手的對象，是名人艾柏納澤・多塞特的獨子。艾柏納澤為人正派嚴謹，是一位信仰堅定、正直的奉獻盤傳遞者；唯獨對抵押品有一種癖好，喜歡取消抵押人贖回物品的權利。他的獨子，年方十歲，臉上有著淡淡的雀斑，他的髮色和你趕火車時向報攤買的雜誌封面顏色一樣。比爾和我猜想，艾柏納澤會把贖金從兩千元殺價到一分錢，不過且待我娓娓道來，才知分曉。

　　距離頂峰鎮兩英里處，有一座覆著雪松林的小山，我們就把糧食儲藏在後山的山洞裡。

　　一日傍晚，待日落之後，我們便架著四輪馬車經過多塞特家。那孩子正在街上玩耍，朝著對街籬笆上的小貓丟石子。

　　比爾對他說：「嗨，小弟弟！你想不想吃糖果，跟我去兜兜風啊？」

　　小男孩朝比爾扔了一塊磚頭，正中他的眼睛。

　　比爾一邊爬過車輪，一邊說：「衝著這塊磚頭，我要那老傢伙多付五百元出來。」

　　小男孩像重量級的美洲黑熊般極力反抗，終於還是被我們押上馬車帶走。我們把他關進山洞，把馬拴在雪松樹上。入夜之後，我再把租來的馬車開回三英里外的小村莊退還，然後步行回到山上。

比爾正在為臉上的擦傷和淤青敷藥，洞口的大石後面燃著一堆營火，小男孩的紅髮上插著兩支鷺鷥羽毛，直盯著沸騰的咖啡壺。當我走過來時，他用樹枝指著我說：

「嘿！該死的白人，膽敢踏進原野霸王紅酋長的營地一步，就要你好看！」

「他沒事了。」比爾說著，一邊捲起褲管檢查小腿前側的傷勢。「我們正在玩印第安人角色扮演。我們要把這場水牛比爾秀，弄得像市政府前放映的巴勒斯坦幻燈片一樣逼真。我演獵人老漢克，是紅酋長的俘虜，天一亮就要被剝頭皮。唷呵！這小子踢得還真重啊。」

是的，各位，這孩子似乎樂在其中，山洞野營的樂趣，讓他忘了自己也是個俘虜。他馬上給我取名為奸細「蛇眼」，並且宣布等他的勇士們戰後歸來，破曉時分就要對我施以火刑。

我們吃了晚餐，小男孩滿嘴培根、麵包和肉汁，開始發表他的晚餐感言：「這種生活還不錯，我從來沒在外面露營過。我養過一隻負鼠，我上次過的是九歲的生日，我討厭上學。吉米・泰柏特的阿姨養的斑點雞，牠生下的蛋被大老鼠吃掉了十六顆。這片樹林裡有真的印第安人嗎？我還要加肉汁。是因為樹木搖晃才刮風的嗎？我家養了五條狗。漢克，你的鼻子為什麼紅通通的？我老爸很有錢喔。星星會不會發燙？我星期六鞭打了愛德‧華克兩次。我不喜歡女生。你一定要用繩子才抓得到蟾蜍。閹掉的牛會叫嗎？橘子為什麼是圓的？這個山洞裡有沒有床可以睡覺？阿摩司‧穆瑞有六根腳趾頭。鸚鵡會說話，但是猴子和魚不會。多少加多少才等於十二呢？」

每隔五分鐘，他就會想起自己是個討人厭的紅番，拿起樹枝當長槍，躡手躡腳地走到洞口，探查可惡的白人偵察兵的蹤跡，三不五時還會發出打仗的吶喊聲，嚇得獵人老漢克直發抖。比爾從一開始就這樣被小男孩恐嚇到現在。

「紅酋長呀，你想不想回家呢？」我對小男孩說。

「哦，回家幹嘛？家裡又不好玩，我又不愛上學。在外面露營比較有趣，你不會把我送回家吧，蛇眼？」小男孩說。

「現在還不會，我們還得在山洞裡待一陣子。」我說。

「太好了！這樣最好，我從來沒玩得這麼盡興過。」小男孩說。

我們大概十一點鐘左右睡覺。我和比爾把毯子和棉被鋪開，讓紅酋長睡在我們中間。我們並不怕他逃走，只要樹枝和樹葉一有動靜，他馬上就聯想到來犯的敵人，從毯子上跳起來拿他的長槍，在我和比爾的耳邊尖叫著：「噓！伙伴。」就這麼地，他整整折騰了我們三個小時，最後連我也睡不安穩，夢到自己遭綁架，被一位兇殘的紅髮海盜綁在樹上。

天才剛亮，我就被比爾一連串駭人的尖叫聲吵醒。那種聲音不像吼叫，不像哭嚎，也不像喊叫、歡呼或嚷嚷，一點也不像一個男人會發出的聲音，反而像是女人看到鬼或毛毛蟲時的尖叫聲，聽起來既不雅又恐怖，有礙顏面。天剛亮就在洞裡聽到一個絕望、肥胖的壯漢無法自拔地尖叫，實在是令人毛骨悚然。

我馬上起身一探究竟，發現紅酋長正坐在比爾的胸口，一手揪著他的頭髮，一手拿著切培根的刀子，當真要執行昨晚的判決，把比爾的頭皮給剝下來。

我奪下小男孩的刀子，逼他躺好睡覺。不過比爾早就崩潰了，他躺在自己的床位上，壓根兒不敢闔眼。我稍微打了個盹，想起紅酋長說過，破曉時分就要把我送上火刑柱燒死，我雖然不緊張也不害怕，但還是坐起了身子，靠在石頭旁抽煙斗。

「山姆，你幹嘛那麼早起？」比爾問。

「我？哦，我的肩膀有點痛，我想坐起來可能會舒服些。」我說。

「別瞞我了！你是怕日出就會被他燒死，只要讓他找到一根火柴，他一定會動手的。真要命是吧，山姆？你覺得有人肯付錢把這小鬼贖回家嗎？」

「當然啦！這小鬼敢這樣無法無天，八成就是被父母給寵壞的。你現在跟紅酋長起床做早餐，我去山頭勘查一下。」我說。

我爬上小山頂，四處張望，期待在頂峰鎮的方向看到村民組成的義勇騎兵隊，攜帶長柄大鐮刀和乾草叉，四處搜尋卑鄙的綁匪。不過映入眼簾的卻是一片靜謐的景象，只有一

個男人牽著一頭褐色的騾子在犁田。沒有人在河裡打撈，也沒有人來來回回向焦急的父母通報找不到孩子的下落。眼前的阿拉巴馬近郊，瀰漫著一股催人欲眠的森林氣息。「說不定，還沒有人發現大野狼已經把畜欄中的柔弱小羊給叼走了。上帝保佑大野狼啊！」我這麼對自己說，然後便下山去找早餐吃。

　　我回到山洞時，發現比爾氣喘吁吁地靠著山洞岩壁，而小男孩手裡拿著一顆椰子大的石頭，作勢要砸向比爾。

　　「他竟然把滾燙的馬鈴薯放到我的背上，還一腳把它踩個稀爛，然後我就賞了他一個耳光。山姆，你身上有沒有槍？」比爾解釋道。

　　我奪走了小男孩的石頭，才平息了這場風波。「走著瞧！」小男孩對比爾說：「誰膽敢欺負紅酋長，就非得付出代價不可。你最好小心點！」

小男孩吃完早餐後，從口袋裡取出一塊捆著繩索的皮革，走到洞外把它攤開。

　　「他在幹什麼？你不擔心他會逃跑嗎，山姆？」比爾焦慮地問。

　　「完全不擔心，這孩子不怎麼戀家，不過我們得想個辦法要到贖金啊。小男孩失蹤的事，似乎沒在頂峰鎮上引起什麼騷動，可能沒人發現小男孩失蹤了，他的家人八成以為他去珍姨媽或哪個鄰居家過夜了。無論如何，今天一定會有人想到他。我們今晚就捎信給他父親，叫他交出兩千元來把兒子贖回去。」

　　話才剛說完，就傳來一陣吆喝聲，彷彿是《聖經》裡大衛擊倒所向無敵的巨人歌利亞一般。而紅酋長正揮舞著剛從口袋裡掏出的彈弓。

　　我機靈地躲開，卻聽到「砰」的一聲重擊，和疑似比爾的哀號聲，像是馬匹脫下馬鞍時會發出的颯颯聲。一顆雞蛋大小的黑色石頭，正中比爾的左耳後方，比爾全身一癱，跨過洗碗用的熱水鍋，跌進了火堆裡。我把他從火堆裡拖出來，在他頭上澆了半小時的冷水。

　　不一會兒，比爾坐起身，摸了摸耳朵後面說：「山姆，你知道我最喜歡的《聖經》人物是誰嗎？」

　　「你放輕鬆，過一會兒就會清醒過來的。」我說。

　　「是希律王」他說：「山姆，你不會丟下我自己逃跑吧？」

我走出山洞，抓住小男孩猛搖，搖到他的雀斑臉喀喀作響為止。

「你再不安分點，我就把你直接送回家，你現在要不要乖一點？」我說。

「我只是開開玩笑，又不是故意要傷害老漢克的，他幹嘛打我？我會乖乖的啦，蛇眼，只要你別送我回家，只要你今天讓我玩『黑衣偵察兵』的遊戲就好。」

「我不知道『黑衣偵察兵』怎麼玩，你跟比爾先生商量去，今天他陪你玩，我要外出談生意，晚一點才會回來。你現在進去跟他示好，向他賠不是，不然你就立刻回家。」我說。

我叫他和比爾握手言和，然後把比爾叫到洞外，告訴他我要去三英里外一個叫白楊谷的小村莊，探聽一下頂峰鎮對綁票事件的反應。最好當天就寄一封強制信給多塞特這老頭兒，逼他拿出贖金，順便交代付款方式。

「山姆，你也知道，以前不管什麼天災人禍，我都不曾棄你於不顧，再危險也吭都不吭一聲，從來沒怕過。我們綁架了這個兩條腿的沖天炮之後，他可把我給整慘了，你不會叫我一個人在這裡陪他吧，山姆？」比爾說。

「我下午就回來了呀，在我回來之前，你先逗逗這孩子，安撫安撫他。我們現在來寫信給多塞特老頭。」我說。

比爾和我備妥紙筆，開始寫信；而紅酋長呢，他裹著一件毛毯，趾高氣昂地走來走去，鎮守洞口。比爾含淚求我把贖金由兩千元減為一千五百元。「不是我不相信愛子心切這回事，可是我們是跟人打交道啊，要一個人付兩千元的代價，來贖回這隻四十磅重、滿臉雀斑的小野貓，根本是違反人性。我想一千五百元比較快成交，剩下的差額我來出。」

好吧，為了讓比爾寬心，我也就同意了。我們共同擬定了下述的信件內容：

艾柏納澤・多塞特先生：

您的兒子在我們手中，我們將他安置在遠離頂峰鎮的地方，任憑您或最厲害的偵探都別想找到他。沒錯，要贖回他的唯一方法為：準備一千五百元的大鈔，於今晚十二點送至下文指定您回信的同樣地點。若您同意上述條件，請於今晚八點半，派人帶著您的回函單獨前來，先渡過貓頭鷹河，往白楊谷的方向走，在他的右手邊有個小麥田，靠近麥田籬笆的地方，有三棵相距一百碼的大樹，在第三棵大樹正對面的籬笆下方，會發現一個小紙盒。

請他將回函置於紙盒內，並即刻返回頂峰鎮。

您要是企圖耍花樣，不照我們的命令去做，就再也見不到令郎的面。

只要您乖乖付錢，令郎將於三小時內安然無恙地回到您的身邊。這是最後通牒，您要是不答應，也沒有商量的餘地。

兩位亡命之徒敬上

我在信封上註明多塞特敬啟，然後把信收在口袋裡。正準備動身時，那小鬼跑過來說：

　　「喂，蛇眼，你說你不在的時候，我可以玩『黑衣偵察兵』的。」

　　「當然可以，比爾先生會陪你玩，這遊戲怎麼玩來著？」我說。

　　「我當黑衣偵察兵，我要騎馬到柵欄那邊向那些移民通風報信，說印第安人打過來了。可是我當膩印第安人了，我要當黑衣偵察兵。」

　　「好吧。這遊戲聽起來沒什麼殺傷力，我想比爾先生會協助你擊退那些可惡的野蠻人的。」我說。

　　「那我要當什麼？」比爾疑神疑鬼地看著小男孩問。

　　「你當馬呀，快點趴在地上，我沒有馬怎麼去柵欄那裡？」黑衣偵察兵說。

　　「在我們得手之前，你就別掃他的興了，放輕鬆點。」我說。

　　比爾趴在地上，眼神活像隻落入陷阱的兔子。

　　「柵欄有多遠啊，小子？」比爾用沙啞的聲音問。

　　「九十英里，我們得快馬加鞭才能及時趕到，唷呴，跑啊！」黑衣偵察兵說。

　　黑衣偵察兵跳上比爾的背，腳跟往比爾側身一踹。

　　「我的天啊，山姆，你可得快點回來啊，我真後悔沒把贖金降到一千元以下。喂，你再踢我，我就起來給你好看。」比爾說。

我走到白楊谷，在一家郵局兼商店的附近坐下，和一些前來做生意的鄉巴佬聊天。有位小鬍子聊到老艾柏納澤‧多塞特之子可能失蹤或被擄的傳聞，而且這件事已經在頂峰鎮鬧得滿城風雨。這正中我的下懷！我買了一些煙草，隨口問問黑眼豌豆的價錢，不作聲色地把信寄了，便趕緊離開。郵政局長說郵車再過一小時就會來把信件送去頂峰鎮。

　　我回到山洞時，比爾和小男孩都不見蹤影。我在山洞附近找了又找，冒險用真音假音一起呼叫，還是都沒有回音。

　　我只好坐在滿是青苔的田埂上抽煙斗，等待事情的發展。

　　大約過了半個小時，我聽到樹叢傳來一陣沙沙聲，比爾踉蹌地從樹叢裡走出來，停在洞口的空地上，小男孩則像一名偵察兵一樣，默默尾隨在後，竊笑不已。比爾停下腳步，把帽子脫下，拿出紅色手帕擦臉，小男孩則停在距離他大約八英尺的地方。

　　「山姆，你可能會認為我是叛徒，可是我也是不得已的。雖然我都這麼大的人了，算是個男子漢，也懂得保護自己，但是我的自負和優越感終究還是有認輸的一天。小男孩跑了，是我讓他回家的，沒戲唱了。」比爾繼續說道：「雖然以前有很多人，為了斂財不惜拿生命當賭注，可是他們也沒像我這樣，承受這麼慘無人道的酷刑啊。雖說作賊要像賊，但好歹也有個限度啊。」

　　「發生什麼事了，比爾？」我問。

　　「我被騎了整整九十英里到柵欄那裡去，一寸也不少。等到移民者安然無恙了，他就賞我燕麥吃，可是拿沙子來代替燕麥，叫人怎麼吞得下去啊。接下來的一個小時，我還得跟他解釋為什麼洞是空的，為什麼道路可以雙向通行，為什麼草是綠的。我跟你說，山姆，換作是誰，都忍無可忍了！於是我便揪住他的衣領，把他給拖下山。他一路上拳打腳踢，把我的小腿踢得青一塊紫一塊，還在我的大拇指上咬了兩口，我的手已經沒有知覺了。」

接著比爾繼續說：「他跑了，跑回家了。我告訴他回頂峰鎮的路，把他向前踢了八英尺，算是送他一程。很抱歉，拿不到贖金了，如果不這麼做，我恐怕要進精神病院了。」

比爾雖然氣喘吁吁，不過臉色紅潤，流露一種說不出的安詳和滿足。

「比爾，你們家有沒有心臟病的病史？」我說。

「沒有，只得過瘧疾，出過一些意外，沒得過慢性病。你問這個幹嘛？」比爾說。

「那你就可以回頭看看了。」我說。

比爾回頭，一見是小男孩，臉色一陣鐵青，便跌坐在地上，胡亂地拔草、折樹枝。這一個小時內，我還真擔心他會精神失常。然後我說我決定速戰速決，以免夜長夢多，只要老多塞特同意我們的條件，午夜之前就能拿到贖金，然後逃之夭夭。聽我這麼說，比爾才振作起來，勉強對小男孩擠出一點笑容，答應等自己恢復精神，就扮演俄國人，陪他演出日俄戰爭的戲碼。

那些付贖金的人，肯定會使出對付職業綁匪的反間計來對付我們，不過我早就有所防備，保證既能拿到贖金又能全身而退。我們指定放置回函和贖金的那棵樹就在籬笆附近，籬笆四周盡是空曠遼闊的田野，要是有警察埋伏，盤算著大老遠就發現穿越田野或沿馬路前來取信的綁匪，那可就大錯特錯啦！因為我八點半就會像一隻蟾蜍一樣躲在樹上，守候著送信的人。

指定的時間一到，一個毛頭小子騎著腳踏車沿路而來，找到籬笆下的紙盒，把一張摺好的紙輕輕地丟了進去，便騎車返回頂峰鎮。

過了一個小時，確定事情進展順利之後，我才滑下樹幹取走紙條，沿著籬笆溜進森林裡，又過了一小時才回到山洞。我打開紙條，挨著燈火念給比爾聽，上面用十分潦草的筆跡寫著：

兩位亡命之徒：

今日接獲兩位大爺的來信，關於小犬贖金之事，我認為索價偏高，特此提供一個反向的建議，兩位一定樂於接受。請將強尼送回寒舍，並支付兩百五十元現金，我便同意讓他回家，兩位也得以解脫。送回時間以晚上為佳，由於小犬失蹤之事眾所皆知，倘若街坊鄰居眼見有人挾小犬前來，恐將採取不利兩位的行動，恕我無法負責。

艾柏納澤・多塞特 敬上

「好一個江洋大盜！虧他寫得出來……」我說。

我瞄了比爾一眼，猶豫著還要不要說下去，我從來沒在這個愚蠢又多嘴的惡棍臉上看過這種神情。

「山姆。」比爾開口了：「兩百五十元畢竟不算什麼，反正我們付得起。這孩子再多待一天，我就要發瘋了。多塞特先生對我們提出這麼便宜的價碼，已經是大發慈悲了，你不會放過這次機會吧？」

「比爾，老實說，我對這小子也不太放心，我們送他回家吧，把贖金付一付就可以閃人了。」我說。

我們當晚就送他回家，還得騙他說他父親替他買了一把鑲銀的長槍和鹿皮鞋，我們第二天會帶他去打獵，他才肯走。

大約十二點鐘，我們來到艾柏納澤家敲門。依照原訂計畫，我們應該在樹下的紙盒裡收取一千五百元的，現在反而是比爾數了兩百五十元，塞進多塞特的手裡。

小男孩一發現我們要將他留在家裡，便像鳴笛一樣嚎啕大哭，還像水蛭般地抱著比爾的腿不放，他的父親費了一番功夫才將他像透氣藥布一樣地從比爾腿上撕下來。

「你能抓住他多久？」比爾問。

「我不像以前那麼強壯了，不過我想十分鐘沒問題。」老多塞特說。

「應該夠了，十分鐘夠我跑過中部、南部和中西部各州，狂奔到加拿大邊境」比爾說。

即使天色那麼黑，比爾那麼胖，我又比他會跑，我還是在頂峰鎮外一英里半的地方，才追上他。

8 鐘擺

「八十一街到了，麻煩讓他們下車。」身穿藍衣的車掌喊著。

一群市民為了擠下車亂成一團，然後另一群人又爭相擠上車。叮，叮！曼哈頓高鐵喀啦喀啦地駛離，約翰‧柏金斯隨著群眾走下車站樓梯。

約翰慢步踱回家，反正他的生活中沒有「搞不好會……」這種事，所以慢慢地走即可。對一個結婚兩年，又住在公寓的男人來說，生活毫無驚喜可言。約翰一邊走著，一邊用黯然的嘲諷口氣，對自己預告這平淡無奇的一天的結局。

凱蒂一定會在門口等他，送上一個帶有冷掉的奶油糖味道的吻。他會脫下大衣，坐在鋪了碎石的躺椅上，閱讀晚報上用排版機打出的日俄戰爭屠殺慘況。晚餐會吃鍋燒肉配沙拉，

沙拉上還會淋上保證不傷皮膚的沙拉醬，還有燉大黃，和一瓶因貼有化學純度認證標籤而臉紅的草莓果醬。晚餐過後，凱蒂會拿出補丁好的棉被，給他看上面用送冰人撕給她的領帶充當的碎布。到了七點半的時候，樓上的胖子會開始做運動，他們必須用報紙把家具蓋住，接住天花板掉落的水泥屑。八點整，住在對面房間的即興歌舞雜耍團團員希齊和慕妮，會在喝酒過後略發酒瘋，開始在房裡翻椅子，幻想漢莫斯坦拿著每週五百元的聘約追著他們跑。接著呢，住在天井對面的那位男士會拿出長笛來吹；瓦斯每晚都會竄到大馬路上遛躂；上菜用的升降機會故障從軌道上滑下來；門房再載札諾威斯基太太的五個孩子過鴨綠江；穿著香檳色鞋子的女士會牽著她的斯開島梗，輕快地下樓，把她星期四的化名貼在電鈴和信箱上；弗洛哥摩爾家的夜生活也會照常進行。

約翰·柏金斯知道這些事情都會發生，他也知道，八點十五分的時候，他會鼓起勇氣去拿他的帽子，而他的太太會語帶牢騷地問說：

「現在你又想上哪兒去啊，約翰·柏金斯？」

「我想去麥可克勞斯基撞球場和那些小伙子打一兩場撞球。」他會這麼回答。

近來打撞球已經成為約翰的例行公事，然後他會到十點、十一點左右才回家。他回到家時，凱蒂有時已經睡著，有時還在等候，準備用「憤怒」這個熔爐，熔去些許婚姻鐵鍊上的鍍金。要是這兩位弗洛哥摩爾公寓的居民站上法庭，和愛神丘比特對簿公堂，丘比特可得好好解釋他為何亂點鴛鴦譜。

今晚，約翰走進家門，情況卻一反常態。凱蒂沒在門口送上熱情洋溢的吻，三個凌亂的房間瀰漫著一股不祥的預兆，凱蒂的物品隨處亂放，鞋子丟在地板中央，捲髮器、髮飾、和服、蜜粉盒四散在梳妝台和梳妝椅上，一點也不像凱蒂的作風。約翰看到梳子上卡了一堆凱蒂的棕色捲髮，心裡不由得一沈，凱蒂向來都把這些梳下來的頭髮收在壁爐上的藍色小花瓶裡，夢想將來編成一塊女用「髮墊」，但今天這麼反常，一定有什麼事讓她這樣匆忙不安。

煤燈的火焰旁掛著一張顯眼的摺紙，約翰取下紙條，發現是太太留下的口信：

> 約翰吾愛：
>
> 　我剛收到母親病危的電報，我要趕搭四點半的火車，哥哥山姆會到車站接我。冰箱裡有冷羊肉。希望她不是扁桃腺炎又發作了。記得付給送牛奶的小弟五十分錢。她的病情去年春天時就惡化了。別忘了寫信給瓦斯公司，告訴他們瓦斯錶的事。你的襪子在最上層的抽屜。我明天會再寫信給你。
>
> 　凱蒂急留。

約翰與凱蒂結褵兩年，無一夜不同眠的。約翰反覆閱讀留言，看得傻眼，他一成不變的生活，竟發生了變動，讓他一時茫然了起來。

凱蒂平常煮飯時穿的紅底黑點的便袍，被孤伶伶地亂扔在椅背上，一副可憐兮兮的模樣。她平日穿的家居服，也被她匆忙地到處亂扔。她最愛吃的奶油糖果的小紙袋也沒綁好，一份日報攤在地上，火車時刻表的那一欄被剪掉一塊長方形的破洞。房間裡的每樣東西都訴說著一種失落，桌子不像桌子、椅子不像椅子，都沒有生命和靈魂了。凱蒂留下的物品毫無生氣，約翰佇在其中，內心一股莫名的孤寂感油然而生。

　　他開始整理房間，盡可能地把房間收拾整齊。可是他一碰觸到凱蒂的衣服，就一陣恐懼似的悸動，凱蒂已經完全融入他的生命裡，像空氣一樣重要卻讓人渾然不覺，因此他從未想過沒有凱蒂的日子會如何。而現在她就這樣毫無預警地消失了，彷彿不曾存在過。就算她只會消失個幾天，頂多一兩個星期，可是對約翰而言，這個太平無事的家園卻彷彿受到死神的召喚一般。

　　約翰從冰箱裡拿出冷羊肉，煮了一壺咖啡，坐下來孤伶伶地用餐，和厚著臉皮貼有純度保證標籤的草莓果醬大眼瞪小眼。此刻他僅存的幸福曙光，似乎只剩眼前的鍋燒肉和淋上褐色沙拉醬的沙拉。他家破人散了。扁桃腺發炎的岳母，把他家的守護神一拳揍得老遠。一個人吃完晚餐後，約翰逕自坐在前面的窗邊。

　　他不想抽菸。窗外的城市對他吶喊，邀他同歡共舞。今晚沒人管他，他可以像那些自由的單身貴族一樣，不用報備就外出狂歡。他可以暢飲通宵，四處遊蕩，縱情玩樂，不會有

憤怒的凱蒂等著教訓意猶未盡的他。只要他高興，他可以到麥可克勞斯基撞球場和那些酒肉朋友大打撞球，直到黎明女神減弱了燈泡的亮度為止。他一度對弗洛哥摩爾公寓的生活感到厭倦，被婚姻的繩索牽絆著，如今凱蒂不在家，就沒人綁著他了。

約翰・柏金斯不習慣分析自己的情感，不過當他坐在長十二英尺、寬十英尺的客廳裡，沒有凱蒂相伴時，他卻敏銳地察覺到自己渾身不自在。他這才知道，凱蒂是他幸福的源泉。他對凱蒂的感情，曾被那些乏味的家務事所掩蓋，如今凱蒂不在家，他才驚覺自己是如此愛著她。要不是那些格言、訓示、預言等等的言論，不時在一旁耳提面命，我們恐怕也要等到歌聲甜美的鳥兒飛去了，才懂得欣賞音樂之美啊。

「我真是笨得可以，才會這樣對待凱蒂。」約翰若有所思地說：「我竟然寧願每晚打撞球，和那些小伙子瞎混，也不願待在家裡陪她。可憐的凱蒂，自己在家已經沒什麼樂子可言了，還有我這樣的老公！約翰・柏金斯啊，你真是差勁透了。我一定要好好彌補她，帶她出去見見世面，從現在起，再也不跟麥可克勞斯基撞球場的那幫人打交道了。」

的確，窗外的城市對約翰吶喊著，邀他一同來嘲弄這個世界。麥可克勞斯基撞球場的那些小伙子每晚無所事事，只是將球打進球袋消磨時間而已。柏金斯陷入失去親人的悔恨裡，任憑什麼娛樂或撞球桿的喀啦聲，都誘惑不了他的靈魂。他曾經擁有凱蒂卻不知珍惜，如今等到伊人已去，他才一心想挽回。滿心悔恨的柏金斯只能追溯著他的墮落史，發現自己和被天使逐出伊甸園的亞當沒兩樣。

約翰的右手邊有一張椅子，椅背上掛著凱蒂的藍色中性襯衫，還維持著她穿過的痕跡，袖子的中間有些細小、獨特的皺摺，是她做家事時弄皺的，一切都是為了給他一個舒適快樂的家呀。衣服上還飄散著細緻、撲鼻的藍鈴草香。約翰拿起這件冷冰冰的薄衫，凝視良久，凱蒂從來不會這麼冷淡的。約翰的眼中湧出了淚水，是淚水沒錯。等凱蒂回家，一切就會改觀了，他要努力彌補他的疏忽，不然沒有她的生活要怎麼過？

門開了，凱蒂拎著一個小背包走了進來，約翰看傻了眼。

「哇！真高興回家了。媽媽的病沒什麼，山姆在車站等我，說她只是稍微發作了一下而已，他們才發完電報，她就沒事了。所以我趕搭下一般火車回來，真想趕快來一杯咖啡啊。」凱蒂說。

此時，沒人聽到三樓前面弗洛哥摩爾家的機器又恢復「正常」，開始喀喀作響。一條輸送帶滑落，一塊彈簧被碰到了，齒輪調整好了，輪子也照常在軌道上運轉。

約翰·柏金斯看著時鐘指著八點十五分，他拿起帽子走到門口。

「現在你又想上哪兒去啊，約翰·柏金斯？」凱蒂語帶牢騷地問。

「我想去麥可克勞斯基撞球場，和那些小伙子打一兩場撞球。」約翰說。

9 綠門

　　假設你剛吃完晚飯，到百老匯遊蕩，一邊盤算著要看好笑的悲劇或是嚴肅的歌舞雜耍劇，一邊花了十分鐘把菸抽完。這時候，突然有隻手鉤住你的臂膀，你回頭看見一位眼神妖媚的美女，身披俄國貂皮，一身珠光寶氣的。她急忙在你手裡塞進一條熱騰騰的奶油捲，亮出一把小剪刀，剪掉你大衣上的第二顆鈕釦，意味深長地丟下一句「平行四邊形」後，便往對街溜走，還不時心神不寧地回頭觀望。

　　你對這種百分之百的的冒險機會有沒有興趣？想必是沒興趣吧。你一定會糗到臉紅，不好意思地把奶油捲丟掉，繼續沿著百老匯走，還不時無奈地摸索著被搶走的扣子，除非你是少數熱愛冒險犯難的人之一，不然必有此反應。

　　世界上絕少有真正的冒險家，書上記載的這一類人物，多半是手法新穎的商人，他們出門在外，追求的無非是金色毛料、聖杯、愛情、財富、地位和名聲。但是他們沒有預設的目的地，和未知的命運不期而遇，最好的例子就是《聖經》中浪子回頭的故事。

勇敢又傑出的半冒險家，則不勝枚舉。從十字軍東征到美國殖民地的擴張，這些半冒險家豐富了歷史和小說的領域，使得歷史小說得以蓬勃發展。但他們原是別有居心的，想得獎，想得分；他們主觀意識強烈，好與人爭，隨時準備出擊，渴望名留青史，又愛挑別人毛病，這些人無法羅列於真正的冒險家之林。

　　「浪漫」與「冒險」，幾乎是一體的兩面，這兩位孿生神靈常在大城市裡尋找信徒。每當我們走在街上，它們會躲在暗處窺視，再偽裝成二十種化身來考驗我們。不知怎麼地，我們總會突然在某扇窗戶內，撇見似曾相識的臉孔；總會在沈睡的大街上，聽見某棟密閉的空屋傳來痛苦害怕的哭聲；計程車司機總在陌生的門口放我們下車，然後這扇門會微笑著開啟，邀我們入內；有時「機會之神」會高高地從它家窗戶丟字條到你我的腳邊；我們在人群中與來去匆匆的陌生人交換眼神，即便是匆匆一撇，都得以察覺其中的憎恨、愛戀或恐懼。要是忽而一陣大雨，我們的傘會遮蔽住月亮星辰；變幻莫測的冒險往往化身迷途的羔羊、寂寞的人、癡狂的舉動、神秘或危險的事物，到處引誘、尋找對象，它讓機會溜過我們的指縫，我們卻鮮少願意把握，勇闖冒險之途。我們被傳統的包袱壓得全身僵硬，日復一日過生活，直到行將就木時，才發現我們所謂的羅曼史，不過是一、兩段平淡的婚姻，或一枚如鎖在抽屜裡的緞面玫瑰花飾，或一輩子跟暖爐過不去。

　　魯道夫・史坦納堪稱一位真正的冒險家，他幾乎每晚都要出門尋奇，尤其隔壁路口最常出現奇人軼事。當他愈想試手氣時，就愈會闖陌生的小徑。他曾在警察局過夜兩次，也當過無數次冤大頭，上了那些唯利是圖的狡猾騙子的當；他的手錶和金錢，都在別人一番阿諛奉承之下給騙走了。可是各種挫折都無損其對冒險的狂熱，只要一有機會，他一定不會放過。

　　有一天晚上，魯道夫又沿著以前的市中心街道溜達，人行道上有兩批人潮，一批急著回家，另一批好動的民眾，見到燈火通明的餐廳向他們虛情假意地招手，家也待不住了，打算上館子用餐。

這位風度翩翩的年輕冒險家沈著而警覺地移動步伐。他白天是鋼琴店的售貨員，領帶不用別針固定，而是用黃水晶環套住。有一次他寫信給雜誌編輯，說黎碧小姐的《茱妮之愛情試煉》是影響他最深的一本書。

他走著走著，在路邊的一間餐廳前，聽到有個玻璃盒傳出牙齒用力嘎嘎作響的聲音，他的興致馬上來了（雖然心裡還是有點七上八下的）。他一看，發現旁邊門上掛著牙科招牌。一位身材高大、奇裝異服的黑人在路上發傳單，他身穿紅色繡花外套，配上黃色褲子和軍帽，只要有人伸手，他便小心翼翼地將傳單遞給他們。

這類的牙科廣告手法，魯道夫見多了，通常他會跳過這些發傳單的人，也不會進去店裡光顧。不過今晚這個非洲黑人以迅雷不及掩耳的速度塞了一張傳單給他，讓他只得收下，對黑人這成功的伎倆苦笑。

魯道夫往前走了幾步，才往傳單瞄一眼，未料一陣驚奇。他興致勃勃地將傳單翻面，傳單的背面是空白的，而傳單正面用墨水寫了兩個字：「綠門」。這時他看到前方三步之遙之處，有人把黑人發的傳單扔掉，他隨之撿起紙條，但那張傳單上面印的卻是牙醫的姓名、地址，和一般「齒板」、「假牙架」的簡介，還心虛地保證手術「無痛」。

冒險心作祟的鋼琴售貨員，停在路口思考了一會兒。他先是穿越過馬路，向前走了一個路口，爾後又回頭往反方向走。他若無其事地從黑人面前經過，隨手又接了一張傳單，向前走了十步路才拿起來看，傳單上用一樣的筆跡寫著「綠門」。走在他前後的行人丟了三、四張傳單在人行道上，空白面朝上，魯道夫把這些傳單翻過來，上面全都印著「牙科診所」的介紹。

魯道夫本來就是「冒險」之神的忠實信徒，鬼靈精怪的「冒險」之神只須召喚他一次就夠了，這次既然一反常態，召喚了他兩次，他當然要一探究竟。

魯道夫慢慢走回黑人站立的地方，旁邊盒子裡的牙齒還在嘎嘎作響。不過這一次，黑人沒發傳單給他。這位衣索匹亞人站在那裡，儘管一身俗艷而滑稽，但仍不失一種原始蠻荒民族的莊嚴。他彬彬有禮地對某些人發傳單，對某些人不發。他每隔半分鐘，嘴裡就會哼一段刺耳的曲調，聽不出來在唱什麼，可能是某齣偉大歌劇的樂章，也可能只是車掌們信口閒談的內容。這一回他不但不發傳單給魯道夫，光亮的大臉似乎還賞了魯道夫一個冷淡、鄙視的表情。

這個表情帶著一種無言的控訴，一副認為他不夠格的樣子，讓這位冒險家有種被刺傷的感覺。不管這張紙片上的神秘字樣代表著什麼意思，都是這個傢伙從人群中選上他的，還連發兩次傳單給他，這會兒怎麼一副宣判他智商不足，沒有魄力解出謎底似的。

這位年輕人從人潮中往路邊靠，對這棟建築很快地上下打量了一番，他相信他的冒險即將從這裡展開。

這棟建築共有五層樓，地下室開了一間小餐廳，一樓的店面關著，應該是賣仕女帽或皮草的。二樓閃爍的霓虹燈管一看就知道是牙科。三樓掛了各行各業的招牌，有看手相的、

裁縫師、音樂家和醫生。再上面一層裝了窗簾，窗台上還放了幾瓶乳白色的牛奶，看來像一般住戶。

審查過後，魯道夫輕快地踏上石階，進入這棟建築物。他沿著鋪了地毯的樓梯向上走了兩段，然後停在樓梯口。走廊上只有兩盞昏暗的煤燈，右邊的那盞煤燈離他比較遠，他往較近的煤燈一看，在微弱的光環中看到一扇綠色的門。他躊躇了一會兒，但他彷彿又看見那位發傳單的黑騙子輕蔑地對著他冷笑，於是他當下便走向綠門敲門。

在這種等待應門的時刻，正好可以探測一下真冒險的跡象。在綠色的門板後面，可能無奇不有！可能有賭徒聚賭，可能有狡猾的流氓不著痕跡地設下圈套，可能有美女設法引領心愛的勇士來到她的大門；危險、死亡、愛情、失望、揶揄——都可能前來回應這膽大包天的敲門聲。

屋內微微地傳來窸窸窣窣的聲音，綠門緩緩地被打開，開門的是一位不到二十歲的少女。少女一臉蒼白，走路搖搖晃晃。她鬆開門栓，軟趴趴地把門推開，一隻手四處摸索。魯道夫把她扶到牆邊一張褪色的沙發上，然後關上門。他就著閃爍不定的煤燈，把房間打量了一下，得到的結論是：一戶家中弄得整整潔潔的窮人家。

少女躺著沒動，像昏了過去一樣。魯道夫急忙在房間裡找桶子，昏倒的人應該放在桶子上打滾——不對，不對，溺水的人才要。他開始用帽子對她搧風，這招果然奏效，她睜開了眼睛，不過那是因為她的鼻子被帽緣給打著了。年輕人發現，在他心中熟悉的面孔中，獨缺這位少女的臉龐：真誠、灰濛濛的眼神，小巧外彎的鼻子，像豌豆藤一樣捲曲的栗子色頭髮。看來他的冒險歷程即將畫下完美的句點，獲得報酬了，只不過她這張臉龐未免消瘦蒼白了些。

少女平靜地看著他，嘴角露出微笑。

「我昏過去了，對不對？唉，誰不會昏倒呢？你試著三天不吃不喝看看！」她虛弱地說。

「天啊！你等我。」魯道夫跳了起來，大喊著。

他推開綠門衝下樓，二十分鐘後回來，用腳踢了踢門，示意女孩開門。只見他兩手抱了一堆從雜貨店和餐廳買的東西，他把東西攤在桌上——有奶油麵包、冷肉、蛋糕、餡餅、泡菜、鮮蠔、烤雞，還有牛奶和熱茶各一瓶。

「你這樣不吃不喝，太不像話了。別再跟人賭這種事了，來吃吧！」魯道夫嚷嚷著。

他把她攙扶到餐桌前坐下，問說：「有沒有杯子可以喝茶？」她回答：「窗戶旁邊的架子上有。」待他端了一個杯子回來，發現她已經用女人精準的第六感，從紙袋裡搜出一條特大號的醃黃瓜來吃，眼中還閃耀著一種欣喜之情。魯道夫笑著搶走她的醃黃瓜，倒了一整杯牛奶，命令她說：「先喝牛奶，再喝茶，然後啃雞翅。你要是乖乖的，明天就給你吃醃黃瓜。現在呢，如果你願意讓我在這裡作客，我們就一起吃晚餐。」

他拉了一把椅子過來。少女喝過熱茶，眼神亮了些，臉色也紅潤多了。她像隻餓昏的野獸般開始大快朵頤，似乎把這年輕人的出現和協助視為理所當然——她看起來不像是不懂規矩的人，可能是因為壓力太大，才讓她覺得自己有權把那些人為的教條拋諸腦後。等她逐漸恢復體力、身體較為舒適之後，她才稍微意識到好歹該有點規矩。她開始訴說自己的一些事情，那是城市中最常聽到的乏味事情之一——可憐的女店員，薪水已經夠微薄了，還不時被扣工錢，店面就是靠這樣來擴充的；後來，一場大病，又讓她丟了工作，人生就此失去希望，然後——這位冒險家就來到綠門前敲門了。

然而，這個故事在魯道夫聽來，卻像《伊里亞德》或《茱妮之愛情試煉》裡的評論一樣令人震撼。

「想不到你竟然吃了這麼多的苦。」他說。

「我真的很命苦呀。」女孩嚴肅地說。

「你在城裡都沒有親人或朋友嗎？」

「一個也沒有。」

「我也是孤伶伶的一個人。」魯道夫隔了一會兒說。

「太好了。」少女立刻脫口而出。不知怎麼地，聽到少女這麼說，魯道夫似乎很高興。

過沒多久，女孩的眼皮垂了下來，深深地嘆了一口氣，說：「我好睏喔，可是我很開心。」

於是魯道夫起身拿帽子，並說：「那我就要道晚安囉，好好睡一覺吧。」

她握著他的手，說了聲「晚安」，但她的眼神清楚地道出她的疑問，既率真又可憐，似乎在等著他開口說些什麼。

「喔，我明天會回來看你有沒有好一點，我可沒那麼好打發。」

對女孩而言，魯道夫怎麼來的似乎並不重要，重要的是他來了，不過到了門口時，女孩還是問道：「你怎麼會來敲我的門呢？」

他看了她一會兒，才想起傳單的事，頓時燃起一陣妒火，這些傳單也有可能被其他一樣愛冒險的人拿去！他當下決定隱瞞真相，不拆穿這個女孩的計謀，他知道她也是窮怕了才會出此下策。

「我們有一個鋼琴調音師住在這棟房子裡，我不小心敲錯門了。」他說。

女孩用微笑目送他離去後，關上綠門。

走到樓梯口時，他停下來好奇地東張西望，接著往走廊的另一頭走去又走回，然後上樓繼續探個究竟。他發現，這棟房子裡的每個房門都是綠色的。

他走出大樓，進入人行道，還是滿腦子疑惑。神奇的非洲人還在原地，魯道夫手裡握著兩張傳單朝他迎面走去。

「你為什麼要發這些傳單給我？這些傳單是什麼意思？」他問。

黑人咧開大嘴露出親切的微笑，並說明他老闆精湛的廣告手法。

「我的老闆就在那裡。」黑人指著街的一頭說：「不過你可能趕不上第一幕了。」

魯道夫順著黑人指的方向一瞧，看到戲院入口上方的電子看板閃著新上映的戲名：「綠門」。

「聽說很精彩呢。發行商付一塊美金，請我在發牙科傳單時，順便幫他發幾張新戲的宣傳單，還是你也要一張牙科的傳單呢？」黑人說。

魯道夫停在自家的轉角喝啤酒、抽雪茄，他點燃雪茄，扣好大衣的鈕釦，把帽子往後拉了拉，一派固執地對著轉角的路燈說：

「我依然相信是命運之神引領我找到她的。」

在這個節骨眼還能做出這種結論，魯道夫·史坦納果然稱得上是「浪漫」和「冒險」的忠實信徒啊。

10 附家具出租的房間

　　位於紐約西南邊的紅磚區，住了一群人，他們就像時鐘一樣，一刻不得閒，一直轉一直轉，來去匆匆。因為無家可歸，反而可以說是四處為家了。他們到處租用附家具的房子，永遠都是過客——不但居無定所，心靈亦無所依歸。他們用爵士調唱著〈甜蜜的家園〉，用紙箱攜帶所有的家當，帽緣上纏繞著藤蔓，一小盆橡膠盆栽對他們而言就是一棵大樹。

　　既然這一區曾住過一千個房客，就應該有一千個故事可說，但可想而知，這些故事多半令人興趣缺缺。不過要說這些漂泊者搬走以後，這裡都沒鬧過鬼，那也很奇怪。

　　有天晚上，一位年輕人在這一區遊蕩，他繞著一棟棟殘破不堪的磚房，挨家挨戶地按門鈴，按到第十二家時，他把

空空如也的手提袋放在台階上，順手撣了撣帽簷和額頭的灰塵。門鈴聲很微弱，聽起來像是在遙遠、空曠的深處迴盪。

這是他按的第十二家門鈴了，來應門的房東太太，讓他聯想起一條不衛生、噁心的蟲子，把核果吃得只剩空殼，繼續尋找能吃的房客來填充空殼。

他詢問是否有房間出租。

「進來吧。」房東太太從喉嚨發出聲音，聽來卻像喉嚨裏了一層毛一樣。「三樓的房客一個星期前剛搬走，你要不要看看房間？」

年輕人跟她上了樓，不知哪兒來的微光沖淡了走廊上的陰影。他們輕悄悄地踩著樓梯上的地毯，看這地毯破爛的程度，想必連織布機都不願承認它是自己所織出來的吧。在這種缺乏陽光又臭氣瀰漫的環境下，地毯似乎已經植物化，它長滿一簇一簇的蘚苔，腳踩上去還像有機體一樣黏答答的。樓梯每個轉角的牆面上，都有一個空的壁龕，可能曾用來擺設盆栽或神像吧。要是擺盆栽，那些植物一定會被這腐敗的空氣給薰死；要是擺設神像，也不難想像，這些神像會被小鬼和惡魔摸黑拖到地下某個房間深處去了。

「就是這一間。」房東太太從毛茸茸的喉嚨發出聲音說：「這間還不錯，很少空著呢。去年夏天的房客還挺有品的，既不鬧事，也準時預付房租。水在走廊盡頭。史普洛斯和慕妮在這裡住過三個月，他們是搞雜耍的，布瑞塔・史普洛斯小姐，你可能聽過這個人，喔，那是她的藝名，當時他們的結婚證書就掛在那個梳妝台上方，還裱得好好的呢。煤氣在這裡，還有很多空間可以放衣櫃。這個房間很搶手，向來不會空很久。」

「這裡住過很多戲子嗎？」年輕人問。

「他們來來去去，沒錯，我的房客大多和戲院有點淵源，先生，因為這附近是戲院區。不過戲子很難在一個地方久住的，是有些來我這裡住過，都來來去去的。」

年輕人租下房間，並預付了一週的房租。他說他很疲倦了，想要立刻住進來，便算好房租付給她。房東太太說房間隨時可以使用，毛巾和水都有現成的。房東太太要離開時，年輕人又問了這一個問題，這是他第一千次問這個問題了：

「有位叫做維許納的年輕女孩，伊露薏絲‧維許納小姐，你記得有這麼一個人來租過房子嗎？她應該是個歌星，皮膚白晰，身高一般，很苗條，頭髮是微紅的金色，左邊眉毛附近有一顆痣。」

「我對這個名字沒印象，那些藝人換藝名和換房間一樣快，況且都是來來去去的，我不記得有這麼一個房客。」

沒有，得到的答案又是沒有。他五個月來馬不停蹄地打聽，得到的答案千篇一律都是「沒有」。不知有多少次，白天時，他向經理、經紀人、學校、合唱團詢問，晚上則混在戲院的觀眾群裡尋找，從卡司堅強的劇院，到低級小歌廳，他都找過，卻又生怕真的在低級歌廳的演員名單裡看到他要找的人。他一直在找他的愛人，這座城市四面環水，因此他相信，她離家之後應該還在城裡，只是這座城市宛如一大片流沙，不停流動，沒有根基，今天還在上層的沙粒，也許明天就埋入底層的沼泥和黏土中了。

這個房間故作殷勤地迎接這位新房客，這種病容憔悴、馬馬虎虎的歡迎法，和娼女虛情假意的微笑沒兩樣。腐朽的家具、破爛的繡花沙發椅套，還有兩張椅子，兩扇窗戶之間有一面寬一英尺的廉價壁鏡，一兩片鍍金的相框，角落裡還有古銅色床架，整個房間就是靠這些物品所反射的光輝，硬裝出一副舒適的模樣。

年輕人懶洋洋地坐在椅子上，頓時這裡像是巴別塔裡的一個房間一樣，開始用各種語言，七嘴八舌地向他訴說各個房客的故事。

髒兮兮的大墊子上有一塊七彩的小地毯，像是花團錦簇的長方形熱帶小島，被波濤洶湧的大海包圍。貼著鮮豔壁紙的牆上，掛滿了那些漂泊者帶來的圖畫，有〈雨格諾教情侶〉、〈第一次爭吵〉、〈婚禮早餐〉，還有〈泉邊少女〉。壁爐前斜斜地蓋著一塊突兀的布幔，活像亞馬遜芭蕾舞團的腰帶，讓它原本莊重的外形稍顯不雅。壁爐上還有些廢棄的小東西，是那些曾受困此地的房客，被幸運的船隻載往某個清新宜人的港口之後，所遺留下來的，包含了一兩個普通花瓶、女演員的照片、一個藥罐，還有零星的幾張紙牌。

　　隨著這些密碼文字愈見清晰可辨，過去的房客所留下的痕跡也開始完整地浮現。梳妝台前的地毯被踩禿了一小塊，可見某個美人曾在這裡歇腳。牆上的小指紋顯示這裡的小房客曾摸索尋覓陽光和空氣。一塊潑濺出來的污漬以炸彈開花的姿態黏在牆上，證明曾有個裝了什麼飲料的玻璃杯或玻璃瓶被砸個粉碎。窗間的壁鏡留有鑽石劃出的潦草字母，拼著「瑪麗」的名字。怎麼好像這裡前前後後的房客都曾一氣之下，一股腦兒地盡情發洩——說不定是被這房間的過度陰冷給激怒的。這些家具斑斑駁駁、傷痕累累；沙發椅被彈簧擠得歪扭變形，像一隻在某種詭異的痙攣發作時被殺害的可怕怪物。還有某次劇烈的暴動，把大理石壁爐給削掉了一大塊。木地板的每一塊木板，用各自的聲調發出痛苦的哀號。令人難以置信的是，這些惡行與傷害竟出自於那些曾以此為「家」的房客之手，很可能是盲目而倖存的居家本能，和對家庭守護神的怨懟，燃起他們心中的熊熊怒火吧。畢竟，可以打掃、布置和珍惜的地方，才叫做「家」。

椅子上的年輕房客任由這些思緒列隊輕踏過他的腦海，房間內響起曾有過的聲音，傳來曾有過的氣味。他聽到房間裡曾有人忍俊不住，一陣起起落落的竊笑聲；房間一時又傳來咒罵聲、骰子的嘎嘎聲、搖籃曲的調子，還有一陣低沈的哭聲；接著上方傳來激昂的五弦琴音；不知哪處的房門砰砰作響；地鐵斷斷續續呼嘯而過；一隻貓在後院籬笆上哀號。他吸了一口房間的空氣，那說不上臭，而是受潮的味道，像是地窖的冷霉味和臭油布、爛木頭混合的氣味。

正當他休息之際，房間突然瀰漫著一股濃烈、香甜的木犀草味，似乎是隨著一陣風飄來的。這氣味濃郁芬芳，真實不虛，彷彿真有個活生生的人在那兒。年輕人忽然大喊：「什麼事啊，親愛的？」他好像聽見有人在叫他，趕忙起身四處張望。濃濃的香氣緊緊圍繞著他，他也分不清是人還是味道，竟伸手想去觸摸。但香味怎麼可能呼喚他？一定是有某種聲音在呼喚他呀，可是剛才觸摸他、圍繞他的，不可能是這個聲音吧？

「她住過這個房間！」他大喊著，急忙尋找她住過的證據。他知道，只要屬於她的或她碰過的東西，他就一定認得出來。這股繚繞不去的木犀草香，是她鍾愛的味道，是她獨有的芬芳，但，到底是從哪裡傳出來的？

這個房間曾被草草地整理過，有六支髮簪散落在單薄的梳妝台桌布上——都是些不起眼的女性用品，他看不出其所以然，便略過不察。他在房裡翻箱倒櫃，找到一條被棄置的破舊小手帕，他把手帕貼在臉上，聞到天芥草肆無憚忌的刺鼻味道，便把它往地上扔去。他在另一個抽屜找到幾顆鈕釦、一張戲院節目單、一張當票、兩顆散落的軟糖，和一本分析夢境的書。最後一個抽屜裡，有一個黑色緞面蝴蝶結，是女用的髮飾，為此他天人交加了一會兒，可是黑緞蝴蝶結也是一般女生常用的髮飾，用來表現端莊的氣質而已，沒什麼特別的個人特質。

接著他又像獵狗搜尋氣味一樣，在房內來回踱步，審視牆壁，趴在地上翻弄地毯隆起的一角，掀起窗簾和布幕，仔細搜查壁爐、桌子和牆角歪七扭八的櫥櫃，只為了尋得一絲她的氣息。雖然他感覺不到她在自己的前後左右，切切地依戀、呼喊著自己，但透過較為微細的知覺，甚至也不需那麼微細，都能察覺得到，確實有人在呼喚他！他再一次大聲回答：「我在這兒，親愛的！」他回過頭，張大眼睛，凝望著空氣，眼前只有木犀草香，沒有形體和顏色，沒有愛意和張開的雙臂。天啊！這香氣到底是打哪兒來的？從什麼時候開始，連香氣也會出聲呼喚了？他尋找著可能的來源。

他在房間的各個縫隙和角落裡找來找去，他找到了一些瓶塞和香菸，隨即一手扔了。有一次，他在地毯的褶縫中找到一根抽過的菸，也被他丟在腳下踩個稀爛，咒罵幾句。他搜遍整個房間，找到一些無聊又低級的小線索，都是一些來來去去的房客所留下。她可能在這裡住過，她的靈魂似乎依然徘徊不去，他卻偏偏尋不著一絲痕跡。

於是他想到了房東太太。

他衝出這個鬧鬼的房間，下樓來到一扇透著光線的房門口，應門的是房東太太。年輕人盡量忍住心中的激動，苦苦哀求道：

「房東太太，請問在我之前誰住過那個房間？」

「先生，我再告訴你一次吧，是史普洛斯和慕妮啊，我說過了嘛，她的藝名是布瑞塔·史普洛斯，私底下是慕妮女士啦。我這房子的名氣還不小，他們裱過的結婚證書就掛在那上面——」

「史普洛斯小姐是個什麼樣的人，我是說，長得怎麼樣？」

「這個嘛，黑頭髮，矮矮壯壯的，長得滿喜感的，他們上週四才搬走。」

「在他們之前呢？」

「哦，是個單身漢，運貨的，還欠我一星期的租金就跑了。在他之前的克勞德太太帶著兩個孩子住了四個月，更早還有個道爾老頭，房租是他兒子出的，他住了六個月。這一年來的房客就這些了，再早的我記不得了，先生。」

他向房東太太道謝之後，便拖著緩慢的步伐回房。這個房間死氣沈沈的，方才為它注入一股生命力的氣味已經散去，木犀草的香味不再，只剩家具儲放已久的腐霉味。

他的希望破滅，讓他連帶著也失去了意志。他坐在那兒凝視著啪吱作響的昏黃煤燈，過沒多久，他走到床邊，將床單割成一條一條的，把它們用刀子塞滿窗邊和門縫。等一切就緒，他熄掉煤燈，將煤氣開到最大，便滿心感謝地躺在床上。

＊　　＊　　＊　　＊　　＊　　＊　　＊

今晚輪到麥克庫爾太太去買啤酒了，她拿罐子裝了酒，便與波蒂太太一同坐在地下室。房東們常在這裡聚會，承受良心的煎熬。

「我今晚把三樓後面的房間租出去了，是個年輕人，差不多兩小時前上床睡覺了吧。」波蒂太太對著一圈綿密的啤酒泡泡說。

「喂，波蒂太太，你有跟他說……」麥克庫爾太太一副崇拜至極的模樣，繼續神秘兮兮地小聲說道：「那種房子你也租得出去，不愧是箇中高手啊，你有跟他實話實說嗎？」

「房間嘛，擺了家具就是要出租的，我沒跟他說，麥克庫爾太太。」波蒂太太用她毛茸茸的嗓音說道。

「真有你的啊，波蒂太太，我們就是靠租房子混飯吃，你真的很會做生意，要是他們聽到這房間曾經有人在床上自殺，誰還敢租啊？」

「就像你說的，我們也要過活啊。」波蒂太太說。

「是啊，波蒂太太，這是個不爭的事實啊。上個禮拜的今天，我才幫你把三樓後面那個房間整理好的，這麼個美人兒，臉蛋很俏的，竟然會開煤氣自殺。」

「要不是左眉旁邊多了顆痣，她的確算是標緻。」波蒂太太深有同感，只是吹毛求疵地說道。「再來一杯吧，麥克庫爾太太？」

11 伯爵與婚禮賓客

　　安迪・唐納文住在第二街，有一天晚上，他在家裡吃飯時，史卡特太太介紹了一位年輕的新房客給他認識。她叫做康薇小姐，身材嬌小，不太引人注目，她穿著一件暗褐色的素面洋裝，有些牽強地專注低頭用著餐。康薇抬起怯懦的眼皮，正眼打量了他一眼，禮貌性地小聲喊了一下他的名字，又繼續低頭吃羊肉。唐納文有風度地頷首笑了一下，這為他搏得了政商之流的形象，但他已經將這位一身暗色衣服的小姐從考慮交往的名單中刪除了。

　　兩個星期後，唐納文坐在屋前的階梯上抽雪茄時，聽到後上方傳來輕輕的沙沙聲，他轉頭看了一眼，又回過頭來。

　　康薇正從門裡出來，她穿了一件廣東縐紗料子的黑色洋裝——廣東縐紗——喔，這可是烏黑薄透的好布料啊。她戴著一頂黑帽子，帽子垂著薄如蛛網的黑紗。她站在樓梯的第一階，戴著黑色絲質手套，全身看不到一點白色或色彩。她的一頭金髮又直又亮，用一個沒有皺摺、亮亮的素面蝴蝶結低低地綁在頸後。她的相貌平平，稱不上漂亮，不過當她睜著灰色的大眼睛，望著對面房子上的天空，眼裡訴說著無限的悲戚與哀愁時，模樣還挺迷人的。

仔細想想吧，小姐們——一身黑色裝扮，選用縐紗料子，而且是廣東縐紗，這樣就對啦。全身黑色裝扮，把閃亮亮的秀髮垂在黑色薄紗下（當然，一定要是金髮），一臉苦命、心事重重的樣子，然後裝出這個模樣：你才要邁入人生的新階段，但年紀輕輕便遭逢巨變，就此意志消沈，只好到公園散散心，而且出門的時機要抓得剛好——喔，這樣準能吸引男人的目光。不過，人家是穿喪服，我這樣說人家，未免太酸溜溜了吧？

當下唐納文決定重新考慮追求康薇小姐。他丟掉手中還剩一吋多的雪茄，那本來可以再抽八分鐘的。他很快地向康薇躬了身。

「今晚天氣真好啊，康薇小姐。」要是氣象局聽到了他這麼言之確鑿的誇張語氣，一定會在桅杆上升起表示晴天的白色方旗子。

「對心情好的人來說，天氣是很好，唐納文先生。」康薇小姐嘆氣道。

唐納文暗自在心底咒罵好天氣，沒心沒肝的天氣！應該下冰雹、刮大風，外加飄大雪，來配合康薇小姐的心情才是。

「希望不是你的哪個親人──過世了才好？」唐納文冒昧地問。

「死神奪走的不是我的親人，而是──唉，我自己難過就好了，我不想害你跟我一起感傷，唐納文先生。」康薇遲疑了一會兒說。

「害我？你怎麼這麼說呢？康薇小姐，我很樂意聽啊，呃，我是說，我很遺憾聽到這種事，我一定比誰都還由衷地同情你的遭遇啊。」唐納文反駁道。

康薇露出微微的一笑，不過這笑容卻比她靜默的表情還淒苦啊。

「唐納文先生，『你笑，世界就跟著你笑；你哭，世界仍顧自笑著。』」她提到了這句話，說道：「這句話我終於懂了，我在城裡沒有親戚朋友，只有你一直對我好，我很感激。」

他在餐桌上曾遞了兩次胡椒給她。

「在紐約，要自己一個人生活，是很不容易的──偏偏在紐約就很容易變成這樣。」唐納文先生說：「不過呢，這個古老的小鎮有時也不會那麼壓迫，它會變得很友善、很美好的。你可以到公園走走啊，康薇小姐，你不覺得這樣會讓你快樂一點嗎？請容我──」

「謝謝，唐納文先生，我很樂意讓你護送，如果你願意欣然接受一個鬱鬱寡歡的人與你為伴的話。」

他們走進市中心的一座古老的公園，這座公園四周都是鐵欄杆，唐納文先生以前常來這裡散步。他們找了一個安靜的地方坐下。

　　年輕人和老年人的悲傷不同：年輕人的悲傷，是有人分擔多少，便能減輕多少；老年人的悲傷，可能再怎麼分擔都減輕不了。

　　快過一個小時之後，康薇小姐才透露說：「我有個未婚夫，我們原本計畫明年春天結婚。唐納文先生，你別以為我在騙你啊，他在義大利有一塊地和一座城堡，是一個如假包換的伯爵，他叫做費南多‧馬茲尼伯爵，他儀態很優雅，我從沒見他失態過。但爸爸當然是反對了，有一次我們私奔，爸爸一路追趕，硬是把我們抓了回來，我還以為爸爸一定會和費南多決鬥的。爸爸是在普吉布西做馬車出租生意的。

　　後來爸爸的態度終於軟化，答應讓我們明年春天結婚。費南多向家父證明自己真的是一位伯爵，家財萬貫。之後他返回義大利整頓城堡，好作為我們的新家。爸爸的自尊心很強，當費南多要給我幾千塊錢，給我當嫁妝時，被他給罵了一頓，他連戒指或禮物也不讓我收。等費南多坐船回義大利之後，我就進城來，在糖果店當收銀員。」

「三天前，我收到一封來自義大利的信，不過是透過普吉布西轉寄的。信上說，費南多在一次船難中喪生了。」

「這就是我會這麼悲傷的原因，唐納文先生，我的心已隨他埋進土裡了。跟我在一起一定很無聊吧，唐納文先生，我對任何人都提不起興趣了。我不該掃你的興，還耽誤你跟那些有好心情又會逗你開心的朋友相聚，你可能想回去了吧？」

唔，小姐們，你要是想看一個男人拿著鐵鎬或鐵鍬奪門而出的話，只管告訴他說你的心已經隨另一個男人進了墳墓吧。年輕男人天生就是盜墓者，這點寡婦最清楚了。看著康薇哭成淚人兒，又穿著黑色喪服，唐納文勢必要設法找回她的心，不過情敵是個死人的話，怎麼說都很不利。

「我真的很替你難過。我們還不用回去，也不准說你在城裡沒有朋友，康薇小姐，我真的很替你難過，非常替你難過，希望你把我當朋友看待。」唐納文先生溫柔地說。

「我的項鍊裡有他的照片，還沒有給任何人看過。不過我把你當朋友，想讓你看一看，唐納文先生。」康薇用手帕擦去眼淚後說。

康薇打開項鍊的墜子給他看，唐納文興致盎然地對著照片注視良久。馬茲尼伯爵的臉很耐人尋味，他的皮膚光滑，看起來聰明、開朗又帥氣，可以想像他應該是個強壯樂觀的領袖人物。

「我房間裡有一張大一點的，還加了框，等我們回去我再給你看。我只能靠這些照片睹物思人了，不過他將永遠活在我的心裡，這是無庸置疑的。」

唐納文先生已經愛上她了，因此決定接受這項艱巨的挑戰——取代悲情伯爵在康薇小姐心中的地位。不過他似乎不認為這是什麼難事，因為他只要扮演悲天憫人的開心果就好，而他確實也頗稱職。接下來的半個小時裡，他們一邊吃冰淇淋，一邊談心事，只不過，康薇眼裡的憂愁卻絲毫未減。

那天晚上，他們在大廳裡道別之前，她跑上樓把照片拿下來給他看。照片不但加了框，還寶貝地用白色絲巾包好，唐納文看了直覺不可思議。

「他回義大利的前夕給我的，項鍊墜子裡就是用這一張縮小的。」康薇說。

「他長得很英俊。」唐納文誠懇地說：「康薇小姐，下週日下午願不願意賞個光，陪我去康尼呢？」

一個月後，他們向史卡特太太及其他房客宣布他們訂婚了，但是康薇小姐還是繼續穿著黑色的衣服。

又過了一週，他們倆坐在市中心公園的同一張椅子上，月光透過樹葉的縫隙照在兩人身上，樹葉一迎風搖曳，兩人的身影就像投影機出來的畫面一樣，搖搖晃晃又模糊不清。唐納文一整天都心不在焉，愁容滿面，康薇見他一直不說話，終於也按捺不住。

「安迪，你怎麼了？你今晚好嚴肅，悶悶不樂的。」

「我沒事，瑪姬。」

「我知道你有心事，難道我還看不出來嗎？你以前不會這樣的，到底怎麼了？」

「真的沒什麼，瑪姬。」

「有，一定有，快告訴我。你一定是在想別的女人。好啊，既然喜歡就去追啊，麻煩你行行好，把你的手拿開。」

安迪明智地回答她：「告訴你也無妨，反正你不會懂的。你聽過麥克·蘇利文吧？大家都叫他『大麥克』·蘇利文。」

「沒聽過。如果是他讓你變成這樣，我也不想認識他。他到底是誰？」瑪姬說。

「他是全紐約最了不起的人物。」安迪用幾近崇拜的語氣說：「他幾乎能任意操控坦慕尼協會，在政壇上呼風喚雨的。他這人很有勢力，誰要是說了反大麥克的話，不出兩秒就會被上百萬人壓在鎖骨上。他不久之前去拜訪英國，英國國王都要對他敬畏三分呢。」

「大麥克算是我的朋友，我在這一帶雖然沒什麼影響力，可是大麥克像對待大人物一樣，把我這麼一個小人物、窮人家當作朋友。我今天在包爾瑞街遇到他，你猜他怎麼來著？他走過來跟我握手，還說：『安迪啊，我一直有在注意你喔，你在你家那邊表現得不錯，我以你為榮。你要喝點什麼？』他抽了一支雪茄，我點了一杯威士忌加汽水，然後告訴他，我再過兩個星期就要結婚了。他對我說：『安迪，記得發帖子給我，免得我忘了，我一定會去給你捧場的。』大麥克是這樣說的，而且他是一個說到做到的人。

瑪姬，你不會懂的，如果大麥克‧蘇利文能來參加我的婚禮，就算要我砍掉一隻手，我也心甘情願啊，這會是我一生中最值得驕傲的日子。當他去參加一個人的婚禮時，這個人這輩子就算是成功了。這也是我今晚看起來有點難過的原因。」

「既然他對你這麼重要，你為何不請他來呢？」康薇輕鬆說道。

「我是有苦衷的，我不能請他來。別問我原因了，我不能告訴你。」唐納文難過地說。

「我不在乎的，一定是政治因素吧。不過你也沒理由對我哭喪著臉啊。」康薇說。

過了一會兒，唐納文才又說道：「瑪姬，我在你的心中和馬茲尼伯爵一樣重要嗎？」

他等了很久，康薇都沒有回答。後來，她才把頭靠在他的肩上哭。她抓著他的手臂，一邊哭一邊抽噎，哭得廣東縐紗都濕了。

「噯呀，你看你！這會兒又怎麼啦？」唐納文把自己的煩惱暫時擱下，安慰著說。

「安迪，我一直在騙你，你不會和我結婚的，也不會再愛我了，可是我還是要把真相告訴你。安迪，根本就沒有什麼伯爵，我一輩子沒交過男朋友，可是其他女生都有，而且開口閉口都是男朋友，男人見她們這樣，反而越是想追。還有啊，安迪，你也知道，我穿黑色本來就比較好看。所以我就去相片館買了那張照片，複製一張小的放在項鍊裡，再捏造了整個關於伯爵的故事，包括他遇難的事，這樣我就能理所當然地穿黑色衣服啊。沒人會愛一個騙子的，你一定會跟我分手，然後我會羞愧得無地自容。噢，我從來沒愛過別人，我只愛過你啊——這就是整件事的來龍去脈。」

然而唐納文並沒有把她推開，反而把她抱得更緊，她抬頭看到安迪臉上露出微笑，似乎他已經明白了。

「安迪，你願意原諒我嗎？」

「我當然會原諒你，沒關係的，過去的事就讓它過去吧。現在真相大白了，瑪姬，我就希望你婚前會對我說實話，這才是好女孩嘛！」

確定安迪不再怪她之後，她才羞怯地笑著說：「安迪，你真的相信伯爵的故事嗎？」

「哦，也不怎麼相信啦。」安迪一邊拿他的雪茄盒，一邊說：「因為呢，你項鍊裡的照片就是大麥克·蘇利文。」

12 一千元

「一千元，在這兒了。」托爾曼律師嚴肅地鄭重說道。

年輕的吉利安一邊數著這疊薄薄的五十元新鈔，一邊被逗得哈哈大笑。

「這個數字還真尷尬啊。」他親切地向律師解釋：「假如是一萬元，還可以放放煙火，出出風頭啊，不然五十元也省事多了。」

「你也聽過你叔叔的遺囑了。」托爾曼律師繼續說著，語調絲毫沒有任何起伏：「不知道你有沒有注意聽，不過我還是提醒你一下吧，當你花掉這一千元之後，記得向我們提交一份開支明細，這是遺囑裡規定的，我相信你會遵照已故的吉利安先生的遺願的。」

「也只好這樣了，不過很難算得剛剛好，難免會多花一點。我可能要請一個秘書，我不太會記帳的。」年輕人委婉地說道。

吉利安到他常去的俱樂部，找一個叫「老布萊森」的人。

四十歲的老布萊森，個性沈著，喜歡獨處。他正坐在角落裡看書，看到吉利安朝他走來，便嘆了口氣，放下書本，摘下眼鏡。

「老布萊森，醒醒啊，告訴你一件有趣的事。」吉利安說。

「拜託你去說給那些打撞球的小子聽吧，我實在受不了你那些無聊的故事。」老布萊森說。

「這次的不一樣，而且我就想跟你說，這種又悽慘又好笑的事，不適合邊打撞球邊聽啦。我剛從我已故叔叔委託的法律事務所回來，那些律師跟合法的海盜沒兩樣。他留了一千元給我，不多也不少，你說一千元能做什麼啊？」

老布萊森一聽，像是蜜蜂聞到醋一樣，興致勃勃地，「我以為去世的賽普提莫斯・吉利安先生，少說也有五十萬的身價啊。」

「就是啊，好笑就在這兒。他把他所有的錢都捐給細菌啦，先是贊助芽胞桿菌的研發，然後再把剩下的錢拿去設立醫院，好消滅這些細菌。還有一兩筆零星的遺產，男女管家各分得一枚戒指和十元，他的姪子我啊，則分得一千元。」吉利安贊同地笑說。

「你一向不愁沒錢花的。」老布萊森說。

「錢可多咧，說到零用錢，我叔叔可是我的救命恩人啊。」吉利安說。

「還有別的繼承人嗎？」老布萊森問。

「沒了。」吉利安對著香菸皺了皺眉頭，不自在地踹了沙發皮套一腳。「有個叫做海頓小姐的，住在我叔叔家，他是她的監護人。這女人不太講話，喜歡音樂，她老爸不巧就是我叔叔的朋友。我忘了說，那個戒指和十元的笑話啊，她也有份呢。要是我也有就好了，十元買兩瓶葡萄酒就沒了，戒指就賞給服務生當小費，輕鬆了事。老布萊森，你不要瞧不起我或講什麼羞辱話唷，你倒是說說看，一千元要怎麼花？」

老布萊森擦擦眼鏡笑了，吉利安一看到他笑，就知道他準備講什麼更惡毒的話了。

「一千元，說多不多，說少不少，可以買到一個幸福的小窩，然後對洛克斐勒這種富豪一笑置之。也可以用一千元把太太送到南方逃命。如果是七、八、九月的話，用一千元買純鮮奶給一百個嬰兒喝，少說也能養活五十個。一千元能在畫廊裡玩半個小時的法羅牌。一千元能幫一個有志氣的小孩完成學業。聽說昨天在拍賣場上，就有一件柯洛的真跡作品以一千元成交。一千元夠你搬到新罕普夏，風風光光地過兩年。你可以租下麥迪遜花園廣場一晚，如果有人要聽的，你可以對他們談談身為推定的不安全感。」老布萊森說。

「老布萊森，你要是別那麼愛說教，人緣就會好點。我是問你，我那一千元要怎麼花。」吉利安維持一貫冷靜地說。

「你嗎？巴比・吉利安，你只有一件事可做，先買顆鑽石墜子送給蘿塔・蘿芮萊小姐，然後再去愛達荷州買個大農場。我建議你找個牧羊場，因為我最討厭羊了。」老布萊森微笑道。

「真是謝了，我就知道你最靠得住，老布萊森，你還真是一針見血啊，我就是想把這筆錢一次花個精光，不然還要一條一條列舉消費明細，頭疼死了。」吉利安起身說道。

他打電話叫了一輛計程車，告訴司機：「到哥倫比亞戲院舞台入口。」

蘿塔・蘿芮萊小姐正拿著粉撲化妝，待會兒的日場幾乎客滿，她也差不多準備好，等著登場了。這時，化妝師跟她提到吉利安先生的名字。

「讓他進來吧。」蘿芮萊小姐接著說：「巴比，什麼事啊？我再過兩分鐘就要上場了。」

「你快附耳過來。」吉利安很快地說：「這樣就對了，不耽誤你兩分鐘的。我送你個墜子之類的小東西如何？我出得起一個壹後面再加三個零。」

「喔，好啊。亞當，把我的右手手套拿來。喂，巴比，你注意到黛拉・史黛西前幾天晚上戴的那條項鍊沒有？聽說是在蒂芬妮買的，價值兩百元耶。不過呢，當然啦——亞當，把我的肩帶往左邊拉一點。」蘿芮萊小姐說。

「蘿芮萊小姐，該唱開場了！」外面提示演員上台的小男童大喊著。

吉利安慢慢地走回等候他的計程車旁。

「如果你有一千元，你會怎麼花。」他問司機。

「開一間沙龍啊。」司機立刻用沙啞的嗓音接口：「我知道有個地方值得投資，就在轉角那棟四層樓的磚房，我已經把它摸得一清二楚了，二樓是中國佬開的雜燴餐廳，三樓是修指甲的，還有外國大使館，四樓是撞球場。如果你想投資的話──」

「哦，不，我只是好奇問一問而已。我是按時包車的，你只管開，我叫你停就停。」

車子沿著百老匯駛過八個路口，吉利安用手杖勾開車門下了車。路邊有個盲人正坐在椅子上賣鉛筆，吉利安逕自朝他走去。

「對不起，請問一下，如果你有一千元，你會拿它來做什麼？」吉利安說。

「你是從剛才那輛車下來的是吧？」盲人問。

「是啊。」吉利安說。

「大白天的，你又搭計程車，應該不是什麼問題人物，就給你看看這個吧。」盲人從口袋裡掏出一本小冊子，吉利安打開一看，是一本存摺，盲人名下有一千七百八十五元的存款。

吉利安把存摺還給盲人，走回車上，對司機說：「我忘了一件事，麻煩你開到百老匯的托爾曼與夏普律師事務所。」

托爾曼律師戴著金邊眼鏡，用好奇又不懷好意的眼光看著他。

「真不好意思，我想請教一個問題，希望不會太冒昧。」吉利安神情愉悅地說道：「在我叔叔的遺囑上，除了留一枚戒指和十元美金給海頓小姐之外，還有沒有其他的？」

「沒有。」托爾曼說。

「多謝了，先生。」吉利安語畢回到車上，跟司機說了叔叔家的地址。

海頓小姐正在書房裡寫信，她一身黑衣，身材嬌小，但你很難不去注意她的眼睛。這時吉利安走進屋裡，覺得疑點重重。

「我剛從托爾曼律師那裡過來，他們看過遺囑了，發現一個……」——吉利安試圖想用一個法律術語——「發現一個修正案，就是附帶說明之類的，好像那老頭子再三考慮後，決定放寬一點，再給你一千元。托爾曼律師要我把錢送過來，在這裡，你最好數數看對不對。」

吉利安把錢放在她桌上，她臉色立刻發白，不停地喊著：「噢！噢！」

吉利安側過身面向窗戶，低聲地說：「我想，你知道我是愛你的。」

　　「對不起。」海頓小姐說著便收了錢。

　　「這樣也打動不了你嗎？」吉利寬心地說。

　　「對不起。」她重複道。

　　「我可以寫一張紙條嗎？」吉利安笑著問道，然後坐在書房裡的大桌子前，海頓小姐拿了紙筆給他之後，就走回自己的寫字桌。

　　吉利安如是記錄了他的花費：

　　　　不肖的羅伯特‧吉利安，為了永恆的幸福，
　　　　已將一千元給予世上最好、最親愛的女人，
　　　　感謝蒼天。

　　他把紙條塞進信封，鞠了躬便走出門。

　　他搭著計程車又來到托爾曼與夏普律師事務所。

　　「我把一千元花掉了，這會兒是前來繳交消費明細的。托爾曼先生，您不覺得空氣裡有夏天的味道了嗎？」他開心地向戴著金邊眼鏡的托爾曼報告，順便把白色信封扔在桌上：「裡面的紙條上說明了一千元的去處。」

　　托爾曼沒碰信封，而是把合夥人夏普叫到保險庫的門邊，一起往保險庫裡搜尋文件，他們像中獎般地搜出了一個蠟封的大信封。兩人用那德高望重的腦袋，對著信封的內容物搖頭晃腦，接著由托爾曼代表發言。

「吉利安先生，你叔叔的遺囑裡有一項附加條款，他私下授權我們，在你繳交一千元的消費明細之後，才能打開這個信封。既然你已經達成約定，我們就要宣讀這項附加條款了，我盡量不用法律術語，讓你大致瞭解這項附註的大意就好了。

上面說，這一千元若是運用得宜，你將得到更多的財產，而夏普先生和我則受託負責裁決。我向你保證，我們會嚴格地盡我們的義務，但也會秉持公平的原則，而不會加以刁難。我們並非待你不公，吉利安先生。我們再回到附加條款上吧，如果這筆錢是以審慎、明智且不圖私利的方式花掉，那我們就有權將存放在我們這兒的五萬元債券轉交給你。不過，已故的吉利安先生也交代得很清楚，如果你像以前一樣，把這筆錢拿去如老吉利安先生所說的——「跟你那些狐群狗黨一起亂花掉」的話，那麼這五萬元就必須立刻支付給他所監護的瑪麗安·海頓。吉利安先生，我和夏普先生現在就來看看你的花費方式，我想你都寫好了吧，希望你對我們要有信心。

托爾曼先生正要伸手拿信封時，吉利安卻搶先一步將它撕碎塞進口袋裡。

「沒關係的，不用麻煩了，反正你們也看不懂我在寫什麼。我把一千元拿去賭馬輸光了，再見了，兩位大爺。」吉利安微笑道。

吉利安離去之時，托爾曼和夏普難過地搖了搖頭，因為他們聽到吉利安等電梯時，嘴裡還愉快地吹著口哨呢。

13 哈格瑞夫的化身術

潘德頓・泰柏少校帶著女兒莉蒂雅，自莫比爾移居華盛頓，他們選的房子位於寄宿區，在最安靜的大道後方五十碼處，是一棟舊式磚房，門廊以白色高柱支撐。院子裡莊嚴的槐木與榆樹成蔭，正值花季的梓樹飄落陣陣花雨，散得草地紅白點點。此外尚有一排排高大的黃楊樹，隔成圍籬和步道。這種南方風味和景致，最對泰柏父女的味兒了。

他們在這棟舒適的私人寄宿房子裡，租了幾間房間，包括泰柏少校專用的書房。他正在為他的書《阿拉巴馬軍隊、法官與法庭軼聞回憶錄》寫最後一個章節。

泰柏少校是傳統的南方人，他過不慣現代生活，也不覺得這種生活有什麼價值可言。他還活在南北戰爭前的時代，當時泰柏家族擁有上千頃的棉花田，全由黑奴耕種。他們家族既闊綽又好客，官邸內出入的都是南方的上流仕紳。儘管時代不同了，泰柏少校仍保有當時的高傲和榮譽心，還遵守著過時的繁文縟節，可想而知，他一身也仍是舊派裝扮。

他穿的衣服是五十年前的樣式了，所以儘管他身材魁梧，但他行那種傳統的屈膝禮「一鞠躬」時，長袍的衣角會掃到地面，連華盛頓人看了都覺得吃驚，他們早就不興這種長袍和寬邊帽了，只有南方的國會議員還作這身打扮。這種高腰蓬裙的樣式，還被其中一位房客命名為「哈伯神父裝」呢。

　　少校一身奇裝異服，襯衫胸襟的打摺又大片又糾結，黑色的蝶形領結老是歪到一邊，但儘管如此，他在瓦德曼太太這棟高級的供膳宿舍裡，仍是廣受歡迎。有些年輕的店員常故意去「激他」，讓他忍不住說起他最愛談的南方傳統和歷史。

　　他特別喜歡引用《軼聞回憶錄》裡的內容。年輕店員很小心不讓他識破他們是故意激他的，別看少校已經六十八歲了，他灰色的眼睛堅定而銳利，任他們再怎麼大膽也會小生怕怕。

　　莉蒂雅小姐是一位三十五歲的老小姐。她個子小小的，身材圓滾滾，梳得服服貼貼頭髮緊緊盤起，顯得更加老氣。她也是一個很舊派的人，只不過不像少校那樣，有著一股內戰前的舊時光輝。她生性節儉，掌管家中一切財務，繳費的事都是由她出面。少校嫌房租、水費很瑣碎，他實在不解，他們三不五時就來收費，何不把帳單累積一段時間——好比等他出版了《軼聞回憶錄》，收到稿費以後——再一次付清呢？不過莉蒂雅小姐會冷靜地繼續手上的縫紉，說道：「只要錢還夠用，我們就付吧，說不定以後他們自個兒嫌麻煩，就會一起收了。」

　　瓦德曼太太的房客大多是店員或商人，白天大都不在家，不過其中有個年輕人，從早到晚大都待在房子裡。這個人叫做亨利・霍普金斯・哈格瑞夫，屋子裡上上下下的房客，都直呼他的全名。他受雇於一家頗受歡迎的雜耍歌舞劇院，這幾年來

雜耍歌舞劇的地位與日俱增，而且哈格瑞夫又是個謙虛有禮貌的人，瓦德曼太太沒有理由不讓他寄宿在這兒。

哈格瑞夫在劇院裡還小有名氣，他是一位精通各種語言的喜劇演員，扮演德國人、愛爾蘭人、瑞典人和黑人都是他的拿手好戲。不過他的野心不僅於此，他最希望能成功演出一齣正統的喜劇。

這位年輕人特別崇拜泰柏少校，只要泰柏少校一開始回憶南方往事，或是講那些生動的軼聞時，哈格瑞夫一定在場作忠實聽眾。

少校私底下管他叫「戲子」，有一段時間，少校故意對他很冷淡，不讓他獻殷勤，但年輕人的態度友善，又那麼愛聽他講故事，因此很快就深得少校的心。

沒多久，這兩人就成了忘年之交。少校固定每天下午把書稿唸給他聽，哈格瑞夫總是知道什麼時候該哈哈大笑，這讓少校十分感動。有一天，少校對莉蒂雅說，年輕的哈格瑞夫既具有洞見，也願意尊重舊政權，而且每次他想談談這些陳年往事時，哈格瑞夫都很捧場。

　　少校和所有的老人家一樣，一談起陳年往事，就會繞著那些細節講個不完。講到以前農場上那種皇家般的風光歲月，他就非得想出幫他看馬的黑奴名字、一些芝麻小事發生的確切日期，或是某一年棉花增產的數量，然後才要繼續講下去。而哈格瑞夫不但不會表現出不耐煩或興趣缺缺的樣子，還會針對當時的生活提出各種問題，而少校絕對有問必答。

　　諸如獵狐行動、負鼠晚餐、鋤頭事件、黑人區的狂歡，方圓五十哩內皆受邀的農場大廳宴會，少校都講過了；有和附近上流人士偶發的衝突，以及少校為了綺蒂·查莫斯和瑞夫班·卡伯森決鬥的事，不過綺蒂後來卻嫁給南加州一個叫史維特的人。還有莫比爾灣獎額驚人的私人遊艇大賽，各種荒誕的信仰、不良的習慣，老黑奴們的高尚情操——少校和哈格瑞夫就這麼天南地北地聊，一次可以耗上好幾個小時。

　　有時候，年輕人表演結束後，連晚上都會上樓找少校，少校則會在門口故作神秘地喚他進門。哈格瑞夫一進門，就會看到小桌子上擺著玻璃酒瓶、糖罐、水果和一大把新鮮綠薄荷。

　　少校一派隆重地說：「哈格瑞夫先生，我突然想到，有個詩人寫過『為疲憊大自然恢復元氣之甜蜜使者』，不過因為職業的關係，你可能很難體會他的意思，其實他指的就是我們南方的一種冰鎮薄荷酒。」

哈格瑞夫充滿興味地看著少校調酒。只見少校施展大師身手，每個步驟都不馬虎；他先以細膩的手法搗碎薄荷，精確地估算成分，再小心翼翼地用鮮紅色的水果點綴，配著周圍綠色薄荷酒，格外顯眼。最後將精挑細選的麥管叮咚一聲丟進去，便熱情而優雅地奉上這杯調酒。

泰柏父女在華盛頓住了四個月了，有一天早上，莉蒂雅小姐發現他們幾乎身無分文了。《軼聞回憶錄》雖然已經完成，但是出版商還不懂得欣賞書中的阿拉巴馬智慧集成。他們在莫比爾的房子被拖欠了兩個月租金，再過三天，他們自己就必須繳交這個月的寄宿房租了，莉蒂雅只好找父親來商量。

「沒錢？」少校不可置信地說：「這點小錢也要時時來煩我，我真是——」

少校掏了掏口袋，只掏出了兩塊錢，然後又把錢放回背心的口袋。

「看來不即刻解決是不行了。」他說：「麻煩你把雨傘拿給我，我現在就進城。前幾天，我們這一區的國會議員傅爾漢將軍向我保證，他能運用影響力讓我的書盡早出版，我現在就去他下榻的飯店求見，看他怎麼安排。」

莉蒂雅帶著一絲感傷，微笑地看著他扣上「哈伯神父裝」離去，少校走到門口還不忘深深一鞠躬。

天黑後少校才回到家。看樣子傅爾漢議員已經和出版商碰過面，出版商看過原稿，表示那些軼事如果能再刪減一半，減少書中一再渲染的地域和階級成見，他或許會考慮出版。

少校氣得發火，不過他是個有教養的人，在莉蒂雅面前必須維持冷靜。

「沒有錢是不行的。」莉蒂雅皺著鼻頭說：「把兩塊錢給我，我今晚打電報給瑞夫叔叔，跟他周轉周轉。」

少校只好從背心口袋裡掏出信封，扔在桌子上，淡淡地說：「說來也許不太明智，但反正錢都這麼少了，所以我就買了今天晚場的戲票，是一齣新的戰爭片，莉蒂雅，你一定不想錯過它在華盛頓地區的首映典禮吧，聽說這齣戲沒有抹黑南方，我承認我自己是很想看。」

莉蒂雅不發一語，只是失望地舉了舉手。

既然票都買了，就去看吧。當晚兩人就進了戲院，聆聽生動的序曲，莉蒂雅的煩惱一時之間都被驅走了。少校穿著一塵不染的亞麻衫，獨特的大衣只露出扣好扣子的部分，一頭白髮往後梳得整整齊齊，看起來非常優雅高貴。《木蘭花》的第一幕開演，舞台布幕一升起便是典型的南方農場場景，泰柏少校的興致馬上來了。

「哇，你看！」莉蒂雅用手推了推他的手臂，指著手裡的節目單。

少校戴上眼鏡，在演員名單裡發現一行字：

韋伯斯特・卡爾漢陸軍上校
——亨利・霍普金斯・哈格瑞夫 飾

「是哈格瑞夫耶，這應該就是他第一次演出所謂的『正統戲劇』了，我真替他高興。」莉蒂雅說。

卡爾漢陸軍上校於第二幕出場，他才一登場，泰柏少校立刻哼了一聲，憤怒地瞪著那位上校，氣得僵在那裡。莉蒂雅支支吾吾不知道說了些什麼，然後揉掉手中的節目單。原來，卡爾漢陸軍上校簡直就是泰柏少校的翻版，尾端捲捲的稀疏白色長髮，貴族般的鼻子，打摺繁複的寬胸襟，歪到一邊的蝶形領結，這些和泰柏少校幾乎完全一模一樣。而且為了刻意模仿，連少校那件獨一無二的大衣，他都訂作了一件：高領、寬衣、高腰、蓬裙，前襬比後襬長一呎，這是少校獨有的衣服樣式。這一刻起，泰柏父女便目不轉睛地看著哈格瑞夫所假扮的高傲少校「在腐敗的舞台上被羞辱」──誠如少校事後所言。

哈格瑞夫抓緊時機，把少校講話的習性、口音、腔調和那些繁文縟節發揮得淋漓盡致，為了加強舞台效果，也稍微誇張來演出。演到少校自認為最足以傲人的那一鞠躬時，台下立刻響起一片熱烈的掌聲。

莉蒂雅僵在座位上，不敢瞄父親一眼。她不時伸手摀住臉頰，像是想笑又不敢笑，只好用手掩住一樣。

哈格瑞夫膽大包天的模仿秀，在第三幕達到高潮，這一幕敘述卡爾漢陸軍上校在他的「密室」裡，招待幾位附近的農場主人。

卡爾漢陸軍上校站在舞台中央的桌子前，這些好友圍著他坐，他一邊朗讀著《木蘭花》劇中獨一無二的經典獨白，一邊以精湛的手法為大夥兒調製冰鎮薄荷酒。

　　泰柏少校聽著別人在轉述他的精彩故事，拿他那些寶貝理論和嗜好來加油添醋，把他巴望出版《軼聞回憶錄》的事拿出來大做文章，連他與卡伯森決鬥的事都不放過，而且比他自己講得還要火爆、狂傲。少校不發一語地坐著，臉色已經氣得發白。

　　這段獨白最後神來一筆，加了一場趣味十足的調酒教學，還兼動作示範。從他靈巧地握住香草──「各位，這種神聖的植物，要是多使了一分力，出來的就是苦味而非香味了」──到精心挑選的麥管為止，泰柏少校之花俏手藝，剎時重現舞台。

　　這一幕結束時，觀眾紛紛起身叫好，哈格瑞夫模仿得維妙維肖、淋漓盡致，讓觀眾都忘了這齣戲的真正主角。在觀眾的千呼萬喚之下，哈格瑞夫走出布幕一鞠躬。看到自己的演出這麼成功，他那一張娃娃臉顯得又亮又紅。

最後，莉蒂雅終於轉過頭去看少校。少校細小的鼻孔像魚鰓一樣抽動，他兩隻手握著椅子扶手，氣得直發抖，準備起身。

「莉蒂雅，我們走，真是太丟臉了。」少校激動得差點說不出話來。

不過莉蒂雅不等他起身，又將他推回座位：「先別走，難道你想秀出真正的大衣，替那件冒牌貨造勢嗎？」於是他們決定等劇終再走。

哈格瑞夫的演出這麼成功，一定拖到很晚才睡吧，早餐和午餐時都沒有見到他出現在餐桌上。

大約下午三點鐘，他敲了少校書房的門，少校開了門，見哈格瑞夫雙手捧著一大疊早報，一副得意洋洋的樣子，根本沒發現少校有什麼異常。

「少校，我昨晚抓住機會把它們全演出來了，而且，我想是很成功的，你聽聽《郵報》上是怎麼說的：

> 他以荒誕誇張的表演方式，將其對昔日南方陸軍上校的構思呈現在觀眾面前，包括奇特的服裝、古怪的習慣用語和食古不化的家族尊嚴。他不但心地善良、講究榮譽，而且單純得可愛，可謂當今舞台劇上最生動的角色。卡爾漢陸軍上校穿著的大衣深具時代性和地方性的特質，哈格瑞夫的表演深扣人心。

才首映就獲得這般評價耶，少校，您覺得怎麼樣？」

「昨晚，我有幸——得以一睹您的大作，先生。」少校的聲音很冷淡，聽起來不太妙。

哈格瑞夫有點不知如何是好。

「您也在場嗎？我不知道您——我不知道您也愛看戲。噢，泰柏少校，您千萬別生氣，我承認確實從您身上得到不少靈感，才能演出成功。不過我只是呈現當時的南方生活而已，並不是衝著您來的，您看觀眾的反應就知道了，去看戲的有一半是南方人，他們會理解的。」哈格瑞夫坦言道。

「哈格瑞夫先生，你這樣羞辱我，我是不會原諒你的。你這麼模仿我、諷刺我，已經重挫本人的自尊心，我真是錯待你了。這位先生，你別以為我這把年紀就不敢把你轟出去，就算你還有一點紳士風度，稍微知道進退應對，我還是要請你離開。」少校從頭到尾都站著說。

哈格瑞夫不知該如何是好，他似乎沒聽懂老少校的話。

「我真的很抱歉冒犯到您，我們北方佬對事情的看法和你們不同，我知道有些人還願意包下半個劇院，將真人真事搬上舞台，好讓觀眾知其一二呢。」

「他們一定不是阿拉巴馬人，先生。」少校高傲地說。

「少校，就我記憶所及，他們或許不是阿拉巴馬人，不過我想引用您書中的幾句話，記得是在米勒吉維爾舉辦的宴會吧，您回敬酒時故意用書面用語說了這段話，：

北方佬是十足的冷血動物，若非與自身利益相關，他們是不會顯露半點熱情的，即使自己或愛人受辱，只要沒損失半毛錢便也無妨。他們施捨起來是很慷慨沒錯，不過少不了要敲鑼打鼓，大肆宣揚一番。

您這番描述，難道會比我昨晚的演出方式中肯嗎？」

　　「我這番話並非憑空捏造的啊。」少校皺眉蹙額地說：「只不過公開演講，稍微誇張一點應該是被允許的。」

　　「那麼公開表演的話……」哈格瑞夫回應道。

　　「這不是重點，你根本是衝著我來的，我無法釋懷，先生。」少校堅持不肯原諒。

　　哈格瑞夫認為自己佔上風了，便面露微笑說：「泰柏少校，您別誤會，我決無冒犯之意。我們做戲子的，靈感來自四面八方，我只是盡量取材，將其呈現於鎂光燈前而已，您就別放在心上了。我來找您另有他事，我們既然都有好幾個月的交情了，我就不拐彎抹角了。我知道您手頭拮据——您別管我怎麼知道的了，這種寄宿房子一定會傳開的——我很想幫您，我常常登場表演，這一季也攢了不少錢，算是小有積蓄，可以借您幾百塊，更多也行，直到您收到——」

　　「住嘴！」少校伸出一隻手臂命令道。

　　「果然被我說中了，你以為用錢就能買回我的自尊嗎？我是怎麼也不會隨便找個朋友借錢的，至於你嘛，先生，你想用錢來彌補嗎？我寧願餓死，也不會任你這樣羞辱的。我再說一次，請你離開。」

哈格瑞夫不發一語地離開。晚餐時，凡德曼太太透露他當天就搬走了，搬到市中心的劇院附近，《木蘭花》已經排定在此連續上演一週。

泰柏父女陷入困境。少校顧慮很多，是不可能在華盛頓區找人借錢。莉蒂雅只好寫信求助瑞夫叔叔，但她擔心叔叔的手頭也很緊，幫不上忙。少校不得已，也只得寫信給凡德曼太太。他信中語意不清，只以「房租遭受拖欠」及「匯款遲未入帳」為由，請求寬貸個幾天，並為此致歉。

然而，此時卻飛來了一筆意外之財，成了父女倆的救星。

一天下午，天色已晚，門僕上樓向泰柏少校通報有位老黑人求見，少校要他把人帶到書房裡來。沒多久，年邁的黑人來到了門口。他握著帽子一鞠躬，一拐一拐地進了書房。他穿著一件體面的寬鬆黑衣，一雙大工作鞋上閃著金屬光澤，與爐灶的色澤相仿。他有一頭濃密灰髮——說白髮比較貼切。黑人一過中年，便很難看出年紀，這個人應該有泰柏少校的歲數了。

「潘德頓元帥，想必你不認不得我了。」他第一句話便這麼說。

少校起身走到他面前，他覺得這口吻頗為熟悉，應該是老農場裡的哪個黑奴吧，不過這些黑奴多半分散著幹活兒，他也記不得這個聲音和長相了。

「確實是認不得了，不過你倒是可以幫我回憶一下。」少校親切地說。

「潘德頓元帥，你記得辛蒂的摩斯嗎？戰後隨即搬走的那位？」

「等等。」少校用指尖搓著額頭說道，他最愛回憶那段美好時光的點點滴滴了，他努力思索著：「辛蒂的摩斯，你是管馬的，負責馴服小馬，沒錯，我想起來了。南方戰敗後，你就改名為──你別提醒我──改名為米歇爾，搬到西部的內不拉斯加去了。」

「是的，是的，先生。」老黑人臉上綻放出笑容：「就是他，的確去了內不拉斯加，就是我沒錯──摩斯‧米歇爾，現在大家管我叫『摩斯‧米歇爾大叔』。我走的時候，老元帥，也就是令尊，給了我一對小騾子，你還記得那些小騾子嗎？潘德頓元帥？」

「我不記得那些小騾了，你知道我在開戰那一年就結了婚，搬到老福林比家去了。坐下，坐下，摩斯大叔，很高興見到你啊，你應該發達了吧？」少校說。

摩斯大叔搬了張椅子，並且小心地把帽子放在椅子腳邊。

「是啊，這些日子我過得還不錯。我剛到內不拉斯加時，那裡的男女老少都跑來看我的小騾子，他們從沒見過這種騾馬，後來我就以三百塊錢把牠們賣掉了，是的，先生，三百塊呀。然後我開了一間鐵匠工坊，賺了點錢，也買了一塊地。我和我老婆生了七個小孩，有兩個夭折，其他的都活得很好。四年前，我的土地上開了一條鐵路，一個小鎮就這麼繁榮起來了。潘德頓元帥，摩斯大叔我現在的身價總值上萬呢。」

「那就好，那就好。」少校誠心地說。

「潘德頓元帥，你孩子呢？那個你喚做莉蒂的小女孩呀，她應該已經長大了，沒人認得出是當年的小女娃兒了吧？」

少校走道門邊喊道：「莉蒂雅，親愛的，你來一下好嗎？」

莉蒂雅看起來的確已經是一個大人了，她略顯不安地從房裡出來。

「喏，你看！我剛才怎麼說的？我就知道這孩子已經長大了。孩子，你不記得摩斯大叔了嗎？」

「莉蒂雅，這位是辛蒂姨媽的摩斯，你才兩歲大時，他就離開桑尼米德，到西部去了。」少校解釋道。

「哦，摩斯大叔，當時我還那麼小，不記得您了。而且就像您說的，我都長那麼大了，我那時候才出生不久呢。可是我雖然不記得你，還是很高興見到你。」莉蒂雅說。

摩斯大叔的出現，的確令她高興，也令少校開心，終於有一個活生生而具體的東西，能將他們與過去的快樂時光連結起來。他們三人坐著聊起往事，回憶農場裡的點點滴滴，少校和摩斯大叔還不時地互相糾正、提示對方。

少校問摩斯大叔為何遠道而來。

「我是特地來這裡參加浸信大會的，我從來不傳教，不過我算是教會裡的長輩，又出得起自己的旅費，他們就派我來了。」摩斯大叔解釋道。

「那您又是如何得知我們在華盛頓的呢？」莉蒂雅問。

「我下榻的旅社有個從莫比爾來的服務員，他說有天早上見您從這棟房子裡出來過。」摩斯大叔摸了摸口袋，又繼續說：「我此行的目的，除了看看老朋友之外，是想償還我欠您的債務的。」

「你欠我的債務？」少校訝異地說。

「是的，先生，一共三百元。」他拿出一疊紙鈔，遞給少校：「當年我要離開時，老元帥對我說：『帶著這些小騾馬吧，摩斯，等你將來有能力時，再還我。』沒錯，先生，老元帥當時是這麼說的。一場戰爭讓老元帥家道中落，後來也過世了，我只好將這筆債還給潘德頓元帥您啊，一共是三百元，摩斯大叔現在有能力償還了，他們買我的土地去造鐵路時，我就有能力還錢了。您算一算數目吧，潘德頓元帥，這就是我賣小騾馬所賺的錢。」

泰柏少校滿眶淚水地用一隻手握住摩斯大叔的手，用另一隻手搭著他的肩膀。

「親愛的、忠心的老僕啊，我也不妨對你實話實說，『潘德頓元帥』上個星期才把他僅有的最後一毛錢花光了。摩斯大叔，既然您有心還債，我們會欣然接受的，就當作是證明你對舊社會制度的忠誠和奉獻吧。莉蒂雅，親愛的，快收下吧，你比我會善用這筆錢的。」少校用顫抖的聲音說道。

「收下吧，小姐，這是您父女倆應得的。」摩斯大叔說。

等摩斯大叔一走，莉蒂雅便放聲大哭，她是喜極而泣，而少校也轉身臉朝著角落，大口大口地抽著他的陶製煙斗。

接著幾天，泰柏父女已恢復往常的平靜與自在。莉蒂雅不再愁容滿面，少校也穿起新的禮服，活像一尊紀念往日黃金歲月的蠟像。另一位出版商讀了他的《軼聞回憶錄》後表示，只要稍加潤飾，讓精彩處再低調一點，一定可以大賣。總之，雖不盡人意，但也令人滿意了。

收到這筆金錢的一週後，女傭送了一封信到莉蒂雅的房間，郵戳顯示發信地點為紐約，但寄件者不明，令莉蒂雅有些納悶。她坐在桌前，用剪刀把信拆開，內容寫道：

泰柏小姐大鑒：

　我想您應該很樂意聽到我的好消息，紐約的一家證券公司願意付我週薪兩百美金，要我演出《木蘭花》裡的卡爾漢陸軍上校。
　我還有一件事想告訴你，不過你最好不要告訴泰柏少校。他真的給了我很多演出的靈感，如果這個角色讓他心裡不太舒服，我很想彌補他，所以我還是想了一個法子，奉上那三百塊。

　亨利·霍普金斯·哈格瑞夫　敬上

　註：我演的摩斯大叔如何啊？

泰柏少校經過大廳時，看到莉蒂雅的房門開著，不禁停下腳步。

「莉蒂雅，今早有我們的信嗎？」少校問。

莉蒂雅將信塞進衣服的褶縫裡，立刻答道：「有，我把《莫比爾年鑑》放在您書房的桌上。」

14 歧路重生

　　吉米·華倫坦正在監獄的鞋店裡賣力地縫補鞋幫，這時警衛前來護送他到辦公室去。今早州長簽了他的特赦令，吉米無精打采地從典獄長手中接過特赦令。他被判刑四年，目前已服刑將近十個月了，他原本以為關三個月就差不多了。像吉米這種在外交遊廣闊的人，即使要吃牢飯，也用不著費事去理頭髮。

　　「那麼，華倫坦先生，你明天早上就可以出獄了，振作起來，好好做人吧。你的心地並不壞，別再破壞保險箱了，要正正當當地過日子啊。」典獄長說。

　　「我？我從來沒破壞過保險箱啊。」吉米驚訝地說。

　　「哦，是是是，我看看你是怎麼被扯進斯普林菲爾德這樁案子的。敢情是怕牽扯出哪位達官貴人，所以不敢提出不在場證明嗎？還是純粹被某個惡劣的老陪審團給誣害了？你們這些喊冤的人，多半不出這兩個理由。」典獄長笑說。

「我？我從來就不曾去過斯普林菲爾德！典獄長。」吉米依然一臉茫然無辜。

「克洛寧，把他押回去，給他一套出獄穿的服裝，明天早上七點再放他到臨時拘留所。華倫坦，要記得我的忠告。」典獄長說。

第二天早上七點十五分，吉米著裝完畢，來到典獄長的辦公室。他穿的衣服是現成的，完全不合身，而鞋子不但硬梆梆的，走起路來還會嘎吱作響。

書記給他一張火車票和五元紙鈔，這是法律規定的，幫助他重建生活，重新當一個好公民。典獄長也送他一根雪茄，並與他握手。囚犯名冊中記上「華倫坦，編號9762，州長特赦」，於是詹姆斯·華倫坦先生便出獄了。

一路上，小鳥啁啾、綠樹迎風搖曳，但吉米並不在乎，逕朝一家餐廳走去。他重獲自由後的第一件事，便是開開心心地吃上一頓。他點了烤雞與白酒，抽了一支雪茄，這支雪茄的等級比典獄長送他的還高。吃飽之後，他悠哉地走到車站，往車站門口的盲人帽子裡丟了二十五分錢，便上了火車。三個鐘頭後，他在州界附近的小鎮下車，進了麥克·道倫咖啡館，和獨坐在吧台後方的麥克握了握手。

「吉米老弟，真抱歉，我們沒能早點把你弄出來。斯普林菲爾德那邊一直抗議，州長差點就不敢簽特赦令了。你還好吧？」麥克說。

「還好，我的鑰匙呢？」吉米說。

他接過鑰匙，走上樓打開後面的房間。一切都跟他離開的時候一樣。地上還留有班・普萊斯偵探的襯衫領扣，那是他們前來逮捕他，把他制伏時，被他扯下來的。

吉米從牆上拉出一張折床，再按下一塊壁板，拖出一個滿是灰塵的皮箱。他打開皮箱，深情地望著這套全東岸最優良的竊盜工具。這套一應俱全的工具組，是用特別冶煉過的鋼鐵所鑄造的，內含最新型的鑽子、穿孔機、曲柄鑽、鑽頭、螺絲鉗、螺旋鑽，和兩三樣吉米自己發明的小東西，他對這套工具頗感自豪。這套工具價值超過九百元，是在一個專賣他們這一行工具的地方訂做的。

不到半個小時後，吉米走下樓穿過咖啡館。他已換上一身優雅合身的服裝，手裡拎著撢過灰塵的乾淨皮箱。

「又有好戲要上場啦？」麥克親切地問。

「你在問我嗎？」吉米用有所疑問的語氣問道：「我不知道你在說什麼。我現在的身分是紐約脆餅與麥片聯合公司的代表。」

吉米這種講話的樣子讓麥克聽了很興奮，麥克當場硬是請吉米喝了一杯鮮奶汽水，因為吉米向來滴酒不沾的。

編號9762的華倫坦出獄一週後，印第安那州的里奇蒙發生了一件保險庫竊案，歹徒的手法細膩，絲毫沒有留下任何線索。保險庫裡的八百元全部遭竊。兩週後，洛根史波特有個先進的專利防盜保險庫，也三兩下就被撬開，其中的一千五百元現金失竊，但所有的證券和銀元都原封不動，這才引起警方的注意。接下來，傑佛遜市一家銀行的老式保險庫也被打開，五千元現金不翼而飛。這下子損失慘重，逼得普萊斯不得不親自出馬。在比較作案手法之後，他發現這幾樁竊案的手法幾乎如出一轍，他調查過犯罪現場，並發表以下聲明：

「這種高超的手法，絕對是吉米·華倫坦所為，他又重操舊業了。你看那個密碼鎖，不費吹灰之力就給拉出來了，只有他有這種螺絲鉗。再看看這些鎖頭的切口，乾淨俐落的，吉米向來只鑽一個孔就夠了，沒錯，他就是我要緝拿的人。這次絕對要他吃足牢飯。」

普萊斯對吉米的作案習慣瞭若指掌，在斯普林菲爾德案發當時，他就研究過吉米的作案手法。吉米一向單獨行動，速戰速決；他人脈很廣，往往能夠逃過法律的制裁。據聞普萊斯已

經掌握住這名在逃嫌犯的行蹤，擁有防盜保險庫的居民才稍為放心了一點。

有一天下午，吉米拎著他的手提箱搭乘郵車，到了艾墨爾便跳下車。艾墨爾是個小鎮，距離盛產鋅礦的阿肯薩斯有五英里遠。吉米像個身手矯健的年輕大四生，一副剛放學回家的模樣，沿著寬敞的人行道走回旅社。

一位剛過街的年輕女郎在街角與他擦肩而過，進了「艾墨爾銀行」。在他們四目交會之時，吉米感到自己像變了個人似的。女郎也低下雙眼，臉頰微泛紅暈；像吉米這樣的年輕人，在艾墨爾並不多見。

吉米看到一個小男孩在銀行階梯上遊手好閒的，一副自己是銀行股東的樣子。他找了男孩，問了鎮上的一些事情，還不時塞錢給他。沒多久，年輕女郎神色莊重地走銀行，也沒注意到拎著皮箱的吉米，便逕自離去。

「那位小姐不就是波麗‧辛普森嗎？」吉米狡猾地問。

「不是，她是安娜貝兒‧亞當斯，這銀行是她老爸開的。你來艾墨爾做什麼？你的錶鍊是黃金做的嗎？我想養一隻牛頭犬，你還有沒有錢？」小男孩說。

吉米到「農莊旅社」，以「瑞夫‧史賓塞」之名訂了一個房間，他靠在櫃臺上，向服務員說明來意，表示他是來艾墨爾勘查開業地點的。吉米想瞭解鎮上鞋業的景氣如何？因為他想開鞋店，不知道時機好不好？

吉米的衣著打扮與風度讓旅社服務員開了眼界，艾墨爾的一般年輕人大多不修邊幅，像他自己已經算是時髦的了，但在吉米面前仍顯得相形見絀。他一面猜測吉米的活結領帶的打法，一面熱心地提供資訊。

沒錯，旅社服務員表示，投資鞋業應該是很有賺頭的，因為艾墨爾沒有鞋子的專賣店，都是委託布店和雜貨店代為販售的。在這小鎮，賣什麼都好，而且這裡不但舒適宜人，居民也很好相處，他希望史賓塞先生能決定在此開業。

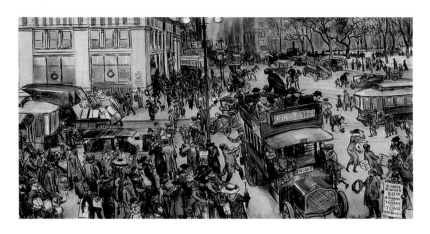

　史賓塞先生表示，他打算先住個幾天，看看情況再說。而且也不用叫腳夫了，他的皮箱這麼重，自己拿就行了。

　愛的感覺說來就來，並且改變了他的一生。過去的吉米‧華倫坦已被燒成灰燼，如今浴火重生的是瑞夫‧史賓塞。他在艾墨爾定居了下來，並且闖出了一番名堂。他開了一家鞋店，生意十分興隆。

　吉米善於交際，結交了不少朋友。他也得償宿願，認識了安娜貝兒‧亞當斯，為她著迷不已。

　過了將近一年，瑞夫‧史賓塞的情況如下：他贏得當地居民的景仰，鞋店生意蒸蒸日上，他與安娜貝兒兩週後即將步入禮堂。亞當斯這位標準苦幹型的鄉下銀行家，也認同了這位準女婿。安娜貝兒對他不但愛慕之至，更是以他為榮。他在亞當斯家中如魚得水，與安娜貝兒已婚的妹妹亦相處融洽，儼然已經成為家庭的一份子了。

　有一天，吉米在房間裡寫下這封信，寄給聖路易斯的一個老友，這個地址很安全，不至於被監視。信上說：

親愛的老朋友：

　　下週三晚上九點，麻煩你到蘇利文家一趟，我要你
為我處理一些瑣事。還有，我想把我的那套工具送給
你，你就算花一千元也買不到一模一樣的，所以我想
你會欣然接受的。比利，我一年前就洗手不幹了，我
開了一家鞋店，正正當當地過日子，而且再過兩週就
要結婚了，新娘子可是世界上最賢慧的女人。比利，
這樣坦坦蕩蕩地過日子，才叫生活！現在就算付我
一百萬，我也不願去偷去搶了。我打算等結婚之後，
就變賣所有家產，搬到西部去，我以前與人結下不少
樑子，到那邊比較不會遭人尋仇。我告訴你，比利，
我老婆是個天使，她對我完全信賴，現在就算給我全
世界，我也不願再幹什麼不正當的勾當了。記得去蘇
利文家跟我碰面，我會把工具帶去。

　　老友吉米

　　吉米寫下此信後的星期一晚上，班·普萊斯搭乘租來的馬
車來到艾墨爾。他在鎮上不動聲色地四處徘徊，終於在史賓塞
鞋店對面的藥局，發現了瑞夫·史賓塞的行蹤。
　　「想與銀行家之女成婚啊，吉米？」普萊斯小聲地自言自
語：「嘿，還未必娶得成咧！」

翌日清晨，吉米在亞當斯家吃早餐。這天他要去小岩城訂做結婚西裝，還要為安娜貝兒買禮物。這是他定居艾墨爾以來，頭一次出城。自從他犯下那幾椿職業水準的竊案之後，已超過一年的光景，所以心想自己應該脫離險境了。

早餐過後，他們一家人一起進城，包含亞當斯、安娜貝兒和吉米，而安娜貝兒的妹妹也帶著兩個女兒同行。一行人經過吉米下榻的旅社時，吉米跑上樓拿了他的皮箱，再繼續前往銀行。吉米的馬車已經備妥在銀行前，道夫·吉布森也在場，準備載他去火車站。

大夥兒走過高高的橡木雕花欄杆，進到銀行大廳。吉米也同他們進去，這位亞當斯的準女婿所到之處，莫不大受歡迎。他的相貌堂堂，態度和藹可親，銀行職員都樂於與他打招呼。這時吉米放下他的皮箱。幸福與青春洋溢的安娜貝戴上吉米的帽子，拿起皮箱說：「我看起來像不像個推銷員啊？哇！瑞夫，這箱子還真重啊，好像裝滿了金磚一樣。」

「這裡面是我打算退還的鍍鎳鞋拔，我想自己送去，可以省一筆運費，我可是很節儉的。」吉米冷靜地說。

艾墨爾銀行才剛買進一款新型保險庫。亞當斯十分引以為豪，堅持開放給大家參觀一下。這個保險庫不大，可是新的門板設計是申請過專利的，內含三組牢固的鋼拴和一個計時鎖，只要一拉把手，三組鋼拴便會自動拴上。亞當斯興致勃勃地向瑞夫解釋它的開關方式，瑞夫假裝洗耳恭聽，露出一副聽不太懂的樣子。而梅和艾嘉莎這兩個孩子，則津津有味地玩著閃亮的金屬拴和有趣的計時鎖。

正當他們全心參觀保險庫時，偵探普萊斯信步而來，將手肘倚著銀行欄杆，隨意張望，並且向銀行出納員表示他只是在等朋友。

此時，銀行內部突然傳來女人的尖叫聲，接著又是一陣騷動。梅這位九歲的小女孩，竟趁著大人沒注意時，玩興大發，把艾嘉莎鎖在保險庫裡，還照著亞當斯示範的方式鎖上鋼拴，亂轉密碼鎖。

老銀行家急忙拉住門把，死命拖拉，嘴裡頻頻唸著：「這門是打不開的，計時器還沒調過，密碼鎖也還沒設定啊。」

艾嘉莎的母親再度歇斯底里地尖叫了起來。

「別吵！大家先靜一靜。」亞當斯舉起顫抖的手說著，接著便扯開嗓門大喊：「艾嘉莎！我在這兒。」由於現場一片靜默，大夥兒隱約聽得到小女孩在黑漆漆的保險庫裡驚聲尖叫。

「我的寶貝啊！她一定嚇壞了！快開門啊！噢，快撬開啊！你們這些男人一點法子都沒有嗎？」艾嘉莎的母親哭道。

「最近也要到小岩城才有人懂得開保險庫啊。我的天啊！瑞夫，我們該如何是好？裡面空氣不足，這孩子撐不了多久的，說不定還會嚇到抽慉啊。」史賓塞聲音顫抖地說。

艾嘉莎的母親用雙手猛搥保險庫門，幾乎崩潰。還有人連爆破這種鬼點子都提出來了。安娜貝兒轉身求助吉米，她雖然害怕，但是並不絕望，因為在她的眼中，她所敬愛的男人是神通廣大的。

「你有辦法嗎，瑞夫？至少試試看好嗎？」

他用銳利的眼神望著安娜貝兒，臉上帶著溫柔、奇怪的微笑說：「安娜貝兒，給我你身上的玫瑰胸針。」

她以為自己聽錯了，但還是從衣服上解開玫瑰別針，交給吉米。吉米先將別針放進背心口袋，然後脫下外套，捲起袖子。從這一刻開始，瑞夫・史賓塞暫時退下，由吉米・華倫坦登場。

　　「大家站遠一點。」他當下命令道。

　　接著吉米將皮箱抬到桌上攤開，剎時起，他彷彿旁若無人似地，以迅捷的手法將這些閃閃發亮的稀奇道具一字排開，一如往常地吹著口哨，開始幹活兒。大夥兒則在一旁看得目瞪口呆。

　　過了一分鐘，吉米就用寶貝鑽子在鋼製的門板上切開一個光滑的切口，以破自己紀錄的十分鐘，撬開了保險庫，並把鎖頭往後一拋。

　　艾嘉莎雖然嚇壞了，但安然無恙，她立刻撲向母親的懷抱。

　　吉米穿上外套，出了欄杆往前門走去，一路上似乎聽到身後熟悉的聲音呼喚著：「瑞夫！」可是他的心意已決。

　　到了門口，一位大漢擋住了他的去路。

　　「你好啊，班！你終於還是來了。我們走吧，我現在已經無所謂了。」吉米仍帶著奇怪的微笑說。

　　不過偵探普萊斯的反應卻十分奇怪。

　　「史賓塞先生，你認錯人了吧，我不認識你，你的馬車還在等你呢。」

　　語畢，普萊斯便轉身朝大街走去。

我多方尋覓
未來的命運。
帶著真誠堅強的心，用愛照亮前方的道路——
奮鬥之中，他們不容我
安排、逃避、支配或創造
我的命運嗎？

——大衛・米諾未發表之詩作

　　歌唱完了，歌詞是大衛寫的，配上鄉下的民謠曲調。這位年輕的詩人請大家喝酒，因此一曲唱畢，酒館餐桌周圍的客人莫不熱烈鼓掌。只有帕比努這位公證人，對著歌詞搖了搖頭，因為他是個博學多聞的人，況且現場也只有他沒喝醉。

　　大衛走出酒館，來到村裡的街上，晚風吹走了他的醉意，他才想起當天和伊芳吵了一架，並且決心離家出走，到外面的世界求取功名。

　　「等我的詩歌傳誦大街小巷之後，她或許會重新思考今天所說的狠話。」他得意地自言自語著。

　　除了還在酒館裡喝酒鬧事的人之外，所有的村民都入睡了。大衛住的小屋是他父親的，他躡手躡腳地走進自己的房間，打包一小疊衣物，然後把包袱綁在棍子上，望著門外從瓦諾延伸出去的馬路。

　　他經過父親的羊舍，這些綿羊晚上都蜷縮在羊舍裡——他白天負責趕羊，想用碎紙寫詩時，就任牠們到處亂跑。他看到伊芳的窗戶還亮著，離家出走的決心稍微有點動搖。燈還亮著，說不定表示她正在後悔發脾氣的事，所以睡不著，說不定今天早上只是──不行！他的心意已決，他不想在瓦諾待下去了，這裡沒人瞭解他，他必須上路追尋自己的命運和未來。

這條路像農夫的犁溝一樣筆直，穿越朦朧月光下的原野，一路綿延三里格。村民都認為，這條路至少可以通到巴黎。這位詩人一路走著，嘴裡不時掛著「巴黎」這個名字。他從未離開瓦諾這麼遠。

左邊的岔路

道路綿延三里格之後，與另一條大路垂直相交，難題出現了。大衛站著猶豫了一會兒，選擇了左邊的岔路。

這條岔路與來時的路相比，意義更顯得重要。路上有輪胎壓過的痕跡，顯示不久前曾有馬車路過。走了半個小時之後，他在一座險峻的山丘下，看到一輛笨重的馬車陷在河床裡，證實方才看到的車輪痕跡不是沒來由的。只見車夫和馬夫合力拉著馬轡，一邊嚷嚷著，路上另有一位高大的黑衣男士，以及一位披著輕盈長斗蓬的纖瘦女子。

大衛見這些僕人不懂技巧，白費力氣，便立刻當起指揮官。他要他們停止對馬叫囂，把力氣使在車輪上，由車夫一人用馬熟悉的聲音喚牠們前進，大衛自己則用強壯的肩膀抵在馬車後方。接著，大家合力一拉，馬車便滑上了堅硬的路面。僕人們也紛紛爬回自己的位置。

大衛把重心放在一隻腳上，站了一會兒。一位身材高大的紳士向他招了招手，說：「上車吧。」這位紳士的嗓門很大，不過講話的技巧和方式，讓他的聲音聽起來很柔和，也讓人聽了會想遵從。大衛猶豫了一下，紳士又對他施令，催他上車。大衛踏上馬車，在黑漆漆的車廂裡，隱約看到一名女子坐在後座。他正打算坐在女士對面時，這位紳士又命令他：「你坐在這位小姐旁邊。」

　　這位紳士將龐大的身軀移到前座，馬車便上山了。這位小姐靜靜地蜷縮在角落裡，大衛分辨不出她的年齡，但是她身上散發的淡淡香氣，這讓詩人相信，這位神秘女子必定是個可人兒。這趟旅程差不多就是他常想像的冒險之旅了，不過他跟身旁這些神秘人士未有交談，因此仍不曉得整個事件將如何發展。

　　一個鐘頭後，大衛往窗外看去，發現馬車已駛進某個城鎮。沒多久，馬車便在一棟大門深鎖、不見一盞燈亮的房子前面停了下來，馬夫跳下馬背，不耐煩地敲著大門。樓上有一扇格子窗打開了，一個戴著睡帽的人探出頭來。

　　「都晚上幾點啦，誰還來打擾我們這些老實的老百姓啊？我們打烊了，這麼晚還在外面溜達，一定不是什麼有錢的旅客。別再敲門了，快走吧。」

　　「開門！快替蒙巴第侯爵閣下開門。」馬夫氣急敗壞地喊著。

　　「啊！真是一千個對不住啊，大爺，我不知道您是——現在很晚了——我馬上替您開門，房子上上下下任您使用就是了。」樓上的人喊道。只聽見屋內鐵鍊和門閂一陣叮叮噹噹的，門便開了。「銀色酒瓶」的店東秉燭立於門檻上，身上半披著一件衣服，渾身發抖著，一方面是寒冷，一方面是害怕。

大衛尾隨侯爵下了馬車，還被命令說：「扶小姐下車。」大衛只好從命。他扶著這位女子下車時，可以感覺到她的小手不住地顫抖。「進屋裡去。」這是他聽到的下一道命令。

酒館的長形餐廳裡，擺著一張幾乎與餐廳同長的橡木桌。這位高大的紳士就近選了一張椅子坐下，疲憊的女子則挑了一個靠牆的座位。大衛並未坐下，他心想現在應該是向大家告辭，繼續上路的大好時機。

「大人，如果我知道您要大駕光臨，一定會有所準備，好好招待的。這——這裡有酒和冷肉，還——還有——」店東深深一鞠躬說。

「蠟燭。」侯爵張開白靜飽滿的手掌，以其獨特的手勢攤開手指說道。

「遵命，大人。」店東拿了六支蠟燭，點好擺在桌上。

「如果閣下不嫌棄，想來點葡萄酒的話，這裡有一桶——」店東繼續說。

「蠟燭。」侯爵又攤開手指說。

「好的，大爺，我馬上去，用飛的去。」

於是大廳裡又點了十二支蠟燭。侯爵的龐大身軀坐滿整張椅子。他一襲黑衣，只有靠近脖子和手腕的地方飾有白色褶邊，連配劍的劍鞘和劍柄都是黑的。他眼神睥睨，一副高高在上的模樣，臉上的八字鬍翹得老高，都快碰到那雙帶著譏諷味兒的眼睛了。

這位小姐則靜靜地坐著。此時，大衛才發覺她很年輕，有著一副我見猶憐的美貌。她的美麗中帶著孤獨，讓大衛望出了神，突然被侯爵的大嗓門給嚇了一跳。

「你的名字和職業？」

「我叫大衛·米諾，是個詩人。」

「你靠什麼為生的？」侯爵說著，鬍子又快翹到眼睛上去了。

「我兼做牧羊人，替父親看管羊群。」大衛抬起頭回答，臉都紅了。

「牧羊人兼詩人，你聽好了，你今晚誤打誤撞，走紅運了。這位小姐叫露西·瓦倫，是我的姪女。她是貴族出身，每年名下可得一萬法郎。至於她的美貌，你自個兒瞧一瞧就知道。若是她的身價還合你的意，只要一句話，她就是你的妻子了。我還沒說完。我原本將她許給維勒莫伯爵，今晚才將她送去成親。賓客都到齊了，牧師也在等，眼看她即將嫁入豪門，誰知典禮儀

式就要開始時，這麼乖巧聽話的女孩竟然惡狠狠地看著我，大罵我是罪人。牧師看得目瞪口呆，她當著牧師的面，拒絕了我為她訂的親事。我當下發了重誓，等離開伯爵的城堡，我要把她嫁給路上遇到的第一個男人，管他是王子、燒碳工還是賊子，都無所謂。而你這個牧羊人，就是我們遇到的第一個男人。她今晚一定要嫁出去，就算不嫁你，也要嫁給別人。你有十分鐘可以考慮，別問東問西了，只有十分鐘，時間很快就過去了。」

侯爵用他白晰的手指大聲地敲著桌子，做出等待的樣子，好像一棟大房子將門窗緊閉，拒絕打擾的模樣。大衛原本有話要說，也只好打住。他轉而走到小姐身邊，對她一鞠躬。

「小姐，您也聽到了，我剛才說我是牧羊的，偶爾也幻想自己是個詩人。如果對詩人的測試，是測試他懂不懂得欣賞和珍惜美的事物，那我現在更深信自己是位詩人了。有什麼我能為您服務的嗎，小姐？」

這位年輕小姐抬頭看著他，眼神冷漠帶著悲傷。她急切需要協助與照顧，長期以來卻求助無門，而眼前這位臉龐率真、通紅的男子，面對這麼冒險的事，竟如此認真；他的體格強壯挺拔，藍色眼眸裡還轉著同情的淚水。一想到這些，她不禁哭了起來。

「先生，您真好心。他是我伯父，也是我唯一的親人。他愛上家母，卻因為我長得酷似母親而恨我，讓我過得生不如死。我一看到他就怕，從來不敢違抗他的命令。那位伯爵的年紀足以當我的父親了，而伯父竟要我嫁給他。先生，請原諒我跟你講我這些苦惱的事情。你一定會謝絕他的瘋狂舉動，但我至少要感謝你這麼仁慈，願意跟我說話，已經許久沒有人對我這樣了。」

此時詩人的眼裡閃爍的已不只是仁慈了。大衛一定是個詩人，因為他早就把伊芳忘得一乾二淨了，現在他眼裡只有這位清新而優雅的美麗陌生女子。她身上帶著撩人的香水味。而大衛深情款款的眼神，也正是她所渴望的。

「我現在只有十分鐘來達成我一生的夢想。小姐，我絕對不是同情你，我是真的愛你。我不能強迫你也愛我，但是請讓我救你出來，逃離這個可怕的魔掌吧。感情可以慢慢培養。我自認還算有前途，不會一輩子牧羊的。現在最重要的，就是全心全意地珍愛你，讓你幸福一點。你願意把命運交到我手上嗎，小姐？」

「噢，你真的願意為了同情而犧牲自己？」

「是為了愛。時間快到了，小姐。」

「你會後悔，會瞧不起我的。」

「我只想讓你快樂，努力讓自己配得上你啊！」

她將纖細的小手從斗蓬裡伸出來，放在他的手裡。

「我願意以身相許，我會愛上你的。告訴他你的決定吧，只要離開他，我才能忘記那雙威嚴的雙眼。」

大衛來到侯爵面前，伯爵動了一下，看了餐廳裡的大鐘一眼。

「還有兩分鐘。牧羊人只花了八分鐘就能決定是否要娶這位美麗富有的新娘！說吧，牧羊人，你願意娶小姐為妻嗎？」

「承蒙小姐看得起，答應做我的妻子了。」大衛站著驕傲地說。

「說得好！你還挺會奉承的嘛，牧羊人。畢竟她有可能遇到更糟糕的對象。現在就快點去找牧師和魔鬼來完婚。」侯爵說。

侯爵用劍柄重重地敲了桌子，店東兩腿發抖，送來更多蠟燭，以配合侯爵突發的念頭。

「找個牧師來，聽到沒有？我十分鐘之內就要看到牧師，否則的話──」

店東丟下蠟燭，拔腿就去。

牧師來了，他睡眼惺忪，講話不清不楚地宣布大衛‧米諾和露西‧瓦倫成為夫妻，然後收了侯爵丟給他的金子，便拖著腳步離開。

「拿酒來。」侯爵對著店東攤開不吉利的手指，命令道。

「斟酒。」酒拿來的時候，他又說道。他站在滿是蠟燭的桌子一端，讓他看起來像一座充滿了怨恨與狂傲的黑山。他瞪著姪女，在他的眼神中，昔日的愛情回憶已經變成像毒一樣的東西了。

「米諾先生，等我把話說完，你就喝了這杯酒。你娶了這個女人，日子不會好過的。這女人和她母親一樣，是個大騙子，是個禍水。她會讓你蒙羞，寢食難安。你看她的眼眸、肌膚和雙唇，充滿誘惑，根本是惡魔的化身，連一個農人都不放過。詩人先生，既然你認為她會為你帶來幸福，就喝下你的酒吧。小姐，我終於可以不必再看到你了。」

侯爵喝了酒。這時女孩突然痛苦地哭了出來，好像受了什麼傷似的。大衛手裡拿著酒杯，向前走了三步來到侯爵面前，他的儀態不太像個牧羊人。

「您方才尊稱我為『先生』，希望這段婚事已拉近了我們兩人的距離——譬如說，社會階級方面——能否容我有這個資格，和您談談一樁小心願呢？」

「說吧，牧羊人。」侯爵輕蔑地說。

「那麼，」大衛說著，把酒杯裡的酒潑向侯爵那雙輕蔑的眼睛：「您應該願意放下身段，與我決鬥吧。」

侯爵一怒之下，咒罵了一聲，像忽然吹響了一聲號角一樣。他從黑色劍鞘裡拔出寶劍，對著在一旁徘徊的店東說：「給這個笨蛋拿劍來！」然後轉向他的姪女，用讓她害怕的聲音大笑道：「你真會給我找麻煩啊，小姐。看來你今晚才剛成婚就要守寡了。」

「我不會用劍啊。」大衛在小姐面前臉紅地坦言。

「我不會用劍啊。」侯爵模仿道。「難不成要拿木棍打？來人！法蘭克斯，拿槍來！」

馬夫從馬車的槍套上取來兩把銀色雕刻、閃閃發亮的大手槍。侯爵將其中一把往桌上一扔，扔到大衛的手邊，然後大喊：「站到桌子另一邊去。牧羊人總會扣扳機吧，能死在我的槍下，是你的榮幸。」

牧羊人與侯爵各自站在長桌的一端，店東嚇得直打顫，見這情況便結結巴巴地說：「閣……閣下，拜託您行行好，別在我的店裡殺人啊！這教我怎麼做生意──」然而，侯爵一臉威脅的表情，嚇得他說不下去。

　　「懦夫，別囉哩巴唆的，幫我們發令開始。」蒙巴第侯爵喊道。

　　店東雙腿一軟，跪在地上，說不出什麼話，他已經嚇得失聲，只是做出乞求的姿勢，哀求他們看在他還要做生意的份上，停止打鬥。

　　「我來發號施令。」小姐以清晰的聲音說道。她走到大衛面前，送上一個香吻。她的眼神閃閃發亮，臉上也有了光澤。她靠在牆邊，而兩個男人舉起手槍，等候她發令。

　　「一、二、三！」

　　兩道槍聲幾乎同時響起，燭光閃爍了一下。侯爵還站著微笑，他把左手放在桌上，手指攤開。大衛也站著，他慢慢地轉頭，尋找他的妻子，接著，便如攤落的長袍，倒地不起。

　　露西小姐發出害怕而絕望的尖叫聲，立刻衝向大衛，彎腰找到他的傷口，露出蒼白、悲痛的表情，輕喊道：「打中心臟，噢，打中心臟了！」

　　「走。」侯爵用宏亮的聲音說：「上馬車，天亮之前仍然要找個活人把你給嫁了，我們遇到的下一個男人，即將成為你的丈夫，管他是強盜還是農夫。如果一路上都找不到人，就把你嫁給幫我開門的。上馬車去。」

高大的侯爵不肯放過她，她再度披上斗蓬，看起來很神秘，馬夫收好武器，一行人便上了馬車。笨重的車輪駛離時，車聲迴繞著整座沈睡中的村莊。「銀色酒瓶」的大廳桌上，仍閃爍著二十四支蠟燭的光芒，慌亂的店東緊握著雙手，望著地上詩人的屍體。

右邊的岔路

道路綿延三里格之後，與另一條大路垂直相交，難題出現了。大衛站著猶豫了一會兒，選擇了右邊的道路。

大衛不知道這條路通往何處，但是他已下定決心，當晚一定要離開瓦諾，遠走高飛。他走了一里格，經過一個大城堡，看來城堡剛舉辦過活動。每扇窗戶都亮著，其中一戶門前的寬大石頭路上，有賓客乘坐的馬車駛過的痕跡。

大衛又走了三里格，感到有點疲倦，便在路邊的松樹枝堆上睡了一會兒，才又繼續踏上未知的旅程。

他在這條大路上走了五天，累了就睡在樹枝或農家的乾草堆上，餓了就吃農家殷勤招待的黑麥麵包，渴了就喝溪水或向牧羊人討水喝。

最後，他走過一座大橋，來到一座詩人雲集的友善城市。這是巴黎，街上人聲鼎沸、車水馬龍，像是在對他唱充滿活力的歡迎歌曲，這一切令他呼吸加速。

他在康堤路租下一間老房子的閣樓，然後坐在木椅上寫詩。這條街從前住的都是達官貴人，現在這一區已然沒落，住了另一批房客。

這些荒廢了的高聳房子還很莊嚴，但裡頭多是布滿灰塵和蜘蛛的空屋。一到晚上，可聽見一間間酒館傳來滋事者吵鬧、打鬥的聲音。這裡曾是上流社會住宅區，如今已成了腐敗、低俗的淫亂之區。不過大衛仍以荷包裡僅存的一點錢，租了一個小窩，白天就著日光，夜晚倚著燭光來寫詩。

一日下午，他從生活水平較低的那一區買了一些食物回來。他拿著麵包、凝乳和一瓶薄酒，走到樓梯的一半時，遇到一位美麗的年輕女子——應該說撞見比較貼切，因為這個女孩正坐在樓梯上休息——她的美超乎任何詩人的想像。這位女子敞開的寬鬆黑斗蓬裡，穿了一件色澤鮮豔的長袍。她的眼神隨著思緒流轉，一會兒睜得圓溜溜的，像個天真無邪的孩子，一會兒子瞇得長長的，像個魅惑的吉普賽人。她一手撩開長袍，露出一隻小巧的高跟鞋，垂著沒繫上的鞋帶。這麼優雅的女子，不適合彎腰綁鞋帶。她渾身充滿魅力，令人無法抗拒。說不定她早就看到大衛走了過來，故意在這裡等他來幫忙的。

噢，先生請見諒，她不是故意擋在樓梯中間的，都是這隻鞋子惹的禍！這隻淘氣的鞋子！唉！它的鞋帶一直掉。噢！如果先生能幫幫忙，該有多好啊！

詩人的手指一邊顫抖，一邊綁著頑固的鞋帶。這位女子可能是位危險人物啊，但她的雙眼瞇得長長的，像個吉普賽人，充滿魅惑，攝住了他。他靠在樓梯扶手上，手裡緊握著剛買的酸酒。

「先生，您真好心。您住在這棟房子裡吧？」她微笑道。

「是的，小姐，我——我想是吧，小姐。」

「那麼，可能住在三樓囉？」

「不，小姐，更高一點。」

這位小姐的手指顫動了一下，但並未顯露不耐煩的神情。

「對不起，我不該問這些的，您別介意好嗎？我的確不該問您住在哪裡的。」

「小姐，沒關係的，我就住在——」

「不，不，別告訴我。是我不對，我只是對這房子和裡頭的一切無法忘懷而已。我以前住在這兒，常來這裡緬懷過去的快樂時光。所以我會問這些事，也是有理由的。」

「沒有理由也無妨。我告訴你，我住在頂樓，住在樓梯轉角的那個小房間。」

「前面那間嗎？」小姐將頭轉向一邊，問道。

「是後面那間，小姐。」

這位小姐如釋重負地吐了一口氣。

「先生，那我就不耽擱您了。」她的眼睛又變成圓溜溜的，像個天真無邪的孩子。「好好照顧我的房子，唉！現在一切只能追憶了。再會了，感謝您的好心。」

她說罷便離開，留下一抹微笑和甜甜的香水味。大衛像在夢遊一樣走上階梯，突然又清醒了過來，女子的微笑和香氣依然繚繞不去。這位素昧平生的女子，給了他一些靈感，那雙眸、那剎時產生的情愫、那鬢髮、那纖細腳上的涼鞋，在他筆下一一化為詩句。

大衛一定是個詩人，因為他早就把伊芳忘得一乾二淨了，現在他眼裡只有這位清新而優雅的美麗陌生女子。她身上的微妙香氣，令他心中產生奇妙的情愫。

　　有一天晚上，這棟房子三樓的房間裡，有三人圍桌而坐。這個房間裡，除了這張桌子、三張椅子和一支點燃的蠟燭之外，便空無一物了。這三人之中，有一位高大的黑衣男子，他有一副輕蔑、高傲的神情，臉上的八字鬍翹得老高，都快碰到那雙帶著譏諷味兒的眼睛了。另外有一名年輕貌美的女子，她的眼睛可以變得圓溜，像個天真無邪的孩子，可以變得細長，像個魅惑的吉普賽人，不過現在她的眼神與其他共謀者相同，銳利而野心勃勃。第三個人可說是個行動家或鬥士，也可說是個膽大包天又耐不住性子的執行官，連呼吸都帶著火藥味與刀槍味。另外兩人稱呼他為「戴瑟羅斯少校」。

　　戴瑟羅斯少校用拳頭敲了敲桌子，按捺住火爆的性子說道：

　　「就是今晚，他去望彌撒的時候。每次計畫了半天，都是空口白話，光是搞什麼秘密集會，討論一堆暗號、密碼和暗語，我已經受不了了。既然要叛國，不如就明目張膽地動手吧，反正法國不能再任由他統治了，我們乾脆在大庭廣眾之下殺了他，不要再偷偷摸摸地設什麼陷阱了。今晚就動手，我說到做到，等他去望彌撒的時候，我親手把他給做掉。」

　　另一位女子轉過頭來，誠摯地看著他。女人雖然傾向於施謀用智，有時也不得不屈從於莽夫之勇。另一名高大男子則摸了摸翹得老高的八字鬍。

「親愛的少校。」他和平常一樣，壓低他的大嗓門說道：「這次我也同意你的看法。等待不是辦法，皇宮的侍衛有許多我們的黨羽，這次的行動應該很安全。」

「今晚。」戴瑟羅斯少校又敲了桌子說：「侯爵，你都聽到了，我會親自下手。」

「可是現在問題來了。」高大男子輕聲說道：「我們必須傳話給皇宮裡的黨羽，還要讓他們知道我們講好的暗號。一定要找個最可靠的人來護送皇家馬車。這種時候，有誰能深入南門，傳信給在那兒站哨的李伯特？只要信傳到他手上，一切就好辦了。」

「我去傳信。」女子說。

「你嗎，伯爵夫人？」侯爵挑起眉毛說：「您那犧牲奉獻的精神是很偉大，但是──」

「聽我說！」這名女子站起身，將手放在桌上，說：「閣樓上住了一位鄉下來的年輕人，我看他老實敦厚，和他放牧的小羊沒兩樣。我在樓梯上碰過他兩三次，我怕他住得離我們聚會的屋子太近，還刻意問過他。只要我一句話，他一定會聽我的。他都在閣樓裡寫詩，而且他應該一直在想著我吧。他不會反抗我的命令的，我會叫他送信去。」

侯爵聽了便起身一鞠躬，說：「我話還沒說完啊，伯爵夫人。我是說：『您那犧牲奉獻的精神是很偉大，但是您的機智與魅力更是偉大啊。』」

正當這些人盤算著陰謀詭計之時，大衛正在潤飾其〈階梯戀人〉一詩中的幾個詩句，他聽到門口傳來怯生生的敲門聲，他開門見到這位女子，心頭直是小鹿亂撞。這位女子氣喘吁吁，眼睛睜得大大的，像個天真無邪的孩子，似乎有事相求。

「先生。」她喘著氣說道：「我遇到困難，不知道該找誰，只好求助於您，您這麼好心又真誠，一定會幫助我的。我一路上從來來往往的人群中奔來找您。先生，家母的生命垂危，我叔叔是皇宮裡的侍衛長，我必須找人去請他回來啊，希望——」

「小姐，你的事就是我的事，告訴我要如何找到你叔叔。」大衛打岔道，他露出熱切的眼神，急於幫助這名女子。

「你到皇宮的南門去，注意，是南門。然後對那裡的侍衛說：『獵鷹已經離巢。』他們就會放你通行，接著你就走到南門入口，重複這個暗號，如果那個人回答：『他隨時可以展開攻擊。』就把信件交給他。先生，這是我叔叔交代的暗號，因為現在整個國家動盪不安，很多人都在密謀要暗殺國王，因此入夜之後，沒有暗號是進不了皇宮的。先生，如果你願意的話，幫我把信交到他手上，家母臨終之前才能見他最後一面啊。」

「把信給我。」大衛急切地說。「這麼晚了，我不能讓你自己回家。我先——」

「不用了，快去吧，分秒必爭啊。」女子的眼睛又變得細長，像吉普賽人一樣百般魅惑：「改天，我會報答您的大恩大德的。」大衛把信塞進衣襟，便走下樓。等他走遠，這名女子才回到三樓的房間。

侯爵的眉毛好像會說話似的，對她做出疑問的神情。

「他去送信了，動作和他看管的羊一樣快，也一樣笨。」

戴瑟羅斯少校又朝桌子敲了一拳，敲得桌子再度搖晃。

「天啊！我忘了帶槍了，我不放心讓別人動手啊。」他大喊。

「拿去。」侯爵從斗蓬裡抽出一把鑲銀雕刻的閃亮大手槍。

「這把可是貨真價實的好槍，你要收好，上面刻有我的徽章，而且我已經被懷疑了。我今晚得離開巴黎，逃遠一點。明日我會在我的官邸等你。伯爵夫人，您先請吧。」

侯爵把蠟燭吹熄，女子也披上斗蓬。兩個男人便輕悄悄地走下樓梯，混入在狹窄的康堤路上遊蕩的人群裡。

大衛加快腳步來到國王的官邸，在南門被侍衛用長戟抵住了胸口，他立刻說出：「獵鷹已經離巢。」

「快過去吧，兄弟。」侍衛說。

大衛走到宮殿南邊的階梯，侍衛們正打算過來抓他，他又講了一次暗語，便沒事了。其中有名侍衛兵走向他，開口說道：「他隨時可以——」不料話還沒說完，侍衛們便受到驚嚇，一陣騷動。一位眼神銳利的英勇男人突然從人群中走了出來，搶走大衛手中的信，還說：「跟我來。」接著便帶他進了大廳，當場把信拆開來看。此時有位身著步兵制服的軍官走過，向他招手示意。「泰特洛少校，將南門和南門入口的侍衛通通給我抓起來關好，換上一些忠心的士兵。」然後他對大衛說：「跟我來。」他們穿過長廊和前廳，來到一間寬敞的房間。房間裡有一位穿著深色衣裳的男士，鬱鬱寡歡地坐在大皮椅上沈思。他對這位沈思中的男人說：

「陛下，我早就告訴過您，皇宮裡的奸細與叛國賊，就和陰溝裡的老鼠一樣多，您還認為我多疑了。這名男子就是那些鼠輩放行進來的，他身上還帶了口信，還好被我給攔截下來。我把他抓來您的面前，好讓您知道，我並沒有多心。」

「我來問問他。」國王起身道，他的眼皮低垂，一副無精打采的樣子。詩人則屈膝行了禮。

「你是打哪兒來的？」國王問。

「我是從伊洛省的瓦諾村來的，陛下。」

「你在巴黎做些什麼？」

「我──我想當個詩人。」

「你在瓦諾村又是做什麼的？」

「我替家父看羊。」

國王又再度起身，這回則張開了眼睛。

「哦！在原野上牧羊嗎？」

「是的，陛下。」

「你住在原野上，一大早還冷颼颼的就出門，徜徉在用籬笆圍住的草地上。羊群自顧自地在山邊漫步，你渴了就喝溪水，餓了就在樹蔭下吃香甜的黑麥麵包，當然還會聽到畫眉鳥在樹林裡高歌囉，是不是這樣啊，牧羊人？」

「一點也沒錯，陛下。還可以聽到蜜蜂在花叢間嗡嗡飛舞，和農人在山上採葡萄時的歌聲。」大衛吐了一口氣道。

「對，對，還有蜂鳴和採果農人的歌聲。」國王不耐煩地說道：「可是能聽到畫眉鳥的歌聲沒錯吧？牠們經常在樹林裡鳴叫，對不對？」

「是的，陛下，只有在伊洛省的樹林裡才會唱得那麼甜美。我曾試著用詩句將其歌聲表達出來。」

「能不能唸幾句來聽聽？」國王熱切地問。「很久以前，我曾聽過畫眉鳥的歌聲，如果你寫得出牠們的歌聲，簡直比一整個王國還有價值啊。況且等你晚上將羊群趕回羊舍之後，還能安安靜靜地一邊吃著美味的麵包，一邊吟詩啊。唸幾句來聽聽吧，牧羊人？」

「我就讀給您聽吧，陛下。」於是大衛便用一種令人恭敬的熱情語調唸道：

> 「懶洋洋的牧羊人，看看你的羊寶寶
> 歡喜雀躍草原上；
> 看看那些冷杉木，搖來搖去微風中，
> 還有牧羊神的牧笛聲。
> 聽我們啁啾在樹梢，
> 看我們俯衝向羊兒，
> 賞我們羊毛做暖巢
> 在那樹枝上──」

這時突然有個刺耳的聲音打斷說：「陛下，如果您不介意，我想對這位不入流的詩人質問幾個問題，還請陛下原諒，我們沒什麼時間了，我是為了陛下的安全著想，不是想冒犯陛下啊。」

「德奧墨公爵，你一向忠心耿耿，怎麼說是冒犯我呢？」於是國王坐回椅子上，眼皮又垂了下來。

「首先，我要把這封信的內容唸給陛下聽聽：『今夜為王太子逝世之週年，如果他依照慣例前去望彌撒，以慰其子在天之靈，獵鷹將在艾斯普蘭納德街的街角展開襲擊。如果發現國王有此打算，請於皇宮西南邊的頂樓放置一盞紅燈，獵鷹會注意的。』」

「你這個農人。」公爵對他厲聲說道：「你都聽到了，說，是誰差你送信來的？」

「公爵大人，信是一位小姐給我的，她說她母親病危，要送信請他叔叔回去看她，我不知道這封信原來是這樣，可是她真的是個美麗善良的女人啊。」

「你倒是形容看看，這女人長什麼模樣，還有你是怎麼當上這個冤大頭的。」公爵命令道。

「形容她！恐怕未必形容得出來呢。嗯，她是陽光，也是綠蔭，她的身材苗條，舉止優雅，宛如赤楊。當你凝視她的雙眸，可以看到她流轉的眼神，時而睜得圓溜，時而瞇得細長，像是在雲縫中窺探的太陽。她來的時候帶著一身優雅，她離去的時候留下一團迷亂與山楂花香。我住在康堤路二十九號，是她找上我的。」大衛微笑著說道。

「我們已經注意這棟房子很久了。」公爵轉身對國王說：「還好有這位詩人的描述，我們大概可以知道惡名昭彰的奎貝多伯爵夫人的樣貌了。」

「陛下與公爵大人，我不太會說話，可不希望因此冤枉什麼好人。先不管她有沒有託我送信，我看過這名女子的眼睛，她簡直像是天使下凡啊。」大衛誠懇地說。

公爵鎮靜地看著他說：「我讓你自己看清楚真相吧。今晚你就扮成國王，坐馬車去望彌撒，你敢不敢試試？」

大衛笑著說：「她的眼睛已經對我證明過了。你要是不相信，我再證明一次也無妨。」

十一點半，公爵親自在皇宮西南邊的一扇窗子內放置一盞紅燈。十一點五十分時，大衛全身穿上國王的裝扮，把頭罩在斗蓬裡，用一隻手遮掩著，慢慢地從皇宮走向等候的馬車。公爵扶他上了馬車，關上車門，馬車便朝教堂呼嘯而去。

艾斯普蘭納德街的街角有一棟房子，由泰特洛少校帶著二十位人馬把關，他們已經做好準備，等謀叛者一出現，他們便立刻攻擊。

然而不知什麼原因，謀叛者的計畫似乎有所改變。當御用馬車來到距離艾斯普蘭納德街還有一個街區的克里斯多夫路時，戴瑟羅斯少校突然帶著他的手下殺出來，朝著馬車與侍衛不斷攻擊。馬車上的侍衛雖然被突如其來的攻擊行動嚇了一跳，依然跳下馬車，英勇奮戰。雙方的打鬥聲驚動了泰特洛少校的人馬，他們立刻趕來支援。但是這個時候，戴瑟羅斯少校臨危之中已經扯開馬車的車門，朝著裡面的黑衣人士開了槍。

現在援軍才抵達現場，滿街盡是人們的哭叫聲與刀槍磨擦的聲音，馬匹早就受驚跑掉了。馬車的座位上躺著可憐詩人裝扮的假國王，他正是死於蒙巴第侯爵的槍下。

主要的大道

　　道路綿延三里格之後，與另一條大路垂直相交，難題出現了。大衛站著猶豫了一會兒，便坐在路邊休息。

　　他不知道這些道路分別通往何處，每一條路似乎都充滿了命運與危險。他坐著坐著，看到一顆閃亮的星星，他與伊芳曾將它命為屬於兩人的星星，這使他憶起了伊芳，開始懷疑自己是否太魯莽了。他何必為了小倆口的幾句口角就棄她而去、離家出走呢？會吃醋不就證明彼此深愛嗎？愛情怎麼會脆弱到被自己的證物給破壞了呢？晚上吵吵，早上氣就消了嘛，現在回去還來得及，瓦諾村民好夢尚酣，沒人比他更清醒了。他的心屬於伊芳，故鄉才是他的幸福所在，才是適合寫詩的好地方。

　　大衛站了起來，抖落一身的不安和任性，他堅定地看著回家的道路。踏上了瓦諾的歸途，他想四處流浪的念頭也就消失了。他經過羊舍，綿羊聽到他的腳步聲，一陣騷動，在羊舍裡奔竄。這種家的聲音，令他心中倍覺溫馨。他靜悄悄地回到自己的房間，躺在房裡，滿心感謝，還好這雙腳當晚就逃離了可怕的命運之路。

　　大衛還真是瞭解女人啊！翌日傍晚，伊芳出現在路上的水井邊，這裡是年輕人聚集、聽牧師講道的地方。儘管她那固執的嘴巴仍然一副不肯讓步的樣子，大衛卻發現她正用眼角的餘光尋找自己的蹤跡。他知道伊芳已經氣消了，沒多久，他們就互相擁吻著，一路走回家。

兩人於三個月後結婚，大衛的父親精明能幹，事業有成，他把兩人的婚禮辦得風風光光的，還傳到三里格外去了。兩位年輕人深受村民的喜愛，街上不僅有人為他們列隊慶祝，草地上也辦了舞會，他們還從德魯克斯請人來表演木偶戲和雜耍特技，以娛嘉賓。

　　一年後，大衛的父親過世，把羊群和屋子留給了他。他也已經擁有全村最賢淑的女人了，伊芳連擠牛奶的桶子和銅製水壺都擦得閃閃發亮——你連路過都會被其反射的陽光照得睜不開眼睛；不過你一定要看看她的院子，等你看到她打理得整整齊齊、花團錦簇的花圃，一定會馬上恢復視力。你或許還能聽到她的歌聲，沒錯，連皮爾‧葛魯諾的鐵工廠上面兩棵栗子樹那麼遠的地方，都聽得到她的歌聲。

　　有一天，大衛打開一個深鎖已久的抽屜，拿出一張紙，開始寫東西。春天再度來臨，觸動了他的心扉。他一定是個詩人，因為他幾乎把伊芳忘得一乾二淨，他現在眼裡只有這塊優雅而充滿魔力的美麗大地。這塊大地從森林和草原飄來芬芳，在詩人心中挑起奇妙的情愫。他白天出去放羊，夜晚將牠們安然無恙地趕回羊舍。不過現在，他正躺在籬笆下，用小紙片寫詩。綿羊走散了，大野狼知道詩不好寫，但羊肉很容易到手。牠們紛紛大膽地從樹林裡跑出來，叼走了羊。

　　大衛的詩越寫越多，他的羊卻越放越少。伊芳管得越來越多，脾氣越來越大，說話也越來越不留情。她的鍋子和水壺逐漸失去光澤，反而是她的眼神變得炯炯有光。她對詩人說，因為他疏於照顧，致使羊群數量減少，還讓這個家庭失去了幸福。於是大衛請了一位牧童幫他看羊，他自己則鎖在閣樓裡繼續寫詩。怎料這個牧童天生也是詩人性格，只不過他不會寫詩，而是終日昏昏沈沈。沒多久，大野狼便發現寫詩與睡眠基本上是同一回事，於是羊群依然不斷減少，伊芳的脾氣也以相對的速度變壞。有時她會站在院子裡，對著樓上窗內的大衛怒罵，連皮爾·葛魯諾的鐵工廠上面兩棵栗子樹那麼遠的地方，都聽得到她的怒罵聲。

仁慈、睿智又愛管閒事的老公證人，帕比諾先生，鼻子轉到哪裡，眼睛就看到哪裡，因此當然也看到這番情景了。他吸了一大口鼻煙壯壯膽，便去找大衛說：

「米諾兄啊，令尊的結婚證書就是我簽的，若是要我簽他兒子的破產證書，我會很難受的。可是我看你破產之期不遠矣，我以老朋友的身分勸勸你啊，你聽我說，我看得出來，你一心只想寫詩。我在德魯克斯有個叫布瑞爾的朋友——喬治·布瑞爾。他家整屋子的藏書，生活的空間才一點點。他是個博學多聞的人，每年都會前往巴黎一趟，而且他自己本身也是作家。他知道地下墓穴是如何建造的，星星是如何命名的，為何千鳥有長長的鳥喙。他對詩歌的意義與形式瞭若指掌，就像你對綿羊的咩咩叫聲決不陌生一樣。我幫你寫封介紹信，你帶著去見他，順便拿幾首自己的詩作讓他鑑定鑑定，這樣你就知道自己該繼續寫詩，還是要好好地照顧你的妻子和事業了。」

「那就麻煩您幫我寫介紹信了，您怎麼不早說呢？」大衛說。

翌日清晨，大衛便將他的寶貝詩作夾在腋下，動身前往德魯克斯。正午時分，他來到了布瑞爾先生的家門前，揩了揩腳上的灰塵。博學的布瑞爾先生戴著閃亮的眼鏡，他打開帕比諾的信，然後像陽光蒸發水氣一般，把內容全讀進腦子裡。他帶大衛進到他的書房，在一片書海裡找了個空位讓他坐下。

　　布瑞爾先生很好心，即使面對一堆和手指長度差不多厚、又捲得亂七八糟的手稿，他也面無懼色。他把這些紙張攤在膝蓋上，然後埋首詩堆，開始一字不漏地閱讀，模樣活像隻鑽進核果裡找果仁吃的蟲子。

　　在這當兒，大衛一人坐在這片文學的書海中搖搖晃晃，這片大海對著他怒吼，他既沒有航海圖，也沒有指南針，不知該航向何處。他想，世界上大概有一半的人都在寫書吧。

　　布瑞爾先生讀完最後一頁後，摘下眼鏡，用手帕擦了擦。

　　「我的老友帕比諾先生還好吧？」他問道。

　　「他的身體健朗得很。」

　　「米諾先生，你養了幾隻羊？」

　　「我昨天數過，有三百零九隻。這些羊的命運頗為坎坷，之前還有八百五十隻的。」

　　「你有妻子，也有家庭，過得舒舒服服的。羊群為你帶來不少財富，你和牠們一起徜徉草原上，生活充滿活力，餓了就吃下令人滿足的甜麵包。你只需維持警覺，便可躺在大地上，聆聽林中畫眉的歌聲。我說到這裡都沒錯吧？」

　　「沒錯。」大衛說。

「你的詩我全都看過了。」布瑞爾先生繼續說道，他的眼神一邊在書海上游移，像是在海平面上尋找船隻。「米諾先生，你看窗外，告訴我你在那棵樹上看到什麼。」

「我看到一隻烏鴉。」大衛看著說。

「世上有一種鳥，每當我想逃避責任的時候，牠就會在一旁鼓勵我偷懶。原來你也認識那種鳥，米諾先生。牠可是空中的哲學家呢，牠願意屈從自己的命運，因此過得很快樂。牠總是一副異想天開的眼神，踏著愉快的腳步，再也沒有別的鳥像牠這樣快樂，飽食終日了。大自然滿足了牠一切的需求，就算自己的羽毛不如黃鸝鳥鮮豔，也不難過。你也聽到大自然賜給牠的聒噪嗓音了是吧？你認為黃鶯有好嗓音就比較滿足嗎？」

大衛站了起來，烏鴉在樹上嘎嘎刺耳地叫個不停。

「謝謝您，布瑞爾先生。但在這些烏鴉的叫聲中，難道連一點黃鶯的歌聲都沒有嗎？」他緩緩地說道。

「我看得很仔細，一字都不漏。先生，你的詩缺乏生命力，你不要再寫詩了。」布瑞爾嘆口氣說道。

「謝謝您，我現在要回去牧羊了。」大衛又說道。

「你先別難過，我們一起吃頓飯，我再詳細地解釋給你聽。」博學的布瑞爾說。

「不了，我得回牧場對我的羊嘎嘎叫了。」詩人說。

大衛把他的詩作夾在腋下，便長途跋涉回瓦諾。他回到村裡的時候，先去了柴格勒開的店，柴格勒是個亞美尼亞的猶太人，他什麼都賣。

「朋友啊，森林裡的大野狼一直騷擾我山丘上的羊，我想買隻手槍來保護我的羊群。你有些什麼貨色？」大衛說。

「米諾兄，今天算我運氣不好，看來要賠本賣你一支手槍了。我上個星期才從一個小販那兒買來一整車的貨物，那是他參加一位皇家門警舉辦的拍賣會所標來的。這些都是從一座大官邸裡挑出來賣的，是一位貴族的財物——我不知道他的爵位是什麼，這人已經因反叛國王而遭到放逐了。這批貨裡有不少手槍，瞧瞧這一把，喔，很有王宮貴族的味道，我就虧個十法郎，賣你四十法郎就好啦。這裡還有支火繩槍——」

「這支就行了。」大衛說道，便把錢扔在櫃臺上。「有裝子彈嗎？」

「我可以幫你裝，一組彈匣再加十法郎。」柴格勒說。

大衛將手槍塞在大衣裡，便走回家。廚房的爐灶還燃燒著，但是伊芳並不在家，她最近經常四處遊蕩，多半是去找鄰居串門子。大衛走進廚房，把詩作全往煤炭裡扔，它們一邊熊熊地燃燒，一邊在煙囪裡發出刺耳的聲響。

「烏鴉的叫聲！」詩人說。

他走上閣樓，關上房門。整座村莊靜悄悄的，許多人都聽到這支大手槍的槍聲。他們看到樓上冒出的煙霧，紛紛聚集了過來。

一群男人將詩人的屍體抬到床上，草草地為這隻可憐的黑烏鴉蓋住破碎的羽毛。女人們大表同情地談論著，有人則跑去通知伊芳。

帕比諾先生是第一個聞風而至的人，他拿起這把手槍，對著上面的銀色雕刻打量著，一邊鑑賞手槍，一邊感到悲痛。

「這種手槍，以及上面的徽章，是屬於蒙巴第侯爵閣下的。」他對旁邊的牧師說。

歐亨利

短篇小說選

原著雙語彩圖本

The Best
Short Stories of
O. Henry

作者 _ 歐‧亨利（O. Henry）
譯者 _ 丁宥榆
封面設計 _ 林書玉
製程管理 _ 洪巧玲
出版者 _ 寂天文化事業股份有限公司
電話 _ +886-2-2365-9739
傳真 _ +886-2-2365-9835
網址 _ www.icosmos.com.tw
讀者服務 _ onlineservice@icosmos.com.tw
出版日期 _ 2020 年 12 月 二版一刷
郵撥帳號 _ 1998620-0 寂天文化事業股份有限公司
訂購金額 600（含）元以上郵資免費
訂購金額 600 元以下者，請外加郵資 65 元
若有破損，請寄回更換

© 2014 by Cosmos Culture Ltd.
All Rights Reserved

國家圖書館出版品預行編目資料

歐亨利短篇小說選（原著雙語彩圖本）(The
Best Short Stories of O. Henry) / 歐‧亨利
（O. Henry）著；丁宥榆 譯 . 一二版 . 一 [臺北
市]：寂天文化，2020.12 面；公分 .

ISBN 978-986-318-957-2 (25K 平裝)

874.57   109019092